Christmas 2005

Dear Friends,

I genuinely love Christmas. I love everything about it—
the decorations, the baking, the shopping and goodwill
toward mankind. My love of the holidays is one reason
I've written a book centered on Christmas almost
every year of my writing career. *Home for the Holidays*
includes two of my favorites: *The Forgetful Bride* and
When Christmas Comes.

The Forgetful Bride is one of my early Christmas stories,
written back in 1991. It's about a woman who meets an
old flame over the holidays. Okay, at the time of their
"romance" she was only eight and she'd refused to kiss
him unless they were married. Now her childhood
husband is back—right in the middle of the Christmas
season—and insists they're actually married.

When Christmas Comes tells the story of what happens
when two people decide to trade homes over the
holidays. Throw a Christmas curmudgeon into a town
obsessed with Christmas, add a few neighborhood kids,
Santa and his elves—and there's Christmas fun to be
had.

Two stories for the price of one. That's the kind of
deal Christmas shoppers are looking for! My wish
is that you'll be able to relax during the holiday
craziness, laugh away the stress and fall in love with life.

Debbie Macomber

P.S. If you enjoyed these stories, please visit my Web site
at www.debbiemacomber.com and leave me a message
on the Guest Book page. If you aren't online, I can be
reached at P.O. Box 1458, Port Orchard, WA 98366.

DEBBIE MACOMBER

HOME
FOR THE
Holidays

MIRA®

MIRA

ISBN 0-7783-2239-4

HOME FOR THE HOLIDAYS

Copyright © 2005 by MIRA Books.

The publisher acknowledges the copyright holder
of the individual works as follows:

THE FORGETFUL BRIDE
Copyright © 1991 by Debbie Macomber.

WHEN CHRISTMAS COMES
Copyright © 1991 by Debbie Macomber.

www.MIRABooks.com

Printed in U.S.A.

CONTENTS

THE FORGETFUL BRIDE

From the Library of:

Elizabeth Bruno

For Patti Knoll
My witty, charming and talented friend

Prologue

"Not unless we're married."

Ten-year-old Martin Marshall slapped his hands against his thighs in disgust. "I told you she was going to be unreasonable about this."

Caitlin watched as her brother's best friend withdrew a second baseball card from his shirt pocket. If Joseph Rockwell wanted to kiss her, then he was going to have to do it the right way. She might be only eight, but Caitlin knew about these things. Glancing down at the doll held tightly in her arms, she realized instinctively that Barbie wouldn't approve of kissing a boy unless he married you first.

Martin approached her again. "Joe says he'll throw in his Don Drysdale baseball card."

"Not unless we're married," she repeated, smoothing the front of her sundress with a haughty air.

"All right, all right, I'll marry her," Joe muttered as he stalked across the backyard.

"How you gonna do that?" Martin demanded.

"Get your Bible."

For someone who wanted to kiss her so badly, Joseph didn't look very pleased. Caitlin decided to press her luck. "In the fort."

"The fort?" Joe exploded. "No girls are allowed in there!"

"I refuse to marry a boy who won't even let me into his fort."

"Call it off," Martin demanded. "She's asking too much."

"You don't have to give me the second baseball card," she said. The idea of being the first girl ever to view their precious fort had a certain appeal. And it meant she'd probably get invited to Betsy McDonald's birthday party.

The boys exchanged glances and started whispering to each other, but Caitlin heard only snatches of their conversation. Martin clearly wasn't thrilled with Joseph's concessions, and he kept shaking his head as though he couldn't believe his friend might actually go through with this. For her part, Caitlin didn't know whether to trust Joseph. He liked playing practical jokes and everyone in the neighborhood knew it.

"It's time to feed my baby," she announced, preparing to leave.

"All right, all right," Joseph said with obvious reluctance. "I'll marry you in the fort. Martin'll say the words, only you can't tell anyone about going inside, understand?"

"If you do," Martin threatened, glaring at his sister, "you'll be sorry."

"I won't tell," Caitlin promised. It would have to be a secret, but that was fine because she liked keeping secrets.

"You ready?" Joseph demanded. Now that the terms were set, he seemed to be in a rush, which rather annoyed

Caitlin. The frown on his face didn't please her, either. A bridegroom should at least *look* happy. She was about to say so, but decided not to.

"You'll have to change clothes, of course. Maybe the suit you wore on Easter Sunday..."

"What?" Joseph shrieked. "I'm not wearing any suit. Listen, Caitlin, you've gone about as far as you can with this. I get married exactly the way I am or we call it off."

She sighed, rolling her eyes expressively. "Oh, all right, but I'll need to get a few things first."

"Just hurry up, would you?"

Martin followed her into the house, letting the screen door slam behind him. He took his Bible off the hallway table and rushed back outside.

Caitlin hurried up to her room, where she grabbed a brush to run through her hair and straightened the two pink ribbons tied around her pigtails. She always wore pink ribbons because pink was a color for girls. Boys were supposed to wear blue and brown and boring colors like that. Boys were okay sometimes, but mostly they did disgusting things.

Her four dolls accompanied her across the backyard and into the wooded acre behind. She hated getting her Mary Janes dusty, but that couldn't be avoided.

With a good deal of ceremony, she opened the rickety door and then slowly, the way she'd seen it done at her older cousin's wedding, Caitlin marched into the boys' packing-crate-and-cardboard fort.

Pausing inside the narrow entry, she glanced around. It wasn't anything to brag about. Martin had made it sound like a palace with marble floors and crystal chandeliers. She couldn't help feeling disillusioned. If she hadn't been so eager to see the fort, she would've insisted they do this properly, in church.

Her brother stood tall and proud on an upturned apple crate, the Bible clutched to his chest. His face was dutifully somber. Caitlin smiled approvingly. He, at least, was taking this seriously.

"You can't bring those dolls in here," Joseph said loudly.

"I most certainly can. Barbie and Ken and Paula and Jane are our children."

"Our children?"

"Naturally they haven't been born yet, so they're really just a glint in your eye." She'd heard her father say that once and it sounded special. "They're angels for now, but I thought they should be here so you could meet them." She was busily arranging her dolls in a tidy row behind Martin on another apple crate.

Joseph covered his face with his hands and it looked for a moment like he might change his mind.

"Are we going to get married or not?" she asked.

"All right, all right." Joseph sighed heavily and pulled her forward, a little more roughly than necessary, in Caitlin's opinion.

The two of them stood in front of Martin, who randomly opened his Bible. He gazed down at the leather-bound book and then at Caitlin and his best friend. "Do you Joseph James Rockwell take Caitlin Rose Marshall for your wife?"

"Lawfully wedded," Caitlin corrected. She remembered this part from a television show.

"Lawfully wedded wife," Martin amended grudgingly.

"I do." Caitlin noticed that he didn't say it with any real enthusiasm. "I think there's supposed to be something about richer or poorer and sickness and health," Joseph said, smirking at Caitlin as if to say she wasn't the only one who knew the proper words.

Martin nodded and continued. "Do you, Caitlin Rose Marshall, hereby take Joseph James Rockwell in sickness and health and in riches and in poorness?"

"I'm only going to marry a man who's healthy and rich."

"You can't go putting conditions on this now," Joseph argued. "We already agreed."

"Just say 'I do,'" Martin urged, his voice tight with annoyance. Caitlin suspected that only the seriousness of the occasion prevented him from adding, "You pest."

She wasn't sure if she should go through with this or not. She was old enough to know that she liked pretty things and when she married, her husband would build her a castle at the edge of the forest. He would love her so much, he'd bring home silk ribbons for her hair, and bottles and bottles of expensive perfume. So many that there wouldn't be room for all of them on her makeup table.

"Caitlin," Martin said through clenched teeth.

"I do," she finally answered.

"I hereby pronounce you married," Martin proclaimed, closing the Bible with a resounding thud. "You may kiss the bride."

Joseph turned to face Caitlin. He was several inches taller than she was. His eyes were a pretty shade of blue that reminded her of the way the sky looked the morning after a bad rainstorm. She liked Joseph's eyes.

"You ready?" he asked.

She nodded, closed her eyes and pressed her lips

tightly together as she angled her head to the left. If the truth be known, she wasn't all that opposed to having Joseph kiss her, but she'd never let him know that because...well, because kissing wasn't something ladies talked about.

A long time passed before she felt his mouth touch hers. Actually his lips sort of bounced against hers. Gee, she thought. What a big fuss over nothing.

"Well?" Martin demanded of his friend.

Caitlin opened her eyes to discover Joseph frowning down at her. "It wasn't anything like Pete said it would be," he grumbled.

"Caitlin might be doing it wrong," Martin offered, frowning accusingly at his sister.

"If anyone did anything wrong, it's Joseph." They were making it sound like she'd purposely cheated them. If anyone was being cheated, it was Caitlin, because she couldn't tell Betsy McDonald about going inside their precious fort.

Joseph didn't say anything for a long moment. Then he slowly withdrew his prized baseball cards from his shirt pocket. He gazed at them lovingly before he reluctantly held them out to her. "Here," he said, "these are yours now."

"You aren't going to *give* 'em to her, are you? Not when she messed up!" Martin cried. "Kissing a girl wasn't like Pete said, and that's got to be Caitlin's fault. I told you she's not really a girl, anyway. She's a pest."

"A deal's a deal," Joseph said sadly.

"You can keep your silly old baseball cards." Head held high, Caitlin gathered up her dolls in a huff, prepared to make a dignified exit.

"You won't tell anyone about us letting you into the fort, will you?" Martin shouted after her.

"No." She'd keep that promise.

But neither of them had said a word about telling everyone in school that she and Joseph Rockwell had gotten married.

Chapter One

For the third time that afternoon, Cait indignantly wiped sawdust from the top of her desk. If this remodeling mess got much worse, the particles were going to get into her computer, destroying her vital link with the New York Stock Exchange.

"We'll have to move her out," a gruff male voice said from behind her.

"I beg your pardon," Cait demanded, rising abruptly and whirling toward the doorway. She clapped the dust from her hands, preparing to do battle. So much for this being the season of peace and goodwill. All these men in hard hats strolling through the office, moving things around, was inconvenient enough. But at least she'd been able to close her door to reduce the noise. Now, it seemed, even that would be impossible.

"We're going to have to pull some electrical wires through there," the same brusque voice explained. She couldn't see the man's face, since he stood just outside her doorway, but she had an impression of broad-shouldered height. "We'll have everything back to normal within a week."

"A week!" She wouldn't be able to service her customers, let alone function, without her desk and phone. And exactly where did they intend to put her? Certainly not in a hallway! She wouldn't stand for it.

The mess this simple remodeling project had created was one thing, but transplanting her entire office as if she were nothing more than a...a tulip bulb was something else again.

"I'm sorry about this, Cait," Paul Jamison said, slipping past the crew foreman to her side.

The wind went out of her argument at the merest hint of his devastating smile. "Don't worry about it," she said, the picture of meekness and tolerance. "Things like this happen when a company grows as quickly as ours."

She glanced across the hallway to her best friend's office, shrugging as if to ask, *Is Paul ever going to notice me?* Lindy shot her a crooked grin and a quick nod that suggested Cait stop being so negative. Her friend's confidence didn't help. Paul was a wonderful district manager and she was fortunate to have the opportunity to work with him. He was both talented and resourceful. The brokerage firm of Webster, Rodale and Missen was an affiliate of the fastest-growing firm in the country. This branch had been open for less than two years and already they were breaking national sales records. Due mainly, Cait believed, to Paul's administrative skills.

Paul was slender, dark-haired and handsome in an urbane, sophisticated way—every woman's dream man. Certainly Cait's. But as far as she could determine, he didn't see her in a similar romantic light. He thought of her as an important team member. One of the staff. At most, a friend.

Cait knew that friendship was often fertile ground for romance, and she hoped for an opportunity to cultivate it. Willingly surrendering her office to an irritating crew of carpenters and electricians was sure to gain her a few points with her boss.

"Where would you like me to set up my desk in the meantime?" she asked, smiling warmly at Paul. From habit, she lifted her hand to push back a stray lock of hair, forgetting she'd recently had it cut. That had been another futile attempt to attract Paul's affections—or at least his attention. Her shoulder-length chestnut-brown hair had been trimmed and permed into a pixie style with a halo of soft curls.

The difference from the tightly styled chignon she'd always worn to work was striking, or so everyone said. Everyone except Paul. The hairdresser had claimed it changed Cait's cooly polished look into one of warmth and enthusiasm. It was exactly the image Cait wanted Paul to have of her.

Unfortunately he didn't seem to detect the slightest difference in her appearance. At least not until Lindy had pointedly commented on the change within earshot of their absentminded employer. Then, and only then, had Paul made a remark about noticing something different; he just hadn't been sure what it was, he'd said.

"I suppose we could move you...." Paul hesitated.

"Your office seems to be the best choice," the foreman said.

Cait resisted the urge to hug the man. He was tall,

easily six three, and as solid as Mount Rainier, the majestic mountain she could see from her office window. She hadn't paid much attention to him until this moment and was surprised to note something vaguely familiar about him. She'd assumed he was the foreman, but she wasn't certain. He seemed to be around the office fairly often, although not on a predictable schedule. Every time he did show up, the level of activity rose dramatically.

"Ah...I suppose Cait could move in with me for the time being," Paul agreed. In her daydreams, Cait would play back this moment; her version had Paul looking at her with surprise and wonder, his mouth moving toward hers and—

"Miss?"

Cait broke out of her reverie and glanced at the foreman—the man who'd suggested she share Paul's office. "Yes?"

"Would you show us what you need moved?"

"Of course," she returned crisply. This romantic heart of hers was always getting her into trouble. She'd look at Paul and her head would start to spin with hopes and fantasies and then she'd be lost....

Cait's arms were loaded with files as she followed the carpenters, who hauled her desk into a corner of Paul's much larger office. Her computer and phone came next, and within fifteen minutes she was back in business.

She was on the phone, talking with one of her most important clients, when the same man walked back, unannounced, into the room. At first Caitlin assumed he was looking for Paul, who'd stepped out of the office. The foreman—or whatever he was—hesitated for a few seconds.

Then, scooping up her nameplate, he grinned at her as if he found something highly entertaining. Cait did her best to ignore him, flipping needlessly through the pages of the file.

Not taking the hint, he stepped forward and plunked the nameplate on the edge of her desk. As she looked up in annoyance, he boldly winked at her.

Cait was not amused. How dare this…this…redneck flirt with her!

She glared at him, hoping he'd have the good manners and good sense to leave—which, of course, he didn't. In fact, he seemed downright stubborn about staying and making her as uncomfortable as possible. Her phone conversation ran its natural course and after making several notations, she replaced the receiver.

"You wanted something?" she demanded, her eyes meeting his. Once more she noted his apparent amusement. She didn't understand it.

"No," he answered, grinning again. "Sorry to have bothered you."

For the second time, Cait was struck by a twinge of the familiar. He strolled out of her makeshift office as if he owned the building.

Cait waited a few minutes, then approached Lindy. "Did you happen to catch his name?"

"Whose name?"

"The…man who insisted I vacate my office. I don't know who he is. I thought he was the foreman, but…" She crossed her arms and furrowed her brow, trying to remember if she'd heard anyone say his name.

"I have no idea." Lindy pushed back her chair and rolled a pencil between her palms. "He is kinda cute, though, don't you think?"

A smile softened Cait's lips. "There's only one man for me and you know it."

"Then why are you asking questions about the construction crew?"

"I...don't know. That guy seems familiar for some reason, and he keeps grinning at me as if he knows something I don't. I hate it when men do that."

"Then ask one of the others what his name is. They'll tell you."

"I can't do that."

"Why not?"

"He might think I'm interested in him."

"And we both know how impossible that would be," Lindy said with mild sarcasm.

"Exactly." Lindy and probably everyone else in the office complex knew how Cait felt about Paul. The district manager himself, however, seemed to be completely oblivious. Other than throwing herself at him, which she'd seriously considered more than once, there was little she could do but be patient. One of these days Cupid was going to let fly an arrow and hit her lovable boss directly between the eyes.

When it happened—and it would!—Cait planned to be ready.

"You want to go for lunch now?" Lindy asked.

Cait nodded. It was nearly two and she hadn't eaten since breakfast, which had consisted of a banana and a cup of coffee. A West Coast stockbroker's day started before dawn. Cait was generally in the office by six and didn't stop work until the market closed at one-thirty, Seattle time. Only then did she break for something to eat.

Somewhere in the middle of her turkey on whole wheat,

Cait convinced herself she was imagining things when it came to that construction worker. He'd probably been waiting around to ask her where Paul was and then changed his mind. He did say he was sorry for bothering her.

If only he hadn't winked.

He was back the following day, a tool pouch riding on his hip like a six-shooter, hard hat in place. He was issuing orders like a drill sergeant, and Cait found herself gazing after him with reluctant fascination. She'd heard he owned the construction company, and she wasn't surprised.

As she studied him, she realized once again how striking he was. Not because he was extraordinarily handsome, but because he was somehow commanding. He possessed an authority, a presence, that attracted attention wherever he went. Cait was as drawn to it as those around her. She observed how the crew instinctively turned to him for directions and approval.

The more she observed him, the more she recognized that he was a man who had an appetite for life. Which meant excitement, adventure and probably women, and that confused her even more because she couldn't recall ever knowing anyone quite like him. Then why did she find him so…familiar?

Cait herself had a quiet nature. She rarely ventured out of the comfortable, compact world she'd built. She had her job, a nice apartment in Seattle's university district, and a few close friends. Excitement to her was growing herbs and participating in nature walks.

The following day while she was studying the construction worker, he'd unexpectedly turned and smiled at something one of his men had said. His smile, she decided, intrigued her most. It was slightly off center and seemed to tease the corners of his mouth. He looked her way more than once and each time she thought she detected a touch of humor, an amused knowledge that lurked just beneath the surface.

"It's driving me crazy," Cait confessed to Lindy over lunch.

"What is?"

"That I can't place him."

Lindy set her elbows on the table, holding her sandwich poised in front of her mouth. She nodded slowly, her eyes distant. "When you figure it out, introduce me, will you? I could go for a guy this sexy."

So Lindy had noticed that earthy sensuality about him, too. Well, of course she had—any woman would.

After lunch, Cait returned to the office to make a few calls. He was there again.

No matter how hard she tried, she couldn't place him. Work became a pretense as she continued to scrutinize him, racking her brain. Then, when she least expected it, he strolled past her and brazenly winked a second time.

As the color clawed up her neck, Cait flashed her attention back to her computer screen.

"His name is Joe," Lindy rushed in to tell her ten minutes later. "I heard one of the men call him that."

"Joe," Cait repeated slowly. She couldn't remember ever knowing anyone named Joe.

"Does that help?"

"No," Cait said, shaking her head regretfully. If she'd ever met this man, she wasn't likely to have overlooked the experience. He wasn't someone a woman easily forgot.

"Ask him," Lindy said. "It's ridiculous not to. It's driving you insane. Then," she added with infuriating logic, "when you find out, you can nonchalantly introduce me."

"I can't just waltz up and start quizzing him," Cait argued. The idea was preposterous. "He'll think I'm trying to pick him up."

"You'll go crazy if you don't."

Cait sighed. "You're right. I'm not going to sleep tonight if I don't settle this."

With Lindy waiting expectantly in her office, Cait approached him. He was talking to another member of the crew and once he'd finished, he turned to her with one of his devastating lazy smiles.

"Hello," she said, and her voice shook slightly. "Do I know you?"

"You mean you've forgotten?" he asked, sounding shocked and insulted.

"Apparently. Though I'll admit you look somewhat familiar."

"I should certainly hope so. We shared something very special a few years back."

"We did?" Cait was more confused than ever.

"Hey, Joe, there's a problem over here," a male voice shouted. "Could you come look at this?"

"I'll be with you in a minute," he answered brusquely over his shoulder. "Sorry, we'll have to talk later."

"But—"

"Say hello to Martin for me, would you?" he asked as he stalked past her and into the room that had once been Cait's office.

Martin, her brother. Cait hadn't a clue what her brother could possibly have to do with this. Mentally she ran through a list of his teenage friends and came up blank.

Then it hit her. Bull's-eye. Her heart started to pound until it roared like a tropical storm in her ears. Mechanically Cait made her way back to Lindy's office. She sank into a chair beside the desk and stared into space.

"Well?" Lindy pressed. "Don't keep me in suspense."

"Um, it's not that easy to explain."

"You remember him, then?"

She nodded. Oh, Lord, did she ever.

"Good grief, what's wrong? You've gone so pale!"

Cait tried to come up with an explanation that wouldn't sound…ridiculous.

"Tell me," Lindy said. "Don't just sit there wearing a foolish grin and looking like you're about to faint."

"Um, it goes back a few years."

"All right. Start there."

"Remember how kids sometimes do silly things? Like when you're young and foolish and don't know any better?"

"Me, yes, but not you," Lindy said calmly. "You're perfect. In all the time we've been friends, I haven't seen you do one impulsive thing. Not one. You analyze everything before you act. I can't imagine you ever doing anything silly."

"I did once," Cait told her, "but I was only eight."

"What could you have possibly done at age eight?"

"I…I got married."

"Married?" Lindy half rose from her chair. "You've got to be kidding."

"I wish I was."

"I'll bet a week's commissions that your husband's name is Joe." Lindy was smiling now, smiling widely.

Cait nodded and tried to smile in return.

"What's there to worry about? Good grief, kids do that sort of thing all the time! It doesn't mean anything."

"But I was a real brat about it. Joe and my brother, Martin, were best friends. Joe wanted to know what it felt like to kiss a girl, and I insisted he marry me first. If that wasn't bad enough, I pressured them into performing the ceremony inside their boys-only fort."

"So, you were a bit of pain—most eight-year-old girls are when it comes to dealing with their brothers. He got what he wanted, didn't he?"

Cait took a deep breath and nodded again.

"What was kissing him like?" Lindy asked in a curiously throaty voice.

"Good heavens, I don't remember," Cait answered shortly, then reconsidered. "I take that back. As I recall, it wasn't so bad, though obviously neither one of us had any idea what we were doing."

"Lindy, you're still here," Paul said as he strolled into the office. He inclined his head briefly in Cait's direction, but she had the impression he barely saw her. He'd hardly been around in the past couple of days—almost as if he was purposely avoiding her, she mused, but that thought was too painful to contemplate.

"I was just finishing up," Lindy said, glancing guiltily toward Cait. "We both were."

"Fine, fine, I didn't mean to disturb you. I'll see you two in the morning." A second later, he was gone.

Cait gazed after him with thinly disguised emotion. She waited until Paul was well out of range before she spoke. "He's so blind. What do I have to do, hit him over the head?"

"Quit being so negative," Lindy admonished. "You're going to be sharing an office with him for another five days. Do whatever you need to make darn sure he notices you."

"I've tried," Cait murmured, discouraged. And she had. She'd tried every trick known to woman, with little success.

Lindy left the office before her. Cait gathered up some stock reports to read that evening and stacked them neatly inside her leather briefcase. What Lindy had said about her being methodical and careful was true. It was also a source of pride; those traits had served her clients well.

To Cait's dismay, Joe followed her. "So," he said, smiling down at her, apparently oblivious to the other people clustering around the elevator. "Who have you been kissing these days?"

Hot color rose instantly to her face. Did he have to humiliate her in public?

"I could find myself jealous, you know."

"Would you kindly stop," she whispered furiously, scowling at him. Her hand tightened around the handle of her briefcase so hard her fingers ached.

"You figured it out?"

She nodded, her eyes darting to the lighted numbers above the elevator door, praying it would make its descent in record time instead of pausing on each floor.

"The years have been good to you."

"Thank you." *Please hurry,* she urged the elevator.

"I never would've believed Martin's little sister would turn out to be such a beauty."

If he was making fun of her, she didn't appreciate it. She was attractive, she knew that, but she certainly wasn't waiting for anyone to place a tiara on her head. "Thank you," she repeated grudgingly.

He gave an exaggerated sigh. "How are our children doing? What were their names again?" When she didn't answer right away, he added, "Don't tell me you've forgotten."

"Barbie and Ken," she muttered under her breath.

"That's right. I remember now."

If Joe hadn't drawn the attention of her co-workers before, he had now. Cait could have sworn every single person standing by the elevator turned to stare at her. The hope that no one was interested in their conversation was forever lost.

"Just how long do you intend to tease me about this?" she snapped.

"That depends," Joe responded with a chuckle Cait could only describe as sadistic. She gritted her teeth. He might have found the situation amusing, but she derived little enjoyment from being the office laughingstock.

Just then the elevator arrived, and not a moment too soon to suit Cait. The instant the doors slid open, she stepped toward it, determined to get as far away from this irritating man as possible.

He quickly caught up with her and she swung around to face him, her back ramrod stiff. "Is this really necessary?" she hissed, painfully conscious of the other people crowding into the elevator ahead of her.

He grinned. "I suppose not. I just wanted to see if I could get a rise out of you. It never worked when we were kids, you know. You were always so prim and proper."

"Look, you didn't like me then and I see no reason for you to—"

"Not *like* you?" he countered loudly enough for everyone in the building to hear. "I married you, didn't I?"

Chapter Two

Cait's heart seemed to stop. She realized that not only the people on the elevator but everyone left in the office was staring at her with unconcealed interest. The elevator was about to close and she quickly stepped forward, stretching out her arms to hold the doors open. She felt like Samson balanced between two marble columns.

"It's not the way it sounds," she felt obliged to explain in a loud voice, her gaze pleading.

No one made eye contact with her and, desperate, she turned to Joe, sending him a silent challenge to retract his words. His eyes were sparkling with mischief. If he did say anything, Cait thought in sudden horror, it was bound to make things even worse.

There didn't seem to be anything to do but tell the truth. "In case anyone has the wrong impression, this man and I are not married," she shouted. "Good grief, I was only eight!"

There was no reaction. It was as if she'd vanished into thin air. Defeated, she dropped her arms and stepped back, freeing the doors, which promptly closed.

Ignoring the other people on the elevator—who were carefully ignoring her—Cait clenched her hands into hard fists and glared up at Joe. Her face tightened with anger. "That was a rotten thing to do," she whispered hoarsely.

"What? It's true, isn't it?" he whispered back.

"You're being ridiculous to talk as though we're married!"

"We were once. It wounds me that you treat our marriage so lightly."

"I…it wasn't legal." The fact that they were even discussing this was preposterous. "You can't possibly hold me responsible for something that happened so long ago. To play this game now is…is infantile, and I refuse to be part of it."

The elevator finally came to a halt on the ground floor and, eager to make her escape, Cait rushed out. Straightening to keep her dignity intact, she headed through the crowded foyer toward the front doors. Although it was midafternoon, dusk was already setting in, casting dark shadows between the towering office buildings.

Cait reached the first intersection and sighed in relief as she glanced around her. Good. No sign of Joseph Rockwell. The light was red and she paused, although others hurried across the street after checking for traffic; Cait always felt obliged to obey the signal.

"What do you think Paul's going to say when he hears about this?" Joe asked from behind her.

Cait gave a start, then turned to look at her tormenter. She hadn't thought about Paul's reaction. Her throat seemed to constrict, rendering her speechless, otherwise she would have demanded Joe leave her alone. But he'd raised a question she dared not ignore. Paul might hear about her so-called former relationship with Joe and might even think there was something between them.

"You're in love with him, aren't you?"

She nodded. At the very mention of Paul's name, her knees went weak. He was everything she wanted in a man and more. She'd been crazy about him for months and now it was all about to be ruined by this irritating, unreasonable ghost from her past.

"Who told you?" Cait snapped. She couldn't imagine Lindy betraying her confidence, but Cait hadn't told anyone else.

"No one had to tell me," Joe said. "It's written all over you."

Shocked, Cait stared at Joe, her heart sinking. "Do…do you think Paul knows how I feel?"

Joe shrugged. "Maybe."

"But Lindy said…"

The light changed and, clasping her elbow, Joe urged her into the street. "What was it Lindy said?" he prompted when they'd crossed.

Cait looked up, about to tell him, when she realized exactly what she was doing—conversing with her antagonist. This was the very man who'd gone out of his way to embarrass and humiliate her in front of the entire office staff. Not to mention assorted clients and carpenters.

She stiffened. "Never mind what Lindy said. Now if you'll kindly excuse me…" With her head high, she marched down the sidewalk. She hadn't gone more than a few feet when the hearty sound of Joe's laughter caught up with her.

"You haven't changed in twenty years, Caitlin Marshall. Not a single bit."

Gritting her teeth, she marched on.

* * *

"Do you think Paul's heard?" Cait asked Lindy the instant she had a free moment the following afternoon. The New York Stock Exchange had closed for the day and Cait hadn't seen Paul since morning. It looked like he really *was* avoiding her.

"I wouldn't know," Lindy said as she typed some figures into her computer. "But the word about your childhood marriage has spread like wildfire everywhere else. It's the joke of the day. What did you and Joe do? Make a public announcement before you left the office yesterday afternoon?"

It was so nearly the truth that Cait guiltily lowered her eyes. "I didn't say a word," she defended herself. "Joe was the one."

"He told everyone you were married?" A suspicious tilt at the corner of her mouth betrayed Lindy's amusement.

"Not exactly. He started asking about our children in front of everyone."

"There were children?"

Cait resisted the urge to close her eyes and count to ten. "No. I brought my dolls to the wedding. Listen, I don't want to rehash a silly incident that happened years ago. I'm more afraid Paul's going to hear about it and put the wrong connotation on the whole thing. There's absolutely nothing between me and Joseph Rockwell. More than likely Paul won't give it a second thought, but I don't want there to be any…doubts between us, if you know what I mean."

"If you're so worried about it, talk to him," Lindy advised without lifting her eyes from the screen. "Honesty is the best policy, you know that."

"Yes, but it could prove to be a bit embarrassing, don't you think?"

"Paul will respect you for telling him the truth before he hears the rumors from someone else. Frankly, Cait, I think you're making a fuss over nothing. It isn't like you've committed a felony, you know."

"I realize that."

"Paul will probably be amused, like everyone else. He's not going to say anything." She looked up quickly, as though she expected Cait to try yet another argument.

Cait didn't. Instead she mulled over her friend's advice, gnawing on her lower lip. "You might be right. Paul will respect me for explaining the situation myself, instead of ignoring everything." Telling him the truth could be helpful in other respects, too, now that she thought about it.

If Paul had any feeling for her whatsoever, and oh, how she prayed he did, then he might become just a little jealous of her relationship with Joseph Rockwell. After all, Joe was an attractive man in a rugged outdoor sort of way. He was tall and muscular and, well, good-looking. The kind of good-looking that appealed to women—not Cait, of course, but other women. Hadn't Lindy commented almost immediately on how attractive he was?

"You're right," Cait said, walking resolutely toward the office she was temporarily sharing with Paul. Although she'd felt annoyed at first about being shuffled out of her own space, she'd come to think of this inconvenience as a blessing in disguise. However, she had to admit she'd been disappointed thus far. She had assumed she'd be spending a lot of time alone with him. That hadn't happened yet.

The more Cait considered the idea of a heart-to-heart

talk with her boss, the more appealing it became. As was her habit, she mentally rehearsed what she wanted to say to him, then gave herself a small pep talk.

"I don't remember that you talked to yourself." The male voice booming behind her startled Cait. "But then there's a great deal I've missed over the years, isn't there, Caitlin?"

Cait was so rattled she nearly stumbled. "What are you doing here?" she demanded. "Why are you following me around? Can't you see I'm busy?" He was the last person she wanted to confront just now.

"Sorry." He raised both hands in a gesture of apology contradicted by his twinkling blue eyes. "How about lunch later?"

He was teasing. He had to be. Besides, it would be insane for her to have anything to do with Joseph Rockwell. Heaven only knew what would happen if she gave him the least bit of encouragement. He'd probably hire a skywriter and announce to the entire city that they'd married as children.

"It shouldn't be that difficult to agree to a luncheon date," he informed her coolly.

"You're serious about this?"

"Of course I'm serious. We have a lot of years to catch up on." His hand rested on his leather pouch, giving him a rakish air of indifference.

"I've got an appointment this afternoon…" She offered the first plausible excuse she could think of; it might be uninspired but it also happened to be true. She'd made plans to have lunch with Lindy.

"Dinner then. I'm anxious to hear what Martin's been up to."

"Martin," she repeated, stalling for time while she invented another excuse. This wasn't a situation she had much experience with. She did date, but infrequently.

"Listen, bright eyes, no need to look so concerned. This isn't an invitation to the senior prom. It's one friend to another. Strictly platonic."

"You won't mention…our wedding to the waiter? Or anyone else?"

"I promise." As if to offer proof of his intent, he licked the end of his index finger and crossed his heart. "That was Martin's and my secret pledge sign. If either of us broke our word, the other was entitled to come up with a punishment. We both understood it would be a fate worse than death."

"I don't need any broken pledge in order to torture you, Joseph Rockwell. In two days you've managed to turn my life into—" She paused midsentence as Paul Jamison casually strolled past. He waved in Cait's direction and smiled benignly.

"Hello, Paul," she called out, weakly raising her right hand. He looked exceptionally handsome this morning in a three-piece dark blue suit. The contrast between him and Joe, who was wearing dust-covered jeans, heavy boots and a tool pouch, was so striking that Cait had to force herself not to stare at her boss. If only Paul had been the one to invite her to dinner…

"If you'll excuse me," she said politely, edging her way around Joe and toward Paul, who'd gone into his office. Their office. The need to talk to him burned within her. Words of explanation began to form themselves in her mind.

Joe caught her by the shoulders, bringing her up short. Cait gasped and raised shocked eyes to his.

"Dinner," he reminded her.

She blinked, hardly knowing what to say. "All right," she mumbled distractedly and recited her address, eager to have him gone.

"Good. I'll pick you up tonight at six." With that he released her and stalked away.

After taking a couple of moments to compose herself, Cait headed toward the office. "Hello, Paul," she said, standing just inside the doorway. "Do you have a moment to talk?"

He glanced up from a file on his desk. "Of course, Cait. Sit down and make yourself comfortable."

She moved into the room, closing the door behind her. When she looked back at Paul, he'd cocked his eyebrows in surprise. "Problems?" he asked.

"Not exactly." She pulled out the chair opposite his desk and slowly sat down. Now that she had his full attention, she was at a loss. All her prepared explanations and witticisms had flown out of her head. "The rate on municipal bonds has been extremely high lately," she said nervously.

Paul agreed with a quick nod. "They have been for several months now."

"Yes, I know. That's what makes them such excellent value." Cait had been selling bonds heavily in the past few weeks.

"You didn't close the door to talk to me about bonds," Paul said softly. "What's troubling you, Cait?"

She laughed uncomfortably, wondering how a man could be so astute in one area and so blind in another. If only he'd reveal some emotion toward her. Anything. All he did was sit across from her and wait. He was cordial enough, gracious even, but there was no hint of anything more. Nothing to give Cait any hope that he was starting to care for her.

"It's about Joseph Rockwell."

"The contractor who's handling the remodeling?"

Cait nodded. "I knew him years ago when we were just children." She glanced at Paul, whose face remained blank. "We were neighbors. In fact Joe and my brother, Martin, were best friends. Joe moved out to the suburbs when he and Martin were in the sixth grade and I hadn't heard anything from him since."

"It's a small world, isn't it?" Paul remarked affably.

"Joe and Martin were typical young boys," she said, rushing her words a little in her eagerness to have this out in the open. "Full of tomfoolery and pranks."

"Boys will be boys," Paul said without any real enthusiasm.

"Yes, I know. Once—" she forced a light laugh "—they actually involved me in one of their crazy schemes."

"What did they put you up to? Robbing a bank?"

She somehow managed a smile. "Not exactly. Joe—I always called him Joseph back then, because it irritated him. Anyway, Joe and Martin had this friend named Pete who was a year older and he'd spent part of his summer vacation visiting his aunt in Peoria. I think it was Peoria.... Anyway he came back bragging about having kissed a girl. Naturally Martin and Joe were jealous and as you said, boys will be boys, so they decided that one of them should test it out and see if kissing a girl was everything Pete claimed it was."

"I take it they decided to make you their guinea pig."

"Exactly." Cait slid to the edge of the chair, pleased that Paul was following this rather convoluted explanation. "I was eight and considered something of a...pest." She paused, hoping Paul would make some comment about how impossible that was. When he didn't, she continued, a little let down at his restraint. "Apparently I was more of one than I remembered," she said, with another forced laugh. "At eight, I didn't think kissing was something nice girls did, at least not without a wedding band on their finger."

"So you kissed Joseph Rockwell," Paul said absently.

"Yes, but there was a tiny bit more than that. I made him marry me."

Paul's eyebrows shot to the ceiling.

"Now, almost twenty years later, he's getting his revenge by going around telling everyone that we're actually married. Which of course is ridiculous."

A couple of strained seconds followed her announcement.

"I'm not sure what to say," Paul murmured.

"Oh, I wasn't expecting you to say anything. I thought it was important to clear the air, that's all."

"I see."

"He's only doing it because...well, because that's Joe. Even when we were kids he enjoyed playing these little games. No one really minded, though, especially not the girls, because he was so cute." She certainly had Paul's attention now.

"I thought you should know," she added, "in case you happened to hear a rumor or something. I didn't want you thinking Joe and I were involved, or even considering a relationship. I was fairly certain you wouldn't, but one never knows and I'm a firm believer in being forthright and honest."

Paul blinked. Wanting to fill the awkward silence, Cait chattered on. "Apparently Joe recognized my name when he and his men moved my office in here with yours. He was delighted when I didn't recognize him. In fact, he caused a commotion by asking me about our children in front of everyone."

"Children?"

"My dolls," Cait was quick to explain.

"Joe Rockwell's an excellent man. I couldn't fault your taste, Cait."

"The two of us *aren't* involved," she protested. "Good grief, I haven't seen him in nearly twenty years."

"I see," Paul said slowly. He sounded…disappointed, Cait thought. But she must have misread his tone because there wasn't a single, solitary reason for him to be disappointed. Cait felt foolish now for even trying to explain this fiasco. Paul was so oblivious about her feelings that there was nothing she could say or do to make him understand.

"I just wanted you to know," she repeated, "in case you heard the rumors and were wondering if there was anything between me and Joseph Rockwell. I wanted to assure you there isn't."

"I see," he said again. "Don't worry about it, Cait. What happened between you and Rockwell isn't going to affect your job."

She stood up to leave, praying she'd detect a suggestion of jealousy. A hint of rivalry. Anything to show he cared. There was nothing, so she tried again. "I agreed to have dinner with him, though."

Paul had returned his attention to the papers he'd been reading when she'd interrupted him.

"For old times' sake," she said in a reassuring voice—

to fend off any violent display of resentment, she told herself. "I certainly don't have any intention of dating him on a regular basis."

Paul grinned. "Have a good time."

"Yes, I will, thanks." Her heart felt as heavy as a sinking battleship. Without knowing where she was headed or who she'd talk to, Cait wandered out of Paul's office, forgetting for a second that she had no office of her own. The area where her desk once sat was cluttered with wire reels, ladders and men. Joe must have left, a fact for which Cait was grateful.

She walked into Lindy's small office across the hall. Her friend glanced up. "So?" she murmured. "Did you talk to Paul?"

Cait nodded.

"How'd it go?"

"Fine, I guess." She perched on the corner of Lindy's desk, crossing her arms around her waist as her left leg swung rhythmically, keeping time with her discouraged heart. She should be accustomed to disappointment when it came to Paul, but somehow each rejection inflicted a fresh wound on her already battered ego. "I was hoping Paul might be jealous."

"And he wasn't?"

"Not that I could tell."

"It isn't as though you and Joe have anything to do with each other now," Lindy sensibly pointed out. "Marrying him was a childhood prank. It isn't likely to concern Paul."

"I even mentioned that I was going out to dinner with Joe," Cait said morosely.

"You are? When?" Lindy asked, her eyes lighting up. "Where?"

If only Paul had revealed half as much interest. "Tonight. And I don't know where."

"You are going, aren't you?"

"I guess. I can't see any way of avoiding it. Otherwise he'd pester me until I gave in. If I ever marry and have daughters, Lindy, I'm going to warn them about boys from the time they're old enough to understand."

"Don't you think you should follow your own advice?" Lindy asked, glancing pointedly in the direction of Paul's office.

"Not if I were to have Paul's children," Cait said, eager to defend her boss. "Our daughter would be so intelligent and perceptive she wouldn't need to be warned."

Lindy's smile was distracted. "Listen, I've got a few things to finish up here. Why don't you go over to the deli and grab us a table. I'll meet you there in fifteen minutes."

"Sure," Cait said. "Do you want me to order for you?"

"No. I don't know what I want yet."

"Okay, I'll see you in a few minutes."

They often ate at the deli across the street from their office complex. The food was good, the service fast, and generally by three in the afternoon, Cait was famished.

She was so wrapped up in her thoughts, which were muddled and gloomy after her talk with Paul, that she didn't notice how late Lindy was. Her friend rushed into the restaurant more than half an hour after Cait had arrived.

"I'm sorry," she said, sounding flustered and oddly shaken. "I had no idea those last few chores would take me so long. Oh, you must be starved. I hope you've ordered." Lindy removed her coat and stuffed it into the booth before sliding onto the red upholstered seat herself.

"Actually, no, I didn't." Cait sighed. "Just tea." Her spirits were at an all-time low. It was becoming painfully clear that Paul didn't harbor a single romantic feeling toward her. She was wasting her time and her emotional energy on him. If only she'd had more experience with the opposite sex. It seemed her whole love life had gone into neutral the moment she'd graduated from college. At the rate things were developing, she'd still be single by the time she turned thirty—a possibility too dismal to contemplate. She hadn't given much thought to marriage and children, always assuming they'd naturally become part of her life; now she wasn't so sure. Even as a child, she'd pictured her grown-up self with a career *and* a family. Behind the business exterior was a woman traditional enough to hunger for that most special of relationships.

She had to face the fact that marriage would never happen if she continued to love a man who didn't return her feelings. She gave a low groan, then noticed that Lindy was gazing at her in concern.

"Let's order something," Lindy said quickly, reaching for the menu tucked behind the napkin holder. "I'm starved."

"I was thinking I'd skip lunch today," Cait mumbled. She sipped her lukewarm tea and frowned. "Joe will be taking me out to dinner soon. And frankly, I don't have much of an appetite."

"This is all my fault, isn't it?" Lindy asked, looking guilty.

"Of course not. I'm just being practical." If Cait was anything, it was practical—except about Paul. "Go ahead and order."

"You're sure you don't mind?"

Cait gestured nonchalantly. "Heavens, no."

"If you're sure, then I'll have the turkey on whole wheat," Lindy said after a moment. "You know how much I like turkey, though you'd think I'd have gotten enough over Thanksgiving."

"I'll just have a refill on my tea," Cait said.

"You're still flying to Minnesota for the holidays, aren't you?" Lindy asked, fidgeting with the menu.

"Mmm-hmm." Cait had purchased her ticket several months earlier. Martin and his family lived near Minneapolis. When their father had died several years earlier, Cait's mother moved to Minnesota, settling down in a new subdivision not far from Martin, his wife and their four children. Cait tried to visit at least once a year. However, she'd been there in August, stopping off on her way home from a business trip. Usually she made a point of visiting her brother and his family over the Christmas holidays. It was generally a slow week on the stock market, anyway. And if she was going to travel halfway across the country, she wanted to make it worth her while.

"When will you be leaving?" Lindy asked, although Cait was sure she'd already told her friend more than once.

"The twenty-third." For the past few years, Cait had used one week of her vacation at Christmas time, usually starting the weekend before.

But this year Paul was having a Christmas party and Cait didn't want to miss that, so she'd booked her flight closer to the holiday.

The waitress came to take Lindy's order and replenish the hot water for Cait's tea. The instant she moved away from their booth, Lindy launched into a lengthy tirade about how she hated Christmas shopping and how busy the malls were this time of year. Cait stared at her, bewildered. It wasn't like her friend to chat nonstop.

"Lindy," she interrupted, "is something wrong?"

"Wrong? What could possibly be wrong?"

"I don't know. You haven't stopped talking for the last ten minutes."

"I haven't?" There was an abrupt, uncomfortable silence.

Cait decided it was her turn to say something. "I think I'll wear my red velvet dress," she mused.

"To dinner with Joe?"

"No," she said, shaking her head. "To Paul's Christmas party."

Lindy sighed. "But what are you wearing tonight?"

The question took Cait by surprise. She didn't consider this dinner with Joe a real date. He just wanted to talk over old times, which was fine with Cait as long as he behaved himself. Suddenly she frowned, then closed her eyes. "Martin's a Methodist minister," she said softly.

"Yes, I know," Lindy reminded her. "I've known that since I first met you, which was what? Three years ago now."

"Four last month."

"So what does Martin's occupation have to do with anything?" Lindy asked.

"Joe Rockwell can't find out," Cait whispered.

"I didn't plan on telling him," Lindy whispered back.

"I've got to make up some other occupation like…"

"Counselor," Lindy suggested. "I'm curious, though. Why can't you tell Joe about Martin?"

"Think about it!"

"I am thinking. I really doubt Joe would care one way or the other."

"He might try to make something of it. You don't know

Joe like I do. He'd razz me about it all evening, claiming the marriage was valid. You know, because Martin really *is* a minister, and since Martin performed the ceremony, we must really be married—that kind of nonsense."

"I didn't think about that."

But then, Lindy didn't seem to be thinking much about anything lately. It was as if she was walking around in a perpetual daydream. Cait couldn't remember Lindy's ever being so scatterbrained. If she didn't know better, she'd guess there was a man involved.

Chapter Three

At ten to six, Cait was blow-drying her hair in a haphazard fashion, regretting that she'd ever had it cut. She was looking forward to this dinner date about as much as a trip to the dentist. All she wanted was to get it over with, come home and bury her head under a pillow while she sorted out how she was going to get Paul to notice her.

Restyling her hair hadn't done the trick. Putting in extra hours at the office hadn't impressed him, either. Cait was beginning to think she could stand on top of his desk naked and not attract his attention.

She walked into her compact living room and smoothed the bulky-knit sweater over her slim hips. She hadn't dressed for the occasion, although the sweater was new and expensive. Gray wool slacks and a powder-blue turtleneck with a silver heart-shaped necklace dangling from her neck were about as dressy as she cared to get with someone like Joe. He'd probably be wearing cowboy boots and jeans, if not his hard hat and tool pouch.

Oh, yes, Cait had recognized his type when she'd first seen him. Joe Rockwell was a man's man. He walked and talked macho. No doubt he drove a truck with tires so high off the ground she'd need a stepladder to climb inside. He was tough and gruff and liked his women meek and submissive. In that case, of course, she had nothing to worry about; he'd lose interest immediately.

He arrived right on time, which surprised Cait. Being prompt didn't fit the image she had of Joe Rockwell, redneck contractor. She sighed and painted on a smile, then walked slowly to the door.

The smile faded. Joe stood before her, tall and debonair, dressed in a dark gray pin-striped suit. His gray silk tie had *pink* stripes. He was the picture of smooth sophistication. She knew that Joe was the same man she'd seen earlier in dusty work clothes—yet he was different. He was nothing like Paul, of course. But Joseph Rockwell was a devastatingly handsome man. With a devastating charm. Rarely had she seen a man smile the way he did. His eyes twinkled with warmth and life and mischief. It wasn't difficult to imagine Joe with a little boy whose eyes mirrored his. Cait didn't know where that thought came from, but she pushed it aside before it could linger and take root.

"Hello," he said, flashing her that smile.

"Hi." She couldn't stop looking at him.

"May I come in?"

"Oh…of course. I'm sorry," she faltered, stumbling in her haste to step aside. He'd caught her completely off guard. "I was about to change clothes," she said quickly.

"You look fine."

"These old things?" She feigned a laugh. "If you'll excuse me, I'll only be a minute." She poured him a cup of coffee, then dashed into her bedroom, ripping the sweater over her head and closing the door with one foot. Her shoes went flying as she ran to her closet. Jerking aside the orderly row of business jackets and skirts, she pulled clothes off their hangers, considered them, then tossed them on the bed. Nearly everything she owned was more suitable for the office than a dinner date.

The only really special dress she owned was the red velvet one she'd purchased for Paul's Christmas party. The temptation to slip into that was strong but she resisted, wanting to save it for her boss, though heaven knew he probably wouldn't notice.

Deciding on a skirt and blazer, she hopped frantically around her bedroom as she pulled on her panty hose. Next she threw on a rose-colored silk blouse and managed to button it while stepping into her skirt. She tucked the blouse into the waistband and her feet into a pair of medium-heeled pumps. Finally, her velvet blazer and she was ready. Taking a deep breath, she returned to the living room in three minutes flat.

"That was fast," Joe commented, standing by the fireplace, hands clasped behind his back. He was examining a framed photograph that sat on the mantel. "Is this Martin's family?"

"Martin…why, yes, that's Martin, his wife and their children." She hoped he didn't detect the breathless catch in her voice.

"Four children."

"Yes, he and Rebecca wanted a large family." Her heartbeat was slowly returning to normal though Cait still felt light-headed. She had a sneaking suspicion that she was suffering from the effects of unleashed male charm.

She realized with surprise that Joe hadn't said or done anything to embarrass or fluster her. She'd expected him to arrive with a whole series of remarks designed to disconcert her.

"Timmy's ten, Kurt's eight, Jenny's six and Clay's four." She introduced the freckle-faced youngsters, pointing each one out.

"They're handsome children."

"They are, aren't they?"

Cait experienced a twinge of pride. The main reason she went to Minneapolis every year was Martin's children. They adored her and she was crazy about them. Christmas wouldn't be Christmas without Jenny and Clay snuggling on her lap while their father read the Nativity story. Christmas was singing carols in front of a crackling wood fire, accompanied by Martin's guitar. It meant stringing popcorn and cranberries for the seven-foot-tall tree that always adorned the living room. It was having the children take turns scraping fudge from the sides of the copper kettle, and supervising the decorating of sugar cookies with all four crowded around the kitchen table. Caitlin Marshall might be a dedicated stockbroker with an impressive clientele, but when it came to Martin's children, she was Auntie Cait.

"It's difficult to think of Martin with kids," Joe said, carefully placing the family photo back on the mantel.

"He met Rebecca his first year of college and the rest, as they say, is history."

"What about you?" Joe asked, turning unexpectedly to face her.

"What about me?"

"Why haven't you married?"

"Uh…" Cait wasn't sure how to answer him. She had a glib reply she usually gave when anyone asked, but somehow she knew Joe wouldn't accept that. "I…I've never really fallen in love."

"What about Paul?"

"Until Paul," she corrected, stunned that she'd forgotten the strong feelings she held for her employer. She'd been so concerned with being honest that she'd overlooked the obvious. "I am deeply in love with Paul," she said defiantly, wanting there to be no misunderstanding.

"There's no need to convince me, Caitlin."

"I'm not trying to convince you of anything. I've been in love with Paul for nearly a year. Once he realizes he loves me, too, we'll be married."

Joe's mouth slanted in a wry line and he seemed about to argue with her. Cait waylaid any attempt by glancing pointedly at her watch. "Shouldn't we be leaving?"

After a long moment, Joe said, "Yes, I suppose we should," in a mild, neutral voice.

Cait went to the hall closet for her coat, aware with every step she took that Joe was watching her. She turned back to smile at him, but somehow the smile didn't materialize. His blue eyes met hers, and she found his look disturbing—caressing, somehow, and intimate.

Joe helped her on with her coat and led her to the parking lot, where he'd left his car. Another surprise awaited her. It wasn't a four-wheel-drive truck, but a late sixties black convertible in mint condition.

The restaurant was one of the most respected in Seattle, with a noted chef and a reputation for excellent seafood. Cait chose grilled salmon and Joe ordered Cajun shrimp.

"Do you remember the time Martin and I decided to open our own business?" Joe asked, as they sipped a predinner glass of wine.

Cait did indeed recall that summer. "You might have been a bit more ingenious. A lemonade stand wasn't the world's most creative enterprise."

"Perhaps not, but we were doing a brisk business until an annoying eight-year-old girl ruined everything."

Cait wasn't about to let that comment pass. "You were using moldy lemons and covering the taste with too much sugar. Besides, it's unhealthy to share paper cups."

Joe chuckled, the sound deep and rich. "I should've known then that you were nothing but trouble."

"It seems to me the whole mess was your own fault. You boys wouldn't listen to me. I had to do something before someone got sick on those lemons."

"Carrying a picket sign that read 'Talk to me before you buy this lemonade' was a bit drastic even for you, don't you think?"

"If anything, it brought you more business," Cait said dryly, recalling how her plan had backfired. "All the boys in the neighborhood wanted to see what contaminated lemonade tasted like."

"You were a damn nuisance, Cait. Own up to it." He smiled and Cait sincerely doubted that any woman could argue with him when he smiled full-force.

"I most certainly was not! If anything you two were—"

"Disgusting, I believe, was your favorite word for Martin and me."

"And you did your level best to live up to it," she said,

struggling to hold back a smile. She reached for a bread-stick and bit into it to disguise her amusement. She'd always enjoyed rankling Martin and Joe, though she'd never have admitted it, especially at the age of eight.

"Picketing our lemonade stand wasn't the worst trick you ever pulled, either," Joe said mischievously.

Cait had trouble swallowing. She should have been prepared for this. If he remembered her complaints about the lemonade stand, he was sure to remember what had happened once Betsy McDonald found out about the kissing incident.

"It wasn't a trick," Cait protested.

"But you told everyone at school that I'd kissed you—even though you'd promised not to."

"Not exactly." There was a small discrepancy that needed clarification. "If you think back you'll remember you said I couldn't tell anyone I'd been inside the fort. You didn't say anything about the kiss."

Joe frowned darkly as if attempting to jog his memory. "How can you remember details like that? All of this happened years ago."

"I remember everything," Cait said grandly—a gross exaggeration. She hadn't recognized Joe, after all. But on this one point she was absolutely clear. "You and Martin were far more concerned that I not tell anyone about going inside the fort. You didn't say a word about keeping the kiss a secret."

"But did you have to tell Betsy McDonald? That girl had been making eyes at me for weeks. As soon as she learned I'd kissed you instead of her, she was furious."

"Betsy was the most popular girl in school. I wanted her for my friend, so I told."

"And sold me down the river."

"Would an apology help?" Confident he was teasing her once again, Cait gave him her most charming smile.

"An apology just might do it." Joe grinned back, a grin that brightened his eyes to a deeper, more tantalizing shade of blue. It was with some difficulty that Cait pulled her gaze away from his.

"If Betsy liked you," she asked, smoothing the linen napkin across her lap, "then why didn't you kiss her? She'd probably have let you. You wouldn't have had to bribe her with your precious baseball cards, either."

"You're kidding. If I kissed Betsy McDonald I might as well have signed over my soul," Joe said, continuing the joke.

"Even as mere children, men are afraid of commitment," Cait said solemnly.

Joe ignored her remark.

"Your memory's not as sharp as you think," Cait felt obliged to tell him, enjoying herself more than she'd thought possible.

Once again, Joe overlooked her comment. "I can remember Martin complaining about how you'd line up your dolls in a row and teach them school. Once you even got him to come in as a guest lecturer. Heaven knew what you had to do to get him to play professor to a bunch of dolls."

"I found a pair of dirty jeans stuffed under the sofa with something dead in the pocket. Mom would have tanned his hide if she'd found them, so Martin owed me a favor. Then he got all bent out of shape when I collected it. He didn't seem the least bit appreciative that I'd saved him."

"Good old Martin," Joe said, shaking his head. "I swear he was as big on ceremony as you were. Marrying us was a turning point in his life. From that point on, he started carting a Bible around with him the way some kids do a slingshot. Right in his hip pocket. If he wasn't burying something, he was holding revival meetings. Remember how he got in a pack of trouble at school for writing 'God loves you, ask Martin' on the back wall of the school?"

"I remember."

"I sort of figured he might become a missionary."

"Martin?" She gave an abrupt laugh. "Never. He likes his conveniences. He doesn't even go camping. Martin's idea of roughing it is doing without valet service."

She expected Joe to chuckle. He did smile at her attempted joke, but that was all. He seemed to be studying her the same way she'd been studying him.

"You surprise me," Joe announced suddenly.

"I do? Am I a disappointment to you?"

"Not at all. I always thought you'd grow up and have a passel of children yourself. You used to haul those dolls of yours around with you everywhere. If Martin and I were too noisy, you'd shush us, saying the babies were asleep. If we wanted to play in the backyard, we couldn't because you were having a tea party with your dolls. It was enough to drive a ten-year-old boy crazy. But if we ever dared complain, you'd look at us serenely and with the sweetest smile tell us we had to be patient because it was for the children."

"I did get carried away with all that motherhood business, didn't I?" Joe's words stirred up uncomfortable memories, the same ones she'd entertained earlier that afternoon. She really did love children. Yet, somehow, without her quite knowing how, the years had passed and she'd buried the dream. Nowadays she didn't like to think too much about a husband and family—the life that hadn't happened. It haunted her at odd moments.

"I should have known you'd end up in construction," she said, switching the subject away from herself.

"How's that?" Joe asked.

"Wasn't it you who built the fort?"

"Martin helped."

"Sure, by staying out of the way." She grinned. "I know my brother. He's a marvel with people, but please don't ever give him a hammer."

Their dinner arrived, and it was as delicious as Cait had expected, although by then she was enjoying herself so much that even a plateful of dry toast would have tasted good. They drank two cups of cappuccino after their meal, and talked and laughed as the hours melted away. Cait couldn't remember the last time she'd laughed so much.

When at last she glanced at her watch, she was shocked to realize it was well past ten. "I had no idea it was so late!" she said. "I should get home." She had to be up by five.

Joe took care of the bill and collected her coat. When they walked outside, the December night was clear and chilly, with a multitude of stars twinkling brightly above.

"Are you cold?" he asked as they waited for the valet to deliver the car.

"Not at all." Nevertheless, he placed his arm around her shoulders, drawing her close.

Cait didn't protest. It felt natural for this man to hold her close.

His car arrived and they drove back to her apartment building in silence. When he pulled into the parking lot, she considered inviting him in for coffee, then decided against it. They'd already drunk enough coffee, and besides, they both had to work the following morning. But more important, Joe might read something else into the invitation. He was an old friend. Nothing more. And she wanted to keep it that way.

She turned to him and smiled softly. "I had a lovely time. Thank you so much."

"You're welcome, Cait. We'll do it again."

Cait was astonished to realize how appealing another evening with Joseph Rockwell was. She'd underestimated him.

Or had she?

"There's something else I'd like to try again," he was saying, his eyes filled with devilry.

"Try again?" she repeated. "What?"

He slid his arm behind her and for a breathless moment they looked at each other. "I don't know if I've got a chance without trading a few baseball cards, though."

Cait swallowed. "You want to kiss me?"

He nodded. His eyes seemed to grow darker, more intense. "For old times' sake." His hand caressed the curve of her neck, his thumb moving slowly toward the scented hollow of her throat.

"Well, sure. For old times' sake." She was astonished at the way her heart was reacting to the thought of Joe holding her…kissing her.

His mouth began a slow descent toward hers, his warm breath nuzzling her skin.

"Just remember," she whispered when his mouth was about to settle over hers. Her hands gripped his lapels. "Old times'…"

"I'll remember," he said as his lips came down on hers.

She sighed and slid her hands up his solid chest to link her fingers at the base of his neck. The kiss was slow and thorough. When it was over, Cait's hands were clutching his collar.

Joe's fingers were in her hair, tangled in the short, soft curls, cradling the back of her head.

A sweet rush of joy coursed through her veins. Cait felt a bubbling excitement, a burst of warmth, unlike anything she'd ever known before.

Then he kissed her a second time…

"Just remember…" she repeated when he pulled his mouth from hers and buried it in the delicate curve of her neck.

He drew in several ragged breaths before asking, "What is it I'm supposed to remember?"

"Yes, oh, please, remember."

He lifted his head and rested his hands lightly on her shoulders, his face only inches from hers. "What's so important you don't want me to forget?" he whispered.

It wasn't Joe who was supposed to remember; it was Cait. She didn't realize she'd spoken out loud. She blinked, uncertain, then tilted her head to gaze down at her hands, anywhere but at him. "Oh…that I'm in love with Paul."

There was a moment of silence. An awkward moment. "Right," he answered shortly. "You're in love with Paul." His arms fell away and he released her.

Cait hesitated, uneasy. "Thanks again for a wonderful dinner." Her hand closed around the door handle. She was eager now to make her escape.

"Any time," he said flippantly. His own hands gripped the steering wheel.

"I'll see you soon."

"Soon," he echoed. She climbed out of the car, not giving Joe a chance to come around and open the door for her. She was aware of him sitting in the car, waiting until she'd unlocked the lobby door and stepped inside. She hurried down the first-floor hall and into her apartment, turning on the lights so he'd know she'd made it safely home.

Then she removed her coat and carefully hung it in the closet. When she peeked out the window, she saw that Joe had already left.

Lindy was at her desk working when Cait arrived the next morning. Cait smiled at her as she hurried past, but didn't stop to indulge in conversation.

Cait could feel Lindy's gaze trailing after her and she knew her friend was disappointed that she hadn't told her about the dinner date with Joe Rockwell.

Cait didn't want to talk about it. She was afraid that if she said anything to Lindy, she wouldn't be able to avoid mentioning the kiss, which was a subject she wanted to avoid at all costs. She wouldn't be able to delay her friend's questions forever, but Cait wanted to put them off until at least the end of the day. Longer, if possible.

What a fool she'd been to let Joe kiss her. It had seemed so right at the time, a natural conclusion to a delightful evening.

The fact that she'd let him do it without even making a token protest still confused her. If Paul happened to hear about it, he might think she really *was* interested in Joe. Which, of course, she wasn't.

Her boss was a man of principle and integrity—and altogether a frustrating person to fall in love with. Judging by his reaction to her dinner with Joe, he seemed immune to jealousy. Now if only she could discover a way of letting him know how she felt...and spark his interest in the process!

The morning was hectic. Out of the corner of her eye, Cait saw Joe arrive. Although she was speaking to an important client on the phone, she stared after him as he approached the burly foreman. She watched Joe remove a blueprint from a long, narrow tube and roll it open so two other men could study it. There seemed to be some discussion, then the foreman nodded and Joe left, without so much as glancing in Cait's direction.

That stung.

At least he could have waved hello. But if he wanted to ignore her, well, fine. She'd do the same.

The market closed on the up side, the Dow Jones industrial average at 2600 points after brisk trading. The day's work was over.

As Cait had predicted, Lindy sought her out almost immediately.

"So how'd your dinner date go?"

"It was fun."

"Where'd he take you? Sam's Bar and Grill as you thought?"

"Actually, no," she said, clearing her throat, feeling more than a little foolish for having suggested such a thing. "He took me to Henry's." She announced it louder than necessary, since Paul was strolling into the office just then. But for all the notice he gave her, she might as well have been fresh paint drying on the office wall.

"Henry's," Lindy echoed. "He took you to Henry's?

Why, that's one of the best restaurants in town. It must have cost him a small fortune."

"I wouldn't know. My menu didn't list any prices."

"You're joking. No one's ever taken me anyplace so fancy. What did you order?"

"Grilled salmon." She continued to study Paul for some clue that he was listening in on her and Lindy's conversation. He was seated at his desk, reading a report on short-term partnerships as a tax advantage. Cait had read it earlier in the week and had recommended it to him.

"Was it wonderful?" Lindy pressed.

It took Cait a moment to realize her friend was quizzing her about the dinner. "Excellent. The best fish I've had in years."

"What did you do afterward?"

Cait looked back at her friend. "What makes you think we did anything? We had dinner, talked, and then he drove me home. Nothing more happened. Understand? Nothing."

"If you say so," Lindy said, eyeing her suspiciously. "But you're certainly defensive about it."

"I just want you to know that nothing happened. Joseph Rockwell is an old friend. That's all."

Paul glanced up from the report, but his gaze connected with Lindy's before slowly progressing to Cait.

"Hello, Paul," Cait greeted him cheerfully. "Are Lindy and I disturbing you? We'd be happy to go into the hallway if you'd like."

"No, no, you're fine. Don't worry about it." He looked past them to the doorway and got to his feet. "Hello, Rockwell."

"Am I interrupting a meeting?" Joe asked, stepping into

the office as if it didn't really matter whether he was or not. His hard hat was back in place, along with the dusty jeans and the tool pouch. And yet Cait had no difficulty remembering last night's sophisticated dinner companion when she looked at him.

"No, no," Paul answered, "we were just chatting. Come on in. Problems?"

"Not really. But there's something I'd like you to take a look at in the other room."

"I'll be right there."

Joe threw Cait a cool smile as he strolled past. "Hello, Cait."

"Joe." Her heart was pounding hard, and that was ridiculous. It must have been due to embarrassment, she told herself. Joe was a friend, a boy from the old neighborhood; just because she'd allowed him to kiss her didn't mean there was—or ever would be—anything romantic between them. The sooner she made him understand this, the better.

"Joe and Cait went out to dinner last night," Lindy said pointedly to Paul. "He took her to Henry's."

"How nice," Paul commented, clearly more interested in troubleshooting with Joe than discussing Cait's dating history.

"We had a good time, didn't we?" Joe asked Cait.

"Yes, very nice," she responded stiffly.

Joe waited until Paul was out of the room before he stepped back and dropped a kiss on her cheek. Then he announced loudly enough for everyone in the vicinity to hear, "You were incredible last night."

Chapter Four

"I thought you said nothing happened," Lindy said, looking intently at a red-faced Cait.

"Nothing did happen." Cait was furious enough to kick Joe Rockwell in the shins the way he deserved. How dared he say something so…so embarrassing in front of Lindy! And probably within earshot of Paul!

"But then why would he say something like that?"

"How should I know?" Cait snapped. "One little kiss and he makes it sound like—"

"He kissed you?" Lindy asked sharply, her eyes narrowing. "You just got done telling me there's nothing between the two of you."

"Good grief, the kiss didn't mean anything. It was for old times' sake. Just a platonic little kiss." All right, she was exaggerating a bit, but it couldn't be helped.

While she was speaking, Cait gathered her things and shoved them in her briefcase. Then she slammed the lid closed and reached for her coat, thrusting her arms into the sleeves, her movements abrupt and ungraceful.

d a mouthful of pizza and Cait was left to wait
moments until he swallowed. "I seem to recall he
explained that the two of us go a long way back."
traightened, too curious to hide her interest. "Did
concerned? Jealous?"

? No, if anything, he looked bored."

ed," Cait repeated. Her shoulders sagged with de-
swear that man wouldn't notice me if I pranced
his office naked."

t's a clever idea, and one that just might work.
you should practice around the house first, get the
f it. I'd be willing to help you out if you're serious
this." He sounded utterly nonchalant, as though
uggested subscribing to cable television. "This is
iends are for. Do you need help undressing?"

took a sip of her wine to hide a smile. Joe hadn't
ed in twenty years. He was still witty and fun-lov-
d a terrible tease. "Very funny."

ey, I wasn't kidding. I'll pretend I'm Paul and—"
u promised you were going to be good."

wiggled his eyebrows suggestively. "I will be. Just
ait."

could feel the tide of color flow into her cheeks.
ickly lowered her eyes to her plate. "Joe, cut it out.
making me blush and I hate to blush. It makes my
ok like a ripe tomato." She lifted her slice of pizza
into it, chewing thoughtfully. "I don't understand
ery time I think I have you figured out you do
ng to surprise me."

what?"

yesterday. You invited me to dinner, but I never
you'd take me someplace as elegant as Henry's.

"Have a nice weekend," she said tightly, not completely understanding why she felt so annoyed with Lindy.
"I'll see you Monday." She marched through the office,
but paused in front of Joe.

"You wanted something, sweetheart?' he asked in a ca-
joling voice.

"You're despicable!"

Joe looked downright disappointed. "Not low and
disgusting?"

"That, too."

He grinned from ear to ear just the way she knew he
would. "I'm glad to hear it."

Cait bit back an angry retort. It wouldn't do any good
to engage in a verbal battle with Joe Rockwell. He'd have
a comeback for any insult she could hurl. Seething, Cait
marched to the elevator and jabbed the button impatiently.

"I'll be by later tonight, darling," Joe called to her just
as the doors were closing, effectively cutting off any protest.

He was joking. He had to be joking. No man in his right
mind could possibly expect her to invite him into her home
after this latest stunt. Not even the impertinent Joe Rockwell.

Once home, Cait took a long, soothing shower, dried
her hair and changed into jeans and a sweater. Friday
nights were generally quiet ones for her. She was munching on pretzels and surveying the bleak contents of her
refrigerator when there was a knock on the door.

It couldn't possibly be Joe, she told herself.

It *was* Joe, balancing a large pizza on the palm of one
hand and clutching a bottle of red wine in the other.

Cait stared at him, too dumbfounded at his audacity
to speak.

"I come bearing gifts," he said, presenting the pizza to her with more than a little ceremony.

"Listen here, you…you fool, it's going to take a whole lot more than pizza to make up for that stunt you pulled this afternoon."

"Come on, Cait, lighten up a little."

"Lighten up! You…you…"

"I believe the word you're looking for is fool."

"You have your nerve." She dug her fists into her hips, knowing she should slam the door in his face. She would have, too, but the pizza smelled *so* good it was difficult to maintain her indignation.

"Okay, I'll admit it," Joe said, his deep blue eyes revealing genuine contrition. "I got carried away. You're right, I am an idiot. All I can do is ask your forgiveness." He lifted the lid of the pizza box and Cait was confronted by the thickest, most mouthwatering masterpiece she'd ever seen. The top was crowded with no less than ten tempting toppings, all covered with a thick layer of hot melted cheese.

"Do you accept my humble apology?" Joe pressed, waving the pizza under her nose.

"Are there any anchovies on that thing?"

"Only on half."

"You're forgiven." She took him by the elbow and dragged him inside her apartment.

Cait led the way into the kitchen. She got two plates from the cupboard and collected knives, forks and napkins as she mentally reviewed his crimes. "I couldn't believe you actually said that," she mumbled, shaking her head. She set the kitchen table, neatly positioning the napkins after shoving the day's mail to one side. "The

least you can do is tell me why you
say that in front of Paul. Lindy had a
me. Can you imagine what she and P.
She retrieved two wineglasses from th
them by the plates. "I've never been
in my life."

"Never?" he prompted, opening
kitchen drawers until he located a cor

"Never," she repeated. "And don't th
to ensure lasting peace."

"I wouldn't dream of it."

"It's a start, but you're going to owe n
this prank, Joseph Rockwell."

"I'll be good," he promised, his eyes t
ilely removed the cork, tested the wine
both glasses.

Cait jerked out a wicker-back chair a
down. "Did Paul say anything after I left

"About what?" Joe slid out a chair an

Cait had already dished up a large
them, fastidiously using a knife to disc
of melted cheese that stretched from the

"About me, of course," she growled

Joe handed her a glass of wine. "Nc

Cait paused and lifted her eyes to
What does that mean?"

"Only that he didn't say much abo

Joe was taunting her, dangling bits :
mation, waiting for her reaction. She :
better than to trust him, but she was
out what Paul had said that she ign
me everything he said," she demand

Joe h
several
said you
Cait :
he look
"Pau
"Bo
feat. "I
arounc
"Th
Maybe
hang
about
she'd
what
Ca
chang
ing ar
"H
"Yc
He
you w
Cai
She qi
You're
face lc
and bi
you. E
somet
"Lik
"Lik
dreame

You were the perfect gentleman all evening and then today, you were so…"

"Low and disgusting."

"Exactly." She nodded righteously. "One minute you're the picture of charm and culture and the next you're badgering me with your wisecracks."

"I'm a tease, remember?"

"The problem is I can't deal with you when I don't know what to expect."

"That's my charm." He reached for a second piece of pizza. "Women are said to adore the unexpected in a man."

"Not this woman," she informed him promptly. "I need to know where I stand with you."

"A little to the left."

"Joe, please, I'm not joking. I can't have you pulling stunts like you did today. I've lived a good, clean life for the past twenty-eight years. Two days with you has ruined my reputation with the company. I can't walk into the office and hold my head up any longer. I hear people whispering and I know they're talking about me."

"Us," he corrected. "They're talking about us."

"That's even worse. If they want to talk about me and a man, I'd rather it was Paul. Just how much longer is this remodeling project going to take, anyway?" As far as Cait was concerned, the sooner Joe and his renegade crew were out of her office, the sooner her life would return to normal.

"Not too much longer."

"At the rate you're progressing, Webster, Rodale and Missen will have offices on the moon."

"Before the end of the year, I promise."

"Yes, but just how reliable are your promises?"

"I'm being good, aren't I?"

"I suppose," she conceded ungraciously, jerking a stack of mail away from Joe as he started to sort through it.

"What's this?" Joe asked, rescuing a single piece of paper before it fluttered to the floor.

"A Christmas list. I'm going shopping tomorrow."

"I should've known you'd be organized about that, too." He sounded vaguely insulting.

"I've been organized all my life. It isn't likely to change now."

"That's why I want you to lighten up a little." He continued studying her list. "What time are you going?"

"The stores open at eight and I plan to be there then."

"I suppose you've written down everything you need to buy so you won't forget anything."

"Of course."

"Sounds sensible." His remark surprised her. He scanned her list, then yelped, "Hey, I'm not on here!" He withdrew a pen from his shirt pocket and added his own name. "Do you want me to give you a few suggestions about what I'd like?"

"I already know what I'm getting you."

Joe arched his brows. "You do? And please don't say 'nothing.'"

"No, but it'll be something appropriate—like a muzzle."

"Oh, Caitlin, darling, you injure me." He gave her one of his devilish smiles, and Cait could feel herself weakening. Just what she didn't want! She had every right to be angry with Joe. If he hadn't brought that pizza, she'd have slammed the door in his face. Wouldn't she? Sure, she would! But she'd always been susceptible to Italian food. Her only other fault was Paul. She did love him. No one seemed to believe that, but she'd known almost from the moment they'd met that she was destined to spend the rest of her life loving Paul Jamison. Only she'd rather do it as his wife than his employee....

"Have you finished your shopping?" she asked idly, making small talk with Joe since he seemed determined to hang around.

"I haven't started. I have good intentions every year, you know, like I'll get a head start on finding the perfect gifts for my nieces and nephews, but they never work out. Usually panic sets in Christmas Eve and I tear around the stores like mad and buy everything in sight. Last year I forgot wrapping paper. My mother saved the day."

"I doubt it'd do any good to suggest you get organized."

"I haven't got the time."

"What are you doing right now? Write out your list, stick to it and make the time to go shopping."

"My darling Cait, is this an invitation for me to join you tomorrow?"

"Uh…" Cait hadn't intended it to be, but she supposed she couldn't object as long as he behaved himself. "You're welcome on one condition."

"Name it."

"No jokes, no stunts like you pulled today and absolutely no teasing. If you announce to even one person that we're married, I'm walking away from you and that's a promise."

"You've got it." He raised his hand, then ceremoniously crossed his heart.

"Lick your fingertips first," Cait demanded. The instant the words were out of her mouth, she realized how ridiculous she sounded, as if they were eight and ten all over again. "Forget I said that."

His eyes were twinkling as he stood to bring his plate to the sink. "I swear it's a shame you're so in love with Paul," he told her. "If I'm not careful, I could fall for you myself." With that, he kissed her on the cheek and let himself out the door.

Pressing her fingers to her cheek, Cait drew in a deep, shuddering breath and held it until she heard the door close. Then and only then did it seep out in ragged bursts, as if she'd forgotten how to breathe normally.

"Oh, Joe," she whispered. The last thing she wanted was for Joe to fall in love with her. Not that he wasn't handsome and sweet and wonderful. He was. He always had been. He just wasn't for her. Their personalities were poles apart. Joe was unpredictable, always doing the unexpected, whereas Cait's life ran like clockwork.

She liked Joe. She almost wished she didn't, but she couldn't help herself. However, a steady diet of his pranks would soon drive her into the nearest asylum.

Standing, Cait closed the pizza box and tucked the uneaten portion onto the top shelf of her refrigerator. She was putting the dirty plates in her dishwasher when the phone rang. She quickly washed her hands and reached for it.

"Hello."

"Cait, it's Paul."

Cait was so startled that the receiver slipped out of her hand. Grabbing for it, she nearly stumbled over the open dishwasher door, knocking her shin against the sharp edge. She yelped and swallowed a cry as she jerked the dangling phone cord toward her.

"Sorry, sorry," she cried, once she'd rescued the telephone receiver. "Paul? Are you still there?"

"Yes, I'm here. Is this a bad time? I could call back later

if this is inconvenient. You don't have company, do you? I wouldn't want to interrupt a party or anything."

"Oh, no, now is perfect. I didn't realize you had my home number…but obviously you do. After all, we've been working together for nearly a year now." Eleven months and four days, not that she was counting or anything. "Naturally my number would be in the Human Resources file."

He hesitated and Cait bent over to rub her shin where it had collided with the dishwasher door. She was sure to have an ugly bruise, but a bruised leg was a small price to pay. Paul had phoned her!

"The reason I'm calling…"

"Yes, Paul," she prompted when he didn't immediately continue.

The silence lengthened before he blurted out, "I just wanted to thank you for passing on that article on the tax advantages of limited partnerships. It was thoughtful of you and I appreciate it."

"I've read quite a lot in that area, you know. There are several recent articles on the same subject. If you'd like, I could bring them in next week."

"Sure. That would be fine. Thanks again, Cait. Goodbye."

The line was disconnected before Cait could say anything else and she was left holding the receiver. A smile came, slow and confident, and with a small cry of triumph, she tossed the telephone receiver into the air, caught it behind her back and replaced it with a flourish.

Cait was dressed and waiting for Joe early the next morning. "Joe," she cried, throwing open her apartment door, "I could just kiss you."

He was dressed in faded jeans and a hip-length bronze-colored leather jacket. "Hey, I'm not stopping you," he said, opening his arms.

Cait ignored the invitation. "Paul phoned me last night." She didn't even try to contain her excitement; she felt like leaping and skipping and singing out loud.

"Paul did?" Joe sounded surprised.

"Yes. It was shortly after you left. He thanked me for giving him an interesting article I found in one of the business journals and—this is the good part—he asked if I was alone…as if it really mattered to him."

"If you were alone?" Joe repeated, and frowned. "What's that got to do with anything?"

"Don't you understand?" For all his intelligence Joe could be pretty obtuse sometimes. "He wanted to know if *you* were here with me. It makes sense, doesn't it? Paul's jealous, only he doesn't realize it yet. Oh, Joe, I can't remember ever being this happy. Not in years and years and years."

"Because Paul Jamison phoned?"

"Don't sound so skeptical. It's exactly the break I've been waiting for all these months. Paul's finally noticed me, and it's thanks to you."

"At least you're willing to give credit where credit is due." But he still didn't seem particularly thrilled.

"It's just so incredible," she continued. "I don't think I slept a wink last night. There was something in his voice that I've never heard before. Something…deep and personal. I don't know how to explain it. For the first time in a whole year, Paul knows I'm alive!"

"Are we going Christmas shopping or not?" Joe demanded brusquely. "Damn it all, Cait, I never expected you to go soft over a stupid phone call."

"But this wasn't just any call," she reminded him. She reached for her purse and her coat in one sweeping motion. "It was was from *Paul*."

"You sound like a silly schoolgirl." Joe frowned, but Cait wasn't about to let his short temper destroy her mood. Paul had phoned her at home and she was sure that this was the beginning of a *real* relationship. Next he'd ask her out for lunch, and then…

They left her apartment and walked down the hall, Cait grinning all the way. Standing just outside the front doors was a huge truck with gigantic wheels. Just the type of vehicle she'd expected him to drive the night he'd taken her to Henry's.

"This is your truck?" she asked when they were outside. She couldn't keep the laughter out of her voice.

"Something wrong with it?"

"Not a single thing, but Joe, honestly, you are so predictable."

"That's not what you said yesterday."

She grinned again as he opened the truck door, set down a stool for her and helped her climb into the cab. The seat was cluttered, but so wide she was able to shove everything to one side. When she'd made room for herself, she fastened the seat belt, snapping it jauntily in place. She was so happy, the whole world seemed delightful this morning.

"Will you quit smiling before someone suggests you've been overdosing on vitamins?" Joe grumbled.

"My, aren't we testy this morning."

"Where to?" he asked, starting the engine.

"Any of the big malls will do. You decide. Do you have your list all made out?"

Joe patted his heart. "It's in my shirt pocket."

"Good."

"Have you decided what you're going to buy for whom?"

His smile was slightly off-kilter. "Not exactly. I thought I'd follow you around and buy whatever you did. Do you know what you're getting your mother? Mine's damn difficult to buy for. Last year I ended up getting her a dozen bags of cat food. She's got five cats of her own and God only knows how many strays she's feeding."

"At least your idea was practical."

"Well, there's that, and the fact that by the time I started my Christmas shopping the only store open was a supermarket."

Cait laughed. "Honestly, Joe!"

"Hey, I was desperate and before you get all righteous on me, Mom thought the cat food and the two rib roasts were great gifts."

"I'm sure she did," Cait returned, grinning. She found herself doing a lot of that when she was with Joe. Imagine buying his mother rib roasts for Christmas!

"Give me some ideas, would you? Mom's a hard case."

"To be honest, I'm not all that imaginative myself. I buy my mother the same thing every year."

"What is it?"

"Long-distance phone cards. That way she can phone her sister in Dubuque and her high-school friend in Kansas. Of course she calls me every now and then, too."

"Okay, that takes care of Mom. What about Martin? What are you buying him?"

"A bronze eagle." She'd decided on that gift last summer when she'd attended Sunday services at Martin's church. In the opening part of his sermon, Martin had used eagles to illustrate a point of faith.

"An eagle," Joe repeated. "Any special reason?"

"Y-yes," she said, not wanting to explain. "It's a long story, but I happen to be partial to eagles myself."

"Any other hints you'd care to pass on?"

"Buy wrapping paper in the after-Christmas sales. It's about half the price and it stores easily under the bed."

"Great idea. I'll have to remember that for next year."

Joe chose Northgate, the shopping mall closest to Cait's apartment. The parking lot was already beginning to fill up and it was only a few minutes after eight.

Joe managed to park fairly close to the entrance and came around to help Cait out of the truck. This time he didn't bother with the step stool, but clasped her around the waist to lift her down. "What did you mean when you said I was so predictable?" he asked, giving her a reproachful look.

With her hands resting on his shoulders and her feet dangling in midair, she felt vulnerable and small. "Nothing. It was just that I assumed you drove one of these Sherman-tank trucks, and I was right. I just hadn't seen it before."

"The kind of truck I drive bothers you?" His brow furrowed in a scowl.

"Not at all. What's the matter with you today, Joe? You're so touchy."

"I am not touchy," he snapped.

"Fine. Would you mind putting me down then?" His large hands were squeezing her waist almost painfully, though she doubted he was aware of it. She couldn't imagine what had angered him. Unless it was the fact that

Paul had called her—which didn't make sense. Maybe, like most men, he just hated shopping.

He lowered her slowly to the asphalt and released her with seeming reluctance. "I need a coffee break," he announced grimly.

"But we just arrived."

Joe forcefully expelled his breath. "It doesn't matter. I need something to calm my nerves."

If he needed a caffeine fix so early in the day, Cait wondered how he'd manage during the next few hours. The stores quickly became crowded this time of year, especially on a Saturday. By ten it would be nearly impossible to get from one aisle to the next.

By twelve, she knew: Joe disliked Christmas shopping every bit as much as she'd expected.

"I've had it," Joe complained after making three separate trips back to the truck to deposit their spoils.

"Me, too," Cait agreed laughingly. "This place is turning into a madhouse."

"How about some lunch?" Joe suggested. "Someplace far away from here. Like Tibet."

Cait laughed again and tucked her arm in his. "That sounds like a great idea."

Outside, they noticed several cars circling the lot looking for a parking space and three of them rushed to fill the one Joe vacated. Two cars nearly collided in their eagerness. One man leapt out of his and shook an angry fist at the other driver.

"So much for peace and goodwill," Joe commented. "I swear Christmas brings out the worst in everyone."

"And the best," Cait reminded him.

"To be honest, I don't know what crammed shopping

malls and fighting the crowds and all this commercialism have to do with Christmas in the first place," he grumbled. A car cut in front of him, and Joe blared his horn.

"Quite a lot when you think about it," Cait said softly. "Imagine the streets of Bethlehem, the crowds and the noise…" The Christmas before, fresh from a shopping expedition, Cait had asked herself the same question. Christmas seemed so commercial. The crowds had been unbearable. First at Northgate, where she did most of her shopping and then at the airport. Sea-Tac had been filled with activity and noise, everyone in a hurry to get someplace else. There seemed to be little peace or good cheer and a whole lot of selfish concern and rudeness. Then, in the tranquility of church on Christmas Eve, everything had come into perspective for Cait. There had been crowds and rudeness that first Christmas, too, she reasoned. Yet in the midst of that confusion had come joy and peace and love. For most people, it was still the same. Christmas gifts and decorations and dinners were, after all, expressions of the love you felt for your family and friends. And if the preparations sometimes got a bit chaotic, well, that no longer bothered Cait.

"Where should we go to eat?" Joe asked, breaking into her thoughts. They were barely moving, stuck in heavy traffic.

She looked over at him and smiled serenely. "Any place will do. There're several excellent restaurants close by. You choose, only let it be my treat this time."

"We'll talk about who pays later. Right now, I'm more concerned with getting out of this traffic sometime within my life span."

Still smiling, Cait said, "I don't think it'll take much longer."

He returned her smile. "I don't, either." His eyes held hers for what seemed an eternity—until someone behind them honked irritably. Joe glanced up and saw that traffic ahead of them had started to move. He immediately stepped on the gas.

Cait didn't know what Joe had found so fascinating about her unless it was her unruly hair. She hadn't combed it since leaving the house; it was probably a mass of tight, disorderly curls. She'd been so concerned with finding the right gift for her nephews and niece that she hadn't given it a thought.

"What's wrong?" she asked, feeling self-conscious.

"What makes you think anything's wrong?"

"The way you were looking at me a few minutes ago."

"Oh, that," he said, easing into a restaurant parking lot. "I don't think I've ever fully appreciated how lovely you are," he answered in a calm, matter-of-fact voice.

Cait blushed and glanced away. "I'm sure you're mistaken. I'm really not all that pretty. I sometimes wondered if Paul would have noticed me sooner if I was a little more attractive."

"Trust me, Bright Eyes," he said, turning off the engine. "You're pretty enough."

"For what?"

"For this." And he leaned across the seat and captured her mouth with his.

Chapter Five

"I...wish you hadn't done that," Cait whispered, slowly opening her eyes in an effort to pull herself back to reality.

As far as kisses went, Joe's were good. Very good. He kissed better than just about anyone she'd ever kissed before—but that didn't alter the fact that she was in love with Paul.

"You're right," he muttered, opening the door and climbing out of the cab. "I shouldn't have done that." He walked around to her side and yanked the door open with more force than necessary.

Cait frowned, wondering at his strange mood. One minute he was holding her in his arms, kissing her tenderly; the next he was short-tempered and irritable.

"I'm hungry," he barked, lifting her abruptly down to the pavement. "I sometimes do irrational things when I haven't eaten."

"I see." The next time she went anywhere with Joseph Rockwell, she'd have to make sure he ate a good meal first.

The restaurant was crowded and Joe gave the receptionist their names to add to the growing waiting list. Sitting on the last empty chair in the foyer, Cait set her large black leather purse on her lap and started rooting through it.

"What are you searching for? Uranium?" Joe teased, watching her.

"Crackers," she answered, shifting the bulky bag and handing him several items to hold while she continued digging.

"You're searching for crackers? Whatever for?"

She glanced up long enough to give him a look that questioned his intelligence. "For obvious reasons. If you're irrational when you're hungry, you might do something stupid while we're here. Frankly, I don't want you to embarrass me." She returned to the task with renewed vigor. "I can just see you standing on top of the table dancing."

"That's one way to get the waiter's attention. Thanks for suggesting it."

"Aha!" Triumphantly Cait pulled two miniature bread sticks wrapped in cellophane from the bottom of her purse. "Eat," she instructed. "Before you're overcome by some other craziness."

"You mean before I kiss you again," he said in a low voice, bending his head toward hers.

She leaned back quickly, not giving him any chance of following through on that. "Exactly. Or waltz with the waitress or any of the other loony things you do."

"You have to admit I've been good all morning."

"With one minor slip," she reminded him, pressing the bread sticks into his hand. "Now eat."

Before Joe had a chance to open the package, the hostess approached them with two menus tucked under her arm. "Mr. and Mrs. Rockwell. Your table is ready."

"Mr. and Mrs. Rockwell," Cait muttered under her breath, glaring at Joe. She should've known she couldn't trust him.

"Excuse me," Cait said, standing abruptly and raising her index finger. "His name is Rockwell, mine is Marshall," she explained patiently. She was not about to let Joe continue his silly games. "We're just friends here for lunch." Her narrowed eyes caught Joe's, which looked as innocent as freshly fallen snow. He shrugged as though to say any misunderstanding hadn't been *his* fault.

"I see," the hostess replied. "I'm sorry for the confusion."

"No problem." Cait hadn't wanted to make a big issue of this, but on the other hand she didn't want Joe to think he was going to get away with it, either.

The woman led them to a linen-covered table in the middle of the room. Joe held out Cait's chair for her, then whispered something to the hostess who immediately cast Cait a sympathetic glance. Joe's own gaze rested momentarily on Cait before he pulled out his chair and sat across from her.

"All right, what did you say to her?" she hissed.

The menu seemed to command his complete interest for a couple of minutes. "What makes you think I said anything?"

"I heard you whispering and then she gave me this pathetic look like she wanted to hug me and tell me everything was going to be all right."

"Then you know."

"Joe, don't play games with me," Cait warned.

"All right, if you must know, I explained that you'd suffered a head injury and developed amnesia."

"Amnesia," she repeated loudly enough to attract the attention of the diners at the next table. Gritting her teeth, Cait snatched up her menu, gripping it so tightly the edges curled. It didn't do any good to argue with Joe. The man was impossible. Every time she tried to reason with him, he did something to make her regret it.

"How else was I supposed to explain the fact that you'd forgotten our marriage?" he asked reasonably.

"I did not forget our marriage," she informed him from between clenched teeth, reviewing the menu and quickly making her selection. "Good grief, it wasn't even legal."

She realized that the waitress was standing by their table, pen and pad in hand. The woman's ready smile faded as she looked from Cait to Joe and back again. Her mouth tightened as if she suspected they really were involved in something illegal.

"Uh..." Cait hedged, feeling like even more of an idiot. The urge to explain was overwhelming, but every time she tried, she only made matters worse. "I'll have the club sandwich," she said, glaring across the table at Joe.

"That sounds good. I'll have the same," he said, closing his menu.

The woman scribbled down their order, then hurried away, pausing to glance over her shoulder as if she wanted to be able to identify them later in a police lineup.

"Now look what you've done," Cait whispered heatedly once the waitress was far enough away from their table not to overhear.

"Me?"

Maybe she was being unreasonable, but Joe was the one who'd started this nonsense in the first place. No one could rattle her as effectively as Joe did. And worse, she let him.

This shopping trip was a good example, and so was the pizza that led up to it. No woman in her right mind should've allowed Joe into her apartment after what he'd said to her in front of Lindy. Not only had she invited him inside her home, she'd agreed to let him accompany her Christmas shopping. She ought to have her head examined!

"What's wrong?" Joe asked, tearing open the package of bread sticks. Rather pointless in Cait's opinion, since their lunch would be served any minute.

"What's wrong?" she cried, dumbfounded that he had to ask. "You mean other than the hostess believing I've suffered a head injury and the waitress thinking we're drug dealers or something equally disgusting?"

"Here." He handed her one of the miniature bread sticks. "Eat this and you'll feel better."

Cait sincerely doubted that, but she took it, anyway, muttering under her breath.

"Relax," he urged.

"Relax," she mocked. "How can I possibly relax when you're doing and saying things I find excruciatingly embarrassing?"

"I'm sorry, Cait. Really, I am." To his credit, he did look contrite. "But you're so easy to fluster and I can't seem to stop myself."

Their sandwiches arrived, thick with slices of turkey, ham and a variety of cheeses. Cait was reluctant to admit how much better she felt after she'd eaten. Joe's spirits had apparently improved, as well.

"So," he said, his hands resting on his stomach. "What do you have planned for the rest of the afternoon?"

Cait hadn't given it much thought. "I suppose I should wrap the gifts I bought this morning." But that prospect didn't particularly excite her. Good grief, after the adventures she'd had with Joe, it wasn't any wonder.

"You mean you actually wrap gifts before Christmas Eve?" Joe asked. "Doesn't that take all the fun out of it? I mean, for me it's a game just to see if I can get the presents bought."

She grinned, trying to imagine herself in such a disorganized race to the deadline. Definitely not her style.

"How about a movie?" he suggested out of the blue. "I have the feeling you don't get out enough."

"A movie?" Cait ignored the comment about her social life, mainly because he was right. She rarely took the time to go to a show.

"We're both exhausted from fighting the crowds," Joe added. "There's a six-cinema theater next to the restaurant. I'll even let you choose."

"I suppose you'd object to a love story?"

"We can see one if you insist, only…"

"Only what?"

"Only promise me you won't ever expect a man to say the kinds of things those guys on the screen do."

"I beg your pardon?"

"You heard me. Women hear actors say this incredible drivel and then they're disappointed when real men don't."

"Real men like you, I suppose?"

"Right." He looked smug, then suddenly he frowned. "Does Paul like romances?"

Cait had no idea, since she'd never gone on a date with Paul and the subject wasn't one they'd ever discussed at the office. "I imagine he does," she said, dabbing her mouth with her napkin. "He isn't the type of man to be intimidated by such things."

Joe's deep blue eyes widened with surprise and a touch of respect. "Ouch. So Martin's little sister reveals her claws."

"I don't have claws. I just happen to have strong opinions on certain subjects." She reached for her purse while she was speaking and removed her wallet.

"What are you doing now?" Joe demanded.

"Paying for lunch." She sorted through the bills and withdrew a twenty. "It's my turn and I insist on paying..." She hesitated when she saw Joe's deepening frown. "Or don't real men allow women friends to buy their lunch?"

"Sure, go ahead," he returned flippantly.

It was all Cait could do to hide a smile. She guessed that her gesture in paying for their sandwiches would somehow be seen as compromising his male pride.

Apparently she was right. As they were walking toward the cashier, Joe stepped up his pace, grabbed the check from her hand and slapped some money on the counter. He glared at her as if he expected a drawn-out public argument. After the fuss they'd already caused in the restaurant, Cait was darned if she was going to let that happen.

"Joe," she argued the minute they were out the door. "What was *that* all about?"

"Fine, you win. Tell me my views are outdated, but when a woman goes out with me, I pick up the tab, no matter how liberated she is."

"But this isn't a real date. We're only friends, and even that's—"

"I don't give a damn. Consider it an apology for the embarrassment I caused you earlier."

"Isn't that kind of sexist?"

"No! I just have certain…standards."

"So I see." His attitude shouldn't have come as any big surprise. Just as Cait had told him earlier, he was shockingly predictable.

Hand at her elbow, Joe led the way across the car-filled lot toward the sprawling theater complex. The movies were geared toward a wide audience. There was a Disney classic, along with a horror flick and a couple of adventure movies and last but not least, a well-publicized love story.

As they stood in line, Cait caught Joe's gaze lingering on the poster for one of the adventure films—yet another story about a law-and-order cop with renegade ideas.

"I suppose you're more interested in seeing that than the romance."

"I already promised you could choose the show, and I'm a man of my word. If, however, you were to pick another movie—" he buried his hands in his pockets as he grinned at her appealingly "—I wouldn't complain."

"I'm willing to pick another movie, but on one condition."

"Name it." His eyes lit up.

"I pay."

"Those claws of yours are out again."

She raised her hands and flexed her fingers in a catlike motion. "It's your decision."

"What about popcorn?"

"You can buy that if you insist."

"All right," he said, "you've got yourself a deal."

When it was Cait's turn at the ticket window, she purchased two for the Disney classic.

"Disney?" Joe yelped, shocked when Cait handed him his ticket.

"It seemed like a good compromise," she answered.

For a moment it looked as if he was going to argue with her, then a slow grin spread across his face. "Disney," he said again. "You're right, it does sound like fun. Only I hope we're not the only people there over the age of ten."

They sat toward the back of the theater, sharing a large bucket of buttered popcorn. The theater was crowded and several kids seemed to be taking turns running up and down the aisles. Joe needn't have worried; there were plenty of adults in attendance, but of course most of them were accompanying children.

The lights dimmed and Cait reached for a handful of popcorn, relaxing in her seat. "I love this movie."

"How many times have you seen it?"

"Five or six. But it's been a few years."

"Me, too." Joe relaxed beside her, crossing his long legs and leaning back.

The credits started to roll, but the noise level hadn't decreased much. "Will the kids bother you?" Joe wanted to know.

"Heavens, no. I love kids."

"You do?" The fact that he was so surprised seemed vaguely insulting and Cait frowned.

"We've already had this discussion," she responded, licking the salt from her fingertips.

"We did? When?"

"The other day. You commented on how much I used to enjoy playing with my dolls and how you'd expected me to be married with a house full of children." His words had troubled her then, because "a house full of children" was exactly what Cait would have liked, and she seemed a long way from realizing her dream.

"Ah, yes, I remember our conversation about that now."

He scooped up a large handful of popcorn. "You'd be a very good mother, you know."

That Joe would say this was enough to bring an unexpected rush of tears to her eyes. She blinked them back, annoyed that she'd get weepy over something so silly.

The previews were over and the audience settled down as the movie started. Cait focused her attention on the screen, munching popcorn every now and then, reaching blindly for the bucket. Their hands collided more than once and almost before she was aware of it, their fingers were entwined. It was a peaceful sort of feeling, being linked to Joe in this way. There was a *rightness* about it that she didn't want to explore just yet. He hadn't really changed; he was still lovable and funny and fun. For that matter, she hadn't changed very much, either….

The movie was as good as Cait remembered, better, even—perhaps because Joe was there to share it with her. She half expected him to make the occasional wisecrack, but he seemed to respect the artistic value of the classic animation and, judging by his wholehearted laughter, he enjoyed the story.

When the show was over, he released Cait's hand. Hurriedly she gathered her purse and coat. As they walked out of the noisy, crowded theater, it seemed only natural to hold hands again.

Joe opened the truck, lifted down the step stool and helped her inside. Dusk came early these days, and bright, cheery lights were ablaze on every street. A vacant lot across the street was now filled with Christmas trees. A row of red lights was strung between two posts, sagging in the middle, and a portable CD player sent forth saccharine versions of better-known Christmas carols.

"Have you bought your tree yet?" Joe asked, nodding in the direction of the lot after he'd climbed into the driver's seat and started the engine.

"No. I don't usually put one up since I spend the holidays with Martin and his family."

"Ah."

"What about you? Or is that something else you save for Christmas Eve?" she joked. It warmed her a little to imagine Joe staying up past midnight to decorate a Christmas tree for his nieces and nephews.

"Finding time to do the shopping is bad enough," he said, not really answering her question.

"Your construction projects keep you that busy?" She hadn't given much thought to Joe's business. She knew from remarks Paul had made that Joe was very successful. It wasn't logical that she should feel pride in his accomplishments, but she did.

"Owning a business isn't like being in a nine-to-five job. I'm on call twenty-four hours a day, but I wouldn't have it any other way. I love what I do."

"I'm happy for you, Joe. I really am."

"Happy enough to decorate my Christmas tree with me?"

"When?"

"Next weekend."

"I'd like to," she told him, touched by the invitation, "but I'll have left for Minnesota by then."

"That's all right," Joe said, grinning at her. "Maybe next time."

She turned, frowning, to hide her blush.

They remained silent as he concentrated on easing the truck into the heavy late-afternoon traffic.

"I enjoyed the movie," she said some time later, resist-

ing the urge to rest her head on his shoulder. The impulse
to do that arose from her exhaustion, she told herself.
Nothing else!

"So did I," he said softly. "Only next time, I'll be the
one to pay. Understand?"

Next time. There it was again. She suspected Joe was
beginning to take their relationship, such as it was, far too
seriously. Already he was suggesting they'd be seeing
each other soon, matter-of-factly discussing dates and
plans as if they were longtime companions. Almost as if
they were married…

She was mulling over this realization when Joe pulled
into the parking area in front of her building. He climbed
out and began to gather her packages, bundling them in
his arms. She managed to scramble down by herself, not
giving him a chance to help her, then she led the way into
the building and unlocked her door.

Cait stood just inside the doorway and turned slightly
to take a couple of the larger packages from Joe's arms.

"I had a great time," she told him briskly.

"Me, too." He nudged her, forcing her to enter the living room. He followed close behind and unloaded her remaining things onto the sofa. His presence seemed to
reach out and fill every corner of the room.

Neither of them spoke for several minutes, but Cait
sensed Joe wanted her to invite him to stay for coffee. The
idea was tempting but dangerous. She mustn't let him think
there might ever be anything romantic between them. Not
when she was in love with Paul. For the first time in nearly
a year, Paul was actually beginning to notice her. She refused
to ruin everything now by becoming involved with Joe.

"Thank you for…today," she said, returning to the door,

intending to open it for him. Instead, Joe caught her by the wrist and pulled her against him. She was in his arms before she could voice a protest.

"I'm going to kiss you," he told her, his voice rough yet strangely tender.

"You are?" She'd never been more aware of a man, of his hard, muscular body against hers, his clean, masculine scent. Her own body reacted in a chaotic scramble of mixed sensations. Above all, though, it felt *good* to be in his arms. She wasn't sure why and dared not examine the feeling.

Slowly, leisurely, he lowered his head. She made a soft weak sound as his mouth touched hers.

Cait sighed, forgetting for a moment that she meant to free herself before his kiss deepened. Before things went any further...

Joe must have sensed her resolve because his hands slid down her spine in a gentle caress, drawing her even closer. His mouth began a sensuous journey along her jaw, and down her throat—

"Joe!" She moaned his name, uncertain of what she wanted to say.

"Hmm?"

"Are you hungry again?" She wondered desperately if there were any more bread sticks in the bottom of her purse. Maybe that would convince him to stop.

"Very hungry," he told her, his voice low and solemn. "I've never been hungrier."

"But you had lunch and then you ate nearly all the popcorn."

He slowly raised his head. "Cait, are we talking about the same things here? Oh, hell, what does it matter? The only thing that matters is this." He covered her parted lips with his.

Cait felt her knees go weak and sagged against him, her fingers gripping his jacket as though she expected to collapse any moment. Which was becoming a distinct possibility as he continued to kiss her....

"Joe, no more, please." But she was the one clinging to him. She had to do something, and fast, before her ability to reason was lost entirely.

He drew an unsteady breath and muttered something she couldn't decipher as his lips grazed the delicate line of her jaw.

"We...need to talk," she announced, keeping her eyes tightly closed. If she didn't look at Joe, then she could concentrate on what she had to do.

"All right," he agreed.

"I'll make a pot of coffee."

With a heavy sigh, Joe abruptly released her. Cait half fell against the sofa arm, requiring its support while she collected herself enough to walk into the kitchen. She unconsciously reached up and brushed her lips, as if she wasn't completely sure even now that he'd taken her in his arms and kissed her.

He hadn't been joking this time, or teasing. The kisses they'd shared were serious kisses. The type a man gives a woman he's strongly attracted to. A woman he's interested in developing a relationship with. Cait found herself shaking, unable to move.

"You want me to make that coffee?" he suggested.

She nodded and sank down on the couch. She could scarcely stand, let alone prepare a pot of coffee.

Joe returned a few minutes later, carrying two steaming mugs. Carefully he handed her one, then sat across from her on the blue velvet ottoman.

"You wanted to talk?"

Cait nodded. "Yes." Her throat felt thick, clogged with confused emotion, and forming coherent words suddenly seemed beyond her. She tried gesturing with her free hand, but that only served to frustrate Joe.

"Cait," he asked, "what's wrong?"

"Paul." The name came out in an eerie squeak.

"What about him?"

"He phoned me."

"Yes, I know. You already told me that."

"Don't you understand?" she cried, her throat unexpectedly clearing. "Paul is finally showing some interest in me and now you're kissing me and telling anyone who'll listen that the two of us are married and you're doing ridiculous things like…" She paused to draw in a deep breath. "Joe, oh please, Joe, don't fall in love with me."

"Fall in love with you?" he echoed incredulously. "Caitlin, you can't be serious. It won't happen. No chance."

Chapter Six

"No chance?" Cait repeated, convinced she'd misunderstood him. She blinked a couple of times as if that would correct her hearing. Either Joe was underestimating her intelligence, or he was more of a...a cad than she'd realized.

"You have nothing to worry about." He sipped coffee, his gaze steady and emotionless. "I'm not falling in love with you."

"In other words you make a habit of kissing unsuspecting women."

"It isn't a habit," he answered thoughtfully. "It's more of a pastime."

"You certainly seem to be making a habit of it with me." Her anger was quickly gaining momentum and she was at odds to understand why she found his casual attitude so offensive. He was telling her exactly what she wanted to hear. But she hadn't expected her ego to take such a beating in the process. The fact that he wasn't the least bit tempted to fall in love with her should have pleased her.

It didn't.

It was as if their brief kisses were little more than a pleasant interlude for him. Something to occupy his time and keep him from growing bored with her company.

"This may come as a shock to you," Joe continued indifferently, "but a man doesn't have to be in love with a woman to kiss her."

"I know that," Cait snapped, fighting to hold back her temper, which was threatening to break free at any moment. "But you don't have to be so...so casual about it, either. If I wasn't involved with Paul, I might have taken you seriously."

"I didn't know you were involved with Paul," he returned with mild sarcasm. He leaned forward and rested his elbows on his knees, his pose infuriatingly relaxed. "If that was true I'd never have taken you out. The way I see it, the involvement is all on your part. Am I wrong?"

"No," she admitted reluctantly. How like a man to bring up semantics in the middle of an argument!

"So," he said, leaning back again and crossing his legs. "Are you enjoying my kisses? I take it I've improved from the first go-around."

"You honestly want me to rate you?" she sputtered.

"Obviously I'm much better than I was as a kid, otherwise you wouldn't be so worried." He took another drink of his coffee, smiling pleasantly all the while.

"Believe me, I'm not worried."

He arched his brows. "Really?"

"I'm sure you expect me to fall at your feet, overcome by your masculine charm. Well, if that's what you're waiting for, you'll have one hell of a long wait!"

His grin was slightly off center, as if he was picturing

her arrayed at his feet—and enjoying the sight. "I think the problem here is that *you* might be falling in love with *me* and just don't know it."

"Falling in love with you and not know it?" she repeated with a loud disbelieving snort. "You've gone completely out of your mind. There's no chance of that."

"Why not? Plenty of women have told me I'm a handsome son of a gun. Plus, I'm said to possess a certain charm. Heaven knows, I'm generous enough and rather—"

"Who told you that? Your mother?" She made it sound like the most ludicrous thing she'd heard in years.

"You might be surprised to learn that I do have admirers."

Why this news should add fuel to the fire of her temper was beyond Cait, but she was so furious with him she could barely sit still. "I don't doubt it, but if I fall in love with a man you can believe it won't be just because he's 'a handsome son of a gun,'" she quoted sarcastically. "Look at Paul— he's the type of man I'm attracted to. What's on the inside matters more than outward appearances."

"Then why are you so worried about falling in love with me?"

"I'm not worried! You've got it the wrong way around. The only reason I mentioned anything was because I thought *you* were beginning to take our times together too seriously."

"I already explained that wasn't a problem."

"So I heard." Cait set her coffee aside. Joe was upsetting her so much that her hand was shaking hard enough to spill it.

"Well," Joe murmured, glancing at her. "You never did answer my question."

"Which one?" she asked irritably.

"About how I rated as a kisser."

"You weren't serious!"

"On the contrary." He set his own coffee down and raised himself off the ottoman far enough to clasp her by the waist and pull her into his lap.

Caught off balance, Cait fell onto his thighs, too astonished to struggle.

"Let's try it again," he whispered in a rough undertone.

"Ah…" A frightening excitement took hold of Cait. Her mind commanded her to leap away from this man, but some emotion, far stronger than common sense or prudence, urged the opposite.

Before she could form a protest, Joe bent toward her and covered her mouth with his. She'd hold herself stiff in his arms, that was what she'd do, teach him the lesson he deserved. How dared he assume she'd automatically fall in love with him. How dared he insinuate he was some…some Greek god all women adored. But the instant his lips met hers, Cait trembled with a mixture of shock and profound pleasure.

Everything within her longed to cry out at the unfairness of it all. It shouldn't be this good with Joe. They were friends, nothing more. This was the kind of response she expected when Paul kissed her. If he ever did.

She meant to pull away, but instead, Cait moaned softly. It felt so incredibly wonderful. So incredibly right. At that moment, there didn't seem to be anything to worry about—except the likelihood of dissolving in his arms then and there.

Suddenly Joe broke the contact. Her instinctive disappointment, even more than the unexpectedness of the action, sent her eyes flying open. Her own dark eyes met his blue ones, which now seemed almost aquamarine.

"So, how do I rate?" he murmured thickly, as though he was having trouble speaking.

"Good." A one-word reply was all she could manage, although she was furious with him for asking.

"Just good?"

She nodded forcefully.

"I thought we were better than that."

"We?"

"Naturally I'm only as good as my partner."

"Th-then how do you rate me?" She had to ask. Like a fool she handed him the ax and laid her neck on the chopping board. Joe was sure to use the opportunity to trample all over her ego, to turn the whole bewildering experience into a joke. She couldn't take that right now. She dropped her gaze, waiting for him to devastate her.

"Much improved."

She cocked one eyebrow in surprise. She had no idea what to say next.

They were both silent. Then he said softly, "You know, Cait, we're getting better at this. Much, much better." He pressed his forehead to hers. "If we're not careful, you just might fall in love with me, after all."

"Where were you all day Saturday?" Lindy asked early Monday morning, walking into Cait's office. The renovations to it had been completed late Friday and Cait had moved everything back into her office first thing this morning. "I must have tried calling you ten times."

"I told you I was going Christmas shopping. In fact, I bought some decorations for my office."

Lindy nodded. "But all day?" Her eyes narrowed suspiciously as she set down her briefcase and leaned against

Cait's desk, crossing her arms. "You didn't happen to be with Joe Rockwell, did you?"

Cait could feel a telltale shade of pink creeping up her neck. She lowered her gaze to the list of current Dow Jones stock prices and took a moment to compose herself. She couldn't admit the truth. "I told you I was shopping," she said somewhat defensively. Then, in an effort to change the topic, she reached for a thick folder with Paul's name inked across the top and muttered, "You wouldn't happen to know Paul's schedule for the day, would you?"

"N-no, I haven't seen him yet. Why do you ask?"

Cait flashed her friend a bright smile. "He phoned me Friday night. Oh, Lindy, I was so excited I nearly fell all over myself." She dropped her voice as she glanced around to make sure none of the others could hear her. "I honestly think he intends to ask me out."

"Did he say so?"

"Not exactly." Cait frowned. Lindy wasn't revealing any of the enthusiasm she expected.

"Then why did he phone?"

Cait rolled her chair away from the desk and glanced around once again. "I think he might be jealous," she whispered.

"Really?" Lindy's eyes widened.

"Don't look so surprised." Cait, however, was much too excited recounting Paul's phone call to be offended by Lindy's attitude.

"What makes you think Paul would be jealous?" Lindy asked next.

"Maybe I'm magnifying everything in my own mind because it's what I so badly want to believe. But he did phone..."

"What did he say?" Lindy pressed, sounding more curious now. "It seems to me he must have had a reason."

"Oh, he did. He mentioned something about appreciating an article I'd given him, but we both know that was just an excuse. What clued me in to his jealousy was the way he kept asking if I was alone."

"But that could've been for several different reasons, don't you think?" Lindy suggested.

"Yes, but it made sense that he'd want to know if Joe was at the apartment or not."

"And was he?"

"Of course not," Cait said righteously. She didn't feel guilty about hiding the fact that he'd been there earlier, or that they'd spent nearly all of Saturday together. "I'm sure Joe's ridiculous remark when I left the office on Friday is what convinced Paul to phone me. If I wasn't so furious with Joe, I might even be grateful."

"What's that?" Lindy asked abruptly, pointing to the folder in front of Cait. Her lips had thinned slightly as if she was confused or annoyed—about what, Cait couldn't figure out.

"This, my friend," she began, holding up the folder, "is the key to my future with our dedicated manager."

Lindy didn't immediately respond and looked more puzzled than before. "How do you mean?"

Cait couldn't get over the feeling that things weren't quite right with her best friend; she seemed to be holding something back. But Cait realized Lindy would tell her when she was ready. Lindy always hated being pushed or prodded.

"The folder?" Lindy prompted when Cait didn't answer.

Cait flipped it open. "I spent all day Sunday reading

through old business journals looking for articles that might interest Paul. I must've gone back five years. I copied the articles I consider the most valuable and included a brief analysis of my own. I was hoping to give it to him sometime today. That's why I was asking if you knew his schedule."

"Unfortunately I don't," Lindy murmured. She straightened, picked up her briefcase and made a show of checking her watch. Then she looked up to smile reassuringly at Cait. "I'd better get to work. I'll come by later to help you put up your decorations, okay?"

"Thanks," Cait said, then added, "Wish me luck with Paul."

"You know I do," Lindy mumbled on her way out the door.

Mondays were generally slow for the stock market—unless there was a crisis. World events and financial reports had a significant impact on the market. However, as the day progressed, everything ran smoothly.

Cait looked up every now and then, half expecting to see Joe lounging in her doorway. His men had started early that morning, but by noon, Joe still hadn't arrived.

Not until much later did she realize it was Paul she should be anticipating, not Joe. Paul was the romantic interest of her life and it annoyed her that Joe seemed to occupy her thoughts.

As it happened, Paul did stroll past her office shortly after the New York market closed. Grabbing the folder, Cait raced toward his office, not hesitating for an instant. This was her golden opportunity and she was taking hold of it with both hands.

"Good afternoon, Paul," she said cordially as she stood

in his doorway, clutching the folder. "Do you have a moment or would you rather I came back later?"

He looked tired, as if the day had already been a grueling one. It was all Cait could do not to offer to massage away the stress and worry that complicated his life. Her heart swelled with a renewed wave of love. For a wild, impetuous moment, it was true, she'd suffered her doubts. Any woman would have when a man like Joe took her in his arms. He might be arrogant in the extreme and one of the worst pranksters she'd ever met; despite all that, he had a certain charm. But now that she was with Paul, Cait remembered sharply who it was she really loved.

"I don't want to be a bother," she told him softly.

He give her a listless smile. "Come in, Cait. Now is fine." He gestured toward a chair.

She hurried into the office, trying to keep the bounce out of her step. Knowing she'd be spending a few extra minutes alone with Paul, Cait had taken special care with her appearance that morning.

He glanced up and smiled at her again, but this time Cait thought she could see a glimmer of appreciation in his eyes. "What can I do for you? I hope you're pleased with your office." He frowned slightly.

For a second, she forgot what she was doing in Paul's office and stared at him blankly until his own gaze fell to the folder. "The office looks great," she said quickly. "Um, the reason I'm here..." She faltered, then gulped in a quick breath and continued, "I went through some of the business journals I have at home and found several articles I felt would interest you." She extended the folder to him, like a ceremonial offering.

He took it from her and opened it gingerly. "Gracious,"

he said, flipping through the pages and scanning her written comments, "you must've spent hours on this."

"It was…nothing." She'd willingly have done a good deal more to gain his appreciation and eventually his love.

"I won't have a chance to look at this for a few days," he said.

"Oh, please, there's no rush. You happened to mention you got some useful insights from the previous article I gave you. So I thought I'd share a few others that seem relevant to what's going on with the market now."

"It's very thoughtful of you."

"I was happy to do it. More than happy," she amended with her most brilliant smile. When he didn't say anything more, Cait rose reluctantly to her feet. "You must be swamped after being in meetings for most of the day, so I'll leave you now."

She was almost at the door when he spoke. "Actually I only dropped in to the office to collect a few things before heading out again. I've got an important date this evening."

Cait felt as if the floor had suddenly disappeared and she was plummeting through empty space. "Date?" she repeated before she could stop herself. It was a struggle to keep smiling.

Paul's grin was downright boyish. "Yes, I'm meeting her for dinner."

"In that case, have a good time."

"Thanks, I will," he returned confidently, his eyes alight with excitement. "Oh, and by the way," he added, indicating the folder she'd worked so hard on, "thanks for all the effort you put into this."

"You're…welcome."

By the time Cait got back to her office she felt numb. Paul had an important date. It wasn't as though she'd expected him to live the life of a hermit, but before today, he'd never mentioned going out with anyone. She might have suspected he'd thrown out the information hoping to make her jealous if it hadn't been for one thing. He seemed genuinely thrilled about this date. Besides, Paul wasn't the kind of man to resort to pretense.

"Cait, my goodness," Lindy said, strolling into her office a while later, "what's wrong? You look dreadful."

Cait tried to swallow the lump in her throat and managed a shaky smile. "I talked to Paul and gave him the research I'd done."

"He didn't appreciate it?" Lindy picked up the Christmas wreath that lay on Cait's desk and pinned it to the door.

"I'm sure he did," she replied. "What he doesn't appreciate is me. I might as well be invisible to that man." She pushed the hair away from her forehead and braced both elbows on her desk, feeling totally disheartened. Unless she acted quickly, she was going to lose Paul to some faceless, nameless woman.

"You've been invisible to him before. What's different about this time?" Lindy fastened a silver bell to the window as Cait abstractedly fingered her three ceramic wise men.

"Paul's got a date, and from the way he talked about it, this isn't with just any woman, either. Whoever she is must be important, otherwise he wouldn't have said anything. He looked like a little kid who's been given the keys to a candy store."

The information seemed to surprise Lindy as much as

it had Cait. She was quiet for a few minutes before she asked, "What are you going to do about it?"

"I don't know," Cait cried, hiding her face in her hands. She'd once jokingly suggested to Joe that she parade around naked in an effort to gain Paul's attention. Of course she'd been exaggerating, but some form of drastic action was obviously needed. If only she knew what.

Lindy mumbled an excuse and left. It wasn't until Cait looked up that she realized her friend was gone. She sighed wearily. She'd arrived at work this morning with such bright expectations, and now everything had gone wrong. She felt more depressed than she'd been in a long time. She knew the best remedy would be to force herself into some physical activity. Anything. The worst possible thing she could do was sit home alone and mope. Maybe she should plan to buy herself a Christmas tree and some ornaments. Her spirits couldn't help being at least a little improved by that; it would get her out of the house, if nothing else. And then she'd have something to entertain herself with, instead of brooding about this unexpected turn of events. Getting out of the house had an added advantage. If Joe phoned, she wouldn't be there to answer.

No sooner had that thought passed through her mind when a large form filled her doorway.

Joe.

A bright orange hard hat was pushed back on his head, the way movie cowboys wore their Stetsons. His boots were dusty and his tool pouch rode low on his hip, completing the gunslinger image. Even the way he stood with his thumbs tucked in his belt suggested he was waiting for a showdown.

"Hi, beautiful," he drawled, giving her that lazy, intimate smile of his. The one designed, Cait swore, just to unnerve her. But it wasn't going to work, not in her present state of mind.

"Don't you have anyone else to pester?" she asked coldly.

"My, my," Joe said, shaking his head in mock chagrin. Disregarding her lack of welcome, he strode into the office and threw himself down in the chair beside her desk. "You're in a rare mood."

"You would be too after the day I've had. Listen, Joe. As you can see, I'm poor company. Go flirt with the receptionist if you're trying to make someone miserable."

"Those claws are certainly sharp this afternoon." He ran his hands down the front of his shirt, pretending to inspect the damage she'd inflicted. "What's wrong?" Some of the teasing light faded from his eyes as he studied her.

She sent him a look meant to blister his ego, but as always Joe seemed invincible against her practiced glares.

"How do you know I'm not here to invest fifty thousand dollars?" he demanded, making himself at home by reaching across her desk for a pen. He rolled it casually between his palms.

Cait wasn't about to fall for this little game. "Are you here to invest money?"

"Not exactly. I wanted to ask you to—"

"Then come back when you are." She grabbed a stack of papers and slapped them down on her desk. But being rude, even to Joe, went against her nature. She was battling tears and the growing need to explain her behavior, apologize for it, when he rose to his feet. He tossed the pen carelessly onto her desk.

"Have it your way. If asking you to join me to look for a Christmas tree is such a terrible crime, then—"

"You're going to buy a Christmas tree?"

"That's what I just said." He flung the words over his shoulder as he strode out the door.

In that moment, Cait felt as though the whole world was tumbling down around her shoulders. She felt like such a shrew. He'd come here wanting to include her in his Christmas preparations and she'd driven him away with a spiteful tongue and a haughty attitude.

Cait wasn't a woman easily given to tears, but she struggled with them now. Her lower lip started to quiver. She might have been eight years old all over again—this was like the day she'd found out she wasn't invited to Betsy McDonald's birthday party. Only now it was Paul doing the excluding. He and this important woman of his were going out to have the time of their lives while she stayed home in her lonely apartment, suffering from a serious case of self-pity.

Gathering up her things, Cait thrust the papers into her briefcase with uncharacteristic negligence. She put on her coat, buttoned it quickly and wrapped the scarf around her neck as though it were a hangman's noose.

Joe was talking to his foreman, who'd been unobtrusively working around the office all day. He hesitated when he saw her, halting the conversation. Cait's eyes briefly met his and although she tried to disguise how regretful she felt, she obviously did a poor job of it. He took a step toward her, but she raised her chin a notch, too proud to admit her feelings.

She had to walk directly past Joe on her way to the elevator and forced herself to look anywhere but at him.

The stocky foreman clearly wanted to resume the discussion, but Joe ignored him and stared at Cait instead, with narrowed, assessing eyes. She could feel his questioning concern as profoundly as if he'd touched her. When she could bear it no longer, she turned to face him, her lower lip quivering uncontrollably.

"Cait," he called out.

She raced for the elevator, fearing she'd burst into tears before she could make her grand exit. She didn't bother to respond, knowing that if she said anything she'd make a greater fool of herself than usual. She wasn't even sure what had prompted her to say the atrocious things to Joe that she had. He wasn't the one who'd upset her, yet she'd unfairly taken her frustrations out on him.

She should've known it would be impossible to make a clean getaway. She almost ran through the office, past the reception desk, toward the elevator.

"Aren't you going to answer me?" Joe demanded, following on her heels.

"No." She concentrated on the lighted numbers above the elevator, which moved with painstaking slowness. Three more floors and she could make her escape.

"What's so insulting about inviting you to go Christmas-tree shopping?" he asked.

Close to weeping, she waved her free hand, hoping he'd understand that she was incapable of explaining just then. Her throat was clogged and it hurt to breathe, let alone talk. Her eyes filled with tears, and everything started to blur.

"Tell me," he commanded a second time.

Cait gulped at the tightness in her throat. "Y-you wouldn't understand." Why, oh why, wouldn't that elevator hurry?

"Try me."

It was either give in and explain, or stand there and argue. The first choice was easier; frankly, Cait didn't have the energy to fight with him. Sighing deeply, she began, "It—it all started when I made up this folder of business articles for Paul…"

"I might've known Paul had something to do with this," Joe muttered under his breath.

"I spent hours putting it together, adding little comments, and…and… I don't know what I expected but it wasn't…"

"What happened? What did Paul do?"

Cait rubbed her eyes with the back of her hand. "If you're going to interrupt me, then I can't see any reason to explain."

"Boss?" the foreman called out, sounding impatient.

Just then the elevator arrived and the doors opened, revealing half a dozen men and women. They stared out at Cait and Joe as he blocked the entrance, gripping her by the elbow.

"Joseph," she hissed, "let me go!" Recognizing her advantage, she called out, "This man refuses to release my arm." If she expected a knight in shining armor to leap to her rescue, Cait was to be sorely disappointed. It was as if no one had heard her.

"Don't worry, folks, we're married." Joe charmed them with another of his lazy, lopsided grins.

"Boss?" the foreman pleaded again.

"Take the rest of the day off," Joe shouted. "Tell the crew to go out and buy Christmas gifts for their wives."

"You want me to do *what?*" the foreman shouted back. Joe moved into the elevator with Cait.

"You heard me."

"Let me make sure I understand you. You want the men to go Christmas shopping for their wives? I thought you just said we're on a tight schedule?"

"That's right," Joe said loudly as the elevator doors closed.

Cait had never felt more conspicuous in her life. Every eye was focused on her and Joe, and it was all she could do to keep her head high.

When the tension became intolerable, Cait turned to face her fellow passengers. "We are not married," she announced.

"Yes, we are," Joe insisted. "She's simply forgotten."

"I did not forget our marriage and don't you dare tell them that cock-and-bull story about amnesia."

"But, darling—"

"Stop it right now, Joseph Rockwell! No one believes you. I'm sure these people can figure out that I'm the one who's telling the truth."

The elevator finally stopped on the ground floor, a fact for which Cait was deeply grateful. The doors glided open and two women stepped out first, but not before pausing to get a good appreciative look at Joe.

"Does she do this often?" one of the men asked, directing his question to Joe, his amusement obvious.

"Unfortunately, yes," he answered, chuckling as he tucked his hand under Cait's elbow and led her into the foyer. She tried to jerk her arm away, but he wouldn't allow it. "You see, I married a forgetful bride."

Chapter Seven

Pacing the carpet in the living room, Cait nervously smoothed the front of her red satin dress, her heart pumping furiously while she waited for Joe to arrive. She'd spent hours preparing for this Christmas party, which was being held in Paul's home. Her stomach was in knots.

She, the mysterious woman Paul was dating, would surely be there. Cait would have her first opportunity to size up the competition. Cait had studied her reflection countless times, trying to be objective about her chances with Paul based on looks alone. The dress was gorgeous. Her hair flawless. Everything else was as perfect as she could make it.

The doorbell sounded and Cait hurried across the room, throwing open the door. "You know what you are, Joseph Rockwell?"

"Late?" he suggested.

Cait pretended not to hear him. "A bully," she said. "A badgering bully, no less. I'm sorry I ever agreed to let you take me to Paul's party. I don't know what I was thinking."

"You were probably hoping to corner me under the mistletoe," he remarked with a wink that implied he wouldn't be difficult to persuade.

"First you practically kidnap me into going Christmas-tree shopping with you," she raged. "Then—"

"Come on, Cait, admit it, you had fun." He lounged indolently on her sofa while she got her coat and purse.

She hesitated, her mouth twitching with a smile. "Who'd ever believe that a man who bought his mother a rib roast and a case of cat food for Christmas last year would be so particular about a silly tree?" Joe had dragged her to no fewer than four lots yesterday, searching for the perfect tree.

"I took you to dinner afterward, didn't I?" he reminded her.

Cait nodded. She had to admit it: Joe had gone out of his way to help her forget her troubles. Although she'd made the tree-shopping expedition sound like a chore, he'd turned the evening into an enjoyable and, yes, memorable one.

His good mood had been infectious and after a while she'd completely forgotten Paul was out with another woman—someone so special that his enthusiasm about her had overcome his normal restraint.

"I've changed my mind," Cait decided suddenly, clasping her hands over her stomach, which was in turmoil. "I don't want to go to this Christmas party, after all." The evening was already doomed. She couldn't possibly have a good time watching the man she loved entertain the woman *he* loved. Cait couldn't think of a single reason to expose herself to that kind of misery.

"Not go to the party?" Joe repeated. "But I thought you'd arranged your flight schedule just so you could."

"I did, but that was before." Cait stubbornly squared her shoulders and elevated her chin just enough to convince Joe she meant business. He might be able to bully her into going shopping with him for a Christmas tree, but this was entirely different. "*She'll* be there," Cait added as an explanation.

"She?" Joe repeated slowly, burying his hands in his suit pockets. He was exceptionally handsome in his dark blue suit and no doubt knew it. He was as comfortable in tailored slacks as he was in dirty jeans.

A lock of thick hair slanted across his forehead; Cait managed—it was an effort—to resist brushing it back. An effort not because it disrupted his polished appearance, but because she had the strangest desire to run her fingers through his hair. Why she'd think such a thing now was beyond her. She'd long since stopped trying to figure out her feelings for Joe. He was a friend and a confidant even if, at odd moments, he behaved like a lunatic. Just remembering some of the comments he'd made to embarrass her brought color to her cheeks.

"I'd imagine you'd want to meet her," Joe challenged. "That way you can size her up."

"I don't even want to know what she looks like," Cait countered sharply. She didn't need to. Cait already knew everything she cared to about Paul's hot date. "She's beautiful."

"So are you."

Cait gave a short, derisive laugh. She wasn't discounting her own homespun appeal. She was reasonably attractive, and never more so than this evening. Catching a glimpse of herself in the mirror, she was pleased to see how nice her hair looked, with the froth of curls circling her head. But she wasn't going to kid herself, either. Her allure wasn't extraordinary by any stretch of the imagination. Her eyes were a warm shade of brown, though, and her nose was kind of cute. Perky, Lindy had once called it. But none of that mattered. Measuring herself against Paul's sure-to-be-gorgeous, nameless date was like comparing bulky sweat socks with a silk stocking. She'd already spent hours picturing her as a classic beauty…tall…sophisticated.

"I've never taken you for a coward," Joe said in a flat tone as he headed toward the door.

Apparently he wasn't even going to argue with her. Cait almost wished he would, just so she could show him how strong her will was. Nothing he could say or do would convince her to attend this party. Besides, her feet hurt. She was wearing new heels and hadn't broken them in yet, and if she did go, she'd be limping for days afterward.

"I'm not a coward," she told him, schooling her face to remain as emotionless as possible. "All I'm doing is exercising a little common sense. Why depress myself over the holidays? This is the last time I'll see Paul before Christmas. I leave for Minnesota in the morning."

"Yes, I know." Joe frowned as he said it, hesitating before he opened her door. "You're sure about this?"

"Positive." She was mildly surprised Joe wasn't making more of a fuss. From past experience, she'd expected a full-scale verbal battle.

"The choice is yours of course," he granted, shrugging. "But if it was me, I know I'd spend the whole evening regretting it." He studied her when he'd finished, then gave her a smile Cait could only describe as crafty.

She groaned inwardly. If there was one thing that drove her crazy about Joe it was the way he made the most outrageous statements. Then every once in a while he'd say something so wise it caused her to doubt her own conclusions and beliefs. This was one of those times. He was right: if she didn't go to Paul's, she'd regret it. Since she was leaving for Minnesota the following day, she wouldn't be able to ask anyone about the party, either.

"Are you coming or not?" he demanded.

Grumbling under her breath, Cait let him help her on with her coat. "I'm coming, but I don't like it. Not one darn bit."

"You're going to do just fine."

"They probably said that to Joan of Arc, too."

Cait clutched the punch glass in both hands, as though terrified someone might try to take it back. Standing next to the fireplace, with its garlanded mantel and cheerful blaze, she hadn't moved since they'd arrived a half hour earlier.

"Is *she* here yet?" she whispered to Lindy when her friend walked past carrying a tray of canapés.

"Who?"

"Paul's woman friend," Cait said pointedly. Both Joe and Lindy were beginning to exasperate her. "I've been standing here for the past thirty minutes hoping to catch a glimpse of her."

Lindy looked away. "I...I don't know if she's here or not."

"Stay with me, for heaven's sake," Cait requested, feeling shaky inside and out. Joe had deserted her almost as soon as they got there. Oh, he'd stuck around long enough to bring her a cup of punch, but then he'd drifted away, leaving Cait to deal with the situation on her own. This was the very man who'd insisted she attend this Christmas party, claiming he'd be right by her side the entire evening in case she needed him.

"I'm helping Paul with the hors d'oeuvres," Lindy explained, "otherwise I'd be happy to stay and chat."

"See if you can find Joe for me, would you?" She'd do it herself, but her feet were killing her.

"Sure."

Once Lindy was gone, Cait scanned the crowded living room. Many of the guests were business associates and clients Paul had worked with over the years. Naturally everyone from the office was there, as well.

"You wanted to see me?" Joe asked, reaching her side.

"Thank you very much," she muttered, doing her best to sound sarcastic and keep a smile on her face at the same time.

"You're welcome." He leaned one elbow on the fireplace mantel and grinned at her boyishly. "Might I ask what you're thanking me for?"

"Don't play games with me, Joe. Not now, please." She shifted her weight from one foot to the other, drawing his attention to her shoes.

"Your feet hurt?" he asked, frowning.

"Walking across hot coals would be less painful than these stupid high heels."

"Then why did you wear them?"

"Because they go with the dress. Listen, would you mind very much if we got off the subject of my shoes and discussed the matter at hand?"

"Which is?"

Joe was being as obtuse as Lindy had been. She assumed he was doing it deliberately, just to get a rise out of her. Well, it was working.

"Did you see her?" she asked with exaggerated patience.

"Not yet," he whispered back as though they were exchanging top-secret information. "She doesn't seem to have arrived."

"Have you talked to Paul?"

"No. Have you?"

"Not really." Paul had greeted them at the door, but other than that, Cait hadn't had a chance to do anything but watch him mingle with his guests. The day at the office hadn't been any help, either. Paul had breezed in and out without giving Cait more than a friendly wave. Since they hadn't exchanged a single word, it was impossible for her to determine how his date had gone.

It must have been a busy day for Lindy, as well, because Cait hadn't had a chance to talk to her, either. They'd met on their way out the door late that afternoon and Lindy had hurried past, saying she'd see Cait at Paul's party.

"I think I'll go help Lindy with the hors d'oeuvres," Cait said now. "Do you want me to get you anything?"

"Nothing, thanks." He was grinning as he strolled away, leaving Cait to wonder what he found so amusing.

Cait limped into the kitchen, leaving the polished wooden door swinging in her wake. She stopped abruptly when she encountered Paul and Lindy in the middle of a heated discussion.

"Oh, sorry," Cait apologized automatically.

Paul's gaze darted to Cait's. "No problem," he said quickly. "I was just leaving." He stalked past her, shoving the door open with the palm of his hand. Once again the door swung back and forth.

"What was that all about?" Cait wanted to know.

Lindy continued transferring the small cheese-dotted crackers from the cookie sheet onto the serving platter. "Nothing."

"It sounded as if you and Paul were arguing."

Lindy straightened and bit her lip. She avoided looking at Cait, concentrating on her task as if it was of vital importance to properly arrange the crackers on the plate.

"You were arguing, weren't you?" Cait pressed.

"Yes."

As far as she knew, Lindy and Paul had always gotten along. The fact that they were at odds surprised her. "About what?"

"I—I gave Paul my two-week notice this afternoon."

Cait was so shocked, she pulled out a kitchen chair and sank down on it. "You did *what?*" Removing her high heels, she massaged her pinched toes.

"You heard me."

"But why? Good grief, Lindy, you never said a word to anyone. Not even me. The least you could've done was talk to me about it first." No wonder Paul was angry. If Lindy left, it would mean bringing in someone new when the office was already short-staffed. With Cait and a number of other people away for the holidays, the place would be a madhouse.

"Did you receive an offer you couldn't refuse?" Cait hadn't had any idea her friend was unhappy at Webster, Rodale and Missen. Still, that didn't shock her nearly as much as Lindy's remaining tight-lipped about it all.

"It wasn't exactly an offer—but it was something like that," Lindy replied vaguely. She set aside the cookie sheet, smiled at Cait and then carried the platter into the living room.

For the past couple of weeks Cait had noticed that something was troubling her friend. It hadn't been anything she could readily name. Just that Lindy hadn't been her usual high-spirited self. Cait had meant to ask her about it, but she'd been so busy herself, so involved with her own problems, that she'd never brought it up.

She was still sitting there rubbing her feet when Joe sauntered into the kitchen, nibbling on a cheese cracker. "I thought I'd find you in here." He pulled out the chair across from her and sat down.

"Has she arrived yet?"

"Apparently so."

Cait dropped her foot and frantically worked the shoe back and forth until she'd managed to squeeze her toes inside. Then she forced her other foot into its shoe. "Well, for heaven's sake, why didn't you say something sooner?" she chastised. She stood up, ran her hands down the satin skirt and drew a shaky breath. "How do I look?"

"Like your feet hurt."

She sent him a scalding frown. "Thank you very much," she said sarcastically for the second time in under ten minutes. Hobbling to the door, she opened it a crack and peeked out, hoping to catch sight of the mystery woman. From what she could see, there weren't any new arrivals.

"What does she look like?" Cait demanded and whirled around to discover Joe standing directly behind her. She nearly collided with him and gave a small cry of surprise. Joe caught her by the shoulders to keep her from stumbling. Eager to question him about Paul's date, she didn't take the time to analyze why her heartrate soared when his hands made contact with her bare skin.

"What does she look like?" Cait asked again.

"I don't know," Joe returned flippantly.

"What do you mean you don't know? You just said she'd arrived."

"Unfortunately she doesn't have a tattoo across her forehead announcing that she's the woman Paul's dating."

"Then how do you know she's here?" If Joe was playing games with her, she'd make damn sure he'd regret it. Her love for Paul was no joking matter.

"It's more a feeling I have."

"You had me stuff my feet back into these shoes for a stupid feeling?" It was all she could do not to slap him silly. "You are no friend of mine, Joseph Rockwell. No friend whatsoever." Having said that, she limped back into the living room.

Obviously unscathed by her remark, Joe wandered out of the kitchen behind her. He walked over to the tray of canapés and helped himself to three or four while Cait did her best to ignore him.

Since the punch bowl was close by, she poured herself a second glass. The taste was sweet and cold, but Cait noticed that she felt a bit light-headed afterward. Potent drinks didn't sit well on an empty stomach, so she scooped up a handful of mixed nuts.

"I remember a time when you used to line up all the Spanish peanuts and eat those first," Joe said from behind her. "Then it was the hazelnuts, followed by the—"

"Almonds." Leave it to him to bring up her foolish past. "I haven't done that since I was—"

"Twenty," he guessed.

"Twenty-five," she corrected.

Joe laughed, and despite her aching feet and the certainty that she should never have come to this party, Cait laughed, too.

Refilling her punch glass, she downed it all in a single drink. Once more, it tasted cool and refreshing.

"Cait," Joe warned, "how much punch have you had?"

"Not enough." She filled the crystal cup a third time—or was it the fourth?—squared her shoulders and gulped it down. When she'd finished, she wiped the back of her hand across her mouth and smiled bravely.

"Are you purposely trying to get drunk?" he demanded.

"No." She reached for another handful of nuts. "All I'm looking for is a little courage."

"Courage?"

"Yes," she said with a sigh. "The way I figure it…" She paused, smiling giddily, then whirled around in a full circle. "There *is* some mistletoe here, isn't there?"

"I think so," Joe said, frowning. "What makes you ask?"

"I'm going to kiss Paul," she said proudly. "All I have to do is wait until he walks past. Then I'll grab him by the hand, wish him a merry Christmas and give him a kiss he won't soon forget." If the fantasy fulfilled itself, Paul would immediately realize he'd met the woman of his dreams, and propose marriage on the spot….

"What is kissing Paul supposed to prove?"

She returned to reality. "Well, this is where you come in. I want you to look around and watch the faces of the other women. If one of them shows signs of jealousy, then we'll know who it is."

"I'm not sure this plan of yours is going to work."

"It's better than trusting those feelings of yours," she countered.

She saw the mistletoe hanging from the archway be-

tween the formal dining room and the living room
Slouched against the wall, hands tucked behind her back,
Cait waited patiently for Paul to stroll past.

Ten minutes passed or maybe it was fifteen—Cait
couldn't tell. Yawning, she covered her mouth. "I think we
should leave," Joe suggested as he casually walked by.
"You're ready to fall asleep on your feet."

"I haven't kissed Paul yet," she reminded him.

"He seems to be involved in a lengthy discussion. This
could take a while."

"I'm in no hurry." Her throat felt unusually dry. She
would have preferred something nonalcoholic, but the
only drink nearby was the punch.

"Cait," Joe warned when he saw her helping herself to
yet another glass.

"Don't worry, I know what I'm doing."

"So did the captain of the *Titanic*."

"Don't get cute with me, Joseph Rockwell. I'm in no
mood to deal with someone amusing." Finding herself hi-
lariously funny, she smothered a round of giggles.

"Oh, no," Joe groaned. "I was afraid of this."

"Afraid of what?"

"You're drunk!"

She gave him a sour look. "That's ridiculous. All I had
is four little, bitty glasses of punch." To prove she knew
exactly what she was doing, she held up three fingers, recognized her mistake and promptly corrected herself. At
least she tried to do it promptly, but figuring out how many
fingers equaled four seemed to take an inordinate amount
of time. She finally held up two from each hand.

Expelling her breath, she leaned back against the wall
and closed her eyes. That was her second mistake. The

world took a sharp and unexpected nosedive. Snapping open her eyes, Cait looked to Joe as the anchor that would keep her afloat. He must have read the panic in her expression because he moved toward her and slowly shook his head.

"That does it, Ms. Singapore Sling. I'm getting you out of here."

"But I haven't been under the mistletoe yet."

"If you want anyone to kiss you, it'll be me."

The offer sounded tempting, but it was her stubborn boss Cait wanted to kiss, not Joe. "I'd rather dance with you."

"Unfortunately there isn't any music at the moment."

"You need music to dance?" It sounded like the saddest thing she'd ever heard, and her bottom lip began to tremble at the tragedy of it all. "Oh, dear, Joe," she whispered, clasping both hands to the sides of her head. "I think you might be right. The punch seems to be affecting me...."

"It's that bad, is it?"

"Uh, yes... The whole room's just started to pitch and heave. We're not having an earthquake, are we?"

"No." His hand was on her forearm, guiding her toward the front door.

"Wait," she said dramatically, raising her index finger. "I have a coat."

"I know. Stay here and I'll get it for you." He seemed worried about leaving her. Cait smiled at him, trying to reassure him she'd be perfectly fine, but she seemed unable to keep her balance. He urged her against the wall, stepped back a couple of paces as though he expected her to slip sideways, then hurriedly located her coat.

"What's wrong?" he asked when he returned.

"What makes you think anything's wrong?"

"Other than the fact that you're crying?"

"My feet hurt."

Joe rolled his eyes. "Why did you wear those stupid shoes in the first place?"

"I already told you," she whimpered. "Don't be mad at me." She held out her arms to him, needing his comfort. "Would you carry me to the car?"

Joe hesitated. "You want me to carry you?" He sounded as though it was a task of Herculean proportions.

"I can't walk." She'd taken the shoes off, and it would take God's own army to get them back on. She couldn't very well traipse outside in her stocking feet.

"If I carry you, we'd better find another way out of the house."

"All right." She agreed just to prove what an amicable person she actually was. When she was a child, she'd been a pest, but she wasn't anymore and she wanted to be sure Joe understood that.

Grasping Cait's hand, he led her into the kitchen.

"Don't you think we should make our farewells?" she asked. It seemed the polite thing to do.

"No," he answered sharply. "With the mood you're in you're likely to throw yourself into Paul's arms and demand that he make mad passionate love to you right then and there."

Cait's face went fire-engine red. "That's ridiculous."

Joe mumbled something she couldn't hear while he lifted her hand and slipped one arm, then the other, into the satin-lined sleeves of her full-length coat.

When he'd finished, Cait climbed on top of the kitchen chair, stretching out her arms to him. Joe stared at her as though she'd suddenly turned into a werewolf.

"What are you doing now?" he asked in an exasperated voice.

"You're going to carry me, aren't you?"

"I was considering it."

"I want a piggyback ride. You gave Betsy McDonald a piggyback ride once and not me."

"Cait," Joe groaned. He jerked his fingers through his hair, and offered her his hand, wanting her to climb down from the chair. "Get down before you fall. Good Lord, I swear you'd try the patience of a saint."

"I want you to carry me piggyback," she insisted. "Oh, please, Joe. My toes hurt so bad."

Once again her hero grumbled under his breath. She couldn't make out everything he said, but what she did hear was enough to curl her hair. With obvious reluctance, he walked to the chair, and giving a sigh of pure bliss, Cait wrapped her arms around his neck and hugged his lean hips with her legs. She laid her head on his shoulder and sighed again.

Still grumbling, Joe moved toward the back door.

Just then the kitchen door opened and Paul and Lindy walked in. Lindy gasped. Paul just stared.

"It's all right," Cait was quick to assure them. "Really it is. I was waiting under the mistletoe and you—"

"She downed four glasses of punch nonstop," Joe inserted before Cait could admit she'd been waiting there for Paul.

"Do you need any help?" Paul asked.

"None, thanks," Joe returned. "There's nothing to worry about."

"But…" Lindy looked concerned.

"She ain't heavy," Joe teased. "She's my wife."

* * *

The phone rang, waking Cait from a sound sleep. Her head began throbbing in time to the painful noise and she groped for the telephone receiver.

"Hello," she barked, instantly regretting that she'd spoken loudly.

"How are you feeling?" Joe asked.

"About like you'd expect," she whispered, keeping her eyes closed and gently massaging one temple. It felt as though tiny men with hammers had taken up residence in her head and were pounding away, hoping to attract her attention.

"What time does your flight leave?" he asked.

"It's okay. I'm not scheduled to leave until this afternoon."

"It is afternoon."

Her eyes flew open. "What?"

"Do you still need me to take you to the airport?"

"Yes…please." She tossed aside the covers and reached for her clock, stunned to realize Joe was right. "I'm already packed. I'll be dressed by the time you get here. Oh, thank goodness you phoned."

Cait didn't have time to listen to the pounding of the tiny men in her head. She showered and dressed as quickly as possible, swallowed a cup of coffee and a couple of aspirin, and was just shrugging into her coat when Joe arrived at the door.

She let him in, despite the suspiciously wide grin he wore.

"What's so amusing?"

"What makes you think I'm amused?" He strolled into the room, hands behind his back, as if he owned the place.

"Joe, we don't have time for your little games. Come on, or I'm going to miss my plane. What's with you, anyway?"

"Nothing." He circled her living room, still wearing that silly grin. "I don't suppose you realize it, but liquor has a peculiar effect on you."

Cait stiffened. "It does?" She remembered most of the party with great clarity. Good thing Joe had taken her home when he had.

"Liquor loosens your tongue."

"So?" She picked up two shopping bags filled with wrapped packages, leaving the lone suitcase for him. "Did I say anything of interest?"

"Oh my, yes."

"Joe!" She glanced quickly at her watch. They needed to get moving if she was to catch her flight. "Discount whatever I said—I'm sure I didn't mean it. If I insulted you, I apologize. If I told any family secrets, kindly forget I mentioned them."

He strolled to her side and tucked his finger under her chin. "This was a secret, all right," he informed her in a lazy drawl. "It was something you told me on the drive home."

"Are you sure it's true?"

"Relatively sure."

"What did I say? Did I declare my undying love for you? Because if I—"

"No, no, nothing like that."

"Just how long do you intend to torment me with this?" She was rapidly losing interest in his little guessing game.

"Not much longer." He looked exceptionally pleased with himself. "So Martin's a minister now. Funny you never thought to mention that before."

"Ah…" Cait set aside the two bags and lowered herself to the sofa. So he'd found out. Worse, she'd been the one to tell him.

"That may well have some interesting ramifications, my dear. Have you ever stopped to think about them?"

Chapter Eight

"This is exactly why I didn't tell you about Martin," Cait informed Joe as he tossed her suitcase into the back seat of his car. She checked her watch again and groaned. They had barely an hour and a half before her flight was scheduled to leave. Cait was never late. Never—at least not when it was her own fault.

"It seems to me," Joe continued, his face deadpan, "that there could very well be some legal grounds to our marriage."

Joe was saying that just to annoy her, and unfortunately it was working. "I've never heard anything more ludicrous in my life."

"Think about it, Cait," he said, ignoring her protest. "We could be celebrating our anniversary this spring. How many years is it now? Eighteen? How the years fly."

"Listen, Joe, I don't find this amusing." She glanced at her watch. If only she hadn't slept so late. Never again would she have any Christmas punch. Briefly she wondered what else she'd said to Joe, then decided it was better not to know.

"I heard a news report of a three-car pileup on the freeway, so we'll take the side streets."

"Just hurry," Cait urged in an anxious voice.

"I'll do the best I can," Joe said, "but worrying about it isn't going to get us there any faster."

She glared at him. She couldn't help it. He wasn't the one who'd been planning this trip for months. If she missed the flight, her nephews and niece wouldn't have their Christmas presents from their Auntie Cait. Nor would she share in the family traditions that were so much a part of her Christmas. She *had* to get to the airport on time.

Everyone else had apparently heard about the accident on the freeway, too, and the downtown area was crowded with the overflow. Cait and Joe were delayed at every intersection and twice were forced to sit through two changes of the traffic signal.

Cait was growing more panicky by the minute. She just had to make this flight. But it almost seemed that she'd get to the airport faster if she simply jumped out of the car and ran there.

Joe stopped for another red light, but when the signal turned green, they still couldn't move—a delivery truck in front of them had stalled. Furious, Cait rolled down the window and stuck out her head. "Listen here, buster, let's get this show on the road," she shouted at the top of her lungs.

Her head was pounding and she prayed the aspirin would soon take effect.

"Quite the Christmas spirit," Joe muttered dryly under his breath.

"I can't help it. I have to catch this plane."

"You'll be there in plenty of time."

"At this rate we won't make it to Sea-Tac before Easter!"

"Relax, will you?" Joe suggested gently. He turned on the radio and a medley of Christmas carols filled the air. Normally the music would have calmed her, but she was suffering from a hangover, depression and severe anxiety, all at the same time. Her fingernails found their way into her mouth.

Suddenly she straightened. "Darn! I forgot to give you your Christmas gift. I left it at home."

"Don't worry about it."

"I didn't get you a gag gift the way I said." Actually she was pleased with the book she'd managed to find—an attractive coffee-table volume about the history of baseball.

Cait waited for Joe to mention *her* gift. Surely he'd bought her one. At least she fervently hoped he had, otherwise she'd feel like a fool. Though, admittedly, that was a feeling she'd grown accustomed to in the past few weeks.

"I think we might be able to get back on the freeway here," Joe said, as he made a sharp left-hand turn. They crossed the overpass, and from their vantage point, Cait could see that the freeway was unclogged and running smoothly.

"Thank God," she whispered, relaxing against the back of the seat as Joe drove quickly ahead.

Her chauffeur chuckled. "I seem to remember you lecturing me—"

"I never lecture," she said testily. "I may have a strong opinion on certain subjects, but let me assure you, I never lecture."

"You were right, though. The streets of Bethlehem must have been crowded and bustling with activity at the time of that first Christmas. I can see it all now, can't you? A rug dealer is held up by a shepherd driving his flock through the middle of town."

Cait smiled for the first time that morning, because she could easily picture the scene Joe was describing.

"Then some furious woman, impatient to make it to the local camel merchant before closing, sticks her nose in the middle of everything and shouts at the rug dealer to get his show on the road." He paused to chuckle at his own wit. "I'm convinced she wouldn't have been so testy except that she was suffering from one heck of a hang-over."

"Very funny," Cait grumbled, smiling despite herself.

He took the exit for the airport and Cait was gratified to note that her flight wasn't scheduled to leave for another thirty minutes. She was cutting it close, closer than she ever had before, but she'd confirmed her ticket two days earlier and had already been assigned her seat.

Joe pulled up at the drop-off point for her airline and gave Cait's suitcase to a skycap while she rummaged around in her purse for her ticket.

"I suppose this is goodbye for now," he said with an endearingly crooked grin that sent her pulses racing.

"I'll be back in less than two weeks," she reminded him, trying to keep her tone light and casual.

"You'll phone once you arrive?"

She nodded. For all her earlier panic, Cait now felt oddly unwilling to leave Joe. She should be rushing through the airport to her airline's check-in counter to get her boarding pass, but she lingered, her heart overflowing with emotions she couldn't identify.

"Have a safe trip," he said quietly.

"I will. Thanks so much...for everything."

"You're welcome." His expression sobered and the ever-ready mirth fled from his eyes. Cait wasn't sure who moved first. All she knew was that she was in Joe's arms, his thumb caressing the softness of her cheek as they gazed hungrily into each other's eyes.

He leaned forward to kiss her. Cait's eyes drifted shut as his mouth met hers.

At first Joe's kiss was tender but it quickly grew in fervor. The noise and activity around them seemed to fade into the distance. Cait could feel herself dissolving. She moaned and arched closer, not wanting to leave the protective haven of his arms. Joe shuddered and hugged her tight, as if he, too, found it difficult to part.

"Merry Christmas, love," he whispered, releasing her with a reluctance that made her feel...giddy. Confused. *Happy*.

"Merry Christmas," she echoed, but she didn't move.

Joe gave her the gentlest of nudges. "You'd better hurry, Cait."

"Oh, right," she said, momentarily forgetting why she was at the airport. Reaching for the bags filled with gaily wrapped Christmas packages, she took two steps backward. "I'll phone when I get there."

"Do. I'll be waiting to hear from you." He thrust his hands into his pockets and Cait had the distinct impression he did it to stop himself from reaching for her again. The thought was a romantic one, a certainty straight from her heart.

Her heart... Her heart was full of feeling for Joe. More than she'd ever realized. He'd dominated her life these past few weeks—taking her to dinner, bribing his way back into her good graces with pizza, taking her on a

Christmas shopping expedition, escorting her to Paul's party. Joe had become her whole world. Joe, not Paul. Joe.

Given no other choice, Cait abruptly turned and hurried into the airport, where she checked in, then went through security and down the concourse to the proper gate.

The flight had already been called and only a handful of passengers had yet to board.

Cait dashed to the counter with her boarding pass. A young soldier stood just ahead of her. "But you don't understand," the tall marine was saying to the airline employee. "I booked this flight over a month ago. I've got to be on that plane!"

"I'm so sorry," the woman apologized, her dark eyes regretful. "This sort of thing happens, especially during holidays, but your ticket's for standby. I wish I could do something for you, but there isn't a single seat available."

"But I haven't seen my family in over a year. My uncle Harvey's driving from Duluth to visit. He was in the marines, too. My mom's been baking for three weeks. Don't you see? I can't disappoint them now!"

Cait watched as the agent rechecked her computer. "If I could magically create a seat for you, I would," she said sympathetically. "But there just isn't one."

"But when I bought the ticket, the woman told me I wouldn't have a problem getting on the flight. She said there're always no-shows."

"I'm so sorry," the agent repeated, looking past the young marine to Cait.

"All right," he said, forcefully expelling his breath. "When's the next flight with available space? Any flight within a hundred miles of Minneapolis. I'll walk the rest of the way if I have to."

Once again, the woman consulted her computer. "We have space available the evening of the twenty-sixth."

"The twenty-sixth!" the young man shouted. "But that's after Christmas and eats up nearly all my leave. I'd be home for less than a week."

"May I help you?" the airline employee said to Cait. She looked almost as unhappy as the marine, but apparently there wasn't anything she could do to help him.

Cait stepped forward and handed the woman her boarding pass. The soldier gazed at it longingly, then moved dejectedly from the counter and lowered himself into one of the molded plastic chairs.

Cait hesitated, remembering how she'd stuck her head out the window of Joe's truck on their drive to the airport and shouted impatiently at the truck driver who was holding up traffic. A conversation she'd had with Joe earlier returned to haunt her. She'd argued that Christmas was a time filled with love and good cheer, the one holiday that brought out the very best in everyone. And sometimes, Joe had insisted, the very worst.

"Since you already have your seat assignment, you may board the flight now."

The urge to hurry nearly overwhelmed Cait, yet she hesitated once again.

"Excuse me," Cait said, drawing a deep breath and making her decision. She approached the soldier. He seemed impossibly young now that she had a good look at him. No more than eighteen, maybe nineteen. He'd probably joined the service right out of high school. His hair was cropped close to his head and his combat boots were so shiny Cait could see her reflection in them.

The marine glanced up at her, his face heavy with defeat. "Yes?"

"Did I hear you say you needed to be on this flight?"

"I have a ticket, ma'am. But it's standby and there aren't any seats."

"Listen," she said. "You can have mine."

The way his face lit up was enough to blot out her own disappointment at missing Christmas with Martin and her sister-in-law. The kids. Her mother… "My family's in Minneapolis, too, but I was there this summer."

"Ma'am, I can't let you do this."

"Don't cheat me out of the pleasure."

As they approached the counter to effect the exchange, the last call for the flight was announced. The marine stood, his eyes wide with disbelief. "I insist," Cait said, her throat growing thick. "Here." She handed him the two bags full of gifts for her nephews and nieces. "There'll be a man waiting at the other end. A tall minister—he'll have a collar on. Give him these. I'll phone so he'll know to look for you."

"Thank you for everything…I can't believe you're doing this."

Cait smiled. Impulsively the marine hugged her, then swinging his duffel bag over his shoulder, he picked up the two bags of gifts and jogged over to the ramp.

Cait waited for a couple of minutes, then wiped the tears from her eyes. She wasn't completely sure why she was crying. She'd never felt better in her life.

It was around six when she awoke. The apartment was dark and silent. Sighing, she picked up the phone, dragged it onto the bed with her and punched out Joe's number.

He answered on the first ring, as if he'd been waiting for her call. "How was the flight?" he asked immediately.

"I wouldn't know. I wasn't on it."

"You missed the plane!" he shouted incredulously. "But you were there in plenty of time."

"I know. It's a long story, but basically, I gave my seat to someone who needed it more than I did." She smiled dreamily, remembering how the young marine's face had lit up. "I'll tell you about it later."

"Where are you now?"

"Home."

He exhaled sharply, then said, "I'll be over in fifteen minutes."

Actually it took him twelve. By then Cait had brewed a pot of coffee and made herself a peanut-butter-and-jelly sandwich. She hadn't eaten all day and was starved. She'd just finished the sandwich when Joe arrived.

"What about your luggage?" Joe asked, looking concerned. He didn't give her a chance to respond. "Exactly what do you mean, you gave your seat away?"

Cait explained as best she could. Even now she found herself surprised by her actions. Cait rarely behaved spontaneously. But something about that young soldier had reached deep within her heart and she'd reacted instinctively.

"The airline is sending my suitcase back to Seattle on the next available flight, so there's no need to worry," Cait said. "I talked to Martin, who was quick to tell me the Lord would reward my generosity."

"Are you going to catch a later flight, then?" Joe asked. He helped himself to a cup of coffee and pulled out the chair across from hers.

"There aren't any seats," Cait said. She leaned back, yawning, and covered her mouth. Why she should be so tired after sleeping away most of the afternoon was beyond her. "Besides, the office is short-staffed. Lindy gave Paul her notice and a trainee is coming in, which makes everything even more difficult. They can use me."

Joe frowned. "Giving up your vacation is one way to impress Paul."

Words of explanation crowded her tongue. She realized Joe wasn't insulting her; he was only stating a fact. What he didn't understand was that Cait hadn't thought of Paul once the entire day. Her staying or leaving had absolutely nothing to do with him.

If she'd been thinking of anyone, it was Joe. She knew now that giving up her seat to the marine hadn't been entirely unselfish. When Joe kissed her goodbye, her heart had started telegraphing messages she had yet to fully decode. The plain and honest truth was that she hadn't wanted to leave him. It was as if she really did belong with him....

That perception had been with her from the moment they'd parted at the airport. It had followed her in the taxi on the ride back to the apartment. Joe was the last person she'd thought of when she'd fallen asleep, and the first person she'd remembered when she awoke.

It was the most unbelievable thing.

"What are you going to do for Christmas?" Joe asked, still frowning into his coffee cup. For someone who'd seemed downright regretful that she was flying halfway across the country, he didn't seem all that pleased to be sharing her company now.

"I...haven't decided yet. I suppose I'll spend a quiet day by myself." She'd wake up late, indulge in a lazy scented bath, find something sinful for breakfast. Ice cream, maybe. Then she'd paint her toenails and settle down with a good book. The day would be lonely, true, but certainly not wasted.

"It'll be anything but quiet," Joe challenged.

"Oh?"

"You'll be spending it with me and my family."

"This is the first time Joe has ever brought a girl to join us for Christmas," Virginia Rockwell said as she set a large tray of freshly baked cinnamon rolls in the center of the huge kitchen table. She wiped her hands clean on the apron that was secured around her thick waist.

Cait felt she should explain. She was a little uncomfortable arriving unannounced with Joe like this. "Joe and I are just friends."

Mrs. Rockwell shook her head, which set the white curls bobbing. "I saw my son's eyes when he brought you into the house." She grinned knowingly. "I remember you from the old neighborhood, with your starched dresses and the pigtails with those bright pink ribbons. You were a pretty girl then and you're even prettier now."

"The starched dresses were me, all right," Cait confirmed. She'd been the only girl for blocks around who always wore dresses to school.

Joe's mother chuckled again. "I remember the sensation you caused in the neighborhood when you said Joe had kissed you." She chuckled, her eyes shining. "His father and I got quite a kick out of that. I still remember how furious Joe was when he learned his secret was out."

"I only told one person," Cait protested. But Betsy had told plenty of others, and the news had spread with alarming speed. However, Cait figured she'd since paid for her sins tenfold. Joe had made sure of that in the past few weeks.

"It's so good to see you again, Caitlin. When we've got a minute I want you to sit down and tell me all about your mother. We lost contact years ago, but I always thought she was a darling."

"I think so, too," Cait agreed, carrying a platter of scrambled eggs to the table. She did miss being with her family, but Joe's mother made it almost as good as being home. "I know that's how Mom feels about you, too. She'll want to thank you for being kind enough to invite me into your home for Christmas."

"I wouldn't have it any other way."

"I know." She glanced into the other room where Joe was sitting with his brother and sister-in-law. Her heart throbbed at the sight of him with his family. But these newfound feelings for Joe left her at a complete loss. What she'd told Mrs. Rockwell was true. Joe was her friend. The very best friend she'd ever had. She was grateful for everything he'd done for her since they'd chanced upon each other, just weeks ago, really. But their friendship was developing into something much stronger. If only she didn't feel so…so ardent about Paul. If only she didn't feel so confused!

Joe laughed at something one of his nephews said and Cait couldn't help smiling. She loved the sound of his laughter. It was vigorous and robust and lively—just like his personality.

"Joe says you're working as a stockbroker right here in Seattle."

"Yes. I've been with Webster, Rodale and Missen for over a year now. My degree was in accounting but—"

"Accounting?" Mrs. Rockwell nodded approvingly. "My Joe has his own accountant now. Good thing, too. His books were in a terrible mess. He's a builder, not a pencil pusher, that boy."

"Are you telling tales on me, Mom?" Joe asked as he sauntered into the kitchen. He picked up a piece of bacon and bit off the end. "When are we going to open the gifts? The kids are getting restless."

"The kids, nothing. You're the one who's eager to tear into those packages," his mother admonished. "We'll open them after breakfast, the way we do every Christmas."

Joe winked at Cait and disappeared into the living room once more.

Mrs. Rockwell watched her son affectionately. "Last year he shows up on my doorstep bright and early Christmas morning needing gift wrap. Then, once he's got all his presents wrapped, he walks into my kitchen—" her face crinkled in a wide grin "—and he sticks all those presents in my refrigerator." She smiled at the memory. "For his brother, he bought two canned hams and three gallons of ice cream. For me it was cat food and a couple of rib roasts."

Breakfast was a bustling affair, with Joe's younger brother, his wife and their children gathered around the table. Joe sat next to Cait and held her hand while his mother offered the blessing. Although she wasn't home with her own family, Cait felt she had a good deal for which to be thankful.

Conversation was pleasant and relaxed, but foremost on the children's minds was opening the gifts. The table was cleared and plates and bowls arranged inside the dishwasher in record time.

Cait sat beside Joe, holding a cup of coffee, as the oldest grandchild handed out the presents. While Christmas music played softly in the background, the children tore into their packages. The youngest, a two-year-old girl, was more interested in the box than in the gift itself.

When Joe came to the square package Cait had given him, he shook it enthusiastically.

"Be careful, it might break," she warned, knowing there was no chance of that happening.

Carefully he removed the bows, then unwrapped his gift. Cait watched expectantly as he lifted the book from the layers of bright paper. "A book on baseball?"

Cait nodded, smiling. "As I recall, you used to collect baseball cards."

"I ended up trading away my two favorites."

"I'm sure it was for a very good reason."

"Of course."

Their eyes held until it became apparent that everyone in the room was watching them. Cait glanced self-consciously away.

Joe cleared his throat. "This is a great gift, Cait. Thank you very much."

"You're welcome very much."

He leaned over and kissed her as if it was the most natural thing in the world. It felt right, their kiss. If anything, Cait was sorry to stop at one.

"Surely you have something for Cait," Virginia Rockwell prompted her son.

"You bet I do."

"He's probably keeping it in the refrigerator," Cait suggested, to the delight of Joe's family.

"Oh, ye of little faith," he said, removing a box from his shirt pocket.

"I recognize that paper," Sally, Joe's sister-in-law, murmured to Cait. "It's from Stanley's."

Cait's eyes widened at the name of an expensive local jewelry store. "Joe?"

"Go ahead and open it," he urged.

Cait did, hands fumbling in her eagerness. She slipped off the ribbon and peeled away the gold textured wrap to reveal a white jeweler's box. It contained a second box, a small black velvet one, which she opened very slowly. She gasped at the lovely cameo brooch inside.

"Oh, Joe," she whispered. It was a lovely piece carved in onyx and overlaid with ivory. She'd longed for a cameo, a really nice one, for years and wondered how Joe could possibly have known.

"You gonna kiss Uncle Joe?" his nephew, Charlie, asked, "'cause if you are, I'm not looking."

"Of course she's going to kiss me," Joe answered for her. "Only she can do it later when there aren't so many curious people around." He glanced swiftly at his mother. "Just the way Mom used to thank Dad for her Christmas gift. Isn't that right, Mom?"

"I'm sure Cait...will," Virginia answered, clearly flustered. She patted her hand against the side of her head as though she feared the pins had fallen from her hair, her eyes downcast.

Cait didn't blame the older woman for being embarrassed, but one look at the cameo and she was willing to forgive Joe anything.

The day flew past. After the gifts were opened—with everyone exclaiming in surprised delight over the gifts Joe had bought, with Cait's help—the family gathered around the piano. Mrs. Rockwell played as they sang a variety of Christmas carols, their voices loud and cheerful. Joe's father had died several years earlier, but he was mentioned often throughout the day, with affection and love. Cait hadn't known him well, but the family obviously felt Andrew Rockwell's presence far more than his absence on this festive day.

Joe drove Cait back to her apartment late that night. Mrs. Rockwell had insisted on sending a plate of cookies home with her, and Cait swore it was enough goodies to last her a month of Sundays. Now she felt sleepy and warm; leaning her head against the seat, she closed her eyes.

"We're here," Joe whispered close to her ear.

Reluctantly Cait opened her eyes and sighed. "I had such a wonderful day. Thank you, Joe." She couldn't quite stifle a yawn as she reached for the door handle, thinking longingly of bed.

"That's it?" He sounded disappointed.

"What do you mean, that's it?"

"I seem to remember a certain promise you made this morning."

Cait frowned, not sure she understood what he meant. "When?"

"When we were opening the gifts," he reminded her.

"Oh," Cait said, straightening. "You mean when I opened your gift to me and saw the brooch."

Joe nodded with exaggerated emphasis. "Right. *Now* do you remember?"

"Of course." The kiss. He planned to claim the kiss she'd promised him. She brushed her mouth quickly over his and grinned. "There."

"If that's the best you can do, you should've kissed me in front of Charlie."

"You're faulting my kissing ability?"

"Charlie's dog gives better kisses than that."

Cait felt more than a little insulted. "Is this a challenge, Joseph Rockwell?"

"Yes," he returned archly. "You're darn right it is."

"All right, then you're on." She set the plate of cookies aside, slid closer and slipped her arms around Joe's neck. Next she wove her fingers into his thick hair.

"This is more like it," Joe murmured contentedly.

Cait paused. She wasn't sure why. Perhaps because she'd suddenly lost all interest in making fun out of something that had always been so wonderful between them.

Joe's eyes met hers, and the laughter and fun in them seemed to disappear. Slowly he expelled his breath and brushed his lips along her jaw. The warmth of his breath was exciting as his mouth skimmed toward her temple. His arms closed around her waist and he pulled her tight against him.

Impatiently he began to kiss her, introducing her to a world of warm, thrilling sensations. His mouth then explored the curve of her neck. It felt so good that Cait closed her eyes and experienced a curious weightlessness she'd never known—a heightened awareness of physical longing.

"Oh, Cait..." He broke away from her, his breathing labored and heavy. She knew instinctively that he wanted to say more, but he changed his mind and buried his face in her hair, exhaling sharply.

"How am I doing?" she whispered once she found her voice.

"Just fine."

"Are you ready to retract your statement?"

He hesitated. "I don't know. Convince me again." So she did, her kiss moist and gentle, her heart fluttering against her ribs.

"Is that good enough?" she asked when she'd recovered her breath.

Joe nodded, as though he didn't quite trust his own voice. "Excellent."

"I had a wonderful day," she whispered. "I can't thank you enough for including me."

Joe shook his head lightly. There seemed to be so much more he wanted to say to her and couldn't. Cait slipped out of the car and walked into her building, turning on the lights when she entered her apartment. She slowly put away her things, wanting to wrap this feeling around her like a warm quilt. Minutes later, she glanced out her window to see Joe still sitting in his car, his hands gripping the steering wheel, his head bent. It looked to Cait as though he was battling with himself to keep from following her inside. She would have welcomed him if he had.

Chapter Nine

Cait stared at the computer screen for several minutes, blind to the information in front of her. Deep in thought, she released a long, slow breath.

Paul had been grateful to see her when she'd shown up at the office that morning. The week between Christmas and New Year's could be a harried one. Lindy had looked surprised, then quickly retreated into her own office after exchanging a brief good-morning and little else. Her friend's behavior continued to baffle Cait, but she couldn't concentrate on Lindy's problems just now, or even on her work.

No matter what she did, Cait couldn't stop thinking about Joe and the kisses they'd exchanged Christmas evening. Nor could she forget his tortured look as he'd sat in his car after she'd gone into her apartment. Even now she wasn't certain why she hadn't immediately run back outside. And by the time she'd decided to do that, he was gone.

Cait was so absorbed in her musings that she barely heard the knock at her office door. Guiltily she glanced up to find Paul standing just inside her doorway, his hands in his pockets, his eyes weary.

"Paul!" Cait waited for her heart to trip into double time the way it usually did whenever she was anywhere near him. It didn't, which was a relief but no longer much of a surprise.

"Hello, Cait." His smile was uneven, his face tight. He seemed ill at ease and struggling to disguise it. "Have you got a moment?"

"Sure. Come on in." She stood and motioned toward her client chair. "What can I do for you?"

"Nothing much," he said vaguely, sitting down. "Uh, I just wanted you to know how pleased I am that you're here. I'm sorry you canceled your vacation, but I appreciate your coming in today. Especially in light of the fact that Lindy will be leaving." His mouth thinned briefly.

No one, other than Joe and Martin, was aware of the real reason Cait wasn't in Minnesota the way she'd planned. Nor had she suggested to Paul that she'd changed her plans to help him out because they'd be short-staffed; obviously he'd drawn his own conclusions.

"So Lindy's decided to follow through with her resignation?"

Paul nodded, then frowned anew. "Nothing I say will change her mind. That woman's got a stubborn streak as wide as a…" He shrugged, apparently unable to come up with an appropriate comparison.

"The construction project's nearly finished," Cait offered, making small talk rather than joining in his criticism of Lindy. Absently she stood up and wandered around her office, stopping to straighten the large Christmas wreath on her door, the one she and Lindy had put up earlier in the month. Lindy was her friend and she wasn't about to agree with Paul, or argue with him, for that matter. Actually she should've been pleased that Paul had sought her out, but she felt curiously indifferent. And she did have work she needed to do.

"Yes, I'm delighted with the way everything's turned out," Paul said, "Joe Rockwell's done a fine job. His reputation is excellent and I imagine he'll be one of the big-time contractors in the area within the next few years."

Cait nodded casually, hoping she'd concealed the thrill of excitement that had surged through her at the mention of Joe's name. She didn't need Paul to tell her Joe's future was bright; she could see that for herself. At Christmas, his mother had boasted freely about his success. Joe had recently received a contract for a large government project—his most important to date—and she was extremely proud of him. He might have trouble keeping his books straight, but he left his customers satisfied. If he worked as hard at satisfying them as he did at finding the right Christmas tree, Cait could well believe he was gaining a reputation for excellence.

"Well, listen," Paul said, drawing in a deep breath, "I won't keep you." His eyes were clouded as he stood and headed toward the door. He hesitated, turning back to face her. "I don't suppose you'd be free for dinner tonight, would you?"

"Dinner," Cait repeated as though she'd never heard the word before. Paul was inviting her to dinner? After all these months? Now, when she least expected it? Now, when it no longer mattered? After all the times she'd ached to the bottom of her heart for some attention from him, he was finally asking her out on a date? Now?

"That is, if you're free."

"Uh…yes, sure…that would be nice."

"Great. How about if I pick you up around five-thirty? Unless that's too early for you?"

"Five-thirty will be fine."

"I'll see you then."

"Thanks, Paul." Cait felt numb. There wasn't any other way to describe it. It was as if her dreams were finally beginning to play themselves out—too late. Paul, whom she'd loved from afar for so long, wanted to take her to dinner. She should be dancing around the office with glee, or at least feeling something other than this peculiar dull sensation in the pit of her stomach. If this was such a significant, exciting, hoped-for event, why didn't she feel any of the exhilaration she'd expected?

After taking a moment to collect her thoughts, Cait walked down the hallway to Lindy's office and found her friend on the phone. Lindy glanced up, smiled feebly in Cait's direction, then abruptly dropped her gaze as if the call demanded her full concentration.

Cait waited a couple of minutes, then decided to return later when Lindy wasn't so busy. She needed to talk to her friend, needed her counsel. Lindy had always encouraged Cait in her dreams of a relationship with Paul. When she was discouraged, it was Lindy who bolstered her sagging spirits. Yes, it was definitely time for a talk. She'd try to get Lindy to confide in her, too. Cait valued Lindy's friendship; true, she couldn't help being hurt that the person she considered one of her best friends would give notice to leave the firm without even discussing it with her. But Lindy must've had her reasons. And maybe she, too, needed some support right about now.

Hearing her own phone ring, Cait hurried back to her office. She was consistantly busy from then on. The New York Stock Exchange was due to close in a matter of minutes when Joe happened by.

"Hi," Cait greeted him, her smile wide and welcoming. Her gaze connected with Joe's and he returned her smile. Her heart reacted automatically, leaping with sheer happiness.

"Hi, yourself." He sauntered into her office and threw himself down in the same chair Paul had taken earlier, stretching his long legs in front of him and folding his hands over his stomach. "So how's the world of finance doing this fine day?"

"About as well as usual."

"Then we're in deep trouble," he joked.

His smile was infectious. It always had been, but Cait had initially resisted him. Her defenses had weakened, though, and she responded readily with a smile of her own.

"You done for the day?"

"Just about." She checked the time. In another five minutes, New York would be closing down. There were several items she needed to clear from her desk, but nothing pressing. "Why?"

"Why?" It was little short of astonishing how far Joe's eyebrows could reach, Cait noted, all but disappearing into his hairline.

"Can't a man ask a simple question?" Joe asked.

"Of course." The banter between them was like a well-rehearsed play. Never had Cait been more at ease with a man—or had more fun with a man. Or with anyone, really. "What I want to know is whether 'simple' refers to the question or to the man asking it."

"Ouch," Joe said, grinning broadly. "Those claws are sharp this afternoon."

"Actually today's been good." Or at least it had since he'd arrived.

"I'm glad to hear it. How about dinner?" He jumped to his feet and pretended to waltz around her office, playing a violin. "You and me. Wine and moonlight and music. Romance and roses." He wiggled his eyebrows at her suggestively. "You work too hard. You always have. I want you to enjoy life a little more. It would be good for both of us."

Joe didn't need to give her an incentive to go out with him. Cait was thrilled at the mere idea. Joe made her laugh, made her feel good about herself and the world. Of course, he possessed a remarkable talent for driving her crazy, too. But she supposed a little craziness was good for the spirit.

"Only promise me you won't wear those high heels of yours," he chided, pressing his hand to the small of his back. "I've suffered excruciating back pains ever since Paul's Christmas party."

Paul's name seemed to leap out and grab Cait by the throat. "Paul," she repeated, sagging against the back of her chair. "Oh, dear."

"I know you consider him a dear," Joe teased. "What has your stalwart employer done this time?"

"He asked me out to dinner," Cait admitted, frowning. "Out of the blue this morning he popped into my office and invited me to dinner as if we'd been dating for months. I was so stunned, I didn't know what to think."

"What did you tell him?" Joe seemed to consider the whole thing a huge joke. "Wait—" he held up his hand

"—you don't need to answer that. I already know. You sprang at the offer."

"I didn't exactly spring," she said, somewhat offended by Joe's attitude. The least he could do was show a little concern. She'd spent Christmas with him, and according to his own mother this was the first time he'd ever brought a woman home for the holiday. Furthermore, despite his insisting to all and sundry that they were married, he certainly didn't seem to mind her seeing another man.

"I'll bet you nearly went into shock." A smile trembled at the edges of his mouth as if he was picturing her reaction to Paul's invitation and finding it all terribly entertaining.

"I did not go into shock." She defended herself heatedly. She'd been taken by surprise, that was all.

"Listen," he said, walking toward the door, "have a great time. I'll catch you later." With that he was gone.

Cait couldn't believe it. Her mouth dropped open and she paced frantically, clenching and unclenching her fists. It took her a full minute to recover enough to run after him.

Joe was talking to his foreman, the same stocky man he'd been with the day he followed Cait into the elevator.

"Excuse me," she said, interrupting their conversation, "but when you're finished I'd like a few words with you, Joe." Her back was ramrod stiff and she kept flexing her hands as though preparing for a fight.

Joe glanced at his watch. "It might be a while."

"Then might I have a few minutes of your time now?"

The foreman stepped away, his step cocky. "You want me to dismiss the crew again, boss? I can tell them to go out and buy New Year's presents for their wives, if you like."

The man was rewarded with a look that was hot

enough to barbecue spareribs. "That won't be necessary, thanks, anyway, Harry."

"You're welcome, boss. We serve to please."

"Then please me by kindly shutting up."

Harry chuckled and returned to another section of the office.

"You wanted something?" Joe asked.

Boy, did she. "Is that all you're going to say?"

"About what?"

"About my going to dinner with Paul? I expected you to be...I don't know, upset."

"Why should I be upset? Is he going to have his way with you? I sincerely doubt it, but if you're worried, invite me along and I'll be more than happy to protect your honor."

"What's the matter with you?" she demanded, not bothering to disguise her fury and disappointment. She stared at Joe, waiting for him to mock her again, but once more he surprised her. His gaze sobered.

"You honestly expect me to be jealous?"

"Not jealous exactly," she said, although he wasn't far from the truth. "Concerned."

"I'm not. Paul's a good man."

"I know, but—"

"You've been in love with him for months—"

"I think it was more of an infatuation."

"True. But he's finally asked you out, and you've accepted."

"Yes, but—"

"We know each other well, Cait. We were married, remember?"

"I'm not likely to forget it." Especially when Joe took

pains to point it out at every opportunity. "Shouldn't that mean…something?" Cait was embarrassed she'd said that. For weeks she'd suffered acute mortification every time Joe mentioned the childhood stunt. Now she was using it to suit her own purposes.

Joe took hold of her shoulders. "As a matter of fact, our marriage means a lot to me. Because I care about you, Cait."

Hearing Joe admit as much was gratifying.

"I want only the best for you," he continued. "It's what you deserve. All I can say is that I'd be more than pleased if everything worked out between you and Paul. Now if you'll excuse me, I need to talk something over with Harry."

"Oh, right, sure, go ahead." She couldn't seem to get the words out fast enough. When she'd called Martin to explain why she wouldn't be in Minnesota for Christmas, he'd claimed that God would reward her sacrifice. If Paul's invitation to dinner was God's reward, she wanted her airline ticket back.

The numb feeling returned as Cait returned to her office. She didn't know what to think. She'd believed… she'd hoped that she and Joe shared a very special feeling. Clearly their times together meant something entirely different to him than they had to her. Otherwise he wouldn't behave so casually about her going out with Paul. And he certainly wouldn't seem so pleased about it!

That was what hurt Cait the most, and yes, she was hurt. It had taken her several minutes to identify her feelings, but now she knew.....

More by accident than design, Cait walked into Lindy's office. Her friend had already put on her coat and was closing her briefcase, ready to leave the office.

"Paul asked me to dinner," Cait blurted out.

"He did?" Lindy's eyes widened with astonishment. But she didn't turn it into a joke, the way Joe had.

Cait nodded. "He just strolled in as if it was nothing out of the ordinary and asked me to have dinner with him."

"Are you happy about it?"

"I don't know," Cait answered honestly. "I suppose I should be pleased. It's what I'd prayed would happen for months."

"Then what's the problem?" Lindy asked.

"Joe doesn't seem to care. He said he hopes everything works out the way I want it to."

"Which is?" Lindy pressed.

Cait had to think about that a moment, her heart in her throat. "Honest to heaven, Lindy, I don't know anymore."

"I understand the salmon here is superb," Paul was saying, reading over the Boathouse menu. It was a well-known restaurant on Lake Union.

Cait scanned the list of entrées, which featured fresh seafood, then chose the grilled salmon—the same dish she'd ordered that night with Joe. Tonight, though, she wasn't sure why she was even bothering. She wasn't hungry, and Paul was going to be wasting good money while she made a pretense of enjoying her meal.

"I understand you've been seeing a lot of Joe Rockwell," he said conversationally.

That Paul should mention Joe's name right now was ironic. Cait hadn't stopped thinking about him from the moment he'd dropped into her office earlier that afternoon. Their conversation had left a bitter taste in her mouth. She'd sincerely believed their relationship was developing into something...special. Yet Joe had gone out of his way to give her the opposite impression.

"Cait?" Paul stared at her.

"I'm sorry, what were you saying?"

"Simply that you and Joe Rockwell have been seeing a lot of each other recently."

"Uh, yes. As you know, we were childhood friends," she murmured. "Actually Joe and my older brother were best friends. Then Joe's family moved to the suburbs and our families lost contact."

"Yes, I remember you mentioned that."

The waitress came for their order, and Paul requested a bottle of white wine. Then he chatted amicably for several minutes, bringing up subjects of shared interest from the office.

Cait listened attentively, nodding from time to time or adding the occasional comment. Now that she had his undivided attention, Cait wondered what it was about Paul that she'd found so extraordinary. He was attractive, but not nearly as dynamic or exciting as she found Joe. True, Paul possessed a certain charm, but compared to Joe, he was subdued and perhaps even a little dull. Cait couldn't imagine her stalwart boss carrying her piggyback out the back door because her high heels were too tight. Nor could she see Paul bantering with her the way Joe did.

The waitress delivered the wine, opened the bottle and poured them each a glass, once Paul had given his approval. Their dinners followed shortly afterward. After taking a bite or two of her delicious salmon, Cait noticed that Paul hadn't touched his meal. If anything, he seemed restless.

He rolled the stem of the wineglass between his fingers, watching the wine swirl inside. Then he suddenly blurted out, "What do you think of Lindy's leaving the firm?"

Cait was taken aback by the fervor in his voice when he mentioned Lindy's name. "Frankly I was shocked," Cait said. "Lindy and I have been good friends for a couple of years now." There'd been a time when the two had done nearly everything together. The summer before, they'd vacationed in Mexico and returned to Seattle with enough handwoven baskets and bulky blankets to set up shop themselves.

"Lindy's resigning came as a surprise to you, then?"

"Yes, this whole thing caught me completely unawares. Lindy didn't even mention the other job offer to me. I always thought we were good friends."

"Lindy *is* your friend," Paul said with enough conviction to persuade the patrons at the nearby tables. "You wouldn't believe what a good friend she is."

"I…know that." But friends sometimes had surprises up their sleeves. Lindy was a good example of that, and apparently so was Joe.

"I find Lindy an exceptional woman," Paul commented, watching Cait closely.

"She's probably one of the best stockbrokers in the business," Cait said, taking a sip of her wine.

"My…admiration for her goes beyond her keen business mind."

"Oh, mine, too," Cait was quick to agree. Lindy was the kind of friend who would trrudge through the blazing sun of Mexico looking for a conch shell because she knew Cait really wanted to take one home. And Lindy had listened to countless hours of Cait's bemoaning her sorry fate of unrequited love for Paul.

"She's a wonderful woman."

Joe was wonderful, too, Cait thought. So wonderful her heart ached at his indifference when she'd announced she would be dining with Paul.

"Lindy's the kind of woman a man could treasure all his life," Paul went on.

"I couldn't agree with you more," Cait said. Now, if only Joe would realize what a treasure *she* was. He'd married her once—well, sort of—and surely the possibility of spending their lives together had crossed his mind in the past few weeks.

Paul hesitated as though at a loss for words. "I don't suppose you've given any thought to the reason Lindy made this unexpected decision to resign?"

Frankly Cait hadn't. Her mind and her heart had been so full of Joe that deciphering her friend's actions had somehow escaped her. "She received a better offer, didn't she?" Which was understandable. Lindy would be an asset to any firm.

It was then that Cait understood. Paul hadn't asked her to dinner out of any desire to develop a romantic relationship with her. He saw her as a means of discovering what had prompted Lindy to resign. This new awareness came as a relief, a burden lifted from her shoulders. Paul wasn't interested in her. He never had been and probably never would be. A few weeks ago, that realization would have been a crushing defeat, but all Cait experienced now was an overwhelming sense of gratitude.

"I'm sure if you talk to Lindy, she might reconsider," Cait suggested.

"I've tried, trust me. But there's a problem."

"Oh?" Now that Cait had sampled the salmon, she

discovered it to be truly delicious. She hadn't realized how hungry she was.

"Cait, look at me," Paul said, raising his voice slightly. His face was pinched, his eyes intense. "Damn, but you've made this nearly impossible."

She looked up at him, her face puzzled. "What is it, Paul?"

"You have no idea, do you? I swear you've got to be the most obtuse woman in the world." He pushed aside his plate and briefly closed his eyes, shaking his head. "I'm in love with Lindy. I have been for weeks...months. But for the life of me I couldn't get her to notice me. I swear I did everything but turn cartwheels in her office. It finally dawned on me why she wasn't responding."

"Me?" Cait asked in a feeble, mouselike squeak.

"Exactly. She didn't want to betray your friendship. Then one afternoon—I think it was the day you first recognized Joe—we, Lindy and I, were in my office and— Oh hell, I don't know how it happened, but Lindy was looking something up for me and she stumbled over one of the cords the construction crew was using. Fortunately I was able to catch her before she fell to the floor. I know it wasn't her fault, but I was so angry, afraid she might have been hurt. Lindy was just as angry with me for being angry with her, and it seemed the only way to shut her up was to kiss her. That was the beginning and I swear to you everything exploded in our faces at that moment."

Cait swallowed, fascinated by the story. "Go on."

"I tried for days to get her to agree to go out with me. But she kept refusing until I demanded to know why."

"She told you...how I felt about you?" The thought was mortifying.

"Of course not. Lindy's too good a friend to divulge your confidence. Besides, she didn't need to tell me. I've known all along. Good grief, Cait, what did I have to do to discourage you? Hire a skywriter?"

"I don't think anything that drastic was necessary," she muttered, humiliated to her very bones.

"I repeatedly told Lindy I wasn't attracted to you, but she wouldn't listen. Finally she told me if I'd talk to you, explain everything myself, she'd agree to go out with me."

"The phone call," Cait said with sudden comprehension. "That was the reason you called me, wasn't it? You wanted to talk about Lindy, not that business article."

"Yes." He looked deeply grateful for her insight, late though it was.

"Well, for heaven's sake, why didn't you?"

"Believe me, I've kicked myself a dozen times since. I wish I knew. I suppose it seemed heartless to have such a frank discussion over the phone. Again and again, I promised myself I'd say something. Lord knows I dropped enough hints, but you weren't exactly receptive."

She winced. "But why is Lindy resigning?"

"Isn't it obvious?" Paul asked. "It was becoming increasingly difficult for us to work together. She didn't want to betray her best friend, but at the same time…"

"But at the same time you two were falling in love."

"Exactly. I can't lose her, Cait. I don't want to hurt your feelings, and believe me, it's nothing personal—you're a trustworthy employee and a decent person—but I'm simply not attracted to you."

Paul didn't seem to be the only one. Other than treating their relationship like one big joke, Joe hadn't ever claimed any romantic feelings for her, either.

"I had to do something before I lost Lindy."

"I agree completely."

"You're not angry with her, are you?"

"Good heavens, no," Cait said, offering him a brave smile.

"We both thought something was developing between you and Joe Rockwell. Like I said, you seemed to be seeing quite a bit of each other, and then at the Christmas party—"

"Don't remind me," Cait said with a low groan.

Paul's face creased in a spontaneous smile. "Joe certainly has a wit about him, doesn't he?"

Cait gave a resigned nod.

Now that Paul had cleared the air, he seemed to develop an appetite. He reached for his dinner and ate heartily. By contrast, Cait's salmon had lost its appeal. She stared down at her plate, wondering how she could possibly make it through the rest of the evening.

She did, though, quite nicely. Paul didn't even seem to notice that anything was amiss. It wasn't that Cait was distressed by his confession. If anything, she was relieved at this turn of events and delighted that Lindy had fallen in love. Paul was obviously crazy about her; she'd never seen him more animated than when he was discussing Lindy. It still shocked Cait that she'd been so unperceptive about Lindy's real feelings. Not to mention Paul's…

Paul dropped her off at her building and saw her to the front door. "I can't thank you enough for understanding," he said, his voice warm. Impulsively he hugged her, then hurried back to his sports car.

Although she was certainly guilty of being obtuse, Cait knew exactly where Paul was headed. No doubt Lindy would be waiting for him, eager to hear the details of their conversation. Cait planned to talk to her friend herself, first thing in the morning.

Cait's apartment was dark and lonely. So lonely the silence seemed to echo off the walls. She hung up her coat before turning on the lights, her thoughts as dark as the room had been.

She made herself a cup of tea. Then she sat on the sofa, tucking her feet beneath her as she stared unseeing at the walls, assessing her options. They seemed terribly limited.

Paul was in love with Lindy. And Joe...Cait had no idea where she stood with him. For all she knew—

Her thoughts were interrupted by the phone. She answered on the second ring.

"Cait?" It was Joe and he seemed surprised to find her back so early. "When did you get in?"

"A few minutes ago."

"You don't sound like yourself. Is anything wrong?"

"No," she said, breaking into sobs. "What could possibly be wrong?"

Chapter Ten

The flow of emotion took Cait by storm. She'd had no intention of crying; in fact, the thought hadn't even entered her mind. One moment she was sitting there, contemplating the evening's revelations, and the next she was sobbing hysterically into the phone.

"Cait?"

"Oh," she wailed. "This is all your fault in the first place." Cait didn't know what made her say that. The words had slipped out before she'd realized it.

"What happened?"

"Nothing. I…I can't talk to you now. I'm going to bed." With that, she gently replaced the receiver. Part of her hoped Joe would call back, but the telephone remained stubbornly silent. She stared at it for several minutes. Apparently Joe didn't care if he talked to her or not.

The tears continued to flow. They remained a mystery to Cait. She wasn't a woman given to bouts of crying, but now that she'd started she couldn't seem to stop.

She changed out of her dress and into a pair of sweats, pausing halfway through to wash her face.

Sniffling and hiccuping, she sat on the end of her bed and dragged a shuddering breath through her lungs. Crying like this made no sense whatsoever.

Paul was in love with Lindy. At one time, the news would have devastated her, but not now. Cait felt a tingling happiness that her best friend had found a man to love. And the infatuation she'd held for Paul couldn't compare with the strength of her love for Joe.

Love.

There, she'd admitted it. She was in love with Joe. The man who told restaurant employees that she was suffering from amnesia. The man who walked into elevators and announced to total strangers that they were married. Yet this was the same man who hadn't revealed a minute's concern about her dating Paul Jamison.

Joe was also the man who'd gently held her hand through a children's movie. The man who made a practice of kissing her senseless. The man who'd held her in his arms Christmas night as though he never intended to let her go.

Joseph Rockwell was a fun-loving jokester who took delight in teasing her. He was also tender and thoughtful and loving—the man who'd captured her heart only to drop it so carelessly.

Her doorbell chimed and she didn't need to look in the peephole to know it was Joe. But she felt panicky all of a sudden, too confused and vulnerable to see him now.

She walked slowly to the door and opened it a crack.

"What the hell is going on?" Joe demanded, not waiting for an invitation to march inside.

Cait wiped her eyes on her sleeve and shut the door. "Nothing."

"Did Paul try anything?"

She rolled her eyes. "Of course not."

"Then why are you crying?" He stood in the middle of her living room, fists planted on his hips as if he'd welcome the opportunity to punch out her boss.

If Cait knew why she was crying nonstop like this, she would have answered him. She opened her mouth, hoping some intelligent reason would emerge, but the only thing that came out was a low-pitched moan. Joe was gazing at her in complete confusion. "I...Paul's in love."

"With *you?*" His voice rose half an octave with disbelief.

"Don't make it sound like such an impossibility," she said crossly. "I'm reasonably attractive, you know." If she was expecting Joe to list her myriad charms, Cait was disappointed.

Instead, his frown darkened. "So what's Paul being in love got to do with anything?"

"Absolutely nothing. I wished him and Lindy the very best."

"So it is Lindy?" Joe murmured as though he'd known it all along.

"You didn't honestly think it was me, did you?"

"Hell, how was I supposed to know? I *thought* it was Lindy, but it was you he was taking to dinner. Frankly it didn't make a whole lot of sense to me."

"Which is something else," Cait grumbled, standing so close to him, their faces were only inches apart. Her hands were on her hips, her pose mirroring his. It occurred to Cait that they resembled a pair of gunslingers ready for a shootout. "I want to know one thing. Every time I turn around, you're telling anyone and everyone who'll listen that we're married. But when it really matters you—"

"When did it really matter?"

Cait ignored the question, thinking the answer was obvious. "You casually turn me over to Paul as if you can't wait to be rid of me. Obviously you couldn't have cared less."

"I cared," he shouted.

"Oh, right," she shouted back, "but if that was the case, you certainly didn't bother to show it!"

"What was I supposed to do, challenge him to a duel?"

He was being ridiculous, Cait decided, and she refused to take the bait. The more they talked, the more unreasonable they were both becoming.

"I thought dating Paul was what you wanted," he complained. "You talked about it long enough. Paul this and Paul that. He'd walk past and you'd all but swoon."

"That's not the least bit true." Maybe it had been at one time, but not now and not for weeks. "If you'd taken the trouble to ask me, you might have learned the truth."

"You mean you don't love Paul?"

Cait rolled her eyes again. "Bingo."

"It isn't like you to be so sarcastic."

"It isn't like you to be so…awful."

He seemed to mull that over for a moment. "If we're going to be throwing out accusations," he said tightly, "then maybe you should take a look at yourself."

"What exactly do you mean by that?" As usual, no one could get a reaction out of Cait more effectively than Joe. "Never mind," she answered, walking to the door. "This discussion isn't getting us anywhere. All we seem capable of doing is hurling insults at each other."

"I disagree," Joe answered calmly. "I think it's time we cleared the air."

She took a deep breath, feeling physically and emotionally deflated.

"Joe, it'll have to wait. I'm in no condition to be rational right now and I don't want either of us saying things we'll regret." She held open her door for him. "Please?"

He seemed about to argue with her, then he sighed and dropped a quick kiss on her mouth. Wide-eyed, she watched him leave.

Lindy was waiting in Cait's office early the next morning, holding two cups of freshly brewed coffee. Her eyes were vulnerable as Cait entered the office. They stared at each other for a long moment.

"Are you angry with me?" Lindy whispered. She handed Cait one of the cups as an apparent peace offering.

"Of course not," Cait murmured. She put down her briefcase and accepted the cup, which she placed carefully on her desk. Then she gave Lindy a reassuring hug, and the two of them sat down for their much-postponed talk.

"Why didn't you tell me?" Cait burst out.

"I wanted to," Lindy said earnestly. "I had to stop myself a hundred times. The worst part of it was the guilt—knowing you were in love with Paul, and loving him myself."

Cait wasn't sure how she would have reacted to the truth, but she preferred to think she would've understood, and wished Lindy well. It wasn't as though Lindy had stolen Paul away from her.

"I don't think I realized how I felt," Lindy continued, "until one afternoon when I tripped over a stupid cord and fell into Paul's arms. From there, everything sort of snowballed."

"Paul told me."

"He...told you about that afternoon?"

Cait grinned and nodded. "I found the story wildly romantic."

"You don't mind?" Lindy watched her closely as if half-afraid of Cait's reaction even now.

"I think it's wonderful."

Lindy's smile was filled with warmth and excitement. "I never knew being in love could be so exciting, but at the same time cause so much pain."

"Amen to that," Cait stated emphatically.

Her words shot like live bullets into the room. If Cait could have reached out and pulled them back, she would have.

"Is it Joe Rockwell?" Lindy asked softly.

Cait nodded, then shook her head. "See how much he's confused me?" She made a sound that was half sob, half giggle. "Sometimes that man infuriates me so much I want to scream. Or cry." Cait had always thought of herself as a sane and sensible person. She lived a quiet life, worked hard at her job, enjoyed traveling and crossword puzzles. Then she'd bumped into Joe. Suddenly she found herself demanding piggyback rides, talking to strangers in elevators and seeking out phantom women at Christmas parties while downing spiked punch like it was soda pop.

"But then at other times?" Lindy prompted.

"At other times I love him so much I hurt all the way through. I love everything about him. Even those loony stunts of his. In fact, I usually laugh as hard as everyone else. Even if I don't always want him to know it."

"So what's going to happen with you two?" Lindy asked. She took a sip of coffee and as she did, Cait caught a flash of diamond.

"Lindy?" Cait demanded, jumping out of her seat. "What's that on your finger?"

Lindy's face broke into a smile so bright Cait was nearly blinded. "You noticed."

"Of course I did."

"It's from Paul. After he had dinner with you, he came over to my apartment. We talked for hours and then…he asked me to marry him. At first I didn't know what to say. It seems so soon. We…we hardly know each other."

"Good grief, you've worked together for ages."

"I know," Lindy said with a shy smile. "That's what Paul told me. It didn't take him long to convince me. He had the ring all picked out. Isn't it beautiful?"

"Oh, Lindy." The diamond was a lovely solitaire set in a wide band of gold. The style and shape were perfect for Lindy's long, elegant finger.

"I didn't know if I should wear it until you and I had talked, but I couldn't make myself take it off this morning."

"Of course you should wear it!" The fact that Paul had been carrying it around when he'd had dinner with her didn't exactly flatter Cait's ego, but she was so thrilled for Lindy that seemed a minor concern.

Lindy splayed her fingers out in front of her to better show off the ring. "When he slipped it on my finger, I swear it was the most romantic moment of my life. Before I knew it, tears were streaming down my face. I still don't understand why I started crying. I think Paul was as surprised as I was."

There must have been something in the air that reduced susceptible females to tears, Cait decided. Whatever it was had certainly affected her.

"Now you've sidetracked me," Lindy said, looking up from her diamond, her gaze dreamy. "You were telling me about you and Joe."

"I was?"

"Yes, you were," Lindy insisted.

"There's nothing to tell. If there was, you'd be the first person to hear. I know," she admitted before her friend could bring up the point, "we have seen a lot of each other recently, but I don't think it meant anything to Joe. When he found out Paul had invited me to dinner, he seemed downright delighted."

"I'm sure it was all an act."

Cait shrugged. She wished she could believe that. Oh, how she wished it.

"You're sure you're in love with him?" Lindy asked hesitantly.

Cait nodded and lowered her eyes. It hurt to think about Joe. Everything was a game to him—a big joke. Lindy had been right about one thing, though. Love was the most wonderful experience of her life. And the most painful.

The New York Stock Exchange had closed and Cait was punching some figures into her computer when Joe strode into her office and closed the door.

"Feel free to come in," she muttered, continuing her work. Her heart was pounding but she dared not let him know the effect he had on her.

"I will make myself at home, thank you," he answered cheerfully, ignoring her sarcasm. He pulled out a chair and sat down expansively, resting one ankle on the opposite knee and relaxing as if he was in a movie theater, waiting for the main feature to begin.

"If you're here to discuss business, might I suggest investing in blue-chip stocks? They're always a safe bet." Cait went on typing, doing her best to ignore Joe—which was nearly impossible, although she gave an Oscar-winning performance, if she did say so herself.

"I'm here to talk business, all right," Joe said, "but it has nothing to do with the stock market."

"What business could the two of us possibly have?" she asked, her voice deliberately ironic.

"I want to resume the discussion we were having last night."

"Perhaps you do, but unfortunately that was last night and this is now." How confident she sounded, Cait thought, mildly pleased with herself. "I can do without hearing you list my no doubt numerous flaws."

"Your being my wife is what I want to talk about."

"Your wife?" She wished he'd quit throwing the subject at her as if it meant something to him. Something other than a joke.

"Yes, my wife." He gave a short laugh. "Believe me, it isn't your flaws I'm here to discuss."

Despite everything, Cait's heart raced. She reached for a stack of papers and switched them from one basket to another. Her entire filing system was probably in jeopardy, but she needed some activity to occupy her hands before she stood up and reached out to Joe. She did stand then, but it was to remove a large silver bell strung from a red velvet ribbon hanging in her office window.

"Paul and Lindy are getting married," he said next.

"Yes, I know. Lindy and I had a long talk this morning." She took the wreath off her door next.

"I take it the two of you are friends again?"

"We were never not friends," Cait answered stiffly, stuffing the wreath, the bell and the three ceramic wise men into the bottom drawer of her filing cabinet. Hard as she tried to prevent it, she could feel her defenses crumbling. "Lindy's asked me to be her maid of honor and I've agreed."

"Will you return the favor?"

It took a moment for the implication to sink in, and even then Cait wasn't sure she should follow the trail Joe seemed to be forging through this conversation. She leaned forward and rested her hands on the edge of the desk.

"I'm destined to be an old maid," she said flippantly, although she couldn't help feeling a sliver of real hope.

"You'll never be that."

Cait was hoping he'd say her beauty would make her irresistible, or that her warmth and wit and intelligence were sure to attract a dozen suitors. Instead he said the very thing she could have predicted. "We're already married, so you don't need to worry about being a spinster."

Cait released a sigh of impatience. "I wish you'd give up on that, Joe. It's growing increasingly old."

"As I recall, we celebrated our eighteenth anniversary not long ago."

"Don't be ridiculous. All right," she said, straightening abruptly. If he wanted to play games, then she'd respond in kind. "Since we're married, I want a family."

"Hey, sweetheart," he cried, throwing his arms in the air, "that's music to my ears. I'm willing."

Cait prepared to leave the office, if not the building. "Somehow I knew you would be."

"Two or three," he interjected, then chuckled and

added, "I suppose we should name the first two Ken and Barbie."

Cait's scowl made him chuckle even louder.

"If you prefer, we'll leave the names open to negotiation," he said.

"Of all the colossal nerve…" Cait muttered, moving to the window and gazing out.

"If you want daughters, I've got no objection, but from what I understand that's not really up to us."

Cait turned around, crossing her arms. "Correct me if I'm wrong," she said coldly, certain he'd delight in doing so. "But you did just ask me to marry you. Could you confirm that?"

"All I want is to make legal what's already been done."

Cait sighed in exasperation. Was he serious, or wasn't he? He was talking about marriage, about joining their lives, as if he were planning a bid on a construction project.

"When Paul asked Lindy to marry him, he had a diamond ring."

"I was going to buy you a ring," Joe said emphatically. "I still am. But I thought you'd want to pick it out yourself. If you wanted a diamond, why didn't you say so? I'll buy you the whole store if that'll make you happy."

"One ring will suffice, thank you."

"Pick out two or three. I understand diamonds are an excellent investment."

"Not so fast," she said, holding out her arm. It was vital she maintain some distance between them. If Joe kissed her or started talking about having children again, they might never get the facts clear.

"Not so fast?" he repeated incredulously. "Honey, I've been waiting eighteen years to discuss this. You're not going to ruin everything now, are you?" He advanced a couple of steps toward her.

"I'm not agreeing to anything until you explain yourself." For every step he took toward her, Cait retreated two.

"About what?" Joe was frowning, which wasn't a good sign.

"Paul."

His eyelids slammed shut, then slowly raised. "I don't understand why that man's name has to come into every conversation you and I have."

Cait decided it was better to ignore that comment. "You haven't even told me you love me."

"I love you." He actually sounded annoyed, as if she'd insisted on having the obvious reiterated.

"You might say it with a little more feeling," Cait suggested.

"If you want feeling, come here and let me kiss you."

"No."

"Why not?" By now they'd completely circled her desk. "We're talking serious things here. Trust me, sweetheart, a man doesn't bring up marriage and babies with just any woman. I love you. I've loved you for years, only I didn't know it."

"Then why did you let Paul take me out to dinner?"

"You mean I could've stopped you?"

"Of course. I didn't want to go out with him! I was sick about having to turn you down for dinner. Not only that, you didn't even seem to care that I was going out with another man. And as far as you were concerned, he was your main competition."

"I wasn't worried."

"That wasn't the impression I got later."

"All right, all right," Joe said, drawing his fingers through his hair. "I didn't think Paul was interested in you. I saw him and Lindy together one night at the office and the electricity between them was so thick it could've lit up Seattle."

"You knew about Lindy and Paul?"

Joe shrugged. "Let me put it this way. I had a sneaking suspicion. But when you started talking about Paul as though you were in love with him, I got worried."

"You should have been." Which was a bold-faced lie.

Somehow, without her being quite sure how it happened, Joe maneuvered himself so only a few inches separated them.

"Are you ever going to kiss me?" he demanded.

Meekly Cait nodded and stepped into his arms like a child opening the gate and skipping up the walkway to home. This was the place she belonged. With Joe. This was home and she need never doubt his love again.

With a sigh that seemed to come from the deepest part of him, Joe swept her close. For a breathless moment they looked into each other's eyes. He was about to kiss her when there was a knock at the door.

Harry, Joe's foreman, walked in without waiting for a response. "I don't suppose you've seen Joe—" He stopped abruptly. "Oh, sorry," he said, flustered and eager to make his escape.

"No problem," Cait assured him. "We're married. We have been for years and years."

Joe was chuckling as his mouth settled over hers, and in a single kiss he wiped out all the doubts and misgivings, replacing them with promises and thrills.

Epilogue

The robust sound of organ music surged through the Seattle church as Cait walked slowly down the center aisle, her feet moving in time to the traditional music. As the maid of honor, Lindy stood to one side of the altar while Joe and his brother, who was serving as best man, waited on the other. The church was decorated with poinsettias and Christmas greenery, accented by white roses.

Cait's brother, Martin, stood directly ahead of her. He smiled at Cait as the assembly rose and she came down the aisle, her heart overflowing with happiness.

Cait and Joe had planned this day, their Christmas wedding, for months. If there'd been any lingering doubts that Joe really loved her, they were long gone. He wasn't the type of man who expressed his love with flowery words and gifts. But Cait had known that from the first. He'd insisted on building their home before the wedding and they'd spent countless hours going over the architect's plans. Cait was helping Joe with his accounting and would be taking over the task full-time when they started their family. Which would be soon. The way Cait figured it, she'd be pregnant by next Christmas.

But before they began their real life together, they'd enjoy a perfect honeymoon in New Zealand. He'd wanted to surprise her with the trip, but Cait had needed a passport. They'd only be gone two weeks, which was all the time Joe could afford to take, since he had several large projects coming up.

As the organ concluded the "Wedding March," Cait handed her bouquet to Lindy and placed her hands in Joe's. He smiled down on her as if he'd never seen a more beautiful woman in his life. Judging by the look on his face, Cait knew he could hardly keep from kissing her right then and there.

"Dearly beloved," Martin said, stepping forward, "we are gathered here today in the sight of God and man to celebrate the love of Joseph James Rockwell and Caitlin Rose Marshall."

Cait's eyes locked with Joe's. She did love him, so much that her heart felt close to bursting. After all these months of waiting for this moment, Cait was sure she'd be so nervous her voice would falter. That didn't happen. She'd never felt more confident of anything than her feelings for Joe and his for her. Cait's voice rang out strong and clear, as did Joe's.

As they exchanged the rings, Cait could hear her mother and Joe's weeping softly in the background. But these were tears of shared happiness. The two women had renewed their friendship and were excited about the prospect of grandchildren.

Cait waited for the moment when Martin would tell Joe he could kiss his bride. Instead he closed his Bible, reverently set it aside, and said, "Joseph James Rockwell, do you have the baseball cards with you?"

"I do."

Cait looked at the two men as if they'd both lost their minds. Joe reached inside his tuxedo jacket and produced two flashy baseball cards.

"You may give them to your bride."

With a dramatic flourish, Joe did as Martin instructed. Cait stared down at the two cards and grinned broadly.

"You may now kiss the bride," Martin declared.

Joe was more than happy to comply.

WHEN CHRISTMAS COMES

For my cousin Paula Bearson, with gratitude.
And special thanks to writer and friend Ann DeFee.

Chapter One

"What do you mean you won't be home for Christmas?" Emily Springer was sure she couldn't have heard correctly. She pressed the telephone receiver harder against her ear, as though that would clarify her daughter's words.

"Mom, I know you're disappointed...."

That didn't even begin to cover it. Emily had scraped and sacrificed in order to save airfare home for her only daughter, a student at Harvard. They always spent the holidays together, and now Heather was telling her she wouldn't be back for Christmas.

"What could possibly be more important than Christmas with your family?" Emily asked, struggling to hide her distress.

Her daughter hesitated. "It's just that I've got so much going on during those two weeks. I'd love to be home with you, I really would, but...I can't."

Emily swallowed past the lump in her throat. Heather was twenty-one; Emily realized her daughter was becoming an independent adult, but for the last eleven years it had been just the two of them. The thought of being separated from her only child over Christmas brought tears to her eyes.

"You've got all the neighbor kids to spoil," Heather continued.

Yes, the six Kennedy children would be more than happy to gobble up Emily's homemade cookies, candies and other traditional holiday treats. But it wouldn't be the same.

"I was home a few months ago," Heather reminded her next.

Emily opened her mouth to argue. True, her daughter had spent the summer in Leavenworth, but she'd been busy working and saving money for school. If she wasn't at her library job, she was with her friends. Emily knew that Heather had her own life now, her own friends, her own priorities and plans. That was to be expected and natural, and Emily told herself she should be proud. But spending Christmas on opposite sides of the country was simply too hard—especially for the two of them, who'd once been so close.

"What about the money I saved for your airfare?" Emily asked lamely, as if that would change anything.

"I'll fly out for Easter, Mom. I'll use it then."

Easter was months away, and Emily didn't know if she could last that long. This was dreadful. Three weeks before Christmas, and she'd lost every shred of holiday spirit.

"I have to hang up now, Mom."

"I know, but...can't we talk about this? I mean, there's got to be a way for us to be together."

Heather hesitated once more. "You'll be fine without me."

"Of course I will," Emily said, dredging up the remnants of her pride. The last thing she wanted was to look pathetic to her daughter—or to heap on the guilt—so she spoke with an enthusiasm she didn't feel. Disappointment pounded through her with every beat of her heart. She had to remember she wasn't the only one who'd be alone, though. Heather would be missing out, too. "What about you?" Emily asked. Caught up in her own distress, she hadn't been thinking about her daughter's feelings. "Will you be all alone?"

"For Christmas, you mean?" Heather said. Her voice fell slightly, and it sounded as if she too was putting on a brave front. "I have friends here, and I'll probably get together with them—but it won't be the same."

That had been Emily's reaction: *It won't be the same.* This Christmas marked the beginning of a new stage in their relationship. It was inevitable—but Christmas was still Christmas, and she vowed that wherever Heather was in future years, they'd spend the holiday together. Emily squared her shoulders. "We'll make it through this," she said stoutly.

"Of course we will."

"I'll be in touch soon," Emily promised.

"I knew you'd be a trouper about this, Mom."

Heather actually seemed proud of her, but Emily was no heroine. After a brief farewell, she placed the portable phone back in the charger and slumped into the closest chair.

Moping around, Emily tried to fight off a sense of depression that had begun to descend. She couldn't concentrate on anything, too restless to read or watch TV. The house felt...bleak. Uncharacteristically so. Maybe because she hadn't put up the Christmas decorations, knowing how much Heather loved helping her.

They had their own traditions. Heather always decorated the fireplace mantel, starting with her favorite piece, a small almost-antique angel that had belonged to Emily's mother. While she did that, Emily worked on the windowsills around the dining room, arranging garlands, candles and poinsettias. Then together, using the ornaments Emily had collected over the years, they'd decorate the Christmas tree. Not an artificial one, either, despite warnings that they were safer than fresh trees.

It sometimes took them half a day to choose their Christmas tree. Leavenworth was a small Washington town tucked in the foothills of the Cascade Mountains, and it offered a stunning array of firs and pines.

This year, without Heather, there would be no tree. Emily wouldn't bother. Really, why go to that much effort when she'd be the only one there to enjoy it. Why decorate the house at all?

This Christmas was destined to be her worst since Peter had died. Her husband had been killed in a logging accident eleven years earlier. Before his death, her life had been idyllic—exactly what she'd wanted it to be. They'd been high-school sweethearts and married the summer after graduation. From the start, their marriage was close and companionable. A year later Heather had arrived. Peter had supported Emily's efforts to obtain her teaching degree and they'd postponed adding to their family. The three of them had been contented, happy with their little household—and then, overnight, her entire world had collapsed.

Peter's life insurance had paid for the funeral and allowed her to deal with the financial chaos. Emily had invested the funds wisely; she'd also continued with her job as a kindergarten teacher. She and Heather were as close as a mother and daughter could be. In her heart, Emily knew Peter would have been so proud of Heather.

The scholarship to Harvard was well deserved but it wasn't enough to meet all of Heather's expenses. Emily periodically cashed in some of her investments to pay her daughter's living costs—her dorm room, her transportation, her textbooks and entertainment. Emily lived frugally, and her one and only extravagance was Christmas. For the last two years, they'd somehow managed to be together even though Heather had moved to Boston. Now this...

Still overwhelmed by her disappointment, Emily wandered into the study and stared at the blank computer screen. Her friend Faith would understand how she felt. Faith would give her the sympathy she needed. They communicated frequently via e-mail. Although Faith was ten years younger, they'd become good friends. They were both teachers; Faith had done her student teaching in Leavenworth and they'd stayed in touch.

Faith—braver than Emily—taught junior-high literature. Emily cringed at the thought of not only facing a hundred thirteen-year-olds every school day but trying to interest them in things like poetry. Divorced for the past five years, Faith lived in the Oakland Bay area of San Francisco.

This news about Heather's change in plans couldn't be delivered by e-mail, Emily decided. She needed immediate comfort. She needed Faith to assure her that she could get through the holidays by herself.

She reached for the phone and hit speed dial for Faith's number. Her one hope was that Faith would be home on a Sunday afternoon—and to Emily's relief, Faith snatched up the receiver after the second ring.

"Hi! It's Emily," she said, doing her best to sound cheerful.

"What's wrong?"

How well Faith knew her. In a flood of emotion, Emily spilled out everything Heather had told her.

"She's got a boyfriend," Faith announced as if it were a foregone conclusion.

"Well, she has mentioned a boy named Ben a few times, but the relationship doesn't sound serious."

"Don't you believe it!"

Faith tended to be something of a cynic, especially when it came to relationships. Emily didn't blame her; Faith had married her college boyfriend and stayed in the marriage for five miserable years. She'd moved to Leavenworth shortly after her divorce. Her connection with Emily had been forged during a time of loneliness, and they'd each found solace in their friendship.

"I'm sure Heather would tell me if this had to do with a man in her life," Emily said fretfully, "but she didn't say one word. It's school and work and all the pressures. I understand, or at least I'm trying to, but I feel so...so cheated."

"Those are just excuses. Trust me, there's a man involved."

Not wanting to accept it but unwilling to argue the point, Emily sighed deeply. "Boyfriend or not," she muttered, "I'll be alone over the holidays. How can I possibly celebrate Christmas by myself?"

Faith laughed—which Emily didn't consider very sympathetic. "All you have to do is look out your front window."

That was true enough. Leavenworth was about as close to Santa's village as any place could get. The entire town entered the Christmas spirit. Tourists from all over the country visited the small community, originally founded by immigrants from Germany, and marveled at its festive atmosphere. Every year there were train rides and Christmas-tree-lighting ceremonies, three in all, plus winter sports and sleigh rides and Christmas parades and more.

Emily's home was sixty years old and one block from the heart of downtown. The city park was across the street. Starting in early December, groups of carolers strolled through the neighborhood dressed in old-fashioned regalia. With the horse-drawn sleigh, and groups of men and women in greatcoats and long dresses gathered under streetlamps, the town looked like a Currier & Ives print.

"Everyone else can be in the holiday spirit, but I won't—not without Heather," Emily said. "I'm not even going to put up a tree."

"You don't mean that," Faith told her bracingly.

"I do so," Emily insisted. She couldn't imagine anything that would salvage Christmas for her.

"What you need is a shot of holiday cheer. Watch *Miracle on 34th Street* or—"

"It won't help," Emily cried. "Nothing will."

"Emily, this doesn't sound like you. Besides," Faith said, "Heather's twenty-one. She's creating her own life, and that's completely appropriate. So she can't make it this year—you'll have *next* Christmas with her."

Emily didn't respond. She couldn't think of anything to say.

"You need your own life, too," Faith added. "I've been after you for years to join the church singles group."

"I'll join when you do," Emily returned.

"Might I remind you that I no longer live in Leaven worth?"

"Fine, join one in Oakland."

"That's not the point, Em," her friend said. "You've been so wrapped up in Heather that you don't have enough going on in *your* life."

"You know that's not true!" Emily could see that talk ing to Faith wasn't having the desired effect. "I called because I need sympathy," Emily said, her tone a bit petulant even to her own ears.

Faith laughed softly. "I've failed you, then."

"Yes." Emily figured she might as well tell the truth. "Of all people, I thought you'd understand."

"I'm sorry to disappoint you, Em."

Her friend didn't *sound* sorry.

"I actually think being apart over the holidays might be good for you—and for Heather."

Emily was aghast that Faith would suggest such a thing. "How can you say that?"

"Heather might appreciate you more and you might just discover that there are other possibilities at Christmas than spending it with your daughter."

Emily knew she'd adjust much more easily if she wasn't a widow. Being alone at this time of year was hard, had been hard ever since Peter's death. Perhaps Faith was right. Perhaps she'd clung to her daughter emotionally, but Emily felt that in her circumstances, it was forgivable.

"I'll be fine," she managed, but she didn't believe it for a moment.

"I know you will," Faith said.

Even more distressed than before, Emily finished the

conversation and hung up the phone. Never having had children, Faith didn't understand how devastating Heather's news had been. And if Emily *was* guilty of relying on her daughter too much, Christmas was hardly the time of year to deal with it. But wait a minute. She'd encouraged Heather's independence, hadn't she? After all, the girl was attending school clear across the country. Surely a few days at Christmas wasn't too much to ask.

Emily decided a walk would help her sort through these complicated emotions. She put on her heavy wool coat, laced up her boots and wrapped her hand-knitted red scarf around her neck. She'd knitted an identical scarf for her daughter, although Heather's was purple instead of red, and mailed it off before Thanksgiving. Finally she thrust her hands into warm mittens. It'd snowed overnight and the wind was cold enough to cut to the bone.

The Kennedy kids—ranging from six years old to thirteen—had their sleds out and were racing down the hill in the park. In order of age and size, they scrambled up the steep incline, dragging their sleds behind them. When they reached the top, they all waved excitedly at Emily. Sarah, the youngest, ran over to join her.

"Hello, Mrs. Springer." The youngster smiled up at her with two bottom teeth missing.

"Sarah," Emily said, feigning shock. "Did you lose those two teeth?"

The girl nodded proudly. "My mom pulled them out and I didn't even cry."

"Did the tooth fairy visit?"

"Yes," Sarah told her. "James said there wasn't any such thing, but I put my teeth under my pillow and in the morning there was fifty cents. Mom said if I wanted to believe in the tooth fairy, I could. So I believed and I got two quarters."

"Good for you."

With all the wisdom of her six years, Sarah nodded. "You've got to believe."

"Right," Emily agreed.

"In Santa, too!"

As the youngest, Sarah had four older brothers and a sister all too eager to inform her that Santa Claus and his helpers bore a strong resemblance to Mom and Dad.

"Do *you* believe, Mrs. Springer?"

Right now that was a difficult question. Emily was no longer sure. She wanted to believe in the power of love and family, but her daughter's phone call had forced her to question that. At least a little…

"Do you?" Sarah repeated, staring intently up at Emily.

"Ah…" Then it hit her. She suddenly saw what should've been obvious from the moment she answered the phone that afternoon. "Yes, Sarah," she said, bending down to hug her former kindergarten student.

It was as simple as talking to a child. Sarah understood; sometimes Emily hadn't. *You've got to believe.* There was always a way, and in this instance it was for Emily to book a flight to Boston. If Heather couldn't join her for Christmas, then she'd go to Heather.

The fact that this answer now seemed so effortless unnerved her. The solution had been there from the first, but she'd been so caught up in her sense of loss she'd been blind to it.

Emily had the money for airfare. All she needed was to find a place to stay. Heather would be so surprised, she thought happily. In that instant Emily decided not to tell her, but to make it a genuine surprise—a Christmas gift.

Emily reversed her earlier conviction. What could've been the worst Christmas of her life was destined to be the best!

Chapter Two

Charles Brewster, professor of history at Harvard, pinched the bridge of his nose as he stared at the computer screen. Stretching his neck to see the clock hidden behind two neatly stacked piles of paper, he discovered that it was three o'clock. Charles had to stop and calculate whether that was three in the afternoon or three at night. He often lost track of time, especially since he had an inner office without windows.

And especially since it was December. He hated the whole miserable month—the short days with darkness falling early, the snow, the distractedness of his students and colleagues. *Christmas.* He dreaded it each and every year. Cringed at the very mention of the holidays. Rationally he knew it was because of Monica, who'd chosen Christmas Eve to break off their relationship. She claimed he was distant and inattentive, calling him the perfect example of the absentminded professor. Charles admitted she was probably right, but he'd loved her and been shocked when she'd walked out on him.

Frowning now, Charles realized it was happening already. Christmas was coming, and once again he'd be forced to confront the memories and the bitterness. The truth was, he rarely thought of Monica anymore except at Christmas. He couldn't help it. Boston during December depressed him. In fact, he associated Christmas, especially Christmas in the city, with unhappiness and rejection. It was as if those emotions had detached themselves from Monica and just become part of the season itself.

Standing up, he strolled out of his office and noticed that all the other History Department offices were dark and empty. It must be three at night, then, which meant he hadn't eaten dinner yet. Funny, he distinctly remembered Mrs. Lewis bringing him a tuna sandwich and a cup of hot coffee. His assistant was thoughtful that way. On the other hand, that might've been the day before. Frankly, Charles no longer remembered. His stomach growled, and he rummaged through his desk drawers for a snack. He located a candy bar, eating it hungrily, with only the briefest consideration of how old it might be.

It was too late to head home now, Charles decided. If he left the building, Security would be on him so fast he wouldn't make it to the front door. He'd have to haul out all his identification and explain why he was still here and... No, it was easier just to stay.

He returned his attention to the computer screen and his work. He'd recently been contracted to write a textbook. He'd agreed to a tight deadline because he knew it would help him get through the holidays. Now he wondered if he'd taken on too much.

The next time he glanced up from the computer, Mrs.

Lewis had stepped into the office. "Professor Brewster, were you here all night?"

Charles leaned back in his chair and rubbed his hand along his face. "It seems I was."

Shaking her head, she placed a cup of hot, black coffee on his desk.

He sipped it gratefully. "What day is this?" It was a question he asked often—so often that it didn't even cause the department secretary's brow to wrinkle.

"Tuesday, December fourteenth."

"It's the fourteenth already?" He could feel the panic rising.

"Yes, Professor. And you have three student appointments today."

"I see." But all Charles saw was trouble. If his mother wasn't pestering him, then it was his students. He sighed, suddenly exhausted. He'd spent the better part of fifteen hours writing his American history text, focusing on the Colonial era, the Revolutionary War and the country's founding fathers. Much of his work that night had been about the relationship between Thomas Jefferson and Aaron Burr. It wouldn't be light reading, but he knew his history and loved it. If he met his deadline, which Charles was determined to do, and turned in the completed manuscript shortly after the first of the year, it would be published and ready for use by the start of the 2006 autumn classes. High aspirations, but Charles knew he could meet the challenge.

"Your mother just phoned again," Mrs. Lewis informed him. She'd left his office and returned to set the mail on his desk.

Charles sighed. His mother's intentions were good, but she worried about him far too much. For years now, she'd been after him to join her in Arizona for the holidays. Personally, Charles would rather have his fingernails pulled out than spend Christmas with his mother. She suffocated him with her concern and irritated him with her matchmaking efforts. Try as he might, he couldn't make her understand that he wasn't interested in another relationship. His one and only attempt at romance had practically demolished him. After Monica's Christmas Eve defection, he'd shielded himself from further involvement. He was content with his life, although his mother refused to believe it. He didn't *want* a relationship. Women made demands on his time; they were a luxury he couldn't afford if he planned to get ahead in his profession. He wanted to write and teach and there simply weren't enough hours in the day as it was. Frankly that suited him just fine.

If Ray would do him the favor of marrying, Charles would be off the hook. Unfortunately his older brother seemed to be a confirmed bachelor. That left Charles—and his mother wasn't giving up without a fight. At every opportunity she shoved women in his path. Twice in the last six months she'd sent the daughters of friends to Boston to lure him out of his stuffy classroom, as she called it. Both attempts had ended in disaster.

"She wants to know your plans for the holidays."

Charles stiffened. This was how their last conversation had begun. His mother had casually inquired about his plans for Labor Day, and the next thing he knew she'd arranged a dinner engagement for him with one of those young women. That particular one had been a twenty-four-year-old TV production assistant in New York; to say they had nothing in common was putting it mildly. "What did you tell my mother?" he asked.

"That you were occupied and unable to take the call."

From the way Mrs. Lewis's lips thinned, Charles guessed she wasn't pleased at having to engage in this small deception. "Thank you," he muttered.

"She insisted I must know about your plans for Christmas," Mrs. Lewis said in a severe voice.

Apprehension shot up his back. "What did you say?"

Mrs. Lewis crossed her arms and stared down at him. "I said I am not privy to your private arrangements, and that for all I knew you were going out of town."

Actually, that didn't sound like a bad plan. He needed an escape, and the sooner the better. If his mother's behavior was true to pattern, she was about to sic some woman on him. As soon as Mrs. Lewis had made that comment about traveling, the idea took root in his mind. It would do him good to get out of the city. He didn't care where he went as long as it was away from Boston, away from his seasonal misery. Someplace quiet would suit him nicely. Someplace where he could work and not worry about what time or day it happened to be.

"Hmm. That has possibilities," he murmured thoughtfully.

The older woman didn't seem to know what he was talking about. His students often wore the same confused look, as if he were speaking in a foreign language.

"Traveling." The decision made now, he stood and reached for his overcoat. "Yes."

Her gaze narrowed. "Excuse me?"

"That was an excellent idea. I'm leaving town for the holidays." All he wanted was peace and quiet; that should be simple enough to arrange.

"Where?" Mrs. Lewis stammered, following him out of his office.

He shrugged. "I really don't care."

"Well, I could call a travel agent for recommendations."

"Don't bother."

A travel agent might book him into some area where he'd be surrounded by people and festivities centered on the Christmas holidays. Any contact with others was out of the question. He wanted to find a place where he'd be completely alone, with no chance of being disturbed. And if possible, he wanted to find a place where Christmas wasn't a big deal.

He told Mrs. Lewis all this, then asked her for suggestions. He turned down Vermont, Aspen, Santa Fe and Disney World.

Disney World!

At her despairing look, he sighed again. "Never mind," he said. "I'll do it myself."

She nodded and seemed relieved.

Later that day, Charles had to admit that finding an obscure location for travel on such short notice was difficult. Taking his briefcase with him, he walked to his condo, not far from the university area. But after he'd showered, heated up a microwave lasagna for his dinner and slept, he tackled the project with renewed enthusiasm. It was now shortly after 8:00 p.m.

After calling half a dozen airlines, he realized he was seeking the impossible. Not a man to accept defeat, Charles went online to do his own investigative work. It was while he was surfing the Internet that he found a site on which people traded homes for short periods.

One such notice was from a woman who'd posted a message: **Desperately Seeking Home in Boston for Christmas Holidays.**

Charles read the message twice, awed by his good fortune. This woman, a schoolteacher in a small town in Washington State, sought a residence in Boston for two weeks over the Christmas holidays. She could travel after December 17th and return as late as December 31st.

The dates were perfect for Charles. He started to get excited. This might actually work without costing him an arm and a leg. Since he didn't have to register in a hotel, his mother would have no obvious means of tracking him. Oh, this was very good news indeed.

Charles answered the woman right away.

From: "Charles Brewster" <hadisbad@charternet.net>
To: "Emily Springer" springere@aal.com
Sent: December 14, 2004
Subject: Trading Places
Dear Ms. Springer,
I'm responding to the DESPERATELY SEEKING IN BOSTON advertisement shown on the Trading Homes Web site. I live in Boston and teach at Harvard. My condo is a two-bedroom, complete with all modern conveniences. You can e-mail me with your questions at the address listed above. I eagerly await your reply.
Sincerely,
Charles Brewster

Before long Charles received a response. Naturally, she had a number of questions. He had a few of his own, but once he was assured that he'd be completely alone in a small Eastern Washington town, Charles agreed to the swap. He supplied references, and she offered her own.

A flurry of e-mails quickly passed between them as they figured out the necessary details. Emily seemed to think she owed him an explanation as to why she was interested in Boston. He didn't tell her that he didn't care about her reasons.

He certainly didn't mention his own. He rather enjoyed the notion of spending time in a town called Leavenworth. If he remembered correctly, a big federal prison was situated in the area. As far as Charles was concerned, that was even better. The less celebrating going on, the happier he'd be. He could spend the holidays in a nice, quiet prison town without any Christmas fuss.

His remaining concern was buying a plane ticket, but once again the online travel sites came to his rescue. Charles had no objection to flying a red-eye, since half the time he didn't know whether it was day or night.

"Everything's been arranged," he announced to Mrs. Lewis the following morning.

She responded with a brief nod. "So you have decided to travel."

"I have."

She held up her hand. "Don't tell me any of the details."

He stared at her. "Why not?"

"In case your mother asks, I can honestly tell her I don't know."

"Excellent idea." He beamed at the brilliance of her suggestion. For once, he was going to outsmart his dear, sweet matchmaker of a mother and at the same time blot Christmas from the calendar. School was closing for winter recess and if she couldn't reach him, she'd assume he wasn't answering his phone, which he rarely did, anyway—even before caller ID. And suppose his mother found some way to get hold of Mrs. Lewis during the Christmas holidays? It wouldn't matter, because Mrs. Lewis didn't know a thing! This was more satisfactory by the minute.

For two blessed weeks in December, he was going to escape Christmas and his mother in one fell swoop.

No question about it, life didn't get any better than this.

Chapter Three

The bell rang, dismissing Faith Kerrigan's last junior-high literature class of the afternoon. Her students were out of the room so fast, anyone might think the building was in danger of exploding. She could understand their eagerness to leave. When classes were dismissed for winter break at the end of the week, she'd be ready— more than ready.

"Faith?" Sharon Carson stuck her head in the doorway. "You want to hit the mall this afternoon?"

Faith cringed. The crowds were going to be horrendous, and it would take a braver woman than she to venture into a mall this close to the holidays. One advantage of being single was that Faith didn't have a lot of Christmas shopping to do. That thought, however, depressed her.

She was an aunt three times over, thanks to her younger sister. Faith loved her nephews, but she'd always dreamed of being a mother herself one day. She'd said goodbye to that dream when she divorced. At the time she hadn't realized it; she'd blithely assumed she'd remarry, but to this point she hadn't met anyone who even remotely interested her. She hadn't guessed it would be that difficult to meet a decent man, but apparently she'd been wrong. Now thirty, she'd begun to feel her chances were growing bleaker by the day.

"Not tonight, Sharon, but thanks."

Her fellow teacher and friend leaned against the door of her classroom. "You're usually up for a trip to the mall. Is something bothering you?"

"Not really." Other than the sorry state of her love life, the only thing on Faith's mind was getting through the next few days of classes.

"Are you sure?" Sharon pressed.

"I'm sure." Faith glanced over at her and smiled. She was tall, the same height as Faith at five foot eight, and ten years older. Odd that her two best friends were forty. Both Emily and Sharon were slightly overweight, while Faith kept her figure trim and athletic. Emily was an undiscovered beauty. She was also the perfect kindergarten teacher, patient and gentle. She looked far younger than her years, with short curly brown hair and dark eyes. Unlike Faith, she wasn't interested in sports. Emily felt she got enough physical exercise racing after five-year-olds all day and had no interest in joining the gym or owning a treadmill. Come to think of it, Faith wasn't sure Leavenworth even had a gym.

Faith ran five miles three times a week and did a seven-mile-run each weekend. She left the races to those who enjoyed collecting T-shirts. She wasn't one of them. The running habit had started shortly after her separation, and she'd never stopped.

"You haven't mentioned Emily lately. What's up with

her?" Sharon asked and came all the way into the room. The summer before, when Sharon and her family had taken a trip north to Washington State, Faith had suggested they visit Leavenworth. As soon as Emily learned Faith's friend would be in the area, she'd insisted on showing them the town. Emily was the consummate host and a fabulous cook. Sharon had come back full of tales about Leavenworth and Emily.

"I talked to her on Sunday." Faith began erasing the blackboard, but paused in the middle of a sweeping motion. "Funny you should mention her, because she's been on my mind ever since."

"I thought you two e-mailed back and forth every day."

"We do—well, almost every day." Faith had sent Emily an e-mail the day before and hadn't heard back, which told her Emily was especially busy. No doubt there'd be a message waiting for her once she got home.

She turned to face Sharon. "I think I might've offended her." Now that she thought about it, Faith realized she probably had. "Emily phoned, which she rarely does, to tell me Heather won't be coming home for Christmas. I told Emily it was time Heather had her own life and to make the best of it." Given the opportunity, she'd gladly take back those words. "I can't believe I wasn't more sympathetic," Faith said, pulling out the desk chair to sit down. She felt dreadful. Her friend had phoned looking for understanding, and Faith had let her down.

"Don't be so hard on yourself," Sharon said. She slipped into one of the student desks.

"Emily doesn't want to be alone over Christmas, and who can blame her?"

"No one wants to be alone at Christmas."

Faith didn't; in fact she'd made plans to visit Penny and join in the festivities with her nephews. "I was completely and utterly insensitive. Poor Emily." No wonder she hadn't answered Faith's e-mail.

"What are you going to do?" Sharon asked.

"What makes you think I'm going to do anything?"

A smile crept over Sharon's face. "Because I know you. I can tell from the look in your eyes."

"Well, you're right. I have an idea."

"What?"

Faith was almost beside herself with glee. "I'm going to surprise Emily and visit her for Christmas."

"I thought you were spending the holidays with your sister."

"I was, but Penny will understand." The truth, Faith realized, was that Penny might even be grateful.

"It's pretty hard to book a flight at this late date," Sharon said, frowning.

"I know.... I haven't figured that out yet." Booking a flight could be a problem, but Faith was convinced she'd find a way, even if it meant flying in the dead of night. There had to be a flight into the Seattle-Tacoma airport at some point between Friday night and Christmas Day.

"My sister-in-law works for a travel agent. Would you like her number?"

"Thanks, Sharon."

They walked to the faculty lounge together and got their purses out of their lockers. Sharon pulled out her cell phone, then scrolled down until she found the number. Faith quickly made a note of it.

"If there's a flight to be had, Carrie will find it," Sharon assured her.

"Thanks again."

"Are you going to call Emily and let her know your plans?" Sharon asked as they left the school building, walking toward the parking lot.

"Not yet. I don't want to get her hopes up if this turns out to be impossible."

"If worse comes to worst, I suppose you could always drive."

"I don't think so." Faith had done it often enough to realize she didn't want to take the Interstate in the middle of winter. The pass over the Siskiyous could be hellish this time of year. It wasn't a trip she wanted to make on her own, either.

"Don't worry—Carrie will get you a flight," Sharon said confidently.

As soon as she was in her car, Faith pulled out her own cell phone and dialed the travel agency. Carrie was extremely helpful and promised to get back to her as soon as she could.

Now that she had a plan, Faith was starting to feel excited. She called her sister soon after she arrived home, and the instant Penny picked up the phone, Faith could hear her three nephews fighting in the background. It sounded as if they were close to killing one another by the time the conversation ended.

Penny had made a token display of disappointment, but Faith didn't think her sister was too distressed. And Faith had to admit she was looking forward to a different kind of holiday herself. One without bickering kids— much as she loved them—and the same old routines. Still, her family was important to her, and she'd promised to visit right after New Year's.

Because she had someplace to go and family to be with, Faith hadn't really listened to what Emily had tried to tell her, hadn't really understood. Emily adored her daughter, of course, but Heather's absence was only part of the problem. What bothered her just as much was the prospect of spending perhaps the most significant holiday of the year by herself. In retrospect, Faith was astonished she hadn't recognized that earlier. She was a better friend than this and she was about to prove it.

After Faith had finished talking to her sister, she immediately sat down at her computer and logged on to the Internet. To her surprise Emily hadn't left her a message. Undeterred, she sent one off.

From: "Faith"<fkerriganinca@network.com>
To: "Emily"<springere@aal.com>
Sent: Thursday, December 16, 2004
Subject: Gift to arrive
Dear Emily,
I haven't heard from you all week. Forgive me for not being more of a friend.
Look for a present to arrive shortly.
Get back to me soon.
Love,
Faith

Half an hour later, the travel agent phoned. "I've got good news and bad news."

"Did you get me a flight?"

"Yes, that worked out fine. I got you into Seattle, but all the flights into Wenatchee are full. That's the bad news." Leavenworth was a few hours outside Seattle, but Faith could manage that easily enough with a rental car.

"I'll book a car," she said.

"I thought of that, too," Carrie went on to explain, "but this is a busy time of year for car rental agencies. The only vehicle available in all of Seattle is a seven-person van."

"Oh." Faith bit her lower lip.

"I reserved it because it was the last car left, but I can cancel the reservation if you don't want it."

Faith didn't take more than a few seconds to decide. "No, I'll take it."

On December twenty-fifth, she intended to be with Emily in Leavenworth. Not only that, she intended to bring Christmas with her—lock, stock and decorations.

Have Yule, will travel.

Chapter Four

In Emily's opinion, everything had worked out perfectly—other than the fact that she hadn't been able to reach Heather to let her know she was arriving. Not that it mattered. Heather would be as thrilled as she was. When Christmas came, the two of them would be together.

Early Sunday morning, Emily caught the short commuter flight out of Wenatchee and landed thirty minutes later at Sea-Tac Airport. Within an hour, Emily was on a nonstop flight from Seattle to Boston.

A mere seven days following her conversation with Heather, Emily was on her way across the entire United States to spend Christmas with her daughter. At the same time Charles Brewster, who sounded like a stereotypical absentminded history professor, was on his way to Leavenworth. Apparently their paths would cross somewhere over the middle of the country, her plane headed east and his headed west.

Emily would spend two glorious weeks with Heather, and Charles would have two weeks to explore Washington State—or do whatever he wanted. They were due to trade back on January first.

Two glorious weeks in Boston. Emily realized Heather had to work on papers and study, but she didn't mind. At least they'd be able to enjoy Christmas Day together and that was what mattered most.

The one negative was that Emily didn't know her daughter's schedule. Emily had repeatedly attempted to contact her, but Heather hadn't returned her messages. Tracy, Heather's roommate, hadn't said anything outright, but Emily had the feeling Heather didn't spend much time in her dorm room. She was obviously working longer hours than she'd let on. Actually, surprising her would be a good thing, Emily thought as she called Heather from Charles Brewster's condo. It would force her to take some time off and—

Surprise her she did.

"Mother," Heather cried into the receiver loudly enough to hurt Emily's eardrum. "You *can't* be in Boston."

Emily realized her arrival was a shock, but Heather seemed more dismayed than pleased.

"I didn't know you had a cell phone," Emily said. It would've saved them both a great deal of frustration had she been able to reach Heather earlier. She'd called the dorm room as soon as she'd landed and Tracy had given Emily a cell number.

"The phone isn't mine," Heather protested. "It belongs to a…friend."

"Ben?"

"No," she said. "Ben is old news."

Information she hadn't bothered to share with her mother, Emily mused. "Where are you?"

"That's not important." Heather sounded almost angry. "Where are *you?*"

Emily rattled off the address, but it didn't sound as if Heather had written anything down. Charles Brewster's condo had proved to be something of a disappointment—not that she was complaining. She'd found it easily enough and settled into the guest room, but it was modern and sterile, devoid of personality or any sign of Christmas.

"I'm so eager to see you," Emily told her daughter. She'd been in town for several hours and they still hadn't connected. "Why don't you come here, where I'm staying and—"

"I'd rather we met at the Starbucks across the street from my dormitory."

"But…" Emily couldn't understand why her daughter wouldn't want to come to her. Her attitude was puzzling, to say the least.

"Mother." Heather paused. "It would be better if we met at Starbucks."

"All right."

"Are you far from there?"

Emily didn't know her way around Boston, but the Harvard campus was within walking distance of the condo. Emily figured she'd find the coffee place without too much trouble, and she told Heather that.

"Meet me there in an hour," Heather snapped.

"Of course, but—"

The line went dead and Emily stared at the receiver, shocked that her own daughter had hung up on her. Or maybe the phone had gone dead. Maybe the battery had run out.…

With a little while before she had to leave, Emily walked

around the condominium with all its modern conveniences. The kitchen was equipped with stainless steel appliances and from the look of it, Emily doubted anyone had so much as turned on a burner. The refrigerator still had the owner's manual in the bottom drawer and almost nothing else. As soon as she could manage it, Emily would find a grocery store.

Everything about the condo was spotless—and barren. Barren was a good word, she decided. Charles Brewster apparently didn't spend much time in his luxurious home. In her opinion his taste in furniture left something to be desired, too. All the pieces were modern, oddly shaped and in her opinion, uncomfortable. She suspected he'd given a designer free rein and then found the look so discordant that he left home whenever possible.

There wasn't a single Christmas decoration. Thank goodness Emily had brought a bit of Christmas cheer with her. The first thing she unpacked was their hand-knit Christmas stockings.

Emily's mother, who'd died a couple of years before Peter, had knit her stocking when Emily was five years old, and she'd knit Heather's, too. It just wouldn't be Christmas without their stockings. She hung them from the mantel, using a couple of paperweights she found in the study to secure them. The angel was carefully packaged in a carry-on. She unwrapped that and set it on the mantel, too. Then she arranged a few other favorite pieces—a tiny sled with a little girl atop, a Santa Heather had bought with her own money when she was ten, a miniature gift, gaily wrapped.

Her suitcases were empty now, but several Christmas decorations remained to be placed about the condo. Emily thought she'd save those until later, when Heather could take part. That way it'd be just like home.

Assuming it would take her no more than thirty minutes to walk to Starbucks, Emily put on her coat, then stepped out of the condo, took the elevator to the marble foyer and hurried onto the sidewalk. Although it was only midafternoon, it resembled dusk. Dark ominous clouds hung overhead and the threat of snow was unmistakable.

Perhaps Heather would suggest a walk across the campus in the falling snow. They could pretend they were back home.

Emily arrived at Starbucks in fifteen minutes and bought a cup of coffee. While she waited for her daughter, she sat at the table next to the window and watched the young people stroll past. Although classes had officially been dismissed for winter break, plenty of students were still in evidence.

A large motorcycle roared past, and Emily winced at the loud, discordant sound. She sipped her coffee, watching the Harley—she assumed it was a Harley because that was the only brand she'd ever heard of. The motorcycle made a U-turn in the middle of the street and pulled into an empty parking space outside the coffee shop. Actually, it wasn't a real space, more of a gap between two parked cars.

The rider turned off the engine, climbed off the bike and removed his black bubblelike helmet. He was an unpleasant-looking fellow, Emily thought. His hair was long and tied at the base of his neck in a ponytail, which he'd flipped over his shoulder. He was dressed completely in black leather, much of his face covered with a thick beard.

A second rider, also dressed in black leather, slipped

off the bike and removed a helmet. Emily blinked, certain she must be seeing things. If she didn't know better, she'd think the second person was her own daughter. But that wasn't possible. Was it?

Heather's twin placed her hand on the man's forearm, said something Emily couldn't hear and then headed into Starbucks alone. The Harley man stayed outside, guarding his bike.

Once the door opened and the girl walked inside, it was all too obvious that she was indeed Heather.

Aghast, Emily stood, nearly tipping over her coffee. *"Heather?"*

"Why didn't you let me know you were coming?" her daughter demanded.

"It's good to see you, too," Emily mumbled sarcastically.

Heather's eyes narrowed. "Frankly, Mother, it's *not* good to see you."

Emily swallowed a gasp. In her wildest imaginings, she'd never dreamed her daughter would say such a thing to her. Without being aware of it, Emily sank back into her chair.

Heather pulled out the chair across from her and sat down.

"Who's your...friend?" Emily asked, nodding toward the window.

"That's Elijah," Heather responded, defiance in every word.

"He doesn't have a last name?"

"No, just Elijah."

Emily sighed. "I see."

"I don't think you do," Heather said pointedly. "You should've told me you were coming to Boston."

"I tried," Emily burst out. "I talked to Tracy five times and left that many messages. Tracy said she'd let you know I'd phoned."

"She did...."

"Then why didn't you return my calls?"

Heather dropped her gaze. "Because I was afraid you were going to send me on a guilt trip and I didn't want to deal with it."

"Send you on a *guilt* trip?"

"You do that, you know? Make me feel guilty."

Despite her irritation, Emily did her best to remain calm. Now she understood why her daughter had insisted they meet at the coffee shop. She didn't want Emily to make a scene, which she admitted she was close to doing.

"I left *five* messages," Emily reminded her.

"I know—but I've been staying with friends and didn't realize you'd phoned until Tracy got in touch with me."

Staying with friends? Yeah, right. Emily's gaze flew out the window. Her daughter and that...that Neanderthal?

"I love him," Heather said boldly.

Emily managed to stay seated. "If that's the case, why don't you bring him inside so we can meet?"

"Because..." Heather hesitated and then squared her shoulders as if gathering her courage. "I didn't want him to hear what you're planning to say."

"About what?" This made no sense whatsoever.

"None of that matters. I'm leaving town with Elijah. In other words, I won't be in Boston over the holidays."

Emily shook her head slightly, wondering if she'd heard correctly. "I beg your pardon?"

"Elijah and I and a couple of other friends are riding down to Florida."

"For Christmas?" Emily *knew* something was wrong with her hearing now. There simply had to be. "On motorcycles?"

"Yes, for Christmas. And yes, on motorcycles. We're sick of this weather and want to spend our holiday on the beach."

Emily was completely speechless.

"You don't have anything to say?" Heather asked angrily. "I figured you'd have lots of opinions to share."

Emily's mouth opened and closed twice while she gathered her thoughts. "I traded homes with a stranger, traveled across the country and now you're telling me you won't be here for Christmas?" Her voice rose on the last word.

Heather's eyes flashed. "That's exactly what I'm saying. I'm of age and I make my own decisions."

Emily's jaw sagged in dismay. "You mean you're actually going to abandon me here—"

"You didn't bother to check your plans with me before you boarded that plane, did you, Mother? That's unfortunate because I've made other arrangements for Christmas. As far as I'm concerned, this problem is all yours."

"You said you had to work." That clearly had been a blatant lie.

"There you go," Heather cried. "You're trying to make me feel guilty."

"If you'd been honest—"

"You don't want me to be honest!" Heather challenged.

The truth of it was, she was right. Emily would rather not know that her daughter was associating with a member of some motorcycle gang.

"Go then," Emily said, waving her hand toward the door. "Have a wonderful time."

Heather leaped out of the chair as if she couldn't get away fast enough. "You can't blame me for this!"

"I'm not blaming you for anything," she said tiredly. Heaven forbid her daughter should accuse her of throwing guilt.

"This is all your own doing."

Emily stared silently into the distance.

"Nothing you say is going to make me change my mind," Heather insisted, as if wanting her to argue.

Emily didn't imagine it would. She felt physically ill, but she held on to her dignity. Pride demanded that she not let her daughter know how badly she'd hurt her.

Rushing out the door, Heather grabbed the black helmet, placed it on her head and climbed onto the back of the motorcycle. Elijah with no last name was already on the bike and within seconds they disappeared down the street.

Emily's opinion of this coming Christmas did an about-face.

This was destined to be the worst one of her life. Not only was she alone, but she was in a strange town, without a single friend. And her daughter had just broken her heart.

Chapter Five

"For heaven's sake, what is this?" Charles stood outside the gingerbread house in the middle of Santa's village feeling total dismay. There had to be some mistake—some vast, terrible mistake. Nothing else would explain the fact that after flying three thousand miles, he'd landed smack-dab in the middle of Christmas Town, complete with ice-skating rink, glittering lights and Christmas music.

He closed his eyes, hoping, praying, this nightmare would vanish and he could settle down in a nice quiet prison community. When he opened them, it was even worse than Charles had imagined. A little kid was staring up at him.

"I'm Sarah," she announced.

He said nothing.

"I lost two teeth." She proceeded to pull down her lower lip in order to reveal the empty spaces in her mouth.

"Is this where Emily Springer lives?" Charles asked, nodding toward the house. He was uncomfortable around children, mainly because he didn't know any.

"She went to Boston to spend Christmas with her daughter," Sarah informed him.

"I know." So he was in the right town. Damn.

"She keeps the key under the flower pot if you need to get inside."

Charles cocked his eyebrows. "She told you that?"

"Everyone in town knows where the key is." As if to prove it, Sarah walked over to the porch, lifted up the pot and produced the key, which she proudly displayed.

A one-horse open sleigh drove past, bells ringing, resembling something straight off a Christmas card. It didn't get any more grotesque than this. Ice skaters circled the rink in the park directly across the street from him. They were dressed in period costumes and singing in three-part harmony.

Rolling his suitcase behind him and clutching his laptop, Charles approached the house. It reminded him of an illustration, too cozy and perfect to be true, with its scalloped edging and colorful shutters. The porch had a swing and a rocking chair. Had he been Norman Rockwell, he would have found a canvas and painted it. Charles sighed heavily. This must be his punishment for trying to avoid Christmas.

"My mom's bringing you cookies," Sarah told him as she followed him up the steps.

"Tell her not to bother."

"She does it to be neighborly."

"I don't want neighbors."

"You don't?"

The little girl looked crushed.

He didn't mean to hurt the kid's feelings, but he wasn't interested in joining a Christmas commune. He simply wasn't socially inclined. All he wanted was to be left alone so he could write—and ignore anything to do with Christmas. Clearly, he'd been mistaken about this town— where was the prison? Keeping to his all-work-and-no-Yule agenda was going to be more of a challenge than he'd planned.

"Thank your mother for me, but explain that I came here to work," he told the little girl, making an effort to mollify her with politeness.

"But it's *Christmas*."

"I'm well aware of the season," he said, stabbing the key into the lock. "Let your mother know I prefer not to be disturbed." He hoped the kid would take the hint, too.

Sarah jutted out her lower lip. "Okay."

Good, she got the message. Charles opened the front door and stepped inside. He should've been prepared…. If Leavenworth was Santa's village, then stepping into this house was like walking into a fairy tale. The furniture was large and old-fashioned and bulky, with lots of lace and doilies. He'd traded homes with Goldilocks. Well, with the Three Bears, anyway. A grandfather clock chimed in the living room and logs were arranged in the fireplace, ready for a match. A knitted afghan was draped across the back of the overstuffed sofa. A green and blue braided rug covered the hardwood floor.

"Oh, brother," Charles sighed, truly discouraged. He abandoned his suitcase and laptop in the entry and walked into the kitchen. Emily had left him a note propped against the holly wreath that served as a center-piece on the round oak table. Charles was almost afraid to read it.

After a moment he reached for it, read it, then tossed it

in the garbage. She'd left him dinner in the refrigerator. All he had to do was heat it in the microwave.

Dinner. Cookies from the neighbor. "Jingle Bells" in a one-horse open sleigh gliding back and forth in front of the house. If *that* wasn't bad enough, the entire street, indeed the whole town, glittered with Christmas lights that blinked from every conceivable corner. This was madness. Sheer madness. He hadn't escaped Christmas; he'd dived headfirst into the middle of it.

The first thing Charles did before he unpacked was pull down every shade on every window he could find. That, at least, blocked out the lights. He found an empty bedroom, set his suitcase on a chair and took out the work materials he needed.

The doorbell chimed and he groaned inwardly, bracing himself for another confrontation with the Christmas kid. Or her mother, bearing gifts of cookies.

It wasn't a woman with a plate of cookies or the child who'd accosted him earlier. Instead there were *six* of them, six children who stared up at him in wide-eyed wonder. They were dressed in winter gear from head to toe, with only their eyes and noses visible behind thick wool scarves and hand-knit hats. Their noses were bright red and their eyes watery. Melting snow dripped puddles onto the porch.

"Do you want to come outside? Go sledding with us?" the oldest of the group asked, his scarf moving where his mouth must be.

"No." Charles couldn't think of anything more to add.

"We have an extra sled you can use."

"I—no, thanks."

"Okay," the second-tallest boy answered.

No one budged.

"You sure?" the first boy asked.

Someone shouted from nearby. An adult voice from what he could tell.

"That's our mom," one of the children said. The little girl from before.

"We were supposed to leave you alone," another girl told him. At least he thought it was a girl.

"You should listen to your mother."

"Do you?"

The kid had him there. "Not always."

"Us neither." The boy's eyes smiled at him and Charles realized he'd made a friend, which was unfortunate.

"Emily said you were a teacher, too."

"I'm writing a book and I won't have time to play in the snow." He started to close the door.

"Not at all?" The oldest boy asked the question with a complete sense of horror.

"It's Christmas," another reminded him.

The woman's voice sounded again, shriller this time.

"We got to go."

"Bye," Charles said and, despite himself, found that he was grinning when he closed the door. His amusement died a quick death once he was back inside the house. Despite his attempt to block out all evidence of Christmas, he was well aware that it waited right outside, ready to pounce on him the minute he peeked out.

Grumbling under his breath, he returned to the kitchen and grudgingly set his dinner in the microwave. Some kind of casserole, duly labeled "Charles." He resisted the urge to call Emily Springer and tell her exactly what he thought of her little Christmas deception. He would, too, if she'd misled him—only she hadn't. He blamed himself for this. Because he'd just realized something—he'd confused Leavenworth, Washington, with Leavenworth, Kansas.

The doorbell chimed once more, and Charles looked at the ceiling, rolling his eyes and groaning audibly. Apparently he was going to have to be more forthright with the family next door. He stomped across the room and hauled open the front door. He wanted to make it clear that he didn't appreciate the disturbances.

No one was there.

He stuck his head out the door and glanced in both directions.

No one.

Then he noticed a plate of decorated cookies sitting on the porch. They were wrapped in red cellophane, which was tied with a silver bow. His first instinct was to pretend he hadn't seen them. At the last second, he reached down, grabbed the plate and slammed the door shut. He turned the lock, and leaned against the wall, breathing fast.

He was in the wrong Leavenworth, but he might as well be in prison, since he wouldn't be able to leave the house, or even open the door, for fear of being ambushed by Christmas carolers, cookies and children.

Not exactly what he'd had in mind...

Chapter Six

Bernice Brewster was beside herself with frustration. For two days she'd tried to reach her son Charles, to no avail. He refused to use a cell phone and the one she'd purchased for him sat in a drawer somewhere. She was sure he'd never even charged the battery.

Growing up in Boston, Charles had been fascinated by history, particularly the original Thirteen Colonies. Now look at him! Granted, that interest had taken him far; unfortunately it seemed to be his *only* interest. If he wasn't standing in front of a classroom full of students—hanging on his every word as she fondly imagined—then he was buried in a book. Now, it appeared, he was writing his very own.

Why, oh why, couldn't her sons be like her friends' children, who were constantly causing them heartache and worry? Instead, she'd borne two sons who had to be the most loving, kindest sons on God's green earth, but... The problem was that they didn't understand one of the primary duties of a son—to provide his parents with grandchildren.

Bernice couldn't understand where she'd gone wrong. If there was anything to be grateful for, it was that Bernard hadn't lived long enough to discover what a disappointment their two sons had turned out to be in the family department.

Charles was the younger of the two. Rayburn, eight years his senior, lived in New York City and worked for one of the big publishers there. He insisted on being called Ray, although she never thought of him as anything but Rayburn. He was a gifted man who'd risen quickly in publishing, although he changed houses or companies so often she couldn't hope to keep track of where he was or exactly what he did. At last mention, he'd said something about the name of the publisher changing because his company had merged with another. The merger had apparently netted him a promotion.

Like his younger brother, however, Rayburn was a disappointment in the area of marriage. Her oldest son was married to his job. He was in his midforties now and she'd given up hope that he'd ever settle down with a wife and family. Rayburn lived and breathed publishing.

Charles, it seemed, was her only chance for grandchildren, slight though that chance might be. He was such a nice young man and for a while, years ago now, there'd been such promise when he'd fallen head over heels in love. Monica. Oh, yes, she remembered Monica, a conniving shallow little bitch who'd broken her son's heart. On Christmas Eve, yet.

What was wrong with all those women in Boston and New York? Both her sons were attractive; Rayburn and Charles possessed their father's striking good looks, not that either had ever taken advantage of that. Bernice suspected Rayburn had been involved with various women, but obviously there'd never been anyone special.

Sitting in her favorite chair with the phone beside her, Bernice wondered what to do next. This was a sorry, sorry state of affairs. While her friends in the Arizona retirement community brought out book after book filled with darling pictures of their grandchildren, she had nothing to show except photos of her Pomeranian, FiFi. There were only so many pictures of the dog she could pass around. Even she was tired of looking at photographs of FiFi.

Bernice petted the small dog and with a brooding sense that something was terribly wrong, reached for the phone. She pushed speed dial for Charles's number and closed her eyes with impatience, waiting for the call to connect.

After one short ring, someone answered. "Hello."

Bernice gasped. The voice was soft and distinctly female. She couldn't believe her ears.

"Hello?"

"Is this the residence of Charles Brewster?" Bernice asked primly. "Professor Charles Brewster?"

"Yes, it is."

Of course it was Charles's condominium. The number was programmed into her phone and Bernice trusted technology. Shocked, she slammed down the receiver and stared, horrified, at the golf course outside.

Charles had a woman at his place. A woman he hadn't mentioned to his own mother, which could mean only one thing. Her son didn't want her to know anything about this…this female. All kinds of frightening scenarios flew into her mind. Charles consorting with a gold digger—or worse. Charles held hostage. Charles… She shook her head. No, she had to take control here.

Still in shock, Bernice picked up the phone again and pushed the top speed-dial button, which would connect her with Rayburn's New York apartment. He was often more difficult to reach than Charles. Luck was with her, however, and Rayburn answered after the third ring.

"Rayburn," Bernice cried in near panic, not giving him a chance to greet her.

"Mother, what's wrong?"

"When was the last time you spoke with your brother?" she demanded breathlessly.

Rayburn seemed to need time to think about this, but Bernice was in no condition to wait. "Something is wrong with Charles! I'm so worried."

"Why don't you start at the beginning?"

"I *am*," she cried.

"Now, Mother…"

"Hear me out before you *Now, Mother* me." The more she thought about a strange woman answering Charles's phone, the more alarmed she became. Ever since that dreadful Monica had broken off the relationship… Ever since her, he'd gone out of his way to avoid women. In fact, he seemed oblivious to them and rejected every attempt she'd made to match him up.

"Your brother has a woman living with him," she said, her voice trembling.

Silence followed her announcement. "Mother, have you been drinking hot buttered rum again?"

"No," she snapped, insulted he'd ask such a thing. "Hear me out. I haven't been able to get hold of Charles for two days. I left messages on his answering machine, and he never returned a single call."

Her son was listening, and for that Bernice was grateful.

"Go on," he said without inflection.

"Just now, not more than five minutes ago, I called Charles again. A woman answered the phone." She squeezed her eyes closed. "She had a…sexy voice."

"Perhaps it was a cleaning woman."

"On a Monday?"

"Maybe it was a colleague. A friend from the History Department."

Bernice maintained a stubborn silence.

"You're sure about this?" Rayburn finally said.

"As sure as I live and breathe. Your brother has a woman in his home—living there."

"Just because she answered the phone doesn't mean she's living with Charles."

"You and I both know your brother would never allow just anyone to answer the phone."

Rayburn seemed to agree; a casual visitor wouldn't be answering his brother's phone.

"Good for him," Rayburn said with what sounded like a chuckle.

"How can you say that?" Bernice cried. "It's obvious that this woman must be completely unacceptable."

"Now, Mother…"

"Why wouldn't Charles tell us about her?"

"I don't know, but I think you're jumping to conclusions."

"I'm not! I just *know* something's wrong. Perhaps she tricked her way into his home, killed him and—"

"You've been watching too many crime shows," Rayburn chastised.

"Perhaps I have, but I won't rest until I get to the bottom of this."

"Fine." Her oldest son apparently grasped how serious she was, because he asked, "What do you want me to do?"

"Oh, Rayburn," she said with a sob, dabbing her nose with a delicate hankie. "I don't know how I'd manage without my sons to look out for me."

"Mother…"

"Take the train to Boston and investigate this situation. Report back to me ASAP."

"I can phone him and handle this in five minutes."

"No." She was insistent. "I want you to check it out with your own eyes. God only knows what your brother's gotten himself into with this woman. I just know whoever it is must be taking advantage of Charles."

"*Mother.* This is Christmas week and—"

"I know what time of year it is, Rayburn, and I realize you have a life of your own. A life that's much too busy to include your mother. But I'll tell you right now that I won't sleep a wink until I hear what's happened to Charles."

There was a pause.

"All right," Rayburn muttered. "I'll take the train to Boston and check up on Charles."

"Thank God." She could breathe easier now.

Chapter Seven

The Boeing 767 bounced against the tarmac and jarred Faith Kerrigan awake. She bolted upright and realized that she'd just landed in Seattle. She glanced at her watch; it was just after seven. She'd had less than four hours' sleep the entire night.

She'd survive. Any discomfort would be well worth the look of joy and surprise on Emily's face when Faith arrived and announced she'd be joining her friend for Christmas.

Remembering that was a better wake-up than a triple-shot espresso. Although the flight—which was completely full—had left the Bay area at 5:00 a.m., Faith had been up since two. Her lone suitcase was packed to the bursting point and she'd stuffed her carry-on until the zipper threatened to pop. After filing off the plane and collecting her suitcase, she dragged everything to the car rental agency. Thankfully, an attendant was available despite the early hour.

Faith stepped up to the counter and managed a smile. "Hi."

"Happy holidays," the young woman greeted her. The name tag pinned to her blouse identified her as Theresa.

With her confirmation number in hand, Faith leaned against the counter and asked, "Will you need my credit card?" She couldn't remember if she'd given the number to her travel agent earlier.

Theresa nodded and slid over a sheaf of papers to fill out. Faith dug in the bottom of her purse for her favorite pen.

The girl on the other side of the counter reminded her of Heather, and she wondered briefly if Theresa was a college student deprived of spending Christmas with her family because of her job.

The phone pealed; Theresa answered immediately. After announcing the name of the agency, followed by "Theresa speaking," she went silent. Her eyes widened as she listened to whoever was on the other end. Then, for some inexplicable reason, the young woman's gaze landed on her.

"That's terrible," Theresa murmured, steadily eyeing Faith.

Faith shifted her feet uncomfortably and waited.

"No...she's here now. I don't know what to tell you. Sure, I can ask, but...yes. Okay. Let me put you on hold."

Faith shifted her weight to the other foot. This sounded ominous.

Theresa held the telephone receiver against her shoulder. "There's been a problem," she said. Her dark eyes held a pleading look.

"What kind of problem?"

The young woman sighed. "Earlier we rented a van exactly like yours to a group of actors and, unfortunately, theirs broke down. Even more unfortunate, we don't have a replacement we can give them. On top of that, it doesn't look like the van they were driving can be easily fixed."

Faith could tell what was coming next. "You want me to give up the van I reserved."

"The thing is, we don't have a single car on the lot to give you in exchange."

Faith would've liked to help, but she had no other means of getting to Leavenworth. "The only reason I reserved the van is because it was the last car available."

"My manager is well aware of that."

"Where is this group headed?" All she needed the van for was to get to Leavenworth. Once Faith reached her destination, she'd be with Emily, who had her own vehicle. She explained that.

"I'm not sure, but my manager said this group gives charity performances across the region. They have appearances scheduled at nursing homes and hospitals."

Great, just great. If she didn't let them have her van, the entire state of Washington would be filled with disappointed children and old people, and it would be all her fault.

"In other words, if we could find a way to get you to Leavenworth, you'd be willing to relinquish the van?" Theresa sounded optimistic. "Let me find out if that's doable."

Faith waited some more while the clerk explained the situation. The young woman had an expressive face. Her eyes brightened as she glanced at Faith and smiled. Cupping her hand over the receiver, she said, "My manager's talking to the actors now, but it seems their next performance is in the general vicinity of Leavenworth."

"So they could drive me there?"

Theresa nodded. "They can drop you off." She smiled again. "My manager said if you agree to this, she'll personally make sure there's a car available for you later, so you can get back to Seattle."

"Okay." This was becoming a bit complicated, but she was willing to cooperate.

"She also wanted me to tell you that because you're being so great about all of this, there won't be any charge for whatever length of time you have one of our cars."

"Perfect." Faith was pretty sure the rental agency must be desperate to ask such a favor of her. Still, it was Christmas, a time for goodwill.

Theresa's attention returned to the phone. "That'll work. Great. Great."

Fifteen minutes later, Faith was driven to the off-site rental facility. Clasping her paperwork and pulling her suitcase, she half-carried, half dragged her carry-on bag.

"Can I help you?" a dwarf asked.

"I'm fine, but thank you," she responded, a little startled.

"I think you must be the woman the agency told us about."

"Us?"

"The others are inside."

"The actors?"

"Santa and six elves. I'm one of the elves."

Faith grinned and, bending slightly forward, offered the man her hand. "Faith."

"Tony."

Soon Faith was surrounded by the five other elves and Santa himself. The actors were delightful. Tony introduced each one to Faith. There was Sam, who played the role of Santa. He was, not surprisingly, a full two feet taller than the other cast members, and he had a full white beard and a white head of hair. He must pad his costume because he was trim and didn't look to be more than fifty. His helpers, all dwarfs, were Allen, Norman,

Betty, Erica and David. And Tony, of course. Before Faith had an opportunity to repeat their names in her mind, the luggage was transferred from the company van to the rental.

"We sure appreciate this," Sam told her as he slid into the driver's seat.

"I'm happy to help," Faith said, and she meant it.

At Sam's invitation, seconded by Tony, Allen and the others, Faith joined him up front; the six elves took the two rear seats.

"Is Leavenworth out of your way?" she asked.

Sam shook his head. "A little, but you won't hear me complaining." He glanced over at Faith. "We have a performance this afternoon in north Seattle at a children's hospital. If you need to be in Leavenworth before tonight, I could let you take the van with Tony. He has a license, but—"

Theresa hadn't mentioned a performance that day, but then she probably hadn't known about it either. Faith hesitated. No doubt Tony should be there for the show. Yes, she was tired and yes, she wanted to see her friend, but nothing was so pressing that she had to be in Leavenworth before five that evening.

"I'm surprising a friend," she admitted. "Emily isn't expecting me. So I don't have to get there at any particular time."

"You mean she doesn't even know you're coming?"

"Nope." Faith nearly giggled in her excitement. "She's going to be so happy to see me."

"Then you don't mind attending the performance with us?"

"Not at all." Although she was eager to get to Leavenworth, Faith didn't feel she could deprive children of meeting Tony.

As it turned out, Faith was completely charmed by the performance. Santa and his helpers were wonderful with the sick children, and Tony even enlisted her to assist in the distribution of gifts. The performance was clearly the highlight of their Christmas celebration.

It wasn't until after four that they all piled back into the van. The elves chatted away, pleased everything had gone so well. Faith learned that Sam and his friends had been doing these charity performances for years. They all worked regularly as actors—with roles in movies, TV productions and commercials—but they took a break at Christmas to bring a bit of joy and laughter into the lives of sick children and lonely old people. Faith felt honored to have been part of it.

"I'm starving," Allen announced not long after they got on the freeway.

Erica and David chimed in. "Me, too."

Not wanting to show up at Emily's hungry, she agreed that they should stop for hamburgers and coffee. Sam insisted on paying for Faith's meal.

"You guys were just great," she said again, biting into her cheeseburger with extra pickles. Emily was going to love them, especially when she learned that they were performing at children's hospitals and retirement homes.

"Thanks."

"What's on the agenda for tomorrow?"

"We aren't due in Spokane until three," Sam told her.

Spokane was a long drive from Leavenworth, and they'd be driving at night. "Do you have hotel reservations?" Faith asked.

"Not until tomorrow," Sam confessed. "Our original plan was to spend the night in Ellensburg."

Faith mulled over this information and knew Emily would encourage her to ask her newfound friends to stay at the house overnight. The place had two extra bedrooms that were rarely used.

"Listen, I'll need to talk it over with my friend, but I'm sure she'd want me to invite you to spend the night." She grinned. "What if you all arrived in costume? I'll be her Christmas surprise—delivered by Santa and his elves. Are you game?"

"You bet," Sam said, and his six friends nodded their agreement.

They all scrambled back into the van, and Tony chuckled from the back seat. "One Christmas delivery, coming right up."

Chapter Eight

Emily was bored and sad and struggling not to break down. There was only one thing left to do—what she always did when she got depressed.

Bake cookies.

But even this traditional cure required a monumental effort. First, she had to locate a grocery store and because she didn't have a car, she'd have to haul everything to the condominium on her own. This was no easy task when she had to buy both flour and sugar. By the time she let herself back into the condo with three heavy bags, she was exhausted.

On the off chance that she might be able to reach Faith, she tried phoning again. After leaving six messages, Emily knew that if her friend was available, she would've returned the call by now. Faith must be at her sister's because she certainly wasn't at home.

Heather's roommate had apparently left town, too, because there was no answer at the dorm. Emily had to accept that she was alone and friendless in a strange city.

Once she began her baking project, though, her mood improved. She doubted Charles had so much as turned on the oven. In order to bake cookies, she'd had to purchase every single item, including measuring cups and cookie sheets. Once the cookies were ready, Emily knew she couldn't possibly eat them all. It was the baking, not the eating, that she found therapeutic. She intended to pack his freezer with dozens of chocolate chip cookies.

Soon the condo smelled delectable—of chocolate and vanilla and warm cookies. She felt better just inhaling the aroma. As she started sorting through her Christmas CDs, she was startled to hear someone knocking at the door. So far she hadn't met a single other person in the entire building. Her heart hammered with excitement. Really, it was ridiculous to be this thrilled over what was probably someone arriving at her door—Charles's door—by mistake.

Emily squinted through the peephole and saw a man in a wool overcoat and scarf standing in the hallway. He must be a friend of Professor Brewster's, she decided. A rather attractive one with appealing brown eyes and a thick head of hair, or what she could see of his hair. She opened the door.

All he did was stare at her.

Emily supposed she must look a sight. With no apron to be found, she'd tucked a dish towel in the waistband of her jeans. Her Rudolph sweatshirt, complete with blinking red nose, had been a gift from her daughter the year before. She wore fuzzy pink slippers and no makeup.

"Can I help you?"

"Where's Charles?" he asked abruptly.

"And you are?"

"His brother, Ray."

"Oh…" Emily moved aside. "You'd better come in because this is a rather long story."

"It would seem so." He removed his scarf and stepped into the apartment. As soon as he did, he paused and looked around. "This *is* my brother's place?"

"Technically yes, but for the next two weeks it's mine. I'm Emily Springer, by the way."

"Hmm. I hardly recognized it." Ray glanced at the mantel where Emily had hung the two Christmas stockings and put the angel. "Would you mind if I sat down?"

"No. Please do." She gestured toward the low-slung leather chair that resembled something one would find on a beach.

Ray claimed the chair and seemed as uncomfortable as she'd been when she'd tried watching television in it.

"You might prefer the sofa," she said, although that meant they'd be sitting next to each other.

"I think I'll try it." He had to brace his hand on the floor before he could lever himself out of the chair. He stood, sniffed the air and asked, "Are you baking cookies?"

She nodded. "Chocolate chip."

"From scratch?"

Again she nodded. "Would you like some? I've got coffee on, too."

"Not yet." He shook his head. "I think you'd better tell me what's going on with my brother first."

"Yes, of course." Emily sat on the other end of the sofa, and turned sideways, knees together, hands clasped. She just hoped she could get through this without breaking into tears. "It all started when my daughter phoned to say she wouldn't be home for Christmas."

"Your daughter lives here in Boston?"

"Yes." Emily moistened her lips. "Heather attends Harvard." She resisted the urge to brag about Heather's scholarship.

"One of my brother's students?"

The thought had never occurred to Emily. "I don't think so, but I don't know." Apparently there was a lot she didn't know about her daughter's life.

"When I learned that Heather wouldn't be coming home for the holidays, I made the foolish decision to come to Boston, only I couldn't afford more than the airfare."

"In other words, you needed a place to stay?"

"Exactly, so I posted a message on a home-exchange site. Charles contacted me and we exchanged e-mails and decided to trade places for two weeks."

"My brother hates Christmas—that's why he wanted out of the city."

Emily's gaze shot to his. "He didn't mention that."

"Well, it's another long story."

"Then I'm afraid Leavenworth's going to be a bit of a shock."

"Explain that later."

"There's not much more to tell you. Charles is living in my home in Leavenworth, Washington, for the next two weeks and I'm here." She stopped to take a deep breath. "And Heather, my daughter, is in Florida with a man who looks like he might belong to the Hells Angels."

"I see."

Emily doubted that, but didn't say so. "Did Charles know you were coming?"

"No. Actually, my mother asked me to visit. She called and you obviously answered the phone. Mother was convinced something had happened to Charles—that he'd gotten involved with some woman and... Never mind. But she insisted I get over here to, uh, investigate the situation."

"She'll be relieved."

"True," Ray said, "but truth be known, I'm a bit disappointed. It would do my brother a world of good to fall in love."

He didn't elaborate and she didn't question him further. Everything she knew about Charles had come from their e-mail chats, which had been brief and businesslike.

Emily stood and walked into the kitchen. Ray followed her. "So you're alone in the city over Christmas?"

She nodded, forcing a smile. "It isn't exactly what I intended, but there's no going back now." Her home was occupied, and getting a flight out of Boston at this late date was financially unfeasible. She was stuck.

"Listen," Ray said, reaching for a cookie. "Why don't I take you to dinner tonight?"

Emily realized she shouldn't analyze this invitation too closely. Still, she had to know. "Why?"

"Well, because we both need to eat and I'd rather have a meal with you than alone." He paused to take a bite of the cookie, moaning happily at the taste. "Delicious. Uh—I didn't mean to sound ungracious. Let me try that again. Would you be so kind as to join me for dinner?"

"I'd love to," Emily said, her spirits lifting.

"I'll catch the last train back to New York, explain everything to my mother in the morning and we'll leave it at that. Now, may I have another one of these incomparable cookies?"

"Of course." Emily met his eyes and smiled. He was a

likable man, and at the moment she was in need of a friend. "When would you like to leave?"

Ray checked his watch. "It's six-thirty, so any time is fine with me."

"I'd better change clothes." She pulled the towel free of her waistband, folded it and set it on the kitchen counter.

"Before you do," Ray said stopping her. "Explain what you meant about my brother being in trouble if he isn't fond of Christmas."

"Oh, that." A giggle bubbled up inside her as she told him about Leavenworth in December—the horse-drawn sleigh, the carolers and the three separate tree-lighting ceremonies, one for every weekend before Christmas.

Ray was soon laughing so hard he was wiping tears from his eyes. Just seeing his amusement made her laugh, too, although she didn't really understand what he found so hilarious.

"If only…if only you knew my b-brother," Ray sputtered. "I can just imagine what he thought when he arrived."

"I guess Charles and I both had the wrong idea about trading homes."

"Sure seems that way," Ray agreed, still grinning. "Why don't I have another cookie while you get ready," he said cheerfully. "I haven't looked forward to a dinner this much in ages."

Come to think of it, neither had Emily.

Chapter Nine

Charles worked at his laptop computer until late in the afternoon. He stopped only when his stomach started to growl. He was making progress and felt good about what he'd managed to accomplish, but he needed a break.

After closing down his computer, he wandered into the kitchen. An inspection of the cupboards and the freezer revealed a wide selection of choices, but he remembered his agreement with Emily. They were to purchase their own food. Emily had been kind enough to prepare yesterday's dinner for him, but he needed to fend for himself from here on out.

There was no help for it; he'd have to venture outside the comfort and security of Emily's house. He'd have to leave this rather agreeable prison and take his chances among the townspeople. The thought sent a chill down his spine.

Peeking through the drapes, Charles rolled his eyes. He was convinced that if he looked hard enough, he'd see Ebenezer Scrooge and the ghost of Marley, not to mention Tiny Tim hobbling down the sidewalk, complete with his crutch, and crying out, "God bless us everyone."

Once he'd donned his long wool coat and draped a scarf around his neck, he dashed out the door. He locked it behind him, although he wondered why he bothered. According to the kid next door, the entire town knew where Emily kept the key. Still, Charles wanted it understood that he wasn't receiving company.

Walking to his rental car, he hurriedly unlocked it and climbed inside before anyone could stop him. With a sense of accomplishment, he drove until he discovered a large chain grocery store. The lot was full, and there appeared to be some sort of activity taking place in front of the store.

Ducking his head against the wind, he walked rapidly across the parking lot toward the entrance.

A crowd had gathered, and Charles glanced over, wondering at all the commotion. He blinked several times as the scene unfolded before him. Apparently the local church was putting on a Nativity pageant, complete with livestock—a donkey, a goat and several sheep.

Just as he scurried by, the goat raised its head and grabbed the hem of his overcoat. Charles took two steps and was jerked back.

The goat was eating his coat. Apparently no one noticed because the three wise men had decided to make an appearance at the same time. Charles tried to jerk his hem free, but the goat had taken a liking to it and refused to let go. Not wanting to call attention to himself, he decided to ignore the goat and proceed into the store, tugging at his coat as he walked. Unfortunately the goat walked right along behind him, chewing contentedly.

Charles had hoped to dash in, collect his groceries and get out, all in fifteen minutes or less. Instead, everyone in the entire store turned to stare at him as he stumbled in, towing the goat.

"Mister, you've got a goat following you." Some kid, about five or six, was kind enough to point this out, as if Charles hadn't been aware of it.

"Go away." Charles attempted to shoo the goat, but the creature was clearly more interested in its evening meal than in listening to him.

"Oh, sorry." A teenage boy raced after him and took hold of the goat by the collar. After several embarrassing seconds, the boy managed to get the goat to release Charles's coat.

Before he drew even more attention, Charles grabbed a cart and galloped down the aisles, throwing in what he needed. He paused to gather up the back of his expensive wool coat, which was damp at the hem and looking decidedly nibbled, then with a sigh dropped it again. As he went on his way, he noticed several shoppers who stopped and stared at him, but he ignored them.

He approached the dairy case. As he reached for a quart of milk a barbershop quartet strolled up to serenade him with Christmas carols. Charles listened politely for all of five seconds, then zoomed into a check-out line.

Was there no escape?

By the time he'd loaded his groceries in the car and returned to Emily's home, he felt as if he'd completed the Boston marathon. Now he had to make it from the car to the house undetected.

He looked around to see if any of the neighborhood kids were in sight. He was out of luck, because he immediately caught sight of six or seven of the little darlings, building a snowman in the yard directly next to his.

They all gaped at him.

Charles figured he had only a fifty-fifty chance of making it to the house minus an entourage.

"Hello, mister."

They were already greeting him and he didn't even have the car door completely open. He pretended not to hear them.

"Want to build a snowman with us?"

"No." He scooped up as many of the grocery bags as he could carry and headed toward the house.

"Need help with that?" All the kids raced to his vehicle, eager to offer assistance.

"No."

"You sure?"

"What I want is to be left alone." Charles didn't mean to be rude, but all this Christmas stuff had put him on edge.

The children stared up at him, openmouthed, as if no one had ever said that to them in their entire lives. The little girl blinked back tears.

"Oh, all right," he muttered, surrendering to guilt. He hadn't intended to be unfriendly—it was just that he'd had about as much of this peace and goodwill business as a man could swallow.

The children gleefully tracked through the house, bringing in his groceries and placing them in the kitchen. They looked pleased when they'd finished. Everyone, that is, except the youngest—Sarah, wasn't it?

"I think someone tried to eat your coat," the little girl said.

"A goat did."

"Must've been Clara Belle," her oldest brother put in.

"She's Ronny's 4-H project. He said that goat would latch on to anything. I guess he was right."

Charles grunted agreement and got out his wallet to pay the youngsters.

"You don't have to pay us," the boy said. "We were just being neighborly."

That "neighborly" nonsense again. Charles wanted to argue, but they were out the door before he had a chance to object.

Once Charles had a chance to unpack his groceries and eat, he felt almost human again. He opened the curtains and looked out the window, chuckling at the Kennedy kids' anatomically correct snowman. He wondered what his mother would've said had he used the carrot for anything other than the nose.

It was dark now, and the lights were fast appearing, so Charles shut the curtains again. He considered returning to work. Instead he yawned and decided to take a shower in the downstairs bathroom. He thought he heard something when he got under the spray, but when he listened intently, everything was silent.

Then the sound came again. Troubled now, he turned off the water and yanked a towel from the rack. Wrapping it around his waist, he opened the bathroom door and peered out. He was just about to ask if anyone was there when he heard a female voice.

"Emily? Where are you?" the voice shouted.

Charles gasped and quickly closed the door. He dressed as fast as possible, which was difficult because he was still wet. Zipping up his pants, he stepped out of the bathroom, hair dripping, and came face to face with— Santa Claus.

Both men shouted in alarm.

"Who the hell are you?" Santa cried.

"What are you doing in my house?" Charles demanded.

"Faith!" Santa shouted.

A woman rounded the corner and dashed into the hallway—then stopped dead in her tracks. Her mouth fell open.

"Who are *you?*" Charles shrieked.

"Faith Kerrigan. What have you done with my friend?"

"If you mean Emily Springer, she's in Boston."

"What?" For a moment it looked as if she was about to collapse.

Immediately six elves appeared, all in pointed hats and shoes, crowding the hallway.

Santa and six elves? Charles had taken as much as a Christmas-hating individual could stand. "What the hell is going on here?" he yelled, his patience gone.

"I…I flew in from the Bay area to surprise my friend for Christmas. She didn't say anything about going to Boston."

"We traded houses for two weeks."

"Oh…no." Faith slouched against the wall.

All six of the elves rushed forward to comfort her. Santa looked like he wanted to punch Charles out.

Charles ran his hand down his face. "Apparently there's been…a misunderstanding."

"Apparently," Faith cried as if that was the understatement of the century.

The doorbell chimed, and when Charles went to answer it, the Kennedy kids rushed past him and over to Faith. Their arms went around her waist and they all started to chatter at once, telling her about Heather not coming home and Emily going to Boston.

Adding to the mass confusion were the six elves, who

seemed to be arguing among themselves about which one of them would have the privilege of bashing in Charles's nose.

Charles's head started to swim. He raised his arms and shouted in his loudest voice, "Everyone out!"

The room instantly went silent. "Out?" Faith cried. "We don't have anywhere to go. There isn't a hotel room between here and Spokane with a vacancy now."

Charles slumped onto the arm of the sofa and pressed his hand against his forehead.

"Where do you expect us to go?" Faith asked. Her voice was just short of hysterical. "I've only had a few hours' sleep and my friends changed their plans to drive me to Leavenworth and the van broke down and now—this."

"All right, all right." Charles decided he could bear it for one night as long as everyone left by morning.

The small group looked expectantly at him. "You can spend the night—but just tonight. Tomorrow morning, all of you are out of here. Is that understood?"

"Perfectly," Faith answered on their behalf.

Not a one of them looked grateful enough. "Count your blessings," Charles snapped.

Really, he had no other choice—besides kicking them out into the cold.

"Thank you," Faith whispered, looking pale and shaken.

Charles glared at the mixed ensemble of characters. Santa, elves, kids and a surprisingly attractive woman stared back at him. "Remember, tomorrow morning you're gone. All of you."

Faith nodded and led Santa and his elves up the stairs.

"Good." First thing in the morning, all these people would be out of this house and out of his life.

Or so Charles hoped. He didn't have the energy to wonder why the tall guy and the six short ones were all in Christmas costume.

Chapter Ten

Early in the evening, Emily and Ray left the condominium. Although it was dark, Ray insisted on showing her the waterfront area. They walked for what seemed like miles, talking and laughing. Ray was a wonderful tour guide, showing her Paul Revere's house and the site of the Boston Tea Party. Both were favorites of his brother's, he pointed out, telling her proudly of Charles's accomplishments as a historian. From the harbor they strolled through St. Stephen's Church and Copp's Hill Burying Ground, which began in 1659 and was the city's second-oldest graveyard. They strolled from one site to the next. Time flew, and when Emily glanced at her watch, she was astonished to discover it was almost eight-thirty.

On Hanover Street, they stopped for dinner at one of Ray's favorite Italian restaurants. The waiter seated them at a corner table and even before handing them menus, he delivered a large piece of cheese and a crusty loaf of warm bread with olive oil for dipping.

"Have I completely worn you out?" Ray asked, smiling over at Emily. He started to peruse the wine list, which had been set in front of him.

Yes, she was tired, but it was a nice kind of tired. "No, quite the contrary. Oh, Ray, thank you so much."

He looked up, obviously surprised.

"A few hours ago, I was feeling utterly sorry for myself. I was staying in one of the most historic cities in our country and all I could think about was how miserable I felt. And right outside my door was all this." She made a wide sweeping gesture with her arm. "I can't thank you enough for opening my eyes to Boston."

He smiled again—and again she was struck by what a fine-looking man he was.

"The pleasure was all mine," he told her softly.

The waiter came with their water glasses and menus. By now, Emily was hungry, and after slicing off pieces of cheese for herself and for Ray, she studied the menu. Ray closed the wine list. After consulting with her, he ordered a bottle of Chianti and an antipasto dish.

As soon as the waiter took their dinner order, Ray leaned back in his seat and reached inside his suit jacket for his cell phone.

"I'd better give my mother a call. I was planning to do it tomorrow, but knowing her, she's waiting anxiously to hear about the strange woman who's corrupted her son."

"You or Charles?" Emily teased.

Ray grinned and punched out a single digit. He raised the small phone to his ear. "Hello, Mother."

His smile widened as he listened for a long moment. "I have someone with me I'd like you to meet."

He had to pause again, listening to his mother's lengthy response.

"Yes, this is the evil woman you feared had ruined your son. She might still do it, too."

"Stop it," Emily mouthed and gently kicked his shoe beneath the table.

"Not to worry—Charles is in Washington State. Here, I'll let Emily explain everything." He handed her the cell phone.

Emily had barely gotten the receiver to her ear when she heard the woman on the other end of the line demand, "To whom am I speaking?"

"Mrs. Brewster, my name is Emily Springer, and Charles and I traded homes for two weeks."

"You're living in Charles's condo?" She didn't seem to believe Emily.

"Yes, but just until after Christmas."

"Oh."

"Charles and I met over the Internet at a site set up for this type of exchange."

"I see." The woman went suspiciously silent.

"It's only for two weeks."

"You're telling me my son let you move into his home sight unseen? And that, furthermore, Charles has ventured all the way to the West Coast?" The question sounded as if it came from a prosecuting attorney who'd found undeniable evidence of perjury.

"Yes... I came to Boston to see my daughter." For the last few days, Emily had tried not to think about Heather, which was nearly impossible.

"Let me speak to Rayburn," his mother said next.

Emily handed the cell phone back to Ray.

Ray and his mother chatted for another few minutes before he closed the phone and stuck it inside his pocket.

By then the wine had been delivered and poured.

Emily reached for her glass and sipped. She enjoyed wine on occasion, but this was a much finer quality than she normally drank.

"Rayburn?" she said, teasing him by using the same tone his mother had used.

He groaned. "If you think that's bad, my little brother's given name is actually Hadley."

"Hadley?"

"Hadley Charles. The minute he was old enough to speak, he refused to let anyone call him Hadley."

Emily smiled. "I can't say I blame him."

"Rayburn isn't much of an improvement."

"No, but it's better than Hadley."

"That depends." Ray sipped his wine and sat up straighter when the waiter brought the antipasto plate. It was a meal unto itself, with several varieties of sliced meats, cheese, olives and roasted peppers.

That course was followed by soup and then pasta. Emily was convinced she couldn't swallow another bite when the main course, a cheese-stuffed chicken dish, was brought out.

When they'd finished, they lingered over another bottle of wine. Ray leaned forward, elbows resting on the table, and they talked, moving from one subject to the next. Emily had hardly ever met a man who was so easy to talk to. He seemed knowledgeable about any number of subjects.

"You're divorced?" he asked, as they turned to more personal matters.

"Widowed. Eleven years ago. Peter was killed when Heather was just a little girl."

"I'm sorry."

"Thank you." She could speak of Peter now without pain, but that had taken years. She was a different woman than she'd been back then, as a young wife and mother. "Peter was a good husband and a wonderful father. I still miss him."

"Is there a reason you've never remarried?"

"Not really. I got caught up in Heather's life and my job. Over the years I've dated now and then, but there was never any spark. What about you?"

He shrugged. "I've been consumed by my job for so long, I don't know what it is to have an ordinary life."

This interested Emily. "I've always wondered what an ordinary life would be like. Does anyone really have one?"

"Good point."

"Did you have any important relationships?"

"I dated quite a bit when I was in my twenties and early thirties. I became seriously involved twice, but both times I realized, almost from the first, that it wouldn't last."

"Sounds like a self-fulfilling prophecy to me."

He grinned as he picked up his wineglass. "My mother said almost those identical words to me. The thing is, I admired both women and, to some extent loved them, but deep down I suspect they knew it wouldn't last, either."

"And it didn't."

"Right. I put long hours into my job and I have a lot of responsibilities. I love publishing. No one's more excited than I am when one of our authors does well."

Emily had plenty of questions about the publishing world, but she knew Ray must have been asked these same questions dozens of times. They had this one evening together, and Emily didn't want to bore him with idle curiosity.

When they'd finished the second bottle of wine, Emily felt mellow and sleepy. Most of the other tables were vacant, and the crew of waiters had started changing tablecloths and refilling the salt and pepper shakers.

Ray noticed the activity going on around them, too. "What time is it?" he asked, sitting up and glancing at his watch with an unbelieving expression.

"It's ten to eleven."

"You're kidding!" He looked shocked.

"Well, you know what they say about time flying, etc."

He chuckled softly. "Tonight certainly was an enjoyable evening—but there's a problem."

"Oh?"

He downed the last of his wine and announced, "I'm afraid the next train doesn't leave for New York until tomorrow morning."

"Oh...right." Emily had entirely forgotten that Ray would have to catch the train.

He relaxed visibly, apparently finding a solution to his problem. "Not to worry, I'll get a hotel room. That shouldn't be too difficult."

Without a reservation, she wondered if that was true. Furthermore, she hated the thought of him spending that extra money on her account. "You don't need to do that."

"What do you mean?"

"Your brother's condo has two bedrooms."

He raised his eyebrows.

"I'm sleeping in the guest room, and I'm sure your brother wouldn't object to your taking his room."

Ray hesitated and looked uncertain. "Are you sure you're comfortable with that arrangement?"

"Of course."

That was easy to say after two bottles of wine. Had Emily been completely sober, she might not have—but really, what could it hurt?

She decided that question was best left unanswered.

Chapter Eleven

Heather Springer wrapped her arms tightly around Elijah's waist, the sound of the wind roaring in her ears. She laid her head against his muscular back and relished the feel of his firm body so close to her own. Three other Harleys, all with passengers, zoomed down the interstate on their way to the white sandy beaches of Florida.

Try as she might, Heather couldn't stop thinking about the bewildered look on her mother's face when she learned Heather had made her own plans for the Christmas holidays.

The least her mother could've done was let her know she was flying to Boston. It was supposed to be a big surprise—well, it definitely was that. Actually, it was more of a shock, and not a pleasant one. Heather had hoped for the proper time to tell her mother about Elijah. That opportunity, unfortunately, had been taken away from her.

Heather sighed. She was grateful when Elijah pulled into a rest area near Daytona Beach. He climbed off the

Harley and removed his helmet, shaking his head to release his long hair.

Heather watched as the other motorcycles pulled into nearby spaces. Heather was proud that Elijah led the way in this adventure. Being with him during the holidays was thrilling, and she wasn't about to let her stick-in-the-mud, old-fashioned mother ruin it.

Elijah was different from any boy Heather had ever dated. The others paled by comparison, especially Ben who was traditional and frankly boring. All he thought about was school and work and getting his law degree. For once, just once, she wanted to think about something besides grades and scholarship money. She wanted to *live*.

She'd met Elijah at Starbucks, and they'd struck up a conversation. That was in early October, and after meeting him everything had changed. Never before had she been in love like this. It was exciting and crazy and new. Elijah's world was completely unlike her own, and she knew their differences were what made him so attractive. He was dark, wild, dangerous—all she'd ever craved. She wanted to share his life, share everything with him. Heather felt pleased that he was introducing her to his friends, but she'd noticed he wasn't interested in meeting hers. That hadn't bothered her until recently. Heather didn't know the other bikers and their girlfriends very well, but she liked them and hoped for the chance to connect.

"Feel that sunshine," Elijah said. He closed his eyes and tilted his face toward the sun.

Heather removed her own helmet and slid off the Harley. "It's not as warm as I thought it would be." She didn't want to complain, but she'd assumed the temperature would be in the seventies; it was closer to the fifties. This wasn't exactly swimming-in-the-ocean kind of weather.

"Once we're in the Miami Beach area you'll be hot enough," Elijah promised. "Until then I'll keep you warm." He circled her waist with his massive arms.

She turned in his embrace, kissing him lightly.

"I thought we'd hang out here for a while," he murmured.

"That sounds good to me." Heather didn't want to admit how much her backside ached, especially when the others didn't seem to have any such complaint. She'd heard one of the girls comment that Heather was walking oddly and then giggle. Heather pretended not to hear. She wasn't one of them, but she badly wanted to be. Given a chance, she'd prove herself, she vowed.

Soon the eight of them were sprawled out on the grass. Elijah lay on his back, his head resting on Heather's lap. She sat leaning against a palm tree.

"You okay?" Elijah asked.

"Of course." She tried to make light of her feelings, rather than confess what she was really thinking.

"You've been pretty quiet."

Heather slipped her fingers through his hair. "I suppose."

"I bet it's your mother."

Heather sighed and realized she couldn't hide her thoughts any longer. "She might've said something, you know."

Elijah nodded. "You couldn't have known she was planning to fly in for Christmas."

Heather twirled a lock of his dark hair around her finger. "She didn't even hint at her plans. It's like she expected me to abandon everything just because she showed up in Boston."

"Parents are unreasonable."

"Yeah." Still, the sick feeling in the pit of her stomach refused to go away.

"It's better with just you and me," he whispered.

Heather didn't bother to mention that there were three other couples tagging along. In the beginning, it was supposed to be just the two of them. But as soon as word got out, several of Elijah's friends had asked to join them. He'd agreed without discussing it with Heather. She hadn't said anything, but she was disappointed.

She'd had their first Christmas together all planned out. Once they reached Miami or the Keys, she'd make this Christmas as special for him as her mother had always made the holiday for her. They'd decorate a tree, sing carols on the beach and open small gifts to each other.

Thinking about her mother depressed her.

"You've got that look again," Elijah muttered, frowning up at her.

"Sorry."

"Forget about her, okay?"

"I'm trying, but it's hard. I wonder what she's doing and who she's with." The thought of her mother all alone tugged at Heather's heart, and despite her best efforts, she couldn't stop feeling guilty. She steeled herself against those emotions. If anyone was to blame for this fiasco, it was her mother, not her!

"You've got to let go of this, or it'll ruin everything," Elijah warned.

"I know."

"You said you and your mother were tight."

"We used to be." Heather knew that nothing would be the same again, and she was glad, she told herself fiercely.

Well, maybe not glad exactly, but relieved that her mother knew about Elijah.

"It's time she understood that you're your own woman and you make your own decisions."

Elijah was repeating the same things she'd told her mother, the same things she'd been saying to herself from the moment they left Boston. "You're right."

"Of course I'm right. She can't dictate to you anymore, you know."

Heather agreed in principle, but that didn't do a thing to ease the knot in her stomach. "I'd feel better if I talked to her."

"You already did."

That was true, but Heather had lingering doubts about their conversation. She'd been shocked and angry when she'd learned her mother was in town. Everything she'd worked toward all these weeks was in danger, and she refused to let her mother ruin her plans.

Elijah studied her, his gaze narrowed. "You've changed your mind, haven't you?"

"About what? Us?" Heather pressed her hands gently against the sides of Elijah's bearded face and stared down at him, letting her love for him fill her eyes. "Oh, Elijah, about us? Never." As if to prove her undying love and devotion, she lowered her mouth to his.

Elijah was a seductive kisser, and he brought his muscular arms around her neck and half lifted his head to meet her lips. His mouth was moist and sensual and before long, any thoughts of her mother vanished completely.

When Elijah released her, Heather kept her eyes closed and sighed softly.

"Are you still worried about your mother?" he teased.

"Mother? What mother?"

Elijah chuckled. "That's what I figured."

Oh, how she loved her motorcycle man.

"You ready to go?" he asked.

The prospect of climbing back on the Harley didn' thrill her, but she tried to sound enthusiastic. "Anytime you say."

Elijah rewarded her with a smile. "And the guys said you'd be trouble."

"Me?"

"College girls generally are."

"So I'm not your first college girl?"

He laughed, but the sound lacked amusement. "I've been around."

She ignored that. She didn't want to hear about any of his other women, because she was determined it would be different with her.

They were good for each other. With Elijah she could throw away her good-girl image and discover her real self. At the same time, she'd teach him about love and responsibility. She didn't know exactly how he made his money, although he always seemed to have enough for gas and beer. But Heather wasn't concerned about that right now; she was determined to enjoy herself.

In one graceful movement Elijah leaped to his feet and stood. As soon as he was upright, the others started to move, too. He was their unspoken leader, their guide to adventure. And Heather was his woman, and she loved it.

Elijah offered Heather his hand, which she took. She brushed the grass and grit from her rear and started back across the grass and the parking lot to where he'd parked the Harley.

Elijah gave Heather her helmet. "You don't need to feel guilty about your mother," he said.

"I don't." But she did. "Still, I think I should call her."

"I thought you said she doesn't have a cell phone."

"She doesn't."

"Do you know where she's staying?"

"No...but—"

"It's out of the question, then, isn't it?"

Heather was forced to agree. Even if she wanted to, she realized in an instant of panic, she had no way of reaching her mother.

Chapter Twelve

*"H*ow much?" Faith Kerrigan couldn't believe what the airline representative on the phone was telling her. According to what he said, her flight back to California would cost nearly twice as much as her original ticket.

"That's if I can find you a seat," he added.

"Oh." Faith could feel a headache coming on. She pressed her fingertips to her temple, which didn't help.

"Do you want me to check for an available flight?" the man asked.

"I—no." Her other option was to wait until there was a rental car available, with a different agency if necessary, and then drive back to California. The fees couldn't possibly be as steep as what the airlines wanted to charge. One thing was certain—she couldn't stay in Leavenworth. She hauled out Emily's phone book and began to call the local car rental places.

This entire Christmas was a disaster. If only she'd talked to Emily before she booked her flight. Oh, no, she groaned to herself, that would have been far too sensible. She'd wanted to surprise her friend. Some surprise! Instead, *she* was the one who'd gotten the shock of her life.

Sam, Tony and the other dwarfs tiptoed around the house as quietly as possible, not wanting to intrude on the curmudgeon. What an unlikable fellow he was! But at least he'd been kind enough not to cast them into the cold dark night. She reminded herself that he'd only delayed it until morning—which made it difficult to maintain much gratitude.

Faith hadn't seen Charles yet. The den door was closed and she could only assume he was on his computer, doing whatever it was he found so important.

"It's time we left," Sam announced once she was off the phone.

Faith still didn't know what she'd do, but the problem was hers and hers alone. Santa and the small troupe of dwarfs gathered around and watched her with anxious expressions.

"Are you sure you'll be safe with *him?*" Tony motioned toward the closed door. Judging by the intense look he wore, he seemed to welcome the opportunity to share his opinion of Charles—with Charles himself.

Faith resisted the urge to kiss his forehead for being so sweet. "I'll be perfectly fine, don't you worry." She hoped she sounded more confident than she felt, but she wanted to send her friends off without burdening them with her troubles.

Sam hesitated, as if he wasn't convinced he should believe her. He scratched his white beard, frowning. "You have a way back to California?"

"Not quite, but I'm working on it. I've called the car rental agency, plus several others. I'm waiting to hear back."

Sam's frown deepened. He seemed about to suggest she join them, but Faith knew that would be impossible.

"You go on," she insisted, "and if I run into any trouble, I'll give you a call." She had his cell phone number. Faith still felt his reluctance, but eventually, after conferring with the others, Sam agreed.

Smiling bravely, she stood on the porch and watched as they climbed into the rental van and backed out of the driveway. She waved until they were out of sight. Her heart sank when she could no longer see them. Soon, far sooner than she was ready, she'd be facing Charles with the unwelcome news from the airlines. Perhaps he'd offer a suggestion, but it was all too clear that he wanted her gone.

Already the two oldest Kennedy children were outside, frolicking in the snow. "Wanna go sledding with us?" Thomas called out to her. He walked toward the park, dragging his sled behind him. His younger brother Jimmy followed, tugging his own sled.

"Maybe later," Faith shouted back. She didn't have the heart to tell him she probably wouldn't be in town much longer.

The cold cut through Faith and she rubbed her hands up and down her arms. She hurried back into the warm comfort of the house, leaning against the closed door as she considered her limited options. She was so deep in thought that it took her a moment to notice Charles standing on the far side of the room.

"Santa and his elves have left?" he asked. "Why were they wearing those outfits, anyway?" He sounded both curious and a touch sardonic.

"Oh—we went to a rest stop and they got changed. We decided it would be part of Emily's Christmas surprise."

"Uh-huh."

Faith avoided eye contact.

"What about you? You're leaving today, too—aren't you?"

Faith raised her index finger and swallowed. "There's… a small problem."

"How small?"

"Well, actually it's a rather large one." She told him how much it would cost to change her flight.

"*How* much?" He sounded as appalled as she was.

"The way it was explained to me is that this would be a new ticket. But the representative said that even if I was willing to pay the change fee, it was unlikely he could find me a seat. I could fly standby, but he told me there are hardly ever any standby seats at this time of year." Faith knew she was giving him more information than necessary, but it was critical that he understand her position.

Charles sighed as if this was too much to take in all at once. "Summarize, please," he snapped—as if she was some freshman in one of his classes, she thought resentfully. "Where does that leave you?"

"Well…I have a rental car…or rather I did until Sam and the dwarfs needed it, so I ended up giving it to them." Again she explained far more than necessary, ending with the tale of the troupe's appearances at hospitals and nursing homes.

"So, you're saying they've left with the one and only van?"

She nodded. "I have calls into several rental agencies now, and they're all looking for a car for me. But rest assured that once I do have a vehicle, I'll be out of here."

"Where will you go?"

She didn't have many options there, either. "Back to California."

Charles had the good grace to look concerned. "You'd be driving at this time of year and in this weather?"

"Do I have a choice?"

He sighed, turned abruptly and walked into the kitchen. "Let me think about this. There's got to be a solution that'd suit both of us."

She was glad he seemed to think there were other options, because she couldn't think of any. The one obvious solution—that she simply stay—was as unpalatable to her as it no doubt was to him.

After a few minutes, Charles returned to the den and closed the door. Apparently he hadn't come up with any creative ideas.

Faith's stomach growled, reminding her that she hadn't eaten since yesterday afternoon. Checking out the refrigerator, she found eggs, cheese and a few vegetables. She whipped up two omelets, then timidly knocked at the den door.

At Charles's gruff reply, she creaked open the door just enough to peer inside. "I made breakfast if you're interested."

"Breakfast? Oh. Yeah, sure."

She didn't need to ask him twice. Maybe half a minute later, Charles joined her at the table. He stared down at his plate, eyes widening as if this was the most delicious meal he'd seen in years.

He sat down and sampled the omelet. "You cook like this all the time?"

Faith wasn't sure what he was asking. "I know my way around a kitchen, if that's what you mean," she said cautiously.

"Every meal?"

"Not always, but I do enjoy cooking."

He ate several more bites, pausing between each one, a blissful expression on his face. "You'd be willing to leave me alone to do my work?"

"If that's a question, I suppose I could manage to keep out of your way." She'd begun to feel hopeful—maybe they *could* compromise.

He studied her narrowly, as if to gauge the truth of her words. "In that case you can stay. You prepare the meals, make yourself scarce, and we'll both cope with this as well as we can. Agreed?"

Faith doubted he knew how gruff and unfriendly he sounded. However... "I could do that."

"Good. I'm here to work. The last thing I'm interested in is Christmas or any of the festivities that seem to have taken over this town. Tell me, are these people crazy? No, don't answer that. Just leave me alone—except for meals, of course."

"Fine."

"I want nothing to do with Christmas. Got that?"

"Yes."

She had no idea what kind of work he was doing, but she'd gladly keep her distance. As for the Christmas part, he'd certainly made his point and she didn't need to hear it again.

"I'll probably have my meals in the den."

"Fine," she said again. As far as she was concerned, the less she had to do with him, the better.

Charles set his fork next to his plate and seemed to be waiting for something more from her.

"I'm willing to make the best of this situation if you are," she finally said. Neither was to blame. They were the victims of a set of unfortunate circumstances.

He nodded solemnly as if to seal their agreement. Then he pushed away from the table and stood. "I will tell you that this is one of the best omelets I've had in years."

She smiled, pleased to hear it. "Thank you." Then she hopped up from the table, taking her plate and cup. "What time would you like lunch?"

"I hadn't thought about it."

"Okay, I'll let you know when it's ready. Fair enough?"

"Certainly." He sounded distracted and eager to get back to his work.

"I'll pick up the groceries," she offered. "It's the least I can do."

His eyes brightened. "That would be appreciated. Just be careful of the goat."

"The goat?"

"Never mind," he muttered and returned to the den.

Chapter Thirteen

Bernice Brewster slept well for the first time in three days. At her age, she shouldn't be worrying about her adult children, but Charles was a concern. For that matter, so was Rayburn. Thankfully her older son had taken her apprehensions to heart and traveled to Boston to check on his younger brother.

Naturally there was a perfectly logical explanation as to why a woman had answered Charles's phone. She should've realized her sensible son wouldn't have some stray woman in the house. Charles was far too intelligent to be taken in by a gold digger. Granted, she'd like nothing better than to see him with the right woman—but there'd be nothing worse than seeing him with the wrong one. Like that Monica. Well, she was a fool and didn't deserve Charles.

Fortunately, Bernice now had the phone number in Washington State where Charles could be reached. She leaned toward the telephone and dialed.

One ring. Two.

"Hello," a female voice answered.

"Hello," Bernice responded, a little uncertainly. She must have written the number down incorrectly. There was only one way to find out and that was to ask. "This phone number was given to me by Emily Springer. Is Charles Brewster there?"

The woman hesitated. "Yes, but he's unavailable at the moment."

Bernice swallowed a gasp and before she could think better of it, slammed down the telephone. Dear heaven, what was happening? Feeling light-headed, she waited until her pounding heart had settled down before she tried to call Rayburn at his apartment. She wanted to know what was going on and she wanted to know right this minute.

When Rayburn didn't answer, she tried his office and learned he was still in Boston.

"Why?" she demanded of his assistant. "Why is he still in Boston?"

"I'm sorry, Mrs. Brewster," the young woman said politely. "Mr. Brewster phoned the office this morning and that's what he said."

"He has his cell phone?" Of course he did, because he'd called her on it the night before.

"I believe he does."

Bernice carefully punched out the cell number and waited. The phone rang four times before her son answered.

"Ray Brewster."

"Rayburn," she gasped, overwhelmed by her children's odd behavior. His greeting had sounded far too friendly, as if he'd been laughing. Well, this was no laughing matter!

"Mother." The sound of her voice sobered him up fast

enough, she noticed. Something very suspicious was going on.

"Where *are* you?" she demanded.

"I'm forty-three years old. I no longer need to check in with you."

How dared he speak to her in that tone! She was about to say so when Rayburn chuckled.

"If you must know, I'm in Boston at Charles's condo."

"There's a *woman* there."

"I already know that, Mother."

Bernice gasped. "You spent the night with her?"

"I was in the same condo, not that it's any of your business."

Bernice pulled out her lace-edged hankie and clenched it tightly. "I...I have no idea where your father and I went wrong that both my sons—"

"Mother, take a deep breath and start over."

Bernice tried, she honestly tried, but her heart was pounding and her head spinning. "I phoned the number you gave me and...another woman answered."

"A woman? Are you sure you had the right number?"

"Of course I'm sure. I asked and she said Charles was unavailable."

"Hold on, let me ask Emily who it might be."

Emily, was it? "I see you're on a first-name basis with this—this house-stealer."

To her chagrin, Rayburn laughed. "Honestly, Mother, I think you missed your calling. You should've been on the stage."

Her husband used to make the same claim, and while she did have a good stage presence, she suspected Rayburn didn't mean it as a compliment.

Bernice could hear him in the background, but hard as she pressed her ear against the receiver, she couldn't make out what was being said.

"Emily says she doesn't have a clue who would be answering the phone at her place. She'll call later and find out if you wish."

"If I *wish?*" Bernice repeated.

"All right, I'll get back to you."

Her son was about to hang up, but she still had more to say. "Rayburn," she shouted. "You behave yourself with this woman, understand?"

"Yes, Mother."

The phone line went dead.

"A woman answered?" Emily repeated after Ray ended the conversation with his mother. "Now, that's interesting."

"Who do you think it might be?"

Emily shrugged. "Don't know, but it'll be easy enough to find out." She went to the telephone and punched out her own number in Washington State.

The line was picked up almost right away. "Hello."

"Faith?" Emily shrieked. "Faith? Is it really you?"

"Emily?"

They both started talking at once, blurting out questions and answers, then each explained in turn. Even then, it took Emily a few moments to discern what had actually happened.

"Oh, no! You came to spend Christmas with me and I'm not there."

"You went to Boston to be with Heather and now she's in Florida?"

"Yes, but I can't think about it, otherwise I'll get too upset."

Faith was sympathetic. "I felt so badly for the way I brushed off your disappointment."

"And now you're trapped in Leavenworth."

"There are worse places to be this time of year," Faith said. She seemed to be in a good frame of mind. "Charles and I have reached an agreement," she went on to say. "I'm staying until after Christmas, and in exchange, I'll keep out of his way and cook his meals."

While her friend put a positive slant on the situation, Emily realized Faith had to be miserable. Alone—or virtually alone—at Christmas.

"What about you?" Faith asked.

"I'm stuck in Boston, but it's really a lovely town." Still, none of that mattered now. "Oh, Faith, what a good friend you are to go to all this trouble for me."

"Well, I tried."

Emily wanted to weep. Despite everything, it seemed she was destined to spend the holidays by herself. Still, she'd had a wonderful evening with Ray and felt attractive and carefree in a way she hadn't in years.

They talked for several minutes longer, making plans to call each other again. When she finished, Emily replaced the receiver and looked over at Ray, smiling.

"I take it she's someone you know?"

Emily told him what had happened. "I was lucky I caught her. Faith was on her way outside to go sledding with the neighbor kids. She's so good with children."

"Faith sounds like a fun-loving person."

"She is."

"She's staying, then?"

Emily nodded. "She and Charles have worked out a compromise." Emily felt guilty about the whole mess. Poor

Charles. All he wanted was to escape Christmas and have time to work without interruption. But, between Faith and the Kennedy children, Emily figured the poor man wouldn't have a moment's peace.

Ray drank the rest of his coffee and set his mug aside. "I guess I'd better head back to New York."

Emily knew it was too much to hope that he'd stay on. "I can't let you go without breakfast," she said brightly.

Ray seemed almost relieved at being given an excuse to linger. "Are you sure I'm not disrupting your plans?"

"Plans? What plans? I'm here for another week and I don't know a soul in town." She opened the cupboard, looking for ideas, and found an old-fashioned waffle iron. She brought it down, oiled it and plugged it in.

"I wondered what happened to Mom's old waffle iron," Ray said as he leaned against the counter. He watched Emily assemble ingredients.

"Are you hungry?" he asked.

She shrugged as she cracked an egg against the side of the bowl. "Not really… The truth is, I'm just delaying the inevitable." It probably wasn't polite to be this truthful, but she was beyond pretense. The minute Ray walked out that door, she'd be alone again and she'd enjoyed his company.

"Actually, I'm not hungry, either."

"You aren't?" The question came out in a rushed whisper.

Ray shook his head. "I was looking for an excuse to stay."

He and Emily exchanged a grin.

"Do we actually need an excuse?" he asked.

Emily didn't know how to answer or even if she should. "Do you have to go back to New York?"

"At the moment I can't think of a single compelling reason."

"Would you be interested in staying in Boston for Christmas? With me?" Normally she wasn't this direct, but she had little to lose and so much to gain.

"I can't imagine anyone I'd rather spend Christmas with."

Chapter Fourteen

On a mission now, Faith walked down Main Street in Leavenworth and headed for her favorite grocery. Even after a number of years away, she was astonished by the number of people who remembered her. Five years earlier, she'd done her student teaching in Leavenworth and worked in Emily's classroom.

Newly divorced, emotionally fragile and struggling to pick up the pieces of her life, she'd come to this out-of-the-way community. The town had welcomed her, and with Emily as her friend, she'd learned that life does continue.

The three months she'd spent with Emily had been like a reprieve for Faith, providing a much-needed escape from her badly bungled life. Once her student teaching was completed, she'd moved back to Seattle and soon afterward graduated with her master's degree in education. Diploma in hand, she'd gone to California to be closer to family.

Although she'd moved away from Leavenworth, Faith had stayed in contact with Emily. Their friendship had continued to grow, despite the physical distance between them and the difference in their ages. In fact, Faith felt she could talk to Emily in ways she couldn't talk to her mother. They were colleagues, but not only that, they'd both experienced the loss of a marriage, albeit for very different reasons and in very different ways.

They made a point of getting together every summer. Usually they met in Seattle or California. The long-distance aspect of the relationship hadn't been a hindrance.

Faith's family and friends were important to her; romance, though, was another matter. She was rather frightened of it. Her marriage had burned her and while she'd like to be settled and married with children, that didn't seem likely now.

As she walked through town, Faith waved at people she recognized. Some immediately waved back; one woman stopped and stared as if she had yet to place her. The living Nativity wasn't scheduled until the afternoon, so she was safe from the goat Charles had mentioned. She'd figured out that the infamous Clara Belle—she remembered Emily's hilarious story about a farm visit with her kindergarten class—had to be the goat in question.

Thinking of Charles made her smile. He was an interesting character. If he hadn't already told her, she would've guessed he was an academic. He fit the stereotype of the absentminded professor perfectly—a researcher who became so absorbed in his work, he needed someone to tell him when and where he needed to be.

He did have a heart, though. Otherwise she'd probably be hitchhiking back to California by now. As long as she made herself invisible, they would manage.

Once inside the store, she got a grocery cart and wandered aimlessly down the aisle, seeking inspiration for dinner. She decided on baked green peppers stuffed with a rice, tomato soup and ground beef mixture. The recipe was her mother's but Faith rarely made it. Cooking for one was a chore and it was often easier to pick up something on the way home from school. Fresh cranberries were on sale, so she grabbed a package of those, although she hadn't decided what to do with them. It seemed a Christmassy thing to buy. She'd find a use for them later.

She'd come up with menus for the rest of the week this afternoon, and write a more complete grocery list then.

On the walk home, Faith discovered the Kennedy kids and about half the town's children sledding down the big hill in the park. If her arms hadn't been full, she would've stopped and taken a trip down the hill herself.

The kids were so involved in their fun that they didn't notice her. Breathless, Faith brought everything into the kitchen. She removed her hat and gloves and draped her coat over the back of a chair. Unpacking the groceries, she sang a Christmas song that was running through her mind.

The door to the den flew open and Charles stood in the doorway glaring at her.

Faith stopped midway to the refrigerator, a package of ground beef in her hand. "Was I making too much noise?" she asked guiltily. In her own opinion, she'd been quiet and subdued, but apparently not.

"I'm trying to work here," he told her severely.

"Sorry," she mouthed and tiptoed back to the kitchen counter.

"You aren't planning to do anything like bake cookies, are you?" He wrinkled his nose as if to say he wasn't interested.

"Uh, I hadn't given it any thought."

"In case you do, you should know I don't want to be distracted by smells, either."

"Smells?" With an effort, Faith managed not to groan out loud.

"The aroma of baking cookies makes my stomach growl."

He wasn't kidding, and Faith found that humorous, although she dared not show it. She was able to stay here only with his approval and couldn't afford to jeopardize her position. "Then rest assured. I won't do anything to make your stomach growl."

"Good." With that, Charles retreated into the den, closing the door decisively.

Faith rolled her eyes. What was she supposed to do all day? Sit in a corner and knit? Play solitaire? If that little bit of commotion had bothered His Highness, then she couldn't see this arrangement working. And yet, what was the alternative?

The awful part was that she felt an almost overwhelming urge to bang lids together. Standing in the middle of the kitchen, she had to bite her lower lip to restrain herself from singing at the top of her lungs and stomping her feet.

This was crazy. Ludicrous. Still, it was all she could do not to behave in the most infantile manner. If she was going to behave like a child, then she might as well join the children. This close to Christmas, they had a lot of pent-up energy.

Dressed in hat, gloves and her coat once again, Faith went outside. The snow on the front lawn was untouched. A fresh layer had fallen overnight, and with time on her hands, she made an impulsive decision to build a snowman. She grinned as she looked at the specimen in the neighbor's yard.

Starting with a small hand-size ball of snow, she rolled it across the lawn, letting it grow larger and fuller with each sweep.

"Do you want me to help?" Sarah asked, appearing at her side.

Sarah was a favorite of Emily's, Faith knew. As the youngest in a big family, she'd learned to hold her own.

"I sure do."

The little girl beamed as Faith resumed the snow-rolling task. "The bottom part of the snowman has to be the biggest," Sarah pointed out, obviously taking on supervisory responsibilities.

"Right."

"Dylan says it's the most important part, too."

Dylan, if Faith remembered correctly, lived down the street and was a good friend to one of the Kennedy boys.

"Are you building a fort?" Thomas shouted, hurrying across the street from the park. He abandoned his sled near the front porch.

"This is a nice friendly snowman," Faith assured him.

Thomas narrowed his eyes. "Looks more like a snow fort to me."

"It's a ball," Sarah primly informed her brother, hands on her hips. "Anyone can see that."

"I don't think so." Thomas raced over to his own yard and started rolling snow. He was quickly joined by his brothers. The boys worked feverishly at constructing their fort.

Sarah and Faith hurried to catch up, changing their tactics. There were four boys against the two of them, but what they lacked in numbers they made up for in cunning. While Faith built their defensive wall, Sarah rolled snowballs, stacking them in neat piles out of sight of her brothers.

"Now, boys," Faith said, standing up and strolling to the middle of the battleground between their two yards. "I'm telling you right now that it's not a good thing to pick a fight with girls."

"Yeah, because they tattle."

"Do not," Sarah screeched.

"Do, too."

Faith stretched out her arms to silence both sides. "Sarah and I were innocently building a friendly snowman for Mrs. Springer's front yard when we were accused of constructing a snow fort."

"It *is* a snow fort," Thomas insisted, pointing accusingly at the wall of snow.

"It became one when you started building yours," Faith said. "But before we go to war, I feel honor bound to look for some means of making peace."

"No way!" Mark cried.

"Hear me out," Faith urged. "First of all, it's unfair. There are more of you than of us."

"I ain't going over to the girls' side," Mark protested.

"We don't want any boys, anyway," Sarah shouted back.

Again Faith silenced them. "You don't want peace?"

"No!" Thomas tossed a snowball straight up and batted it down with his hand as if to prove his expertise.

"Forget it," Mark seconded.

"Then we have to make it a fair fight."

The boys were silent, apparently waiting for one of them to volunteer. No one did.

"I suggest that in order to even things up, the boys' side is restricted to the use of one hand. Agreed?"

The boys grinned and nodded.

"Your left hand," she added.

Their laughter and snickers quickly died out. "Ah, come on..."

Not giving the group a chance to argue, Faith tossed the first snowball, which landed just short of the snow fortification. Before the boys had time to react, she raced back to Sarah. The little girl was crouched behind the shelter and had accumulated a huge pile of snowballs.

Soon they were all laughing and pelting each other with snow. Faith managed to land several wildly thrown snowballs, but she was on the receiving end just as often. At one point she glanced toward the house and saw Charles looking out the living-room window.

Oh, no. Even a snowball fight was too much racket for him. Unfortunately, the distraction cost her. Thomas, who was fast becoming accustomed to pitching snowballs left-handed, scored a direct hit. The snowball struck her square in the chest. Snow sprayed up into her face, and Faith made a show of sputtering.

"Gotcha," Thomas cried and did a jig of triumph, leaping up and down with his arms above his head.

Faith glanced at the house again and saw Charles laughing. She did a double take. The man could actually laugh? This was news. Perhaps he wasn't so stuffy, after all. Perhaps she'd misread him entirely.

Was that possible?

Chapter Fifteen

"This is the Old North Church?" Emily stood outside Christ Church, made famous in the Longfellow poem. "The 'one if by land, two if by sea' church?"

"The very one," Ray assured her. "Boston's oldest surviving religious structure."

Emily tilted back her head and looked to the very top of the belfry. "If I remember my history correctly, a sexton…"

"Robert Newman."

She nodded. "He warned Paul Revere and the patriots that the British were coming."

"Correct. You may go to the head of the class."

Emily had always been fascinated by history. "I loved school. I was a good student," she said. A trait her daughter had inherited.

"I can believe it," Ray said, guiding her inside the church.

They toured it briefly, and Emily marveled as Ray dramatically described that fateful night in America's history.

"How do you know so much about this?"

Ray grinned. "You mean other than through Charles,

who's lived and breathed this stuff from the time he was a kid?"

"Yes."

"The truth is that, years ago, I edited a book—a mystery novel, actually—in which the Old North Church played a major role in the plot."

Emily was so enraptured by Boston's history that she'd forgotten Ray was an important figure in New York publishing.

"As a matter of fact, I have plenty of trivia in the back of my mind from my years as a hands-on editor."

As they walked, Ray described a number of books he'd edited and influential authors he'd worked with. Apparently he no longer did much of that. Instead he had a more administrative role.

Emily found it very easy to talk to Ray, and the hours melted away. It seemed they'd hardly left the condominium, but it was already growing dark. She admired the Christmas lights and festive displays, which weren't like those in Leavenworth, but equally appealing.

They stopped for a seafood dinner and then walked around some more, taking in the sights and sounds of the season. As Emily told him about Leavenworth, Ray grew more amused with each anecdote. "I wish I could be there to see Charles's reaction."

Emily continued to feel guilty about Ray's brother—and about Faith—but she couldn't have known. Her one wish was that Faith and Charles would be as compatible as she and Ray.

Being with him these last few days before Christmas made all the difference in the world. If not for Ray, she'd probably be holed up in the condo baking dozens of cookies and feeling sorry for herself.

"Despite all the mix-ups, I'm glad I'm here," she told him.

"I'm glad you're here, too," Ray said. "I'm enjoying your company so much. Do you want to know what else I'm enjoying?"

Emily could only guess. "Being in Boston again?"

"Well, that too. But what I mean is that I'm completely free of phone calls."

The first thing Ray had done, once he'd contacted his office and informed his assistant that he wouldn't be returning until after the holidays, was turn off his cell phone.

"You might have missed an important call," she reminded him.

"Tough. Whoever's in the office can handle it this time. I'm unavailable." He laughed as he said it.

Emily laughed because he did, but from the little she'd learned about his work, it was a hectic series of meetings and continual phone calls. Ray must be under constant pressure, dealing with agents' and authors' demands, in addition to various vice presidents, sales and marketing personnel, advertising firms and more. Although he held a prominent position with the company and obviously interacted with many people, he seemed as lonely as she was. He'd told her that aside from his work and a few social commitments, he had no reason to rush back to New York. Indeed, he seemed eager to stay here in Boston.

"Coffee?" he asked when they reached the Starbucks where she'd had her last encounter with Heather.

Emily hesitated, but then agreed. After all these hours of walking, she was exhausted and her feet hurt. Yet, at the same time, she was invigorated by everything she'd seen and done—and utterly charmed by Ray.

While he stepped up to the counter to order their

drinks, she secured a table. As luck would have it, the only vacant one was the same table she'd occupied while waiting to meet her daughter. Her thoughts inevitably flashed to Heather, and Emily wondered where she was now and what she was doing. No, it was probably best not to know.

A few minutes later, Ray joined her with two tall cups of coffee. He slipped into the seat across from her. "Time like this is a luxury for me," he said.

"I want you to know how much I appreciate—"

He took her hand, stopping her. "What I'm trying to say, I guess, is that I've avoided it."

Emily frowned, uncertain she understood his meaning.

"I loved being with you today, talking and laughing with you. The truth is, I can't remember any day I've enjoyed more in a very long while."

"But I'm the one who's indebted to you."

"No," he said emphatically. "*I'm* the one who owes *you*. I'd forgotten," he said quietly, "what it's like to give myself a free day. To do something that's not related to work." He paused. "There seems to be a great deal in my life that I've let slide. I needed this wake-up call."

"In other words, I'm an alarm clock?"

He grinned. "You're more than that."

They were flirting with each other, she realized. Normally, conversations such as this terrified her. She'd married her high-school sweetheart and had rarely dated since Peter's death. Her daughter, sad as it was to admit, had more experience with men than she did.

Despite her determination not to, she was worrying about Heather again. Tears filled her eyes.

"Are you okay?"

Embarrassed, she nodded. Wiping the tears from her

cheeks, she offered him a watery smile. "I was just thinking about my daughter."

"She's with friends, isn't she?"

"So she says." Emily rolled her eyes.

"Everyone has to grow up sooner or later, and among other things, that means learning how to judge other people's intentions." He shrugged. "Some lessons are more painful than others."

Sniffling a little, Emily agreed. "I can't think about Heather, otherwise I'll get upset. It's just that I had all these plans for the two of us over Christmas."

"What kind of plans?"

It seemed a little silly to tell Ray about them now. "I packed our favorite Christmas ornaments, so we could decorate a tree the same way we do every year."

"You and I could get a tree."

"You'd be willing to do that?"

"It's Christmas, isn't it? I haven't put up a tree in years."

"No tree?"

He chuckled. "Too much bother to do it on my own, but I'd love to help you. First thing in the morning, we'll buy a tree."

Her spirits brightened instantly.

"Anything else?"

"I always roast the traditional turkey, but I felt that since we were in Boston we should cook lobster. I love lobster tail with lots of melted butter. I've never prepared a whole lobster, though. I thought it'd be fun to go to a fish market and pick one out."

"That sounds like an excellent idea. Lobster for two."

"This is great!" Emily crowed happily.

After finishing their coffee, they walked back to the condominium hand in hand. By the time they rode up in the elevator, Ray had his arm around her. Being this close to him felt…natural. She rested her head against his shoulder.

Ray unlocked the door and swung it open, but he didn't immediately reach for the light switch. When Emily stepped into the living room, Ray turned her into his arms. He closed the front door with his foot, and they stood in near darkness, the only light seeping in through the blinds. She leaned against him, eyes drifting shut.

Ray's palm cradled her cheek, his touch gentle. He rubbed his thumb across her lips and Emily sighed, wanting him to kiss her, afraid he wouldn't—yet afraid he would.

Standing on her toes, she slipped her arms around his neck and whispered, "Thank you for the most wonderful day."

"Thank *you*." His lips found hers then, and it was sweet and sensual all at once.

He brought her full against him as their mouths met again and again, one unhurried kiss following another. Emily's senses spun out of control but she pulled back, fearful of what might happen if they allowed this to continue.

Ray exhaled shakily. "I'm not sure that was a good idea, but I'm not sorry. Not at all…"

Emily kissed the side of his jaw. "Me, neither," she whispered.

She felt his smile. "Don't worry, Ray, I promise not to ravish you," she teased.

"Damn."

"Well…" Emily laughed softly. "I could reconsider."

It was Ray's turn to be amused. "You ready for the lights?"

"I suppose."

When Ray touched the switch, the room instantly went from dark to bright. But he didn't immediately release her.

When they separated and moved farther into the room, Emily noticed the flashing message light on the phone. Ray noticed it, too. Emily's hopes soared—could it be Heather?—but then she remembered that her daughter didn't know where she was staying.

Ray pushed the caller ID button and groaned. "Four calls," he muttered, "and they're all from my mother."

Chapter Sixteen

Southern Florida in December was paradise. There was no other word for it. The beach was flawless, the water blue and clear and warm, the sunshine constant. It was as close to heaven as anyone who'd spent a winter in Boston could imagine.

What Heather didn't know was why she felt so miserable in such a perfect setting. She had every reason in the world to be happy, but she wasn't. To make matters worse, Elijah was growing irritated with her moods.

"Get me a beer," her hero called from where he was stretched out beneath a palm tree on the beach, one of his stalwart companions beside him.

Heather got up from the beach towel where she was sunbathing and walked back into their motel room. She opened the small refrigerator and brought out a cold beer. Without a word she delivered it to Elijah. He looked at his friend, nodded, and the other man stood up and left.

"Let's talk," Elijah said, patting the sand next to him.

"About what?" Heather crossed her arms stubbornly.

"Sit down," he ordered. He pointed at the empty space his friend had just vacated.

Reluctantly Heather joined him.

"All right," he muttered after opening the beer. He took a long swig and wiped the back of his hand across his mouth. "What's wrong?"

"Nothing."

"Don't give me that. You haven't been yourself since we left Boston."

Heather didn't say anything. He knew she felt terrible about leaving her mother behind. If he couldn't figure it out, then she wasn't going to tell him.

"I thought you'd like Florida." Elijah made it sound like an accusation, as if he'd done everything humanly possible to provide for her happiness.

"What's not to like?"

Elijah nodded. "Exactly—so what's the problem?"

"You're right. I'm not happy."

He wrapped his arm around her neck, the cold beer bottle dangling between two fingers. "What is it, babe?"

Heather cringed at his use of the word *babe,* but she'd given up trying to convince Elijah to call her anything else. What particularly irritated her was that she suspected it was the term he used with all his girlfriends.

"If you must know, I'm worried about my mother."

Elijah tightened his grip around her neck by taking another healthy swig of beer. "I thought we already talked that out."

"We talked." He seemed to think it was a closed subject. Heather wished it was, but none of this was turning out the way she'd hoped. The motel was a dump, she was sick of fast food, the other women didn't like her, and...

"What is it now?"

She shook her head, letting her long hair swing. "Nothing."

"Don't give me that," he said again. "You've been in a piss-poor mood from the get-go." He spread his arms and looked out at the rolling waves of the ocean. "Here we are in paradise and you're whining about your mother." He made it sound ludicrous.

Maybe it was, but Heather couldn't help herself. "I'm just worried about her."

"You're *worried* about Mommy?" Now he made it seem like one big joke and that infuriated her even more.

"You don't have a clue," Heather cried. Vaulting to her feet, she tore down the beach, kicking up sand. A few minutes later, she was out of breath and started walking, her eyes filled with tears.

"Wait up," Elijah shouted.

She was surprised he'd come after her. Heather waited for him and then fell into his arms, weeping softly. Elijah held her in his muscular embrace.

"All right, babe, tell me all about it."

"You don't understand."

He kissed the side of her neck. "I can't be happy when you're miserable, you know."

And that made Heather remember why she loved him. Taking a deep breath, she tried to explain.

"Mom was born and raised in this dinky town in Washington State. This is her first trip to the East Coast."

"Get out of here! Her first trip?"

Heather nodded. "I left her all by herself."

"She loves you, right?"

"Of course. She's my mother."

"And you love her?"

"Of course—why else would I feel so awful?"

"Don't you think she'd want you to be happy?" Elijah asked as if following his logic was a simple thing.

"Yes, I suppose, but…" Heather felt confused and unsure. "I wish it was that easy."

"It is," he argued. "Just don't think about her."

"She's probably miserable and alone, and I did this to her."

"Babe," he said, more gruffly this time. "You didn't ask her to fly to Boston, did you?" When she shook her head, he muttered, "Then get a grip. The others are starting to complain."

"Who?"

"Peaches, for one."

Heather had tried to make friends with the women but they were impossible. She was a college girl, so they disliked and mistrusted her on sight.

"Peaches would complain about me no matter what I said or did."

"That's not true," Elijah asserted.

"Yes, it is. It's the same with the others." She didn't mention the way the other girls had made fun of her. Heather wasn't accustomed to riding on a motorcycle for long periods of time and suffered a bad case of TB, better known as tired butt.

"Walk with me," Heather suggested, tugging at his arm.

Elijah hesitated. His only concession to the beach was a sleeveless T-shirt. Even in the Miami sunshine, he wore his leather pants and boots.

"Just for a little way," Heather coaxed.

Elijah glanced over his shoulder and then nodded. "Not far, all right?"

"Sure." At the moment Heather would have promised him anything. They hadn't been alone since they'd left Boston. Even the motel room was shared with another couple. Naturally she was stuck with Peaches, who made no effort to hide her disdain for Heather.

They walked for a while, until Elijah decided they'd gone far enough, and sat down in the sand. "Tell me about *your* mother," Heather said, pressing her head against his shoulder.

Elijah was silent for a moment. "Not much to tell. She's a regular mother, or I think she would've been if she'd stayed around."

"I'm sorry." Heather felt bad for bringing up unhappy memories.

"It was a bummer after she left, but I survived."

"What was Christmas like for you?"

Elijah pulled out his pack of cigarettes, lit one up and took a drag before responding. "It wasn't any Santa down the chimney, if that's what you mean."

"How so?"

"Did I mention my dad took off a year before my mother?"

"No." Heather felt worse than ever.

"No big deal. We had good foster parents, and the state always made sure we had at least one gift under the tree."

Heather slid her arm around his waist.

"What about you?" he asked.

"You don't want to know."

"Sure I do," he countered.

Heather wasn't sure where to start. "I told you about Leavenworth, right?"

"Yeah, it's a Bavarian kind of town, you said."

"Right. Christmas is a big deal there and with my mother, too. I think she always wanted to make up for the fact that my dad died when I was young, so she really did the Christmas thing up big. We had dozens of traditions." Heather grew sad again, just thinking about all she was missing.

"You're a big girl now," Elijah told her. "Traditions are for kids."

Heather nodded but she wanted to tell him that people didn't outgrow their need for a Christmas stocking or decorating a tree or hot apple cider on Christmas Eve.

Elijah sighed. "Are you okay now?"

She shrugged. "I guess."

"Good." He stabbed his cigarette into the sand and then stood. Extending his hand to her, Elijah helped Heather to her feet.

"Thank you," she whispered, kissing him.

"That's much better," he said. He placed one arm around her waist and drew her close. "Forget about your mother."

Heather doubted she could. Despite everything, she knew her mother was all alone in Boston, completely miserable without her.

Chapter Seventeen

Faith basted the roasting chicken and closed the oven door as quietly as possible. Rather than mash the potatoes with the mixer, she decided to use the hand utensil in an effort to cut down on noise. As far as she could discern, the cranky professor had enjoyed her cooking the night before. The stuffed green peppers had disappeared in short order.

By six, the house was dark and dreary. Faith went from room to room, drawing the curtains and turning on lights. She played solitaire for an hour. Then she finished the dinner preparations and set the table for one. Before serving herself, she sautéed the green beans with bacon bits and onion, sliced the gelatin salad and carved the roast chicken. Then she lit two candles on the dining-room table and filled her own plate from the dishes in the kitchen. The closed den door discouraged her from letting Charles know dinner was ready. Once she'd eaten, she'd make up a plate for him and leave it on the kitchen counter; he could warm it up in the microwave when he was hungry. That was what she'd done yesterday.

Faith sat down at the far end of the dining-room table and spread the linen napkin across her lap. Emily always used real cloth napkins. Faith admired that about her friend. Living on her own, Faith tended to treat meals as a necessary evil, but when she dined with Emily, meals were an event to be savored and shared. So, in Emily's house and in Emily's honor, Faith would keep up this tradition.

Reaching for the merlot she'd bought that day, she started to pour herself a glass, then stopped, the bottle suspended, when she realized Charles had emerged from the den. He stood in the dining room, looking a bit disoriented. He stared at her as if he'd forgotten she was in the house.

Faith stood. "Would you like me to get you a plate?"

Charles frowned at the grandfather clock. "I had no idea it was six-thirty." The clock marked the half hour with a resounding clang, punctuating his words. "Uh, do you mind if I join you?" he asked.

Faith was too shocked to reply. "P-please do," she stuttered after an embarrassingly long pause.

Charles went into the kitchen for a plate and served himself from the various dishes she'd prepared, then returned to the dining room. He sat at the opposite end of the table.

They remained awkward with each other. He made a polite comment about the food; she responded with equal politeness.

Silence! Faith desperately wished she had the nerve to put on a Christmas CD—maybe a Celtic Christmas recording Emily had. Or an instrumental of classic carols.

She cleared her throat. "Would you like some merlot?" she offered. She preferred red wine to white, which was why she chose to drink a red with chicken.

"Thank you."

Before she could stand, he got up and retrieved a second wineglass from the kitchen, poured his wine and sat down.

An uneasy silence settled between them once again. Faith picked up her fork and resumed eating.

"How did your snow war end yesterday afternoon?" Charles asked in a casual voice.

"Successfully—for the girls," Faith told him in cordial tones. "The boys surrendered when they saw they were outwitted and overpowered by us."

Charles nodded. "I had a feeling the boy team needed my assistance."

This time, Faith managed to hide her shock.

He glanced at her and grinned—actually grinned. "My aim is excellent, if I do say so myself."

"Oh." She couldn't think of a thing to say. What suddenly filled her mind was a vision of Charles Brewster throwing snowballs, surrounded by a swarm of young boys.

"So you survived the adventure unscathed."

"I sure did." She wasn't telling him how much her shoulders ached and she'd ended up taking aspirin before retiring last night, nor did she mention that she'd soaked in a hot tub for twenty minutes. Today she'd gone shopping, list in hand, and when she returned, she'd lounged in front of the fireplace with a good book and a cup of warm cocoa, keeping as still as possible.

"You enjoyed seeing me get plowed, didn't you?" she asked, again in the most conversational of tones.

"Dare I admit that I did?" He smiled once more, and it transformed his face, reminding Faith of her reaction to his laughter the day before. *Had* she been wrong about him?

"I wish you had joined us," she told him impulsively.

"I was tempted."

"Why didn't you?"

He shrugged and lifted his wineglass. "Mainly because I've got work to do—but that isn't the only reason I'm here." He gestured at the window. "Hard as it is to believe, I came here to avoid Christmas."

Had her mouth been full, Faith would have choked. "You came to *Leavenworth* to avoid Christmas?"

He shrugged again. "I thought it would be a nice quiet prison community."

"That's Leavenworth, Kansas."

"I eventually remembered that."

Faith couldn't keep from laughing.

"I'm delighted you find this so amusing."

"Sorry, I don't mean to make fun of your situation, but it really is kind of funny."

"It's your situation, too," he said. "You're stuck here, just like I am."

Faith didn't need any reminders. "What are you working on?" she asked in an effort to change the subject.

"I'm a history professor at Harvard, specializing in the early-American era."

It made sense that he taught at Harvard, Faith supposed; he lived in Boston, after all.

"I'm contracted to write a textbook, which is due at my publisher's early in the new year."

"How far are you with it?"

"Actually it's finished. I was almost done when I arrived, and my goal is to polish the rough draft in the remaining time I'm here."

"Will you be able to do that?"

"I'm astonished at all the writing I've accomplished since

I got here. I finished the rough draft about fifteen minutes ago." He couldn't quite suppress a proud smile.

"Then congratulations are in order," she said, raising her wineglass to salute him.

Charles raised his glass, too, and they simultaneously sipped the merlot.

"Actually, early American history is a favorite subject of mine," Faith told him. "I teach English literature at the junior-high level but I include some background in American history whenever I can. Like when I teach Washington Irving. The kids love 'The Legend of Sleepy Hollow.'"

"Don't we all?"

After that, they launched into a lively discussion, touching on the Boston Tea Party, Longfellow's poetry, writings of the Revolutionary War period and the War of 1812.

"You know your history," he said. "And your American literature."

"Thank you." She heard the admiration in his voice and it warmed her from the inside out. "I like to think I can hold my own in snowball fights and battles of wits and words."

"No doubt you can." Charles stood and carried both plates into the kitchen. "Shall we finish our wine in the living room?" he surprised her by asking.

"That would be lovely."

The fire had died down to embers, so Charles added another log. He sat in the big overstuffed chair and stretched out his long legs, crossing them at the ankle. Faith sat on the rug by the fireplace, bringing her knees up to her chin as she reveled in the warmth.

"I've always loved this town," she said.

"Thus far, I haven't been very impressed," Charles said,

a little sardonically. "But my predicament hasn't turned out to be nearly as disastrous as I feared."

Faith couldn't have held back a smile if she tried. "I don't think I'll ever forget the look on your face when I showed up with Santa and the elves."

"I don't think I'll ever forget the look on yours when I walked out of that bathroom."

"I was expecting Emily."

"I wasn't expecting anyone."

They both laughed.

"You're not nearly so intimidating when you laugh."

"Me, intimidating?" Charles asked as if she were joking.

"You can be, you know."

He seemed puzzled by that, shaking his head.

"I suspect you don't get angry often," she went on, "but when you do…"

"When I do," he said, completing her thought, "people know it."

He'd certainly made his feelings known shortly after her arrival. "I really appreciate your letting me stay," she told him.

"Actually, after a meal like that and last night's too, I think I'm the fortunate one."

"I've enjoyed cooking the last couple of days. I don't do much of it anymore. Usually I grab something on my way home from school."

"Me, too," he said. "You live alone?"

Faith nodded. "I've been divorced for more than five years." She was too embarrassed to admit how short-lived her marriage had been. "What about you?"

"I've never been married."

"Are you involved with anyone?" Faith asked the question before she had time to think about what it might reveal.

Charles shook his head. "No, my work's always been my life."

Suddenly the room seemed to grow very warm. Faith looked up and found Charles studying her as if seeing her for the first time.

Uncomfortable under his scrutiny, Faith came gracefully to her feet. "I'd better do the dishes," she said.

"Wait." Charles stood, too. "I'll help."

"No, really, that isn't necessary." Faith didn't understand *why* it was so important to put distance between them, but it was. She knew that instinctively. They'd shared a wonderful meal, found common ground, discussed history and even exchanged a few personal facts. They were attracted to each other. She felt it; he felt it, too, Faith was sure, and it unnerved her.

"Okay," Charles said. He stood no more than a foot away from her.

The tension between them seemed to throb like a living thing. It took Faith a moment to realize that Charles was responding to her statement about not needing help with the dishes.

She started to walk away, abandoning her wine, when he caught her hand. She stood frozen, half-facing the kitchen, her fingers lightly held in his. She sensed that if she turned back, he'd probably kiss her. He'd given her the choice.

Slowly, almost against her will, Faith turned. Charles drew her into the circle of his arms and brought his mouth down on hers.

The kiss was wonderful. They strained against each other, wanting, needing to give more, receive more, *feel* more.

When it was over, they stared at each other as if equally perplexed.

"Wow," Faith mumbled.

"You're telling me!"

Charles pulled her back into his embrace and held her tightly. "I'm ready to be wowed again. How about you?"

Faith's heart fluttered with excitement. This was the best surprise yet, she mused, as she closed her eyes and tilted her mouth toward his.

Chapter Eighteen

Emily had the bacon sizzling and muffins baking by the time Ray came out of his brother's bedroom. His hair was still wet from the shower, and he wore a fresh set of clothes. Emily assumed they'd come out of Charles's closet, because Ray hadn't brought a suitcase. Apparently the two brothers were close enough in size for Ray to wear his brother's clothes.

"Good morning," she greeted him cheerfully.

Ray muttered something indistinguishable and stumbled over to the coffeepot. He poured himself a mug. "Are you always this happy in the morning?" he asked, after his first restorative sip.

"Always," Emily said, just as cheerfully as before.

Ray stared at her. "I've heard there are two kinds of people in the world. Those who wake up and say 'Good Morning, God' and those who say 'Good God, Morning.'"

Emily laughed. "You don't need to tell me which one you are."

"Or you." He settled on the stool by the counter,

propped up his elbows and slowly sipped his coffee. When he'd finished his first cup, he was smiling again and eager for breakfast.

Emily set their plates on the counter and joined him, bringing the coffeepot for refills.

"Are you still interested in getting a Christmas tree?" she asked, as Ray dug into his bacon and eggs.

"Definitely, but first I think I'd better call my mother."

They'd listened to the messages the night before. Bernice Brewster made it sound imperative that she speak to her oldest son *immediately*.

After breakfast, Ray went to retrieve the portable phone.

"It's barely six in Arizona," she warned.

"Mom's an early riser and trust me—she's waiting with bated breath to hear from me."

He knew his mother well, because almost as soon as he'd dialed, Bernice was on the line. While they exchanged greetings, Emily scraped off the plates and set them in the dishwasher. She could only hear one end of the conversation, but Ray seemed to have trouble getting a word in edgewise. After a while, he placed the receiver carefully on the counter and walked away. He leaned against one of the stools, arms crossed, and waited patiently for his mother to finish her tirade. Even from the other side of the kitchen, Emily could hear the woman ranting.

"Ray," she whispered, half amused and half shocked at what he'd done.

He poured himself a third mug of coffee and shrugged elaborately.

After a few minutes, he lifted the receiver and pretended to be outraged. "Yes, Mother. Yes, of course, it's *dreadful.*" He rolled his eyes. "What do I plan to do about it? Frankly, nothing. Charles is over twenty-one and for that matter, so am I. Have a wonderful Christmas—your gift should arrive by the 24th. I'll be in touch. Bye now." He listened a few seconds more and then turned off the phone.

"Did you, uh, reassure your mother?" Emily asked.

"I doubt it." Ray chuckled. "She wanted to know what's going on with Charles. I didn't tell her, because basically I don't know. Besides, hard though it is for my mother to grasp, it's none of her business who Charles is with."

Still, Emily understood the other woman's concerns. "She's worried that both her sons are with strange women." She gave a short laugh. "Not *strange,* but strangers."

He smiled, too. "You know, frankly I think she'd be overjoyed if she met you. You're exactly the kind of woman she's wanted to introduce me to all these years."

Emily wasn't sure what to make of his comment. "Is that good or bad?"

"Good," he assured her and briefly touched her cheek. "Very good."

As soon as they'd cleaned up the kitchen, they put on their winter coats and ventured outside. The sky was dull gray, threatening snow. Arms linked, they walked several blocks until they found a Christmas-tree lot.

"Merry Christmas." The lot attendant, a college student from the look of him, wandered over when they entered. He didn't seem especially busy, Emily noticed, but with only three days until Christmas most people had their trees up and decorated.

"Hello," Emily said, distracted by Ray who was straightening a scraggly fir that leaned against the makeshift wire fence. She shook her head at the pathetic little tree with its broken limbs and one bald side.

"Do you want your tree tall or small?" the young man asked. His breath made foggy wisps in the air.

"Medium-sized," Emily said.

He stared at her with narrowed eyes. "Would you mind telling me where you got that scarf?"

Emily turned away from the Christmas trees to look at the young man. "I knit it. Why?"

He shrugged. "I had a friend who had a similar one. That's all."

A chill raced down Emily's spine. "Your friend wouldn't happen to be Heather Springer, would she?"

"Yeah," he said excitedly. "How'd you know?"

"She's my daughter."

"You're Heather's mother?" He whipped off his glove and thrust out his hand. "I'm Ben Miller," he told her. "Heather and I were in art history together."

Ben Miller…Ben Miller… She had it! "Didn't you and Heather date for a while?"

"Yeah." He replaced his glove and rubbed his hands together. "I apparently wasn't…dangerous enough for her."

"Dangerous?"

"Never mind," Ben shook his head. "She's seeing Elijah now. Elijah with no last name." He spit out the words. "From what I hear, she's headed down to Florida with him and a bunch of his no-account friends."

The urge to defend Heather rose quickly, but died within the space of a single heartbeat. Emily could tell that he'd been hurt by Heather's actions—just as she herself had been. "Heather'll be back soon, I'm sure," she murmured. It was the best she could do.

"You came out to spend Christmas with her and she left anyway?" Ben sounded thoroughly disgusted.

"Yes…"

"You know, when Heather told me her plans for Christmas, I assumed it wouldn't take her long to see that she's making a mistake."

Emily'd hoped so, too.

"But if she could turn her back on her own mother at Christmas, then she isn't the person I thought she was." Ben's eyes hardened. "To tell you the truth, I don't care if I ever see her again." He walked over to another section of the lot. "There are a couple of nice trees over here," he said, all business now.

Emily and Ray followed him.

"Give her time," Emily said, squeezing his forearm with one mittened hand.

Ben glanced at her. "She isn't interested in me anymore."

Emily hung her head, fearing her daughter hadn't given her a single thought, either.

Sensing her mood, Ray placed his hand on Emily's shoulder. "You okay?" he asked.

She nodded. Nothing she said or did now would make a difference to what Heather had done or how Emily felt about it. But Ben seemed like a decent, hardworking young man and she felt bad that her daughter had so obviously hurt him.

"With Christmas this close, we don't have much to choose from," Ben apologized. He picked through several trees, then chose a tall, full one. "This is probably a little bigger than you wanted, but it's the best I've got."

Ray looked skeptical and circled the tree. "What do you think?" he asked Emily.

"It's perfect." She winked at Ben.

"We'll take it," Ray said and reached for his wallet.

Without a car they were forced to carry the tree back to the condominium. They walked in single file, Ray holding the trunk in one hand and a stand in the other, and Emily behind him, supporting the treetop. They must've been something of a spectacle, because they got lots of stares along the way.

Once inside the condo, they saw the message light blinking again. Ray checked the caller ID and groaned. "It's my mother. Again."

"Are you going to call her back?"

"Of course, but not anytime soon."

Emily smiled. While Ray fit the tree in the stand, she took out the decorations she'd brought from Seattle.

"You got all that in a single suitcase?" Ray marveled when she spread everything out.

"Two very large suitcases if you must know. Don't forget the stuff already on the mantel."

He shook his head, but Emily could tell he was enjoying this.

The living room was compact, and after a long debate, they decided the best place for the tree was by the window, although that entailed moving the furniture around.

"It's beautiful," Emily told him. She handed him the first decoration—a felt snowman complete with knitted scarf. "I made that for Heather the year she was in kindergarten," Emily explained.

Ray placed it on a tree limb and picked up a second ornament. "Does every one of these have some significance?"

Emily nodded. "Each and every one."

"That's wonderful."

She was surprised he'd appreciate her sentimentality. "You don't think I'm silly to treasure these ornaments?"

"Not at all. You've given your daughter a lovely tradition."

At the mention of Heather, Emily bit her lip, overwhelmed by sadness.

Ray wrapped his arms around her. "My guess is she's got just enough freedom to be miserable," he said softly.

Emily doubted it, but she was grateful for his encouragement.

"Everything's going to work out for the best," he assured her. "Just wait and see."

Emily hoped he was right.

Chapter Nineteen

Faith woke up to the sound of Charles rummaging around in the kitchen. Grabbing her housecoat, she hurried down the stairs.

"Morning," he said, grinning sheepishly. "I hope I didn't wake you."

Faith rubbed the sleep from her eyes. He had to be joking. But then she glanced at the kitchen clock and couldn't believe she'd slept this late. It was the deepest, most relaxed sleep she'd had in months. She hadn't realized how tired she'd been.

"Coffee?" Charles lifted the glass pot.

"Please." She tightened the belt of her velour robe and sat down at the table, shaking the hair away from her face. Charles brought her a mug, which he'd filled with coffee. She added cream and held it in both hands, basking in the warmth that spread through her palms. They'd spent the most enjoyable evening talking and drinking wine and…

"What are your plans for today?" he asked.

Faith hadn't given it much consideration. "Maybe I'll walk into town a bit later."

Charles mulled that over. "Would you object to company?"

"You?" she gasped.

He shrugged in a self-conscious manner. "Unless you'd rather I didn't come with you."

"But I—what about your work?" Naturally she'd enjoy his company but Charles had insisted he was in Leavenworth to work and didn't want to be distracted from his purpose.

"I was up early this morning and got quite a bit done."

"Oh."

"I felt I should leave the project for a while, now that the rough draft is done. I'd like to give my mind a rest."

"Oh." All at once Faith seemed incapable of words consisting of more than one syllable.

"So—it seems I have the luxury of some free time."

"Oh." She sipped her coffee. "But I thought you hated Christmas?"

"I do. For…various reasons. It's far too commercial. The true meaning's been lost in all the frenzy of the season."

"Christmas is what each one of us makes it," Faith felt obliged to tell him.

"Exactly."

Faith swallowed. "I was going into town to do some shopping. Uh, Christmas shopping," she added. She met his eyes as she looked for some indication that he'd be interested in accompanying her. Men were notoriously impatient when it came to browsing through stores. And an avowed Christmas-hater…

He didn't say anything for a moment, then set his mug

aside. "I see. Well, in that case, I've got other projects I can work on."

"Oh." She couldn't disguise her disappointment.

Charles frowned. "*Would* you like my company?"

"Very much," she said quickly.

"Then I read you wrong."

"I'm just afraid it wouldn't interest you," she explained.

"I'd enjoy being out in the fresh air. I'll get my coat." He was like a kid eager to start a promised adventure.

"Whoa." Faith raised one hand. "Give me time. I've got to shower and dress, and I wouldn't mind a little something to eat first."

"Okay." He seemed amenable enough to that.

Faith wasn't quite sure what had prompted the change in him, but she wasn't complaining. She poured cereal and milk into a bowl, and ate every bite. Drinking the last of her coffee, she hurried back up the stairs and grabbed her jeans, a sweater and fresh underwear. She showered, dressed and dried her hair. When she came out of the bathroom, she found her boots, put them on and laced them up.

"Charles?" He didn't seem to be anywhere around. "Charles," she called, more loudly this time.

By chance she happened to glance out the window— to discover him surrounded by half a dozen neighborhood boys and Sarah. The children were apparently trying to talk him into something, but Charles clearly wasn't interested. Several times he shook his head and gestured dismissively with his gloved hands.

Faith threw on her coat and dashed out of the house, fastening her buttons as she went. She could see that Charles had begun to sweep the snow off the porch steps and had apparently been interrupted in his task by the children.

"Hi, Faith," Thomas called out. "You want to go sledding with us?"

"Ah..." She looked to Charles for some indication of his feelings. "What about you?"

Charles shook his head. "The last time I was on a sled, I was thirteen years old and too young to know better."

"It's fun," Thomas Kennedy promised.

"Go down the hill just once and you'll see what we mean." Mark's young voice was filled with excitement.

"You just gotta," Sarah insisted, tugging at Charles's hand.

Several of the older kids had lost interest in persuading Charles; they were already across the street, pulling their sleds.

"Come on," Faith said. "You need to do this or you'll lose face with the kids."

"Faith, I'm not sure it's a good idea."

"It'll be fun. You'll see."

"Faith, listen, I'm not entirely comfortable with this."

"They'll pester you until you give in, you realize?"

Charles seemed to need more convincing. "I'll go first," she told him. "Just do what I do, and you won't have a problem."

"People can get killed sledding," he mumbled to no one in particular.

She looked both ways before crossing the street. "People get killed on their way to work, too."

"This isn't encouraging."

"I'll go first," she said again.

"No," he countered as they trudged up the hill. "If this has to be done, I'll do it."

Thomas proudly showed Charles how to lie flat on the sled and how to steer with his arms. Charles still seemed unsure, but he was enough of a sport to lie prone, his feet hanging over the sled. He looked up at Faith with an expression that said if he died, it would be her fault.

"Are your life insurance premiums paid up?" she teased.

"Very funny," he grumbled.

Faith laughed, but her amusement soon turned to squeals of concern as the sled started down the snowy hill. Because of his weight, Charles flew downward at breakneck speed. His momentum carried him much farther than the children and straight toward the playground equipment.

"Turn!" she screamed. "Charles, turn the sled!" He couldn't hear her, so she did the only thing she could— and that was run after him. She stumbled and fell any number of times as she vaulted down the hill. Before long, she was on her backside, sliding down the snow and slush with only the thin protection of her jeans. The icy cold seeped through her clothes, but she didn't care. If anything happened to him, she'd never forgive herself.

Charles disappeared under the swing set and continued on for several feet before coming to a stop just short of the frozen pond.

"Charles, Charles!" Faith raced after him, oblivious now to her wet bottom and the melting snow running down her calves.

Charles leaped off the sled. His smile stretched from ear to ear as he turned toward her. "That was *incredible!*"

"You were supposed to stop," she cried, furious with him and not afraid to let him know it.

"Then you should have said so." He was by far the calmer one.

"You could've been hurt!"

"Yes, I know, but weren't you the one who said I could just as easily die on my way to work?"

"You're an idiot!" She hurled herself into his arms, nearly choking him. She felt like bursting into tears of relief that he was safe and unhurt.

Charles clasped her around the waist and lifted her off the ground. "Hey, hey, I'm fine."

"I know…I know—but I expected you to stop where the kids do."

"I will next time."

"Next time?"

"Come on," he said, and set her down. "It's your turn."

"No, thanks." Faith raised both her hands and took a step backward. "I already had a turn. I went down the hill on my butt, chasing after you."

He laughed, and the sound was pure magic. He kissed her cold face. "Go change clothes. As soon as you're ready we'll go into town."

"Are you staying in the park?"

Charles nodded. "Of course. A man's got to do what a man's got to do."

Shaking her head, she sighed. What on earth had she created here? One ride down the hill, and Charles Brewster was a thirteen-year-old boy all over again.

Chapter Twenty

Heather could hardly hear a thing over all the noise in the Hog's Breath Tavern in Key West, Florida. Peaches was eyeing Elijah with the voluptuous look of a woman on the prowl. Heather gazed across the room rather than allow herself to be subjected to such blatant attempts to lure Elijah away.

Slipping off the bar stool, she squeezed past crowded tables in a search for the ladies' room. This entire vacation wasn't anything like she'd imagined. She'd pictured sitting with Elijah on a balmy beach, singing Christmas carols and holding each other close. His idea of fun was riding twelve hours a day on his Harley with infrequent breaks, grabbing stale sandwiches in a minimart, and drinking beer with people who disliked and distrusted her.

Inside the restroom, Heather waited in line for a stall. Once she was hidden by the privacy of the cubicle, she buried her face in her hands. It was time to admit she'd made a mistake—hard as that was on her pride—but she'd had about as much as she could take of Elijah and his so-called friends.

When she left the ladies' room, Elijah was back at the bar with a fresh beer, which he raised high in the air when he saw her, evidently to tell her where he was. As if she hadn't figured it out by now. If Elijah didn't have a beer in his hand, then he was generally with a woman and most of the time it wasn't her.

"Babe," he said, draping his arm around her neck. "Where'd you go?"

"To the powder room."

He slobbered a kiss on the corner of her mouth. "Want another beer?"

"No, thanks."

"Hey, this is a party."

Maybe—but she wasn't having any fun. "So it seems."

His smile died and a flash of anger showed in his eyes. "What's your problem?"

Frankly, at this point there were too many to list. "Can we talk?" she asked.

"Now?" He glanced irritably around.

"Please."

"Sure, whatever." Frowning, he slid off the stool. With his arm still around her neck, he led the way outside. "You don't like Key West?" he asked as soon as they were outside. His tone suggested that anyone who couldn't have a good time in this town was in sad shape.

"What's not to like?" This had become her standard response. And she did like Key West. But the things she wanted to do—take history walks, visit Hemingway House, check out bookstores—were of no interest to the others.

"Well, then?" Elijah took another swallow of beer and pitched the bottle into a nearby trash can. "You've been in a sour mood ever since we got here."

"Maybe I don't like you clinging to Peaches."

His laugh was short and abrupt. "You're jealous. Damn, I should've figured as much."

"Not really." She hadn't fully analyzed her feelings. The only emotion she'd experienced watching the two of them had been disgust. That, and sadness at her own misguided choices.

"So what's the big deal?" he demanded.

"There isn't one."

They stopped walking and faced each other. Elijah crossed his arms, leaning against his motorcycle as the din of raised voices and loud music spilled out from the Hog's Breath. Elijah looked longingly over his shoulder, as if he resented being dragged away from all the fun. The partyers continued their revelry, apparently not missing either of them.

"Dammit, tell me what you want."

His impatience rang in her ears. "What are your—our plans for Christmas Day?"

"Christmas Day?" Elijah said. He seemed confused by the question. "What do you mean?"

"You know, December twenty-fifth? Two days from now? What are we going to do to celebrate Christmas?"

He looked at her, his eyes blank. "I haven't thought that far ahead. Why?"

"Why?" she repeated. "Because it's important to me."

He considered this. "What would you like to do?"

Her throat clogged with emotion as she remembered the way she'd celebrated Christmas with her mother, all the special traditions that had marked her childhood. She hadn't realized how much she'd miss those or how empty the holidays would feel without her family.

"I was hoping," Heather said, being as forthright and honest as she could, "that we'd find a small palm tree on the beach and decorate it like a real Christmas tree."

This seemed to utterly baffle Elijah. "Decorate it with what? Toilet paper?"

"I...don't know. Something. Maybe we could find sea shells and string those and cut out paper stars."

Elijah shrugged. "Would that make you happy?"

"I...I don't know. I dreamed of sitting in the sand with you and looking up at the night sky, singing Christmas carols."

Elijah rubbed his hand over his face. "I don't sing, and even if I did, I don't know the words to any of those carols. Well, maybe the one about the snowman. What the hell was his name again? Frisky?"

"Frosty."

"Yeah, Frosty."

"But you can hum, can't you?" Heather had a fairly decent voice. It didn't matter if he sang or not; all that mattered was being together and in love and sharing something important. Maybe creating a new tradition of their own...

"Heather, listen," Elijah said as he unfolded his arms and slowly straightened. "I'm not the kind of guy who decorates palm trees with paper stars or sings about melting snowmen."

"But I thought—"

"What?" He slapped his hand against the side of his head in frustration. "*What* were you thinking?"

"I like to party, too, but a steady diet of it grows old after a while."

"Says who?"

"Me," she cried. She'd never asked Elijah where he got his money, but she was beginning to think she should. "You didn't even consult me about having all these other people along."

"Hey," Elijah snapped, thrusting up both palms in a gesture of surrender. "You didn't *consult* me about all this Christmas junk you're so keen on, either."

He was right, but his sarcasm didn't make her feel any better. "I thought it would be just the two of us."

"Well, it isn't. I've got friends, and I'm not letting any woman get between me and my people."

"Your…people?"

"You know· what I mean."

Unfortunately, Heather was beginning to understand all too well.

"Peaches warned me about college girls," he muttered.

"Ben warned me about you," she returned.

"Who the hell is Ben?"

"A friend." Heather wanted to kick herself for not listening, but it was too late for that.

"College girls are nothing but trouble."

"You didn't used to think that," Heather reminded him. "Not about me." From the moment they met, he'd said he didn't want to get involved with a college girl, and she'd taken that as a challenge to change his mind. She'd wanted to prove…what? She didn't know. Possibly how incredibly foolish she could be.

"I didn't used to think about a lot of things," Elijah said emphatically. "I've got a weakness for good girls, but the first thing they want to do is change me. Thing is, I'm content just the way I am. I'm not ever going to sit under any

Christmas tree and sing silly songs. The sooner you accept that, the better."

Heather looked down the road and nodded. "I'm never going to be happy living like this." Her wide gesture took in the bar, the motorcycles, a group of hysterically laughing people clambering out of a cab.

"Like what?"

"Like this," she said. "Life is more than one big party, you know?"

"No, I don't," he countered.

"Fine." It wouldn't do any good to argue. "I'm leaving."

"You won't get any argument from me, but I'm not taking you to Boston, if that's what you want."

"No." She'd never ask that of him. "I'll catch a bus to Miami in the morning and fly back."

"What about money?" he asked, and the way he said it made it clear she was on her own.

"I'll be fine."

Elijah snorted. "Mommy's credit card to the rescue, right?"

Heather did have an emergency credit card her mother had given her, and she'd be forced to use it. In three years, she'd never had reason to do so, but she did now. Still, she was determined to pay back every last penny.

"Yes, Mommy's credit card. I'm fortunate to have a mother."

Elijah considered that for a moment, then nodded in agreement. "That's probably the reason you're in college. You had parents who gave a damn about you."

"I'm sorry it didn't work out for us," she told Elijah, sad now.

He shrugged casually. "Don't worry about it. We had a few good times."

"No hard feelings?"

Elijah shook his head. "You'll be all right, and so will I."

Heather knew that what he said was true. She should also have known, when she left Boston, that this arrangement would never work. Now she had two days to get back there and find her mother. Her poor, desperate mother in a strange town, without any friends…

Chapter Twenty-One

The phone rang as Ray and Emily sat by the Christmas tree, both cross-legged, sipping wine and listening to a Christmas concert on the radio.

"Don't answer that," he warned. "It might be my mother."

Emily smiled and hopped up to check caller ID. "It's my phone number back in Washington," she said, picking up the receiver. "Hello?"

"Emily? It's Faith."

"Oh, Faith," Emily said, instantly cheered. "It's so good to hear from you."

"Is everything all right?" her friend asked.

"Everything is positively wonderful." Emily looked over to where Ray sat with his wineglass.

"It is here, too," Faith confessed.

"What about Charles?" Emily was sure she hadn't heard her friend correctly. Faith actually sounded happy, but that couldn't be possible, since she was stuck with a Christmas-hating curmudgeon.

"Oh, Emily, Charles has been just *great*. He wasn't in the beginning, but then I realized he's just like everyone else, only a little more intense."

"Really?"

"Yes. In fact, this morning he went sledding with the Kennedy kids. Thomas talked him into it. He was reluctant at first, but once he got started there was no stopping him."

"Charles?" Although they'd never met, Emily had heard enough about Ray's brother to find this bit of news truly astonishing.

"Then Charles and I walked downtown and browsed the stores and he bought the cutest little birdhouse for your yard. It's got a snowy roof and a bright-red cardinal on top."

"*Charles* did that?"

"Yes, and then we had a fabulous lunch. He's working now, or at least that's what he said he was doing, but I think he's taking a nap."

Emily smiled. This definitely wasn't the man Ray had described. From everything he'd told her, Charles was the classic absentminded professor, as stuffy and staid as they come. And he hated Christmas. Something—or someone—had turned his world upside down, and Emily had a very good idea who that might be.

"Faith," Emily murmured, "are you interested in Charles? As a man?"

Her friend didn't answer right away. "Define interested."

"Romantically inclined."

That caught Ray's notice; he stood and walked over to the phone, sitting down on a nearby stool.

"I don't know." Faith's answer revealed her indecision. "Well, maybe." She sounded uncertain, as if she was surprised by her feelings and a little troubled. This relationship must be developing very quickly; Emily could identify with that.

"I think it's wonderful that the two of you are getting along so well."

"He's not at all the way he first seemed," Faith told her. "First impressions can be deceptive, don't you think?"

"Of course."

"But I didn't phone to talk about myself." Faith seemed even more flustered now. "I just wanted to see how you're doing."

Emily's gaze drifted to Ray. "Like I said, this is turning out to be a wonderful Christmas."

Her announcement was followed by a short pause. "Charles's brother is still there?"

"Yes." Emily didn't elaborate.

"So the two of you are hitting it off?"

"We are. We're getting along really well."

As if to prove how well, Ray came to stand behind Emily. He slipped his arms around her waist and kissed the back of her neck. Tiny shivers of delight danced down her spine and she closed her eyes, savoring his warmth and attention.

"Have you heard from Heather?" Faith asked.

Emily's eyes flew open. "Not a peep, but I don't expect to since she doesn't have this phone number."

"I guess she'll call after Christmas," Faith said.

Emily managed a few words of assent, then changed the subject. "It was so sweet of you to come to Leavenworth for Christmas. I just wish you'd let me know."

"And ruin the surprise?" Faith teased.

"Just like I surprised Heather."

Faith laughed softly. "I'll check in with you later. Bye for now."

"Okay. Talk to you soon." Emily hung up the phone and sighed as she turned to Ray to explain the call. "As you could tell, that was Faith."

"What's all this about my brother?"

He released her and Emily leaned against the kitchen counter. "Charles apparently spent the morning sledding with the neighborhood kids."

Ray shook his head, frowning. "That's impossible. Not Charles. He'd never knowingly choose to be around kids."

"That's not all. After sledding, the two of them went Christmas shopping—and he bought me a gift. A birdhouse."

Ray's frown grew puzzled. "This is a joke, right?"

"Not according to Faith."

"Charles? My *brother*, Charles?"

"The very same. Apparently she tired him out, because he's napping."

"I've got to meet this friend of yours. She must be a miracle worker." He paused. "You're sure about all this?"

"That's what Faith told me, and I've never known her to exaggerate."

"Something must've happened to my brother. Maybe I should call him myself."

"Don't you think this is a good thing?" Emily asked. "Judging by everything you've said, your brother seems to have a single focus. His work. He wanted to escape Christmas and finish his book."

Ray nodded, but his expression had started to relax. "It's interesting when you put it that way," he said thoughtfully.

"How so?"

"It sounds as if you're describing me."

This surprised Emily. From the beginning, she'd viewed Charles as an introvert, in contrast to Ray, who was personable and outgoing.

"For years now, Christmas has meant nothing but a few extra days off. Every year, I send the obligatory gift to my mother—usually the latest big mystery and maybe a new coffee-table book with lots of scenic pictures. I attend a few parties, have my assistant mail out greeting cards, make a restaurant reservation for the twenty-fifth. But I haven't felt any real spirit until today. With you."

Emily's heart warmed at his words.

"I never go for even an hour without thinking about work or publishing. We've spent the entire day together, and I haven't once missed hearing my cell ring."

Emily had no idea their Christmas-tree adventure had meant so much to him. He'd seemed eager to hear about her homemade decorations and the traditions she had with her daughter. Later she'd felt a bit silly to be talking so much and certain she'd bored him with her endless stories. She was glad she hadn't.

Ray looked away as if he'd said more than he intended. "Are you ready for dinner? What about that Mexican place we passed?"

"I'm starving." Mexican food sounded divine and the perfect ending to a perfect day.

"Me, too. That's what you get for walking my feet off this afternoon," he said. "Now you have to feed me."

After they'd finished putting the final touches on the tree, they'd gone out for a light lunch of pizza and salad, then walked and walked. They'd had no real destination, but enjoyed being out of doors. They'd talked incessantly and Emily was surprised they had so much to discuss. She was a voracious reader and Ray questioned her about her favorite books and authors. Emily had questions of her own about the publishing industry, which fascinated her. She noticed, though, that neither of them talked much about their private lives. Their conversations skirted around their thoughts and feelings, but the more time they spent together, the more they revealed.

Chapter Twenty-Two

Faith replaced the telephone receiver, and a happy feeling spread through her. What had felt like a disaster a few days earlier now seemed to be working wonderfully well—for her *and* her dearest friend.

As if her thoughts had awakened him, Charles opened the door to the den and stepped out, still yawning.

"Just as I suspected," Faith teased. "You *were* napping."

"I intended to revise the first chapter," he muttered, rubbing his eyes, "but the minute I sat down in that warm, quiet room, I was lost. Thank goodness there's a comfortable sofa in there or I would've fallen asleep with my head on the keyboard."

Faith had taken more than one nap in Emily's comfortable den, perhaps her favorite room in the house. In the early years, it had been Heather's bedroom, but as she grew up, Heather had wanted more privacy and claimed the room at the top of the stairs. Emily had transformed her daughter's former bedroom into a library, with books in every conceivable place. A desk and computer took up one wall, and the worn leather couch another. A hand-knit afghan was draped over its back for those times when reading led to napping.... She'd spent many a lazy winter afternoon on that couch, Faith recalled.

"What have you been up to?" Charles asked.

"I called Emily in Boston to see how she's doing," she told him.

Charles poured a mug of coffee. "Is she having any problems?"

"No. In fact, it seems your brother's decided to stay on."

"Stay on what?"

"In Boston with Emily."

Charles's eyes widened as he stared at her. "Let me see if I'm hearing you right. My brother didn't return to New York?"

"Nope." Faith loved the look of absolute shock. She wondered if Ray had shown the same degree of astonishment when he learned how well his brother had adjusted to Leavenworth and being with her.

"Has something happened in New York that I don't know about?" Charles asked.

"What do you mean?"

"Has the city been snowed in or has there been a train strike? That sort of thing?"

"Not that I've heard. I had the radio on earlier and they didn't mention anything. Why?"

"Why? Because my brother is a dyed-in-the-wool workaholic. Nothing keeps him away from his desk."

"Well, he's taking a few days off to spend with Emily."

Charles took a sip of coffee, as though he needed time to mull over what she'd told him. "Your friend must be one hell of a woman."

"She is." That was the simple truth.

Still distracted, Charles pulled out a kitchen chair and sat down. He glanced around and seemed to notice for the first time that she'd been busy. "You put up those decorations?"

"I didn't think you'd mind." She felt a bit uneasy about that now. Emily had a number of Christmas things she hadn't bothered to display this year; she'd obviously taken the rest of them to Boston. Faith had brought a few of her own decorations, as well. While everything was quiet, she'd unpacked the special ones and displayed them throughout the house. The tiny Christmas tree with red velvet bows stood on the mantel, and so did a small manger scene that Heather had loved since childhood. Emily's Christmas teapot, white china with holly decorations, now held pride of place on the kitchen counter.

Charles wandered into the dining room, Faith on his heels. "What's this?" he asked, motioning toward the centerpiece on the dining-room table.

"A cottonball snowman. Heather made it for Emily when she was eight. She was so proud of it, which is why Emily's kept it all these years."

Charles seemed puzzled, as if he couldn't quite grasp the beauty of the piece. Bells chimed softly from outside and Faith looked out the large picture window to see the horse-drawn sleigh gliding past.

"Charles, let's go for a sleigh ride," she said impulsively. For Faith, it was a highlight of the first and only Christmas she'd spent in Leavenworth—until now. It was the Christmas following her divorce. The sleigh ride, which she'd taken alone, had comforted her. That, and Emily's friendship, had made a painful Christmas tolerable, even pleasant. Her sleigh ride had shown her that being alone could bring its own contentment, its own pleasures. And spending Christmas Day with Emily and Heather had taught her that friendship could lend value to life.

Charles seemed startled by her invitation, then shook his head. "No, thanks."

"It's even more fun than sledding," she coaxed.

Still he declined.

"Well, come and stand in line with me while I wait my turn."

For a moment she thought he'd refuse, but then he nodded. "As long as the line isn't too long."

"Okay."

Dressed in their coats, boots, scarves and gloves, they strolled downtown, walking arm in arm. Night had settled over the small town, and festive activities abounded. The carolers in period costumes were out, standing on street corners singing. The Salvation Army band played Christmas music in the park, as ice skaters circled the frozen pond. Glittering multicolored lights brightened the streets and the town was bustling with shoppers.

Fortunately, the line for the sleigh ride wasn't too long and while she waited, Charles bought them cups of creamy hot chocolate. "I'm so glad I remembered the sleigh ride," she said, holding her hot chocolate with gloved hands.

"Why's that?" Charles asked.

She shrugged, sipping at her chocolate. "I think I mentioned that I did my student teaching in Leavenworth—that's when I met Emily. Those months were hard on me emotionally. I'd only recently been divorced and I was feeling pretty bad. Before me, no one in my family had ever gotten a divorce."

"No one?"

"Not in my immediate family. My parents, grandparents and sister were all happily married, and it really hurt my pride to admit that I'd made a mistake. I blamed myself because I hadn't listened when my parents warned me about Douglas."

"What happened?"

"My husband had a problem—he needed the approval and love of other women. Even now, I believe he loved me to the best of his ability, but Douglas could never be tied to a single woman."

"I see."

"I forgave him the first time he was unfaithful, although it nearly killed me, but the second time I knew this would always be a pattern with him. I thought—I hoped that if I got out of the marriage early enough, I'd be all right, but…I wasn't. I'm not."

Charles moved closer to her, and Faith looked down, tears blurring her eyes. She blinked them away and tried to compose herself, sipping the hot cocoa.

"Why aren't you all right? What do you mean?" he asked.

"I can't trust men anymore. I'm afraid of relationships. Look at me," she whispered. "Five years later, and I rarely date. All my dreams of marriage and family are gone and—" Resolutely she closed her mouth. What had possessed her to tell him this? "Listen," she told him, forcing a cheerful note into her voice, "forget I said anything."

Charles didn't answer right away. "I don't know if I can."

"Then pretend you have. Otherwise I'm going to feel embarrassed."

"Why should you?"

She shook her head. She hardly ever mentioned her divorce, not to anyone. Yet here she was, standing in the middle of this vibrant town in the most joyous season of the year, fighting back tears—spilling her heart to a man she hardly knew.

The sleigh glided up to the stop and the bells chimed as the chestnut mare bowed her head. The driver climbed down from his perch and offered Faith his hand. "Just one ticket," she said, about to give him the money.

"Make that two," Charles said, paying the driver. Without explaining why he'd changed his mind, he stepped up into the sleigh and settled on the narrow bench next to Faith.

The driver leaped back into the seat and took the reins.

Faith spread the woolen blanket over their laps. "What made you decide to come?" she asked.

He stared at her for a long moment. "I don't know... I just didn't want to leave you." He slid his arm around her shoulders and held her close. Warmth seeped into her blood. She hadn't realized how cold she was, but now Charles Brewster sat beside her in a one-horse open sleigh, two days before Christmas, and she felt warm, happy...and complete.

Chapter Twenty-Three

Emily woke the morning of Christmas Eve and stared up at the bedroom ceiling, musing that this was by far the most unusual Christmas of her life.

Not since the first Christmas following Peter's death had she dealt with such complex emotions during the holidays. For one thing, she'd been forced to acknowledge that Heather was an adult now, making her own decisions without the counsel of her mother.

As if *that* wasn't strange enough, Emily was in emotionally unfamiliar territory, living with a man she'd only known a few days. She sat up in bed and reviewed their time together. Ray was a hotshot New York publisher badly in need of a vacation, a career bachelor by all accounts. She was a widow and a small-town kindergarten teacher. Their meeting was accidental, as amusing as it was unexpected. They got along well, laughed together, and enjoyed each other's company. Much as she wanted to continue the relationship, Emily was realistic enough to accept that in a few days they'd both go back to their individual lives, three thousand miles apart. She decided then and there to make the most of their remaining time together.

After a quick shower, she dressed and emerged from the bedroom to discover that Ray was already up and reading the morning paper. The coffee was made. When she entered the kitchen, he lowered the newspaper and smiled.

"What's on the agenda for today?" he asked.

Emily wasn't sure. Back in Leavenworth, she'd be delivering charity baskets in the afternoon. Then, after a dinner of homemade clam chowder with Heather, followed by hot apple cider, she'd get ready for the Christmas Eve service at church. Home again, they'd go to bed, looking forward to a lazy Christmas morning, when they'd open their gifts and enjoy a late breakfast.

"I don't know what to do today," she said, feeling at a loss. "This year is completely unlike any I've ever experienced."

"What would you *like* to do?"

They'd spent their days sightseeing, and while Emily had thoroughly enjoyed this tour of American history, she wanted to concentrate on the season now.

"I'd like to bake cinnamon rolls," she said, coming to the decision quickly. "I do every year, specially for breakfast on Christmas morning. I think that would put me in the holiday spirit more than anything."

"Sounds fantastic. While you're doing that, I'll shop for our Christmas dinner. What shall we have?"

Emily shrugged. "A turkey might be a bit much for just the two of us."

"Didn't you say something about lobster earlier?" Ray asked.

She nodded, smiling. "Lobster would be perfect."

Emily must've realized she'd want to bake bread, because she'd tossed in a packet of yeast when she'd bought the supplies for her cookie-baking venture. She began to systematically search the kitchen cupboards for bowls and pans.

When Ray finished reading the paper, he put on his overcoat. On his way out the door, he came into the kitchen, where Emily was busy assembling ingredients. The recipe was a longtime family favorite, one she knew by heart. Ray took her by the shoulders and turned her so she couldn't avoid looking at him.

"I know this Christmas isn't anything like you anticipated, and I'm sorry about that. But it's the best Christmas I've had since I was a kid—the year my dad got me the red racing bike I so desperately wanted."

"Oh, Ray," she whispered, "that's the nicest thing anyone's said to me in a long, long time." Unable to resist, she slipped her arms around his waist and hugged him. She hadn't been this intimate with a man in years, nor had she felt such longing. He didn't kiss her and, although she was disappointed, she applauded his restraint. There'd be time later to enjoy the sweetness of each other's company.

Whistling, Ray left the condo, and as soon as she'd mixed the dough, Emily set it in a slightly warmed oven to rise. Pulling on her coat, gloves and scarf, she hurried out the door. She wanted to buy Ray a Christmas gift and while she was at it, she needed to stop at the grocery store.

The weather was exactly as it should be: cold and clear, with snow falling lightly. Everyone seemed to be bustling about, intent on last-minute Christmas shopping. There was an infectious spirit of joy and goodwill wherever she went.

Ninety minutes later, when Emily returned to the condo, her arms were laden with packages and groceries. She hummed a Christmas carol as she waited for the elevator. She hoped Ray had returned, too, but when she walked inside, the condo was silent and empty.

As quickly as she could, she unloaded her packages, hung up her coat and hid Ray's present in the bedroom to be wrapped that afternoon. She turned on the gas fireplace, and gentle flames flickered over the artificial log. She went to the radio next, and an instant later, the condo was filled with the glorious sounds of holiday music.

Ray didn't come back for another hour; among his purchases was a couple of deli sandwiches. Emily had been so busy, she'd forgotten to eat breakfast and it was now well past lunchtime.

"I think I should probably put these lobsters in water," he said, setting a large box on the counter. He filled the sink. "Should I add salt?"

"Salt?"

"They live in salt water. They might need it."

"I don't think so." Emily was preoccupied with unwrapping the sandwiches. Not until she turned around did she notice two huge lobsters looking directly at her. "They're alive!" She felt sorry for them and while Ray carried their sandwiches to the table, she released the rubber bands holding their claws together. Poor things, it seemed a shame to keep them prisoner.

Ray got two cold sodas from the refrigerator. "I wasn't sure about getting live lobsters, but I figured I could always exchange them if you'd rather."

"Ah…" Emily was afraid to admit she'd never cooked a

live lobster in her life. Nor had she ever eaten anything more than a lobster tail. "This should be...well, a challenge."

"We'll figure it out," Ray said.

Emily agreed. They were both hungry and didn't attempt conversation until they'd finished lunch. To all outward appearances, they were like a long-married couple anticipating each other's needs. Ray handed her a napkin, she gave him the pepper mill, all without exchanging a word.

"Since neither of us knows that much about cooking lobsters, perhaps I *should* exchange these for cooked ones," Ray suggested once they'd eaten.

"That might be best." She took their empty plates into the kitchen and let out a small cry.

"What?" Ray demanded.

"One of the lobsters is missing."

"What do you mean, missing?"

"There's only one in the sink."

"That's impossible."

"I'm telling you there's only one lobster in the sink."

Ray entered the kitchen and stared into the sink. "One of the lobsters is missing."

Emily placed her hand on her hip. "The editor's eye misses nothing," she teased.

"Where could it have gone?"

"That's for you to find out. I've got dough to knead." She moved to the oven and was about to remove the bowl when she felt something attach itself to her pant leg. Glancing down she saw the lobster.

"Ah...Ray." She held out her leg. "I found the lobster."

"I can see that." He squatted down and petted the creature's head as if it were his favorite pet.

"You might want to detach him from my pant leg."

Ray frowned. "How did the rubber band get off his claws?"

"Er…I took them off. It seemed cruel."

"I see."

"Ray, this is all very interesting, but I'd prefer not to be worrying about this lobster crawling up my leg." She was trying hard not to giggle.

"If you have any ideas on how to remove him, let me know."

Emily tried to shake her leg, but the lobster was firmly affixed. Ray started to laugh then, and she found it impossible not to join him.

"What are we going to do?" she asked between giggles.

"I don't know." Ray bent down and tugged at her jeans, but the lobster wasn't letting go. "Maybe you should take off your pants."

"Oh, sure."

"I'm not kidding."

By then, they were nearly hysterical with laughter. Emily leaned against the kitchen counter, her hand over her mouth, tears running down her cheeks. Ray sat on the floor.

"You've got yourself quite a mess here."

"Just return me with the lobster." Emily could picture it now: Ray walking into the fish market, with her slung over his shoulder, the lobster dangling from her pant leg.

They burst into laughter again.

There was a knock at the door, and Ray, still laughing, left the room. It must be one of the neighbors, Emily supposed, someone else who lived on this floor. She went with Ray, not about to let him escape without helping her first.

They had their arms around each other and were nearly doubled over with laughter when he opened the door.

An older woman stood on the other side, wearing a fur coat and an elaborate hat with a protruding feather. Cradled in the folds of her fur was a white Pomeranian. The dog took one look at Emily and growled.

"Ray!"

"Mother!"

After a few seconds' silence, he asked, "How did you get in?"

"Some nice young man opened the door for me." She glared at Emily. "And who's this?" Bernice Brewster demanded.

Ray looked at Emily and started laughing all over again. "Do you mean Emily or were you referring to the lobster?"

Chapter Twenty-Four

Faith hoped it would snow on Christmas Eve; to her disappointment the day was cold and bright, but there was no sign of snow. Charles had gone out on some errand, and she'd stayed home, her favorite Christmas CD playing as she flipped through Emily's cookbooks, looking for Christmas dinner ideas. Really, she should've thought about this earlier. Charles had suggested a roast, and she was beginning to think that was a good plan. Since she'd never made a turkey, she was a little intimidated by the prospect.

Sipping a cup of coffee, she read through one recipe after another, searching for inspiration. The more she read, the hungrier she got.

The phone rang, and she sighed, half wondering if she should answer. It wouldn't be for her. Still, habit and curiosity demanded she pick up the receiver.

"Merry Christmas," she greeted the unknown caller.

"Mom?" a small quizzical voice returned.

"Heather?"

"You're not my mother," Heather cried.

"This is Faith."

"Faith!" Heather sounded beside herself. "What are you doing in Washington? Where's my mom?"

"I came to surprise your mother, only she isn't here."

"Mom's still in Boston?"

"Yes," Faith said. "Where are you?"

"Boston."

Faith frowned. "I thought you went to Florida with some guy on a Harley."

"I did, but we…we had a parting of the ways. Where's my mother?"

"She's staying in Charles Brewster's condominium. I don't have the address but I understand it isn't that far from the Harvard campus."

"Not Professor Brewster?"

"One and the same. Why?"

"You mean to say he's in Leavenworth, and you are, too?" Heather asked incredulously.

Faith smiled at the comedy of errors. "Yes. I arrived shortly after Charles did. I came with Santa and the elves and then—"

"Who?"

"Never mind, it's complicated. But listen, everything's fine. Charles has been absolutely marvelous about all of this. He agreed to let me stay here until my original departure date." Faith hated to think what might've happened if he'd insisted she leave. She might still have been at the airport, waiting for a standby seat.

"You're talking about *Professor* Brewster?"

"Yes. Professor Charles Brewster."

"You say he's been…marvelous?" Heather seemed genuinely surprised.

"Yes." In fact, he'd been more than that, but Faith wasn't about to share any of the details with Heather.

"He *isn't* marvelous," Heather insisted. "He gave my roommate a C when she worked hard on every assignment and studied for every test. Well, okay, she fell asleep in his class, but who can blame her? The guy's boring."

"I happen to think he's a fascinating man," Faith said sharply, "so please keep your complaints to yourself."

"Faith?" Heather said, her voice dropping. "Are you…interested in Dr. Brewster?"

"That's none of your business."

Heather gave a short, abrupt laugh. "You are! I don't believe it. Just wait until Tracy hears this. Does the professor feel the same way about you? No, don't answer that 'cause I'll bet he does." She laughed again, as if this was the funniest thing she'd heard in weeks.

"It isn't that amusing," Faith said, surprised by her need to defend Charles.

But Heather had already moved on to her own concerns. "So Mom's still in Boston," she said.

"Yes, she couldn't fly home without paying a high-priced penalty."

"That's wonderful." Heather sighed with relief. "Don't say anything to her, okay?"

"Yes, but there's something you—"

"I want to surprise her, so promise you won't say a word."

Faith leaned against the kitchen counter and raised her eyes to the ceiling, resisting the urge to laugh. "You have my word of honor. I won't let her know."

"Great. Thanks, Faith. Say hello to the professor for me."

"Sure."

"I'm going to be my mom's Christmas surprise." With that, Heather terminated the call.

Faith's smile grew. Heather was about to discover a surprise of her own.

Just then, the front door opened and Charles staggered into the house, his arms stacked high with packages. Blindly he made his way into the dining room, piling the festively wrapped gifts on the table. Bags hung from his arms, and he set those next to the boxes.

"Good grief!" Faith rushed forward to help him. "What have you done?"

"I went shopping." His smile was as bright as sun on snow. He looked downright boyish, with a swath of brown hair falling over his brow, his eyes sparkling.

"Who are all these gifts for?"

"The Kennedy kids get a bunch of them and there are a couple in here for you and…" He seemed decidedly pleased with himself.

"Charles." He resembled Scrooge the day after his nightmare, rushing about buying gifts. Faith half listened for Tiny Tim.

"I got something else for Emily, too, in appreciation for trading places with me."

This was quite a switch from his initial attitude. "The way I remember it, you said you'd walked into the middle of a Christmas nightmare." Faith couldn't restrain a smile. "And then I showed up."

"That was no nightmare," he said softly. "That was a gift."

Faith didn't know what to say. His intensity flustered her and she felt the heat rush into her cheeks. After the sleigh ride, something had happened between them, something that was difficult to put into words. She sensed that sharing her pain and the bitter disappointment of her divorce had, in some strange way, released *him*. Charles hadn't said anything, but Faith realized words were often inadequate when it came to conveying emotions. She'd noticed the changes in him last night and even more so this morning.

"You got presents for the Kennedy kids?" she asked, pointing to the packages.

He nodded. "Did you know their dad got laid off last month?"

The kids hadn't said anything to her, but apparently they had to Charles.

"They didn't tell me, either," he told her before she could comment, "but I overheard Mark and Thomas talking about it. And then, early this morning, I saw someone deliver a food basket to the house. With six children, it's got to be tough this time of year."

"What a sweet thing to do. If you want, I'll help you write up gift cards and deliver them."

He nodded and the boyish, pleased look was back. "I enjoyed myself today. I didn't know Christmas could be this much fun. It's always been a time I dreaded."

"But why?"

Charles glanced away. "It's a long story, and a boring one at that."

"Involving a woman, no doubt."

He shrugged.

Faith waited expectantly. She'd shared her pain with him; the least he could do was trust her enough to divulge his.

"I see," she said after an awkward moment. She turned back to the kitchen.

Charles followed her. "If you want to know—"

"No, it isn't necessary," she broke in. "Really."

"It was a devastating experience, and I'd prefer not to discuss it."

"I understand," she said and she did. Faith reassured him with a smile, gathering up the cookbooks and replacing them on the shelf.

"Her name was Monica."

Faith pretended not to hear.

"I loved her and I was sure she loved me."

"Charles, really, you don't need to explain if you'd rather not."

He threw off his coat and sat at the table. "But I would. Please." He gestured to the chair across from him.

Faith pulled it out and sat down. He took her hands, holding them in his own. "I adored her and assumed she felt the same way about me. I bought an engagement ring and planned to give it to her on Christmas Day. Thankfully I never had the opportunity to ask her to marry me."

"Thankfully?"

Charles's fingers tightened around hers. "She told me on Christmas Eve that she found me dull and tedious. I learned later that she'd met someone else."

Faith knew he didn't want her sympathy and she didn't offer it. "I think she was an extremely foolish woman."

Charles raised his eyes until they met hers. "I *am* dull and tedious."

"No," she countered swiftly. "You're brilliant and absent-minded and quite possibly the kindest man I know."

A slow smile touched his mouth. "And you," he said. "You're the most marvelous woman I've ever met."

Chapter Twenty-Five

"Alone at last," Ray muttered as he shut the condo door. He'd walked his mother outside and waited with her until the taxi arrived to take her to the Four Seasons Hotel.

"Ray!" Emily said. "Your mother is hilarious."

"Believe me, I know. She's also meddling and demanding."

"But she loves you and worries about you."

"I should be worrying about *her*," Ray said. "I can't believe she'd fly here without telling me."

"She tried," Emily reminded him. "If I remember correctly, she left four messages, none of which you returned."

Ray looked up at the ceiling and rolled his eyes. "Guilty as charged."

"She does have impeccable timing, though, doesn't she?" Emily doubted she'd ever forget the expression on Bernice's face when Emily appeared at the front door with a lobster attached to her pant leg. The Pomeranian had started barking like crazy, and pandemonium had immediately broken out. Bernice wanted answers and Emily wanted the lobster off her leg and the dog had taken an immediate dislike to both the lobster and Emily. FiFi had leaped out of Bernice's arms, grabbing hold of Emily's other pant leg, and she was caught in a tug-of-war between the lobster and the lapdog.

Everything eventually got sorted out, but until Ray was able to rescue Emily and assure his mother that all was well, it had been a complete and total circus.

"This isn't the way I intended to spend Christmas Eve," Ray said.

"It was wonderful," Emily told him. His mother had known exactly what to do with the lobsters and she'd taken over in the kitchen, issuing orders and expecting them to be obeyed. Ray and Emily had happily complied. That evening, the three of them had feasted on the lobsters and a huge Caesar salad.

After dinner, they'd gathered in front of the fireplace, sipping wine and listening to Christmas music, and Bernice had delighted Emily with tales of her two sons growing up. Emily had enjoyed the evening immensely. And while he might complain, Ray seemed to take pleasure in their visit with his mother, too.

"She insists on taking us out for Christmas dinner," Ray said.

"That would be lovely."

"I'll bet you've never eaten at a hotel on Christmas Day in your life."

"True, but nothing about this Christmas is normal."

Ray walked over to where she stood by the tree. "Do you mind sharing the day with my mother and me?"

Emily smiled. "I consider myself fortunate to be with you both." She was sorry she couldn't be with her daughter, but she'd come a long way since Heather had announced she wouldn't be flying home for the holidays. She was far more prepared to accept Heather's independence, for one thing; it was a natural, healthy process and it was going to happen anyway, so she saw no point in fighting it.

"You're right, this isn't the Christmas Eve I expected," she added, "but I've had such a fabulous time in Boston and I owe it all to you."

"I should be the one thanking you," he whispered, drawing her into his arms. His kisses were gentle but thorough, coaxing and sensual. Emily's knees were weak by the time he released her.

"I have something for you," he said, stroking her arms. He seemed unable to stop touching her, and Emily was equally loath to break away from him.

"I have something for you, too," she told him.

"Me first."

"Okay." They separated and went to their respective bedrooms to retrieve their gifts. A few minutes later, as they sat beneath the Christmas tree, he handed her a small beribboned box. Emily stared at the beautifully wrapped present and then at Ray.

"Open it," he urged.

Her pulse going wild, she tore away the red satin bow and the wrapping paper. The jeweler's box surprised her. This looked expensive.

"Ray?" Her eyes flew up to meet his.

"Open it," he said again.

Slowly, Emily lifted the lid and swallowed a gasp. Inside was a cameo, about the size of a silver dollar.

"It's on a chain," Ray said.

"I love cameos," she whispered, and wondered how he could possibly have known. "Did I mention that?" She had two precious cameos that were among her most treasured possessions. The first had belonged to her grandmother and the second, a small one about the size of a dime, held an even deeper significance. Peter had given it to her on their fifth wedding anniversary. Now she had a third.

"I didn't know, but I saw this one and somehow I was sure you'd like it."

"Oh, Ray, I do. Thank you so much."

He helped her remove it from its plush bed. Emily turned her back to him and lifted her hair so he could connect the chain. This cameo was the most perfect gift he could possibly have given her. The fact that he'd sensed, after such a short acquaintance, how much it would appeal to her, was truly touching.

"This is for you," she said shyly, handing him her present. The day before, they'd strolled past an antique store that specialized in rare books. That morning, she'd gone inside to investigate and discovered a first edition of the science-fiction classic *Dune* by Frank Herbert. It was autographed, and because this was Christmas Eve, she'd been able to talk the dealer down to a reasonable price.

In one of their many conversations, Ray had said that he'd enjoyed science fiction as a teenager. She watched as he eagerly ripped off the paper. When he saw the novel, his eyes grew wide.

"It's autographed," she told him, smiling.

Ray's mouth sagged open. "I loved *Dune* as a kid. I read it so many times the pages fell out."

Reverently he opened the book. "How did you know?"

The whispered question revealed his own astonishment that she could find him such a fitting gift.

"I listened."

"You listened with your heart." His fingertips grazed her cheek as his eyes held hers. Slowly he glided his hand around the nape of her neck and brought her closer to thank her with a kiss.

Emily opened her lips to his. Their kisses were warm, moist, each more intense than the one before. Ray leaned back, gazing at her for several breath-stopping moments. Then he wrapped his arms around her and held her hard against him.

"Ray?"

He answered her with another kiss, and any sensible thoughts she might have had vanished the moment his lips met hers. He lowered her to the carpet, leaning over her.

Emily slid her arms around his neck. Excitement tingled through her, and passion—so long dormant, so deeply buried—came to life.

Ray's hand cupped her breast and she gasped with pleasure. She was afraid and excited at the same time. He began to unfasten her blouse and when she saw that his fingers trembled, she gently brushed them aside and unbuttoned it herself. Just as she reached the last button, there was a knock at the door.

Ray looked at her. Startled, Emily looked at him.

"Your mother?" she asked.

He shrugged and got to his feet. "I doubt it." He walked across the room. "Whoever it is, I'll get rid of them." From her vantage point, she couldn't see the door, but she could hear him open it.

Emily waited. At first nothing happened, and then she heard Heather's shocked voice.

"Who are you?"

"Ray Brewster. And you are?"

Heather sidestepped Ray and walked into the condo. Emily quickly bunched her blouse together and stared up at her daughter's horrified expression.

"Mother?" Heather screeched.

Emily was sure her face was as red as the lobster she'd had for dinner that very night.

Chapter Twenty-Six

When Faith woke on Christmas morning, it was snowing, just as she'd hoped. Tossing aside the covers, she leaped out of bed, thrust both arms into her housecoat and bounded down the stairs. Happiness bubbled up inside her—it was Christmas Day!

From their short time together, Faith knew Charles wasn't a morning person, but she couldn't bear to let him sleep in on a morning as special as this.

After putting on the coffee and waiting impatiently for enough of it to filter through to fill a cup, she swiftly removed the pot and stuck the mug directly under the drip. Then, coffee in hand, she walked down the hallway to the room in which Charles slept.

Knocking at the door, she called, "Wake up, it's Christmas! You can't escape me this morning."

She could hear him grumbling.

"Charles, it's *snowing!* Come on, get up now."

"What time is it, anyway?"

"Seven-thirty. I have coffee for you. If you want, I can bring it in."

"Do I have a choice?"

She laughed and admitted that he really didn't. If he chose to sleep longer, she'd simply rattle around the kitchen making lots of noise until he got up.

"All right, all right, come in."

He didn't sound too pleased, but Faith didn't care. When she creaked open the door, she discovered Charles sitting up in bed. His hair was disheveled and a book had fallen onto the floor.

"Merry Christmas," she said, handing him the coffee.

His stare was blank until he took his first sip. "Ahh," he breathed appreciatively. Then he gave her an absent grin. "Merry Christmas, Faith. Did Santa arrive?"

"Oh…I didn't think to look."

"Let me finish my coffee and shower, and then I'll take a peek under the tree with you."

"You're on," she said and backed out of the room before she could do something silly and completely out of character—like throw her arms around his neck and kiss him. With the two of them alone in Emily's cozy house, the atmosphere had become more and more intimate….

A half hour later, Faith had dressed and was frying bacon for their breakfast when Charles appeared. He wore a dress shirt and sweater vest.

"Merry Christmas!" he said again.

"You, too." She made an effort not to look at him for fear she'd be too easily distracted.

"So, did you check under the tree?" Charles asked.

"Not yet." She slid the bacon onto the platter and wiped her hands.

"You look very nice," Charles said. "I generally don't notice much of anything before ten. I don't know if it's the day or if it's you." His comment was as casual as if he were discussing the weather.

"Me?" she whispered.

"You're an attractive woman." He cleared his throat. "Very attractive."

"Oh."

"It's true."

Flustered now, she offered him a tentative smile. "Breakfast is ready." She carried the crisp bacon over to the kitchen table, which she'd already set using a poinsettia-covered tablecloth. The juice was poured and the toast made; scrambled eggs were heaped in a dish. A quiche lorraine sat in the center of the table. And she'd brewed fresh coffee, the aroma pervading the room. She'd prepared far more than the two of them could possibly eat, but she supposed the quiche would make a nice lunch tomorrow.

"I'm so glad it's snowing," she said excitedly.

"Why wouldn't it snow today? It's snowed every day since I got here."

"Not true," she countered, but then admitted he was right. It *had* snowed every day at some point. Watching the thick white flakes drifting down was a holiday ideal. She felt like a child again.

"Oh, my," she said, unaware that she'd spoken aloud.

"What?"

Faith shook her head, not wanting to answer. She realized that she'd forgotten what it felt like to be happy. It was as though a fog had lifted and the world had become newly vivid, the colors clear and pure. Her gaze flew across the table and she looked at Charles. She knew immediately that he was responsible for her change of attitude. Spending these days with him had opened her to the joy of the season and the promise of love. The divorce had robbed her of so much, shredded her self-confidence, undercut trust and faith and made her doubt herself. It had taken her a long time to deal with the loss, but she was stronger now. She could expect good things in her life. She could anticipate happiness.

"Faith?" he asked with a quizzical expression. "What is it?"

She glanced quickly away and dismissed his question with another shake of her head. "Nothing important."

"Then tell me."

She smiled. "I was just thinking how happy I am to be here, having breakfast with you on Christmas morning."

Charles let the comment rest between them for a long moment. "With me?"

She giggled because he sounded so shocked. "Yes, Charles, with you. Is that so strange?"

"As a matter of fact, yes. I'm not accustomed to anyone enjoying my company."

"Well, I do." She reached for an extra strip of bacon to create a distraction for herself.

Charles set his fork aside and sat back in his chair, staring across the table as if she'd taken his breath away.

Faith grew uncomfortable under his scrutiny. "What is it?" she demanded.

He grinned. "I was just thinking that I could love you."

"Charles!"

"This isn't a joke—I'm completely sincere. I'm halfway in love with you already. But I know what you're going to say."

"I'm sure you don't."

"Yes, I do," he insisted. "You're thinking it's much too soon and I couldn't possibly know my feelings yet. Two weeks from now, our encounter will be just a memory."

That *was* what she was thinking, although Faith badly wanted to stay in touch with Charles once they parted. But there was more to her reaction than that.

"I'm just so happy," she said, "and I realized I haven't been in a long time."

"Happy with me?"

She nodded.

"Could we…you know, call each other after the holidays?" He seemed almost afraid of her response.

"I'd like that."

His eyes sparkled with undisguised pleasure. "I was recently approached by Berkeley about a teaching position," he confided. "Is that anywhere close to you?"

"It's very close."

He took in that information with a slight nod. "Good. That's good."

The doorbell chimed, and Faith dropped her napkin on the table, rising to her feet. "I'll get it." She suspected it was one or more of the Kennedy kids, coming to thank Charles for the gifts. She wondered what he'd bought her; from all the hints he'd been dropping, she suspected it was something special. She'd found a small antique paperweight for him, and that, too, was under the tree.

When she opened the door, it wasn't the Kennedy kids she saw. Instead, there stood Sam with the six dwarfs crowding around him. The dwarfs looked as if all they needed was a word of encouragement before rushing inside and attacking Charles en masse.

"Sam!" she cried and was instantly crushed in a big hug.

"We came to check up on you," Tony said, peering inside the house.

"Yes," Allen added. "We wanted to make sure Scrooge was good to you."

"Everything's fine," she assured her friends, bringing them into the house—and bringing them up to date. By that time, Charles had joined them in the living room.

Santa's elves peered up at him suspiciously.

Tony took a step closer. "She said you've had an attitude adjustment. Is that true?"

Charles nodded, a solemn expression on his face. "Faith won me over."

Sam chuckled. "We thought we'd give you a ride back to Seattle, Faith, so you can catch your flight tomorrow afternoon."

"I'll drive her." Charles moved to her side, placing his arm around her shoulders.

"We're just finishing breakfast but there's plenty if you haven't eaten."

"We haven't," Sam said promptly, and the seven of them rushed into the kitchen.

"Can you stay for dinner?" Charles asked, surprising Faith with the invitation.

"No, no, we don't want to intrude. Besides, we have to head out soon for flights of our own. The only reason we came was to make sure everything was all right with Faith."

"I'm having a wonderful Christmas," Faith told her friends.

And I'm going to have a wonderful life.

Chapter Twenty-Seven

"I've never eaten at the Four Seasons in my life," Emily said anxiously, "Christmas or not." She was sure there'd be more spoons at a single place setting than she had in her entire kitchen.

"It's where Mother always stays when she's in town," Ray told her. His hand rested on the small of her back as he directed her into the huge and elegantly decorated hotel lobby, dominated by a massive Christmas tree.

Emily glanced around, hoping to see Heather. Her daughter had been shocked to find her and Ray together. Although mortified that Heather had caught her half-undressed—well, with her blouse unfastened, anyway—Emily had hurriedly introduced them. Then, summoning all the panache she could muster, she'd announced that she hadn't slept with him.

Her cheeks flamed at the memory of how she'd managed to embarrass all three of them in one short sentence.

"Do you see Heather?" Emily asked, scanning the lobby.

"No," Ray murmured, "but I'm not looking for her."

The two people she held so dear hadn't exactly gotten off on the right foot, and Emily blamed herself.

Ray had tried to explain that the condo actually belonged to his brother, Professor Brewster, but Heather had been too flustered and confused to respond. The scene had been awkward, to say the least. Complicating everything, Heather had immediately stumbled out.

She'd rushed after Heather to invite her to the hotel for Christmas dinner. Her daughter had pretended not to hear, then stepped into the elevator and cast Emily a disgusted look. She'd shaken her head disapprovingly, as if the last place on earth she wanted to be was with her mother and that...*man*.

Emily had gone back into the apartment with her stomach in knots. She still felt ill; her stomachache hadn't abated since last night and she'd hardly been able to force down any breakfast.

"She'll be here any minute," Ray told her.

"Do you think so?" Emily's voice swelled with anticipation and renewed hope.

Ray exhaled loudly. "Actually, I was referring to my mother."

"Oh." Her shoulders deflated.

"Heather will make her own decision," Ray said, giving her shoulder a reassuring squeeze.

"I know." Emily had already realized that, but it was hard not to call her and smooth things out, despite Heather's rude behavior. To be estranged from her only child on Christmas Day was almost more than Emily could bear. If she hadn't heard from her by early evening, she knew she'd break down and call.

"Rayburn!" His mother stepped out of the elevator,

minus FiFi the Pomeranian. She held out her arms to her son as she slowly glided across the lobby. Several heads turned in their direction.

"Mother likes to make an entrance," Ray said under his breath.

"So I noticed."

Bernice Brewster hugged Ray as if it'd been years since their last meeting, and then shifted her attention to Emily. Clasping both of Emily's hands, the older woman smiled benevolently.

"I am so pleased that my son has finally found someone so special."

"Mother, stop it," Ray hissed under his breath.

Emily quite enjoyed his discomfort. "Ray's the special one, Mrs. Brewster."

"I do agree, but it takes the right woman to recognize what a prize he is."

"What time is the dinner reservation?" Ray asked in an obvious attempt to change the subject.

"Three-thirty," his mother informed him. "I do hope you're hungry."

"I'm famished," Emily said, although it wasn't true. Worried as she was about Heather, she didn't know if she could eat a single bite. "I, uh, hope you don't mind, but I invited my daughter to join us…. She didn't know if she could make it or not."

Ray gripped her hand at the telltale wobble in her voice.

"Is anything wrong, my dear?" Mrs. Brewster asked.

"I—Heather and I had a bit of a disagreement."

"Children inflict those on their parents every now and then." Ray's mother looked pointedly in his direction. "Isn't that right, Rayburn?"

Ray cleared his throat and agreed. "It's been known to happen. Every now and then, as you say."

"Don't you worry," the older woman said, gently patting Emily's forearm. "We'll ask the maître d' to seat us at a table for four and trust your daughter has the good sense to make an appearance."

"I hope she does, too."

Ray spoke to the maître d' and they were led to a table with four place settings. Emily was surprised by the number of people who ate dinner in a restaurant on Christmas Day. Aujourd'hui was full, with a long waiting list, if the people assembled near the front were any indication.

The maître d' seated Mrs. Brewster, and Ray pulled out Emily's chair. She was half seated when she saw Heather. Her daughter rushed into the restaurant foyer, glancing around the tables until she caught sight of Emily. A smile brightened her pretty face, and she came into the room, dragging a young man. It took Emily only a moment to recognize Ben.

Emily stood to meet her daughter.

"Mom!" Heather threw her arms around Emily's neck. "I'm so glad I found you."

Emily struggled with emotion. "I am, too." She could hardly speak since her throat was clogged with tears.

"Hi," Heather said, turning to Ray. She extended her hand. "We sort of met last night. I'm Heather."

Ray stood, and they exchanged handshakes. "Ray." He motioned to his mother. "This is my mother, Bernice Brewster."

"And this is Ben Miller," Heather said, slipping her arm around the young man's waist. She pressed her head against his shoulder, as if they were a longtime couple.

Emily was curious about what had happened to Elijah No-Last-Name, but figured she'd learn the details later.

"Please," Mrs. Brewster said, gesturing to the table. "I would like both of you to join us."

Immediately an extra chair and place setting were delivered to the table, and not a minute later everyone was seated.

"This place is really something," Heather said with awe. "You wouldn't believe some of the roadside dumps I ate at while I was in Florida. Thanks so much for including us."

"It's good to see you again," Emily said, smiling at Ben.

The college student grinned, and answered Heather's unspoken question. "Your mother and Ray bought a Christmas tree from me a few days ago."

"Oh."

"When did you two…" Emily began, but wasn't sure how to phrase what she wanted to ask.

"When I left last night, I was pretty upset," Heather confessed, reaching for her water glass. She didn't drink from it but held on to it tightly. "I don't really know why I took off the way I did." She turned to Ray's mother. "I guess I didn't expect to find my mother with a man, you know?"

"Rayburn isn't just a regular run-of-the-mill man," Bernice said with more than a trace of indignation.

"I know—well, at first I didn't, but I'm over that now." Heather drew in a deep breath. "When I left the condo, I wasn't sure where to go or what to do, so I started walking and—"

"I saw her," Ben interrupted, "kind of wandering aimlessly down the street."

"You were still at the Christmas-tree lot?" Ray asked.

Ben nodded. "For those last-minute shoppers. Technically I should've closed about an hour earlier, but I didn't have anywhere to be, so I stuck around."

"It was a good thing, too," Heather said, her eyes brimming with gratitude. "I don't know what I would've done without Ben."

"I closed down the lot, and then Heather and I found somewhere to have coffee and we talked."

"Ben told me just what I needed to hear. He said I was being ridiculous and that my mother was entitled to her own life."

The waiter appeared then, and handed everyone elegant menus. Heather paused until he'd finished.

"It's just that I never thought my mother would ever be interested in a man other than my father," she continued in a low voice as Bernice perused the wine list. "I was... shocked, you know?"

Beneath the table, Ray took Emily's hand and they entwined their fingers.

"You *are* interested in Ray, aren't you?" Heather asked her mother.

The entire room seemed to go silent, as though everyone was waiting for Emily's reply. "Well..."

Mrs. Brewster leaned closer. So did Ray.

"I—I guess you could s-say I'm interested," she stammered. Now that the words were out, she suddenly felt more confident. "As a matter of fact, yes, I am. Definitely. Yes."

Mrs. Brewster released a long sigh. "Is it too early to discuss the wedding?"

"Yes." Ray and Emily spoke simultaneously and then both smothered their laughter.

"We've just met," Ray reminded everyone. "Let's not get ahead of ourselves, okay?"

"But you are smitten, aren't you?" Ray's mother asked with such eagerness that Emily couldn't disappoint her.

"Very much," she said, smiling at the old-fashioned word.

"And Rayburn?"

"I'm smitten, too."

"Good." Mrs. Brewster turned to Heather next. "I think a pale green and the lightest of pinks for the wedding colors, don't you agree?"

Heather nodded. "Perfect."

"May or June?"

Heather sneaked a look at her mother and winked. "June."

Ray brought his head closer to Emily's and spoke behind the menu. "They're deciding our future. Do you object?"

Emily grinned, and a warm, happy feeling flowed through her. "Not especially. What about you?"

Ray grinned back. "I've always been fond of June."

"Me, too."

"My mother will drive us both crazy," he warned.

"I like her," Emily whispered. "I even like FiFi."

Ray studied Bernice and then sighed. "Mother *is* a sweetheart—despite everything."

The waiter approached the table. "Merry Christmas," he said formally, standing straight and tall, as if it was his distinct pleasure to serve them on this very special day of the year.

"May I offer you a drink to start off with?"

"Champagne!" Bernice called out. "Champagne all round."

"Champagne," the others echoed.

"We have a lot to celebrate," Bernice pronounced. "Christmas, a homecoming—and a wedding."

Epilogue

"This is so festive, isn't it?" Faith had seen pictures of Rockefeller Center, but that didn't compare to actually standing here, watching the skaters in their bright winter clothes. Some were performing elaborate twirls and leaps; others clung timidly to the sides. They all seemed to be having a good time.

"I knew you'd love it," Emily said.

"What I'd love to do is skate." Not that she would in what Charles referred to as her "delicate" condition. She rubbed her stomach with one hand, gently reassuring her unborn child that she wouldn't do anything so foolish when she was six months pregnant. In the other hand she held several shopping bags from Saks.

The two friends continued down the avenue, weaving in and out of the crowd. Emily, too, carried packages and bags.

"I still can't imagine you living in New York City and actually loving it, especially after all those years in Leavenworth," Faith said. She was happy for Emily and Ray, but she'd been astonished when Emily had announced last spring that she was moving across the country.

"What I discovered is that New York is just a collection of small communities. There's Brooklyn and SoHo and the Village and Little Italy and Harlem and more."

"What about teaching? Is that any different?"

Emily shook her head. "Children are children, and the kindergartners here are just like the ones in Leavenworth. Okay, so they might be a bit more sophisticated, but in many ways five-year-olds are the same everywhere."

"What's new with Ray?"

Emily's lips turned up in a soft smile. "He works too hard. He brings his work home with him and spends far too many hours at the office, but according to everyone I've met, he's better now than ever."

"Better?"

Her friend blushed. "Happier."

"That," said Faith, "is what regular sex will do for you."

"Faith." Emily nudged her and laughed.

"It certainly worked with Charles."

"If you're going to talk about your love life, I don't want to hear it."

Faith enjoyed watching Emily blush. She'd never seen her this radiant. Life had certainly taken an interesting turn for them both, she reflected. Just a year earlier, they'd been lonely and depressed, facing the holidays alone. A mere twelve months later, each was married—and, to pile happiness on top of happiness, they were practically sisters now. Faith's baby was due in March, and Charles was about as excited as a man could get at the prospect of becoming a father.

His mother was pretty pleased with herself, too. Faith and Emily had both come to love Bernice Brewster. She'd waited nearly seventy years for daughters, and she lavished her daughters-in-law with gifts and occasional bits of motherly wisdom and advice. Well, perhaps more than occasional, but Faith had no objection and she doubted Emily did, either.

"When will Heather get here?" Faith asked, looking forward to seeing her.

"Tomorrow afternoon. She's taking the train down."

"How is she?"

Emily rearranged her shopping bags. "Heather's doing really well."

"Did you ever find out what happened with Elijah and the ill-fated Florida trip? I know she didn't want to talk about it for a while…."

Emily frowned. "Apparently he drank too much and he didn't like to eat in real restaurants. His idea of fine dining was a hot dog at a roadside stand. In addition to all that, he apparently had a roving eye, which Heather didn't approve of."

"That girl always was high maintenance," Faith teased. "What about her and Ben?"

"Who knows?" Emily said with a shrug. "She claims they're just friends but they seem to spend a lot of time together. Ben's going on to law school after graduation."

"Good for him."

"He might come down and spend Christmas with us, too."

"You'll have a houseful, with Heather and maybe Ben." Despite the invitation to spend Christmas in New York at their apartment, Charles and Faith had booked a room at the Warwick Hotel. Bernice was due to arrive, as well. She, of course, would be staying at the Plaza.

Faith doubted there was anyplace more romantic than New York at Christmastime.

She and Emily walked into the Warwick and down the steps to the small lobby. Ray and Charles stood when they came into the room. Even now, after all these months, Faith's heart fluttered at the sight of her husband. His eyes brightened when he saw her. The unexpected happiness she'd discovered last Christmas had never left. Instead, it had blossomed and grown. She was loved beyond measure by a man who was worthy of her devotion.

"Looks like you bought out Saks Fifth Avenue," Charles said as he took the packages from her hands.

"Just the baby department, but Charles, I couldn't help myself. Everything was so cute."

"Buying anything is a big mistake," Ray told them, helping Emily with her shopping bags. "Mother's waited all these years to spoil her first grandchild. My guess is she has stock in Toys 'R' Us by now."

"Don't forget a certain aunt and uncle, too," Emily murmured.

Faith wrapped her arm around Charles's and laid her head against his shoulder.

Emily read her perfectly. "Listen, why don't you two go to your room and rest for a little while? Faith needs to put her feet up and relax. Ray and I will have a drink and catch up. Then, when you're ready, we'll go out for dinner."

Faith nodded, grateful for her friend's sympathy and intuition.

Charles led the way to the elevator. He didn't speak until they were inside. "You overdid it, didn't you?"

"Only a bit. I'll be fine as soon as I sit down with a cup of herbal tea."

Her husband tucked his arm protectively around her and waited until they were back in the room to kiss her.

Then he ordered tea.

"Did you two have a chance to visit?" Ray asked as Emily removed her coat and slung it over the back of her chair. They'd entered the bar, securing a table near the window. "Or was shopping at the top of your priority list?"

"Actually, we did some of both. It's just so good to see Faith this happy."

The waitress came by, and Ray ordered a hot buttered rum for each of them.

"I can't believe the changes in her," Emily said. "She's so much more confident."

"I was going to say the same thing about Charles," her husband said with a bemused grin. "I hardly recognize my own brother. Until he met Faith, all he cared about was history—in fact, I think he would've preferred to live in the eighteenth century. I feel like I finally have a brother again."

The waitress brought their drinks and set them on the table, along with a bowl of salted nuts.

"Do you suppose they're talking about us in the same way?" Emily asked. "Are we different people now than we were a year ago?"

"I know I am," Ray said.

"I think I am, too."

Emily reached for a pecan, her favorite nut, and then for no discernible reason started to laugh.

"What's so funny?"

"Us. Have you forgotten the day we met?"

Ray grinned. "Not likely."

"I was so miserable and upset, and then you happened along. I glommed on to you so fast, I can only imagine what you must've thought."

"*You* glommed on to me?" he repeated. "That's not the way I remember it." Ray grabbed a handful of nuts. "As I recall, I found out that my brother had traded homes with this incredibly lovely woman. The explanation was reasonable. All I had to do was reassure my mother everything was fine and catch the train back to New York."

Emily lowered her eyes and smiled. "I'm so glad you ended up staying."

"You think I missed the last train by accident?"

"You didn't?"

"Not by a long shot. As my mother would say, I was smitten. I still am."

"That's comforting to hear."

"Christmas with you last year was the best of my life."

"Except for the Christmas you got the red racer."

"Well, that was my second-best Christmas."

"And this year?"

"When Christmas comes, I'll let you know."

"You do that," Emily whispered, raising her glass in a toast to the most wonderful Christmas gift of her life.